DESERT FLOWERS

PAUL PEN

Translated by Simon Bruni

D1115716

amazon crossing

Previously published as *La casa entre los cactus* by Plaza & Janés Editores S.A. in Spain in 2017. Translated from Spanish by Simon Bruni

First published in English by AmazonCrossing in 2017.

Published by AmazonCrossing, Seattle

www.apub.com

Amazon, the Amazon logo, and AmazonCrossing are trademarks of Amazon.com, Inc., or its affiliates.

ISBN-13: 9781542046053
ISBN-10: 154204605X

Cover design by David Drummond

Printed in the United States of America

DESERT
FLOWERS

For Roberto, my house among the cactuses.

SOMEWHERE IN THE BAJA CALIFORNIA DESERT, MEXICO

Sometime in the Sixties

Rose opened her eyes certain that something bad had happened. She slid her hand over the mattress to alert her husband.

"Elmer," she whispered.

He turned away.

"Wake up." She pinched his back. "Someone's in the house."

Elmer replied with a snore.

Rose got out of bed. She tiptoed to the door, treading on the spots where the floor didn't creak.

She pressed her ear against the wood.

She heard herself swallow.

Holding her breath, she wrapped her fingers around the handle. She turned it, paying attention to each click of the mechanism, then opened the door just enough for one eye to peek out. The moonlight that flooded the room spilled through the crack, between her legs, pouring a silvery band onto the hallway floor.

All her daughters' bedroom doors were closed.

So was the bathroom door.

Relieved, she let out the air she'd been holding in.

Then Melissa's door swung open, blown by the night breeze.

The hinges squeaked.

"Melissa!" Rose yelled, coming out of the room. She released the door with such force that the handle hit the wall. Her footsteps rumbled in the hallway. She turned on the light in Melissa's bedroom. From shelves, rows of stones with eyes observed her.

The bed was empty.

"Melissa!"

She lifted the sheet, looked under the bed. She swiveled around with her hands on her head, dizzy in a room that seemed enormous.

"They've taken her," she whispered.

She pressed her hands against her belly, twisting her nightgown as if her daughter had been snatched from her just after birth.

Elmer appeared in the doorway.

"They've taken her, Elm," she told him. "They've taken Melissa."

"Nobody's been taken."

"So where is she?"

The question ended in a sob. Elmer held her against his bare chest, protecting her in his arms, calming her with his body's warmth. She rubbed her face against her husband's chest hair, let herself be rocked by his strong heartbeat. "They've taken her from us."

Elmer led her to the bedroom window. He invited her to look outside, guiding her chin with his fingers. A single bulb glowed at the top of a wooden post, projecting a field of light onto the desert's reddish sand. It also cast its light on Elmer's pickup, parked near a cactus taller than the vehicle.

"See?" he said. "There's nothing out there, there's nobody."

Beyond the post, everything was dark. Only the moonlight made it possible to make out the silhouettes of the rocks and cacti that filled the landscape as far as the eye could see.

"Nobody's going to come all this way."

Rose looked at the empty bed. "So where's my daughter?"

She felt her absence in her chest, in her belly.

"I'm here, Mom." Melissa spoke from the doorway. In her hands she carried a rock with eyes. She directed a question at her father. "Again?"

Elmer nodded.

"I went out to speak to the cactuses, Mom." She pointed to her dust-covered slippers as proof. "Although the only one who paid any attention to me was Needles. I don't know what the matter is with Pins today."

Rose hugged her. "I was so frightened," she whispered in Melissa's ear. "I love you all so much."

She breathed in the smell of her daughter's hair, filling the void in her chest. Over her shoulder, she asked Elmer if she'd woken the rest of the girls with all the racket.

"They didn't even notice," he answered.

Melissa closed her eyes and covered them with her hands to show her sisters she wasn't going to cheat.

"Are you sure you can't see anything?" they asked at the same time.

"How could I?"

Melissa heard both of them laugh. She pictured them waving their arms around in front of her, feigning that they were going to thump her, or pulling faces to make her react.

"Come on, stop that. Go hide."

Four feet padded around her. The sand crunched under their shoes as they moved away. Melissa could hear that they'd synchronized their steps so that their feet landed at the same time—an attempt to minimize any sounds that might give away where they were going. When they reached the agreed-upon place, she heard them leap.

"Ready?" she asked.

"No, wait."

Her sisters spoke in synchrony. Consonants and vowels coincided so closely that it could have been a single person speaking. They were experts in doing it. Melissa imagined them smoothing down their hair, checking every crease in their dresses, agreeing on the exact way they'd show a hand or foot when asked, whether their fingers would be together or apart. She took a deep breath. The desert smelled like hot stone. Just as she shifted her weight from one hip to the other, the girls finished preparing themselves.

"Ready!" they both called at the same time.

Melissa opened her eyes. Her pupils adjusted without effort to the twilight. Dozens of cacti, all of them taller than she, rose from the land around her. The rocks were the deep orange that was normal for that time of the evening. Some kind of reptile hid under one of the stones when she moved. Her sisters' simultaneous giggles came from behind two giant cacti. Both had enormous central trunks from which branches that looked like bent arms emerged on either side.

"I'm going to start," she warned her sisters.

"*Three commands and one step forward, more than that and you'll be ignored,*" they sang in unison.

"First command: I want to see the palms of your right hands."

A hand appeared from behind the central trunk of each cactus, some ten feet from her. She observed them closely. At that distance she couldn't make out the lines on the palms, which were always a good clue. She narrowed her eyes, trying to discern the shape of each little finger. She'd set out to guess correctly on the first command, but it was almost impossible from so far away.

"I'm taking one step forward."

"*More than that and you'll be ignored,*" they chanted, chuckling.

Melissa moved toward the cacti as the girls' hands disappeared behind the trunks.

"Second command?" they asked at the same time.

"Left arms."

They both showed them. A yard closer than before, Melissa could make out the creases in her sisters' wrists. She could also see the identical mole on the pale skin of each of the forearms. She tried to make out the difference between the thickness of each thumb.

"Third command?" the girls asked in unison.

"Wait, I'm still looking."

Seeing the elbows would've helped, but getting them to turn their arms would count as another command, and she wanted to look at another feature that might give her a better chance of guessing right.

"Third order," she announced. "I want to see your left feet."

Two shoes sprouted from the bases of both cacti like creeping flowers. They were white, fastened with straps over the insteps. Melissa regretted her strategy—the girls had pulled their pink socks up as far as they would go. One of them had been stung by a scorpion on that ankle, and the scar would've been the clue she needed.

"I see you've cottoned on to that one."

The girls laughed, thinking they'd won. Then Melissa noticed that one of the socks was less tight against its wearer's leg. Melissa had stretched the elastic herself two afternoons ago, when she'd thrown herself to the ground to grab the little girl as they played among the rocks. It was enough information to solve the enigma.

"Daisy on the left and Dahlia on the right."

The girls remained silent. She imagined them exchanging incredulous looks from cactus to cactus, shrugging their shoulders, perhaps mouthing some words.

"No way," they said at the same time from their hiding places.

"Did I guess right?" Melissa already knew the answer. "Go on, come out."

They emerged from behind the cacti.

"I was right!"

"There's no way you could know. We're the same."

7

The girls examined each other from top to bottom, compared the arms and hands that they'd shown, inspected their shoes. Dahlia looked at her twin sister's baggier sock but didn't identify it as the telltale clue. She whispered something in Daisy's ear.

"You cheated," they said at the same time.

"I don't cheat. I'm just smarter than you two."

"Yeah, sure," they added.

It still surprised Melissa how easily the two girls spoke at the same time, using the same words. Sometimes they whispered to each other before coming out with an identical sentence, but sometimes they did it naturally, without preparing. She laughed when she saw them pull up their socks to the same height, adjust the bands on their shoes to the same hole, realign the straps on their white dresses so they showed the same amount of shoulder. Daisy had even picked up a handful of the reddish sand that covered the ground and made a mark on her sister's dress, copying the one on her own, just above the large-petaled flower they had embroidered on both.

"Let's play again," they requested in unison.

"No, it's late. I can barely see."

Melissa gestured at the horizon. The sun had disappeared. A coyote howled somewhere in the desert. A column of dust rose from the ground in the distance. It faded into the sky above the tallest cacti as it approached them.

"Daddy!" yelled the twins.

They held hands and headed home with synchronized strides. Melissa followed behind them. A large stone caught her attention before she reached the track. It was the size of the melon they'd had for dessert a few days ago. She picked it up, feeling its contours, and stroked a right-angled bulge. She held the stone at eye level to inspect it from the front.

"What's that?" the twins asked, looking back.

She showed them the rock and its unusual bulge.

"Another one?" they said.

"This one looks like it has a nose."

The twins walked on indifferently, but Melissa was pleased with her discovery. It wasn't easy to find a rock with such an obvious face. She held the stone in her hands, resting it against her belly. They walked on until Dad's pickup truck passed in front of them without stopping. Melissa closed her mouth and eyes before the dust storm reached her. The twins shrieked with excitement and spat sand through their laughter.

Dad stopped the vehicle in front of the house. It was the only home in sight. At twilight, when the exterior took on the same purple tone as the landscape, it seemed to camouflage itself and disappear among the cacti.

As if it didn't exist.

Dad got out of the truck and slammed the door shut. The girls rushed up to him. They hugged him around the waist, each of them mounting a leg.

"Did you bring anything for us from town?" they yelled.

"Whoa now, let me walk."

The twins ignored him. Dad walked with heavy strides to one side of the truck. He picked up some bags from the cargo area.

"I'm serious, if you don't let go, I'll leave everything here and by tomorrow the coyotes will have taken everything."

Dad looked at the stone in Melissa's hands for a few seconds. Then he asked her to help him with the girls. She left the rock with a nose on the ground and tickled the twins until they let go of their father. She offered to carry some of the bags.

"Don't worry," he replied, carrying several at once. "I just need you to keep those two out of the way. And get that one there"—he gestured with his chin at the pickup's cab—"to quit reading."

Dad shot off toward the house. He walked quickly to shorten the journey, his forearms swelling under the weight of the paper bags he carried on either side of his body, his veins thick like blue worms. He climbed the three steps to the porch without looking at them.

Daisy and Dahlia stood on tiptoes and peered into the vehicle, grabbing hold of the open window frame on the driver's side. "Hi, Iris, what're you reading?"

Melissa recovered her rock and rounded the truck, past the back where large metal letters spelled out FORD, until she reached the passenger's window, which was open. Iris was reading a thick book, open on the loose-fitting skirt that covered her legs to below the knees. Most of the pages were on her left thigh, so she was about to finish. The slight movement of her head from the end of one line to another made her blonde ponytail swing gently.

"What're you reading?" said Dahlia.

"What're you reading?" said Daisy.

When they hadn't agreed on their words beforehand and one of the twins said something ahead of the other, the second twin would repeat it. Iris aimed a raised finger at them without taking her eyes from the text, telling them to be quiet. The girls looked at each other and did up imaginary zippers on their lips. She passed the final page, where the writing reached only halfway down. As she finished the book, she gasped in surprise. In fright. Then she looked up and blinked to return to the world, as if coming out of a dream. Her mouth was open.

"What happened?" asked Daisy.

"What happened?" asked Dahlia.

Iris didn't respond. It was as if she'd run out of words even though she'd just read thousands of them.

"What's the matter?" Melissa pressed her.

Given the time her sister was taking to answer, she guessed some impassioned declaration was about to be made. Iris didn't read books, she lived them, and everything she knew about the world, which wasn't much, she had learned through them.

"The matter is that this world we live in is a very twisted place," she finally answered, indignant at whatever had happened in those pages. "And that I don't know why I try to read books written nowadays when what I really like are the classics from last century. The ones about love, about nice things . . . not this." She closed the book and held it up as if it were irrefutable proof of what she was claiming.

Melissa read the title on the cover.

"What does 'twisted' mean?" the twins asked in unison.

"Twisted is something strange, disturbing, and ugly," Iris explained. "Like what happens in this book. Like you two speaking at the same time."

"We're not twisted."

Each word was perfectly in time, and they celebrated the coincidence by letting go of the truck to jump up and down with their arms in the air. They hugged as if they'd won the game of hiding behind the cacti.

Dad arrived back at the truck to collect more bags.

Melissa opened the door for her sister. They walked back to the house together with the twins ahead of them, laying the same foot at the same time on each step up to the porch.

"What's that?" Iris asked about the stone.

"Look, it's like it has a nose." Melissa ran her finger over it. "And it has a very manly forehead."

"Manly? Now that *does* interest me." Iris stopped to examine the rock more closely. "You're right, it is a bit masculine," she conceded with a smile. "But it's no use to me."

"Did you see any boys in town?"

"Boys? In that town? If only. All I saw was three old men. All short, with moustaches. And they only speak Spanish."

"Nothing interesting?"

"Nothing. I don't know why we fight over who goes."

"Because it'll always be better than spending the day here doing the same thing."

"I'm not so sure."

"If you want, I'll go every month from now on."

"Don't get ahead of yourself." Iris punched Melissa on the shoulder.

They reached the steps, and from the top of them the twins spoke.

"And why can't we go to the town?"

"Because you're too little," Dad replied as he came out the front door on his third trip to the pickup.

Before the screen door could close, a hand stopped it.

"So . . . I have a bunch of daughters, and not one of them is capable of helping me set the table?"

The twins whispered to each other.

"It's just that the world's a very twisted place, Mommy."

The girls burst into laughter and dodged past Mom's legs on their way into the house. She was drying her hands on an apron embroidered with a picture of a stone sun. She gave Iris and Melissa a questioning look.

"I just taught them the word," Iris explained. "It was this book's fault. It has stunned, moved, and astonished me."

Mom made a face to reproach Iris for the way she showed off her vocabulary. She looked at the book cover.

"I don't know why you need to read such ugly things," she said, "considering how perfect our home, our family, and our lives are."

She looked to the horizon, at the acres of open space. Melissa watched her aim a broad smile at the landscape and everything in it: the cacti, the rocks, her daughters' footsteps in the sand, her husband bringing in the shopping. Then she slapped Iris with the book to get her inside. Melissa waited for them to go in. When the mosquito screen closed in front of her, leaving her alone on the porch, she responded to her mother's comment while nobody could hear her.

"Yeah, sure . . . a perfect life."

Iris left the twisted book on a shelf in the kitchen. She'd read every novel on that bookshelf. For a bookend she used a jar filled with coins and bills. When she turned around she saw her father outside, trying to open the screen door with his foot, his arms laden with more bags. She ran to open it for him, dodging the twins, who were taking silverware and napkins to the table. Dad thanked her, blew the hair from his eyes, and reached the kitchen counter. He put the items down near the faucet while Mom checked the shopping.

"And the rice?" she asked.

He pulled a heavy sack from the bottom of a bag, and she kissed him on the cheek. Iris liked seeing how her parents would show their love for each other at any moment, with spontaneous gestures of affection among packs of meat and bread or when Dad came into the bathroom while Mom was brushing her teeth. It was an everyday love that was rarely spoken of in the books that she read, which were more given to passionate romances where one of the lovers usually ended up dead.

"Why are you sighing?" Mom asked her, cutting open a corner of the bag of rice with scissors.

Iris shook her head.

"You two scare me with your adolescence." Mom also gestured at Melissa with the scissors to include her in the remark.

"Me? Don't lump me in with her." Melissa stuck her tongue out at Iris, happy not to be her age yet. Iris screwed up her nose, happy she was no longer Melissa's age. At the table, Daisy and Dahlia said something into each other's ears.

"What've you brought for us, Daddy?"

"You'll see." He was on his way out the door again. "Your stuff's in the last bag."

The girls applauded.

"You kids finish setting the table, and don't interrupt your father," Mom interceded. "He's tired enough as it is after driving all day."

Iris took a pitcher of water from the refrigerator while the twins laid out the six sets of tableware. With synchronized movements they arranged the glasses first, then the napkins, and finally the silverware.

Melissa let the arrangement be but made a space for her rock with the nose. "He's going to have dinner with us," she said.

When Iris considered her sisters' work to be done, she placed the pitcher in the center of the table. Ice cubes clinked against the glass. Seeing how the twins were still checking that the cutlery was centered on the napkins with pinpoint precision, Iris winked at Melissa and moved a few of the knives out of place. They put them back without stopping to tell her off and smiled with satisfaction when the symmetry was restored.

"You two are crazy," Iris said.

Mom turned around at the sink. "Don't say that to them."

Dad arrived back in the kitchen, this time carrying only one bag.

"How's the city?" Melissa asked.

"Awful as ever. And it's not a city: it's a poky little town with six stores," he said.

"At least there're people there," said Melissa. "People with eyes. People who speak. I wish I could go every day and spend the day talking to people."

"With those ugly little people?"

Mom cuffed Iris for the comment.

"It's true," Iris said in her own defense. "There isn't a single good-looking boy there."

"I don't care about that," Melissa said. "What I need is to talk."

"Then you'd better start learning Spanish, because only the man in library speaks English. Just enough to get me the books Dad asks him for. And all that about not caring about boys? Let's see what you have to say in"—Iris went up to her sister and touched her breasts, assessing their growth—"in about two years."

Melissa blushed and cuffed her. Dad separated them as if they were fighting, though they were laughing.

"When you learn to drive, that is if I teach you one day, you'll be able to go to the town whenever you want."

"And what if we walk?" asked the twins.

"It'll take you four days and you'll die of heatstroke, thirst, and hunger."

The twins drank from their water glasses as if they'd walked that distance just by thinking about it.

"Sure, as if you'd let us go even if we did learn to drive," Melissa said. "You don't even let us go with you to the gas station."

"Do you think any of the other guys take their children to work?"

Melissa shrugged.

"Anyways," Iris broke in, "if it's about learning to drive, I could go already." She winked at her mother, who was standing at the sink.

"What was that?" Dad asked. "Why's she winking at you?"

Mom gave Iris a scolding look.

"What?" he insisted.

Prolonging the silence would only make Dad more impatient, so Iris came clean. "Mom's taught me to drive a little."

"You're not serious."

"Just a bit. With the Dodge," Mom explained. "She knows how to accelerate and brake, that's all. The first time, we rammed into a cactus."

"Don't exaggerate!" Iris argued.

"The first time?" Dad asked. "So there've been more than one?"

Mother and daughter laughed.

The twins whispered into each other's ears before speaking.

"You're going to learn to drive before we do, and leave for the city," they said. "You're going to leave us here on our own."

"It's not a city," their father corrected them.

"Please don't leave us on our own," Dahlia said.

"Please don't leave us on our own," Daisy said.

"We'll get eaten by the coyotes and the birds with the weird necks," said Dahlia.

15

"We'll get eaten by the coyotes and—"

Melissa covered Daisy's mouth with her hand so she couldn't repeat the full sentence.

"No one's going to leave you on your own," Dad reassured them. "Anyway, those birds with the weird necks, which are called vultures, only eat dead meat. And you're in no danger because you seem very alive to me." He waited for a reaction from the girls as he approached the table. "Or are you not?" He tickled their bellies, making them writhe with laughter. "See? No vulture's going to eat little girls who squirm that much."

They showed the relief the information brought them by wiping imaginary sweat from their foreheads. But Iris saw Daisy's face turn from reassurance to worry.

"But if they eat dead meat, then they're going to eat Edelweiss," Daisy said.

"But if they eat dead meat, then they're going to eat Edelweiss," repeated Dahlia.

A shower of rice fell onto the floor, the grains reaching Iris's feet. Melissa covered the girls' mouths, but they were already quiet. Mom bent down with an apology and began sweeping up the mess with a brush.

"It's OK." Her trembling hands said otherwise. "I'm fine."

Dad asked Iris to help Mom. He took care of the twins.

"That won't happen," he told them. "Vultures can't dig, so they're not going to take Edelweiss. She'll always be out there with us."

The twins whispered to each other. "We preferred it when she was here for real and we could play with her."

Iris comforted her mother by squeezing her hand as they knelt to clean up the rice. Mom dried her nose and forced a smile. "I'll get used to it," she whispered.

"So, does anyone want to open the bag of special stuff from the town? Or shall we leave it for next weekend?"

Iris noticed the relief in Mom's face. She was grateful for the change of subject. Dad always knew how to make her feel better.

16

"We do!" cried the little girls.

They ran to their dad, who was searching in the bottom of the bag for the surprise he'd brought them from the town's stationery store. Iris observed their excitement as she threw two handfuls of rice in the trash.

"What colors are they?"

"What colors are they?"

Dad prolonged the moment by moving his hand around inside the bag.

"I've brought you red beads"—he took out a plastic jar filled with them—"and green and purple and orange ones."

The twins eagerly gathered all the jars and passed them to each other, openmouthed. They celebrated the haul by deciding what they'd do with each color. The green would be for cactus drawings, the red for the sky, the purple for some flowers, and the orange for the rocks and Daddy's truck.

"And Iris chose these hairpins for you," Dad announced.

He gave Dahlia a pair of green ones. Daisy waited for hers, excited. When she received a white pair, she turned them down. Dahlia returned hers.

"We don't want them. They're not the same," they said in unison. "We have to look the same."

"Not always, girls, just when—"

"We have to look the same," they cut in.

Dad gave Mom an inquiring look.

"It's a phase," she said. "They'll get over it."

Iris was about to suggest an idea to solve the problem, but her father was a step ahead of her. He separated the joined pairs of hairpins and created two new pairs, each with one green and one white pin. He offered a mixed pair to each girl.

"And now?"

"Now they're the same. How did you do it?"

"Magic!"

"Magic!"

Dad pinched their noses.

"It's not magic. Sometimes you just have to make an extra effort so that things are the way you want. We can all achieve what we want to achieve, whatever gets in our way." He gave Mom a look that Iris ascribed romantic connotations to. "Got it?"

The girls nodded and went back to the table.

"And you?" Mom asked Iris from the sink, holding her hands under the water to wash away the rice dust. "What've you brought?"

Before she could answer, her three sisters replied in chorus: "A book."

"Yup, another book, so what? One of the kind I like, to get the sour taste out of my mouth from that last one." She took it out of the bag and read the title out loud. "*Pride and Prejudice*. I hope it's full of love"—she went up to Melissa and whispered to her—"and *more*."

"I heard you." Mom's straightened finger pointed at her from the sink. Then she turned to dad. "She's not serious, is she?"

He shook his head.

"Let me see that."

Iris handed the book to Mom, who examined the cover and read the synopsis on the back, then returned it. She must not have found a reason for concern.

"All day long with your head stuck in those books, fantasizing about other lives. Sometimes I wonder whether you appreciate everything that your father and I do for you, how wonderful our life is."

Dad massaged her shoulder.

"We appreciate what we have," said the twins.

"And I do, too, Mom," added Iris. Then she spoke to the little girls. "But you'll be sixteen one day, too, and you'll feel like doing more than making pictures with beads. You'll feel like meeting a boy." Iris stretched out her arms toward the windows and spoke as if reciting. "And since you won't find a young man in these barren, cactus-filled lands, you'll have to make do with reading the passionate love stories of the characters in books. Books that, luckily, you won't have to order, one by one, from a man in a bookshop lost in this forgotten corner of Mexico, because your eldest sister will have collected them for you on that bookshelf."

The twins listened, wide-eyed. Then they whispered to each other.

"Our eldest sister was Edelweiss."

Mom's shoulders dropped again. Melissa changed the direction of the conversation.

"If you want I'll introduce you to Needles," she told Iris. "Or Pins. I reckon Pins is more your type."

"Very funny," Iris replied. "But what I yearn for is a real boy."

Mom clicked her tongue at her.

"Speaking of Needles and Pins . . ." Dad handed Melissa the paper bag.

"Did you bring clothes?"

Dad nodded. She got up from her chair to peer into the bag and smiled when she saw what it contained. She pulled out an old shirt, taking care not to unfold it. She also took out a pair of torn, faded jeans, which she positioned under the shirt, forming a human figure on the table. Finally, she took a cap from the bottom of the bag.

"It's from your gas station." She showed everyone the logo printed on the front, the same as the one Dad had embroidered on his coveralls. "I wonder how I'll manage it. I'll need a ladder to put this on."

Mom announced that dinner was ready.

Sitting at the table, Melissa struck up a conversation with the twins about hairpins, rocks with faces, and glue for beads. Dad told Mom all about his monthly trip to the town. Iris opted to open her book, position it beside her plate, and read with her elbows on the table, chewing over the pages. There was a moment when Mom looked at her, but she didn't press her to improve her posture or stop reading. Instead she took Dad's hand, and they both observed her as if she were the most beautiful thing they had ever seen. When she began to feel uncomfortable and gave them an embarrassed look, they turned to the twins with an identical expression. The twins had organized their french fries in rows and were eating them one by one. Then their parents focused on Melissa, who was holding a french fry to the place where the rock would have had a mouth and imitating the noise it would make as it chewed.

Mom rested her head on Dad's shoulder. He kissed her on the forehead. They sighed at the family scene before them. Iris turned her attention back to her book.

Melissa opened her bedroom door with difficulty. Her hands were busy with the rock and the men's clothing Dad had brought her. When she was in, she dropped the clothing on the bed. She placed the stone on the desk, without bothering to move aside the magazine cuttings and pencil drawings that covered it. She looked around the room for her scissors. They weren't on the shelves over the headboard. Or on either of the bedside tables. She rummaged through the papers on the desk, and pieces of magazine fell onto the floor. She found them under one of her sketches, a family portrait, one that hadn't convinced her. The ones she thought were good were pinned to the wall opposite her bed, which was almost completely covered in family memories captured in pencil. Each morning, the pictures glowed in front of her like an altarpiece, illuminated by the dawn's pale yellow light—it was a sight she was grateful for on the days when she woke up certain that she didn't belong to this place. With the scissors in her hand, she took more magazines from the desk drawer. They were copies of *Cine avance* that Dad would bring from the gas station when they were left on the shelf for more than two months without being bought. They talked about movies in a language she couldn't read. She only recognized the names of actors and actresses, cities in the United States, and the original English titles of films. Melissa especially liked finding portraits of the actor Rock Hudson, as there was no person with a more fitting name to donate a pair of eyes to her stones. She flicked through several pages, scissors at the ready, waiting to find him. She was out of luck, so she made do with a picture of James Dean, cutting the eyes from a full-page photograph. From the same drawer, she took a bottle of white glue, and with a paintbrush she applied it to the paper. She stuck the eyes just above the bulge on the rock that resembled a nose.

"You can see me at last," she said. "I'm Melissa. I'll introduce you to everyone else later."

Daisy and Dahlia spoke behind her.

"Aren't we enough for you?"

"Why do you say that?" She rummaged through the drawer until she found a different paintbrush from the one she'd used for the glue. "Of course you're enough, but I want to have other friends. Can't I have any friends other than you two?"

She unscrewed the lid on a bottle of black tempera while the girls whispered to each other.

"You have Iris, too. And Mommy and Daddy. And Edelweiss is still outside."

"I know, but what if, say, I want to talk to someone in the middle of the night? Who do I speak to? You're all asleep then."

The girls shrugged.

"Well, there you go."

Melissa tried to paint a smile on the rock, but its topography altered the course of the brushstroke, and she ended up tracing a distorted mouth. She judged it acceptable. She liked her stones to have their own personality, and if this one wanted to express itself with a funny face, so be it. She turned it around so that it looked at her sisters.

"Say hello. His name's James."

The girls waved. "He's sad," they said.

"No he's not. He's just a bit serious," Melissa contended. Then she whispered near the stone's ear. "This is Daisy and Dahlia."

The girls exchanged little smiles.

From the living room came the beginning of a song.

"Music!" they yelled.

They ran downstairs.

"I'm going, too," Melissa explained to James. "I hope you don't mind. You won't be on your own."

She left the stone in one of the few empty spaces that remained on the shelves above the headboard, beside ten other stones with stuck-on eyes and painted smiles. The wood was already sagging under the weight of them. With her fingers, Melissa tightened one of the fastening nuts that loosened every time the stones were moved. She named them all by way of an introduction.

"James, look, this is Marlon, this is John, this is Clark, and this is Rock. These are Cary, Gregory, and another Rock. And those are Natalie and Doris, with one more Rock." She snapped her fingers to end the string of names. "Say hello to James, everyone. He's going to stay in the bedroom with you."

Melissa fell silent.

Listening.

"They're Dad's old records," she said in reply to a question.

She nodded at the stones.

"Sure I will."

She smiled at Gregory.

"Soon. The sooner I go, the sooner I'll be back. The music won't last long anyway."

With no further explanation, Melissa went downstairs.

Iris heard her sister go down the stairs. She was sitting in front of the dressing table in her bedroom, completing her hundred strokes a day with the hairbrush. Mom said it was the best way to maintain the natural shine of blonde hair, the color that all the sisters shared in different tones. On stroke number eighty-three, she put down the brush to follow Melissa and join the family by the record player. Before reaching the stairs, she spotted an open magazine on her sister's desk. It showed an image of a man with his arms almost bare.

Iris's pulse accelerated.

When she walked up to it, she discovered that the actor was wearing a white T-shirt with very short sleeves. She licked her lips. With her finger, she went over the arms' muscles, the curve of the shoulders. She felt the actor's pectorals on the page, his abdomen. She was tempted to touch lower down. She ran the tip of her finger over the picture, daring herself to go a little further. She felt her cheeks flush hot. Her breathing quickened just thinking of touching that part of the pants. When she finally mustered the courage to explore lower down, she realized the picture had had its eyes cut out. Those holes in the face neutralized her desire. She left the room.

She found the rest of the family in the living room. Her parents were dancing, rocking to the music coming from the record player, Dad holding Mom around the waist, her hands on his neck. With their faces within kissing distance, Dad whispered the song lyrics.

"I want to live with you among the flowers. With them and me you'll never be alone . . ."

Mom's eyes were bright. "I want this to last forever," she said.

In her mother's voice, Iris identified the note of fear it sometimes took on. She'd read about the constant fear that stalks mothers from the moment they give birth, but the intensity of the worry that could suddenly well up in Mom suggested a certainty that something bad was going to happen.

"It *will* last forever, Rose, I promise you," Dad whispered in her ear. "We're just fine."

Iris felt uncomfortable when she heard what seemed like a secret.

Mom rested her face against Dad's chest. With her eyes closed, she let out a sigh that ended in a smile, as if she completely trusted Dad's words.

"*The future and this place it's only ours . . .*" he sang.

Copying their parents, Dahlia made Daisy her dance partner. They danced holding each other like adults, laughing. They kept treading on the little rug that always slipped underfoot, laughing harder every time they slid and had to improvise an emergency dance step to stop themselves from falling.

When the needle on the record player reached the end of the song, Melissa returned it to the beginning of the groove and gave Iris an exaggerated bow.

Iris took the hand her sister offered her. "If only you were a real boy," she whispered when she knew her parents wouldn't hear. "I'd hand my soul to Charon if it meant I could turn your arms into a man's."

"Do you really have to use those words to say things?"

"I have a large vocabulary and I make use of it. Please forgive me if it bothers you."

"It doesn't bother me. And if you need a man"—Melissa deepened her voice to make it sound masculine—"you can call me Bob."

Iris raised her eyebrows. "I need a real man, not my little sister putting on voices and using the name from a record sleeve."

She gestured at the cover on the floor, near the turntable. The name Bob Davis was on it, along with a portrait of the singer and a bunch of flowers. The sisters laughed as they performed dance moves that were more energetic and complex than the song called for. Trying to copy their movements, the twins slipped on the rug, falling on the floor at the same time, onto their backsides. They burst into giggles that infected the whole family. Iris pressed her hand against her belly to relieve the abdominal pain. Then the little girls both noticed the guitar that hung from the wall. They said something into each other's ears before suggesting it out loud.

"Play the guitar, Daddy!"

Mom stopped dancing. Dad stood looking at the floor. Iris saw Edelweiss's name inscribed on the instrument. Her sister had carved it on one side of the sound box herself. Edelweiss could spend entire days with that guitar, finding infinite melodies with the five chords she knew.

"No, girls," Dad replied, without looking up. "I can't. Not yet."

The song ended for the second time. Amid the silence that filled the living room, Iris heard the wind whistle through the needles of the cacti outside.

Mom kissed Dad on the cheek.

"Maybe we should get to bed," she said. "You're tired from your trip to the town, and you have to work early tomorrow."

But Dad asked the twins to put the song back on. They cheered and began dancing again as soon as the music started. Iris urged her partner to start moving again. Their parents were persuaded to rejoin the dance as well. Dad intoned the lyrics very close to Mom's lips.

"And any place I'm with you feels like home."

Iris's gaze returned to the name engraved on the guitar. She thought about the other wood that Dad had carved with the same name a little over a year ago: the cross driven into the ground behind the house. She imagined her big sister on the other side of the window of that very living room, under the rocks, among the cacti, observing from the darkness the orangey light coming from the house that had been her home, unable now to join in a family dance or to play her guitar. Iris's eyes filled with tears.

"I miss her, too," Melissa said. With a finger, she wiped away her sister's tears.

They danced in each other's arms until the song ended.

At dawn, the cacti's shadows were so long they looked like hands dragging along the ground, eager to touch the horizon. Leaning against the doorjamb, Rose observed the display of colors with which the desert welcomed the sun.

"I'll never get tired of looking at this landscape," she said to her husband.

"Right now I don't have time to look at anything."

He zipped the gas station coveralls up to the top with a tug. Rose used a hand to smooth down the material on the front, the embroidered badge that said ELMER. She covered the last two letters to read the name as she often said it.

"I did warn you last night, Elm. You should've gone to bed earlier."

Rose rubbed her eyes. She gathered her hair in a ponytail that she held in place with her hand, waiting for the morning air to cool her neck. She let it fall, having felt no improvement. Even at dawn, the breeze was weak and warm.

"What's the point of all of this if I can't enjoy them when I get home?" he asked.

Rose waited until he was within reach to answer his question in the way it deserved: with a kiss, her hand against a jaw that was rougher than the sandpaper he kept in his toolbox. The ceiling creaked over their heads from the girls' movements. Rose recognized Melissa's dragging footsteps. She must have woken sad again. She also identified Iris's. She always walked on tiptoes as if she could take flight at any moment. The twins' gallop thundered toward the stairs.

"They've caught you," she warned Elmer with her lips against his.

He tried to escape in time, but the little girls reached him as if they'd tobogganed down the stairs.

"You're going already, Daddy?"

"You're going already, Daddy?"

"Hi, Mom."

"Hi, Mom."

Rose opened the screen door and invited the three of them out to put on their morning performance, the one in which Elmer struggled to the truck with a girl hanging on to each leg. She watched them from the handrail on the porch. Elmer advanced like an astronaut exploring a planet with stronger gravity than Earth's.

"We love you so much, Daddy."

"We love you so much, Daddy."

He pretended to cut his throat with his fingers, complaining at the nuisance, but Rose knew that he enjoyed their morning routine.

"Ugh, they stink of gas," Dahlia said about the coveralls.

"I like the smell." Daisy pressed her nose against the material and breathed in.

"You can't like it, because I don't like it."

"Maybe you can't not like it because I do like it."

The twins got into one of the arguments that started every time they differed on something, be it which of their three dresses they were going to wear on a given day, the age at which they planned to get married, or whether they liked the smell of gasoline. As was always the case with these disputes, neither managed to convince the other.

"When're you back, Daddy?" they asked, synchronizing again as if the argument had never happened.

"You know when. When the sun's disappearing over there."

He gestured in the rough direction of where the sun went down at that time of year. Rose watched the shadow of her husband's arm join those of the cacti, another hand eager to touch the horizon.

"Oh no, that's forever."

"Oh no, that's forever."

They hugged him more tightly. He looked to Rose for help.

"Come on, girls, he has to go now," she called from the porch.

The hinges on the screen door squeaked behind her, and Iris and Melissa arrived beside her. They leaned on the handrail.

Iris was holding her new book with a finger between pages, marking the place where she'd stopped reading. "There go the girls, facing up to the personal tragedy that afflicts them each morning," she said.

Elmer resorted to tickling them to get them to let go of him.

"Come on. I have to rush off, and Mom's calling you." His voice reached the porch loud and clear. "Don't make things difficult on the last day of class."

Rose let her shoulders drop, fearing Melissa's reaction to those words. She'd wanted to give her the news herself, at breakfast.

The twins magnified the information by leaping with joy. "Last day of class!" they yelled in unison.

"Is that true?" Melissa asked, her voice as weak as the morning breeze.

Rose nodded with a sigh.

Melissa slammed the door as she went back into the house. The bang caught the attention of Elmer and the little girls, who interrupted their celebration.

"Didn't she know?" he asked from where he stood near the truck.

Rose shook her head, crossing her arms. Elmer shrugged an apology but took advantage of the twins' distraction to climb into the pickup. Daisy and Dahlia returned to the porch, escaping the dust cloud the truck created.

"It's the last day of class! We're hungry!"

"It's the last day of class! We're hungry!"

They ran to the kitchen as if they could make breakfast themselves. Rose took Iris by the hand, and they followed the girls in. They found them in the kitchen, sitting on the floor near the refrigerator. Their eyes were fixed on each other as they repeated gestures in a learned sequence. One raised her eyebrows, so did the other. Dahlia stuck out her tongue, Daisy stuck out her tongue. They filled their cheeks with air at the same time and emptied them with two-handed slaps.

Iris interrupted the performance by holding her book between them. She told them to get up. Then she took four bowls from a cupboard to serve breakfast.

Melissa was sitting at the table. She was looking out the window with her head resting on a hand, her eyes lost in the distance. "When were you planning on telling me?" she asked.

"When you stop making such a fuss about it."

A tear slid down Melissa's cheek, then down her forearm, until it reached the tabletop. With her thumb, she was stroking one of her rocks, as if it really were alive. Rose put a hand over her daughter's.

"It's just three months," she said. "You'll be starting another term in no time, and then Socorro will come every day, like she always does. You'll be free to enjoy the summer. Don't you want that?"

Melissa shook her head, pursing her lips. Rose looked to Iris for support.

"Don't look so desolate, it's no big deal. It's as if you were Fantine in *Les Misérables*." Iris served her sister a bowl of cereal. "If our teacher was a good-looking guy, I'd understand you, share in your sorrow, but Socorro's an old woman and we won't miss much if we don't see her for a while."

Melissa clicked her tongue. Rose knew how much it upset her when Iris tried to solve her problems by imposing her approach to life on her, especially since Iris reduced everything to matters of love.

"She's someone from outside," Melissa said. "Pretty much the only person we speak to. I like her, and I'll miss her all summer. If you don't get it, then leave me in peace." She turned her attention outside, sniffing.

Rose was touched by the way Melissa frowned, as if she'd spent her entire life trying to decipher the meaning of the landscape that was her home, trying to accept it but unable to do so. She knew that many children go through a phase when they rebel against their world, their home, their family, but there was something deeper in her daughter's longing.

And she didn't like it.

It scared her.

"We have Dad's workmate's son's birthday in August," Rose said to try to console her. "We'll go visit them like we always do."

Melissa gave her an incredulous look, a look that said she didn't know her daughter very well if she thought their annual visit to a family that didn't speak English was any consolation.

"A boy as alone as we are." Melissa dried her nose with the back of her hand. "And he's weird."

She offered some cornflakes to her stone with eyes. She crushed the cereal against the painted-on mouth, as if the rock were munching it.

"How old's that boy now?" Iris asked.

"I don't know, eleven. Twelve."

"No good to me, then."

Rose tried to cuff Iris for the inappropriate remark, but Iris evaded her with a smile. She sat the twins at the table and served them milk.

The little girls whispered to each other.

"We're really happy that Socorro won't be coming anymore," they said at the same time, "so we don't have to hide."

Melissa dropped her spoon against the rim of her bowl, expressing her anger.

"Of course *you* want her to come, because *you* don't have to hide," Dahlia said.

"But we don't want to hide," Daisy added.

Melissa rebuffed their comments with a deep sigh.

"So, who's hiding today?" Rose asked the twins.

They each indicated the other.

"It's Dahlia's turn," Iris pointed out.

"And Dahlia is . . ." Rose waved a straight finger between them, as if trying to figure out which of the two was Dahlia. In reality, she could tell them apart even from behind, but she liked to reward the effort the girls made to look the same for four hours a day. "Is it you?"

She pointed at the wrong twin on purpose. They laughed, delighted to have created the confusion.

"No, Mommy, that's Dahlia." Daisy directed her mother's finger toward her sister.

"It's you? Really? It's getting harder and harder to tell you apart," Rose said. "So you're hiding today, and Daisy's staying here for the class. Then you'll tell your sister everything you learn from the teacher, won't you?"

"Yes, Mommy, as *always*."

"Yes, Mommy, as *always*."

The weary tone in the girls' words made Melissa smile. "You girls really do like teasing your mother, don't you?"

The twins laughed with their spoons in their mouths, spattering each other with milk.

Iris brought two cups of coffee. She left one on the table, and the other one she drank standing next to the window, her book under her arm. Rose took a sip of coffee, observing her two eldest daughters. They were both looking at the same landscape but seemed in different worlds.

As soon as Dahlia had finished her last spoonful of cereal, Rose urged her to get up. "Come on, Socorro's about to arrive. And the rest of you, start getting your books out."

Melissa stood and took three books from the shelf.

"But we won't have a lesson, will we?" asked Iris. "Seeing as it's the end of the term."

Melissa dropped the books on the table: one on economics, another on natural sciences, and the one handwriting book the twins took turns with.

"We won't, will we, Mom?" Iris persisted.

Rose was already leaving the kitchen and didn't respond. She climbed the stairs, guiding Dahlia by the hand. They went into the bedroom she shared with Daisy.

"Will we really not have to hide anymore tomorrow?" the girl asked.

"Well, until next term."

"Whew, that's *foreeever*."

She drew out the word for as long as she could, as if the summer really was eternal. She ran excitedly to the window and breathed in the air from outside.

"I love summer, Mommy. It's when the cactuses are prettiest. With all those white flowers. I'm going to pick them all. I'm going to spend the entire summer picking flowers."

"Well, I don't know how you'll manage that. The cactuses only flower this month."

"Just one month?" Dahlia looked serious, as if deliberating how she would deal with the setback. "Then I'll collect all of them in a month. And I'm going to make myself a dress with them. And one for you. And one for Daisy. One for Iris. And one for Melissa. Maybe it'll cheer her up. And I want to make another one for Edelweiss as well. We're all going to look so pretty in white. Well, not Edelweiss. But I can leave them on top of her grave and—"

Rose covered her mouth. The grave of her eldest sister had no place on the innocent lips of such a young girl. It was against the natural order of things. She took Dahlia away from the window and pulled the curtains.

"Nice and quiet now, until Socorro leaves."

The little girl held a finger to her lips. She took off her shoes to keep her feet from making noise and winked at Rose. From under one of the room's two identical beds, she took out a piece of cardboard so wide she could barely reach both ends with outstretched arms. She placed it on the bed. It showed a drawing of a landscape similar to the one that surrounded the house: cacti, rocks, the sun, and some clouds were traced in pencil. Dahlia had already filled half of the shapes with colored beads, but there was still a lot of work to do.

"It's looking great," Rose said.

"I've done better ones."

Dahlia gestured at the dozen or so similar works of art that hung from the walls. There were pictures of animals, imaginary creatures, landscapes, and faces more or less resembling the family's. Melissa had sketched them on pieces of cardboard of different sizes so that the twins could color them, bead by bead, during the hours they spent hiding. The ones Dahlia pointed at now were a portrait of Rose that she had yet to finish because the town had run out of the brown glass seed beads she needed for the eyes, and a smaller picture in which the word MOMMY occupied the entire surface. That one was hanging over her bed's headboard. Daisy had another one over hers, the letters colored differently. Rose felt touched whenever she imagined the girls' little hands applying glue to the cards, selecting the beads, and sticking them on, one after the other, to spell out the five letters that together described her most important role in life.

"They're my favorites, too," she said.

Dahlia smiled, and from the bedside table she took the orange jar that Elmer had brought her yesterday. "It's sundown." She pointed at the sky on the card.

Then she asked Rose to bring her ear close so she could tell her a secret. "I'm faster than Daisy."

From under her sister's bed she took out an identical drawing with fewer beads stuck to the card. "See?"

Rose couldn't help smiling. Dahlia returned the other picture to its place, proud that she was ahead. Then she climbed onto the bed, sat with her legs crossed in front of the desert Melissa had drawn, and extracted a first handful of orange beads.

Rose was spellbound by the beauty she saw in her daughter.

"You'd better watch out or Socorro will catch us," Dahlia reproached her.

"I'm going, I'm going."

She left the room and locked the door from the outside. She pictured her daughter filling the circle that would be the sun with glue, creating dusk with her hands. She could almost feel the warmth of that fictitious sun in her chest, the warmth of her girls' love, before the fear of loss clouded everything over. It always appeared at moments of total happiness like this. She left the key in the lock and went downstairs, repeating to herself that everything was fine. With each step peace, and her smile, gradually returned.

Sitting at the kitchen table, which served as a desk, Melissa saw Mom walk in. She was smiling the way she did when she admired the scenery from the screen door, grateful for everything. Mom tipped her head to question whether she was feeling better, and Melissa nodded, even if it wasn't true.

"Let's see if the rest of you can apply yourselves like Melissa does," she said to the others.

Iris was leaning against the counter, engrossed in her book. She was nibbling on a cookie without taking her eyes away from the page.

"Hey, you with the book."

Iris kept reading.

"Hello? Can you hear me?"

Mom had to tap her twice on the shoulder to make her react.

"What is it?"

"What it is that you have class."

"There's no class today, it's the last day of the term," Daisy said from under the table.

Mom lifted the tablecloth, squatting.

"That's something your sister made up. You have class today like any other day"—she stood and turned to Iris—"which is why I'll be paying her the same today as I always do."

"You save enough with the two-for-one deal you've invented." Iris gestured at Daisy on the floor. "That poor lady has four students and thinks she only has three."

Mom looked serious. She took the big basket she used in the vegetable garden from a cupboard. From a drawer she pulled the gardening gloves.

She found her straw hat hanging behind the door. She put it on, looking at Iris.

"When you work and have a tough time earning money, I'm sure you'll understand your parents. Now sit down for your lesson, please."

Daisy obeyed Mom's command, too. She came out of her hiding place and sat in front of the handwriting book, opposite Melissa. She must have seen that her older sister was still sad, because she stroked her hand to comfort her. Iris sat at one end of the table. She opened the economics textbook and over its pages opened *Pride and Prejudice*.

"I have to get out to the garden before the sun burns everything. Iris, you're in charge of making sure Socorro teaches class."

"Look. You can tell her yourself."

The sand crunched under the tires of the teacher's truck.

"Daisy, you're Lily now," said Mom.

It was the name the twins shared when Socorro was in the house. It made it easier for everyone to avoid making a mistake.

"I know, Mommy."

Melissa made out the teacher's silhouette behind the wheel. The front door opened soon after.

"*Híjole*, this heat," Socorro said as she came in.

She wore her gray hair gathered in a bun that made her seem taller. She wore longer clothes and thicker fabrics than the temperature called for. As ever, she acknowledged Melissa first, with a wink. Melissa made herself comfortable in her chair, stretching her back. She was beginning to feel happier. Then the teacher greeted Mom.

"Good morning, Rose. Off to the garden again? I'm so happy to see you do so well with it. I don't know how you do it. Everything I plant dies in all this sunshine. My husband's already told me to give up. The best place for growing chilies and *cebollas* is the market, he said to me the other day. Can you believe it? I must be the worst *esposa* in the state."

Socorro spoke fluent English, but she still said some words in Spanish. Sometimes she did it because she couldn't remember the English word, but she once admitted to Melissa that her real intention was for the girls to learn a little of the language of the country where they lived. As a Mexican, she was offended by a gringo couple living here almost twenty years without teaching the language to their daughters.

"So what's the deal with your girls sat here looking so settled today?" she asked, raising her eyebrows. "You don't think we're going to spend the whole time here inside on the last day of the term, do you?"

Melissa saw Iris give Mom a smile. Their mother opened her mouth to say something, but Daisy got in ahead of her.

"Mom says you have to teach class the same because she's paying you the same."

"Oh, really? She said that?" Socorro looked at Mom. "Well, I say life's too short. We've been studying all year, and it would be criminal not to go out and smell those flowers the cactuses grace us with this time of year."

Mom was silent while she pulled on her gardening gloves. She adjusted the material in the spaces between her fingers without speaking.

"In any case, if your mother thinks you'll only get value for your *dinero* learning a lesson from your books, I'll teach you lesson *veintitrés* from this book outside."

She opened Melissa's science textbook to a page that showed a diagram of a flower. Arrows indicated the scientific names of its parts. Mom glanced over it.

"The flowers of the *cardón* are perfect for differentiating between these parts because they're *bien grandototas*," Socorro added, smiling at Melissa every time she used a Spanish word.

"What's a *cardón*?" asked Daisy.

"*Cardón* is what we Mexicans call those tall cacti that surround your house," she answered. Then she turned to Mom. "So, what do you think about a lesson in the open air?"

Mom adjusted the last finger on the right-hand glove. "All right, you win."

Daisy vanished in front of Melissa. One second she was there, and the next she was running around outside, the screen door shaking in its frame. Iris closed her economics book so enthusiastically that dust was lifted from the table. She sought out Mom's and Melissa's eyes to gloat over her small victory. She went out onto the porch, where she was welcomed by Daisy yelling that she was going to make necklaces out of the flowers. Mom left the kitchen through the back door, the one that provided quicker access to the garden and the little chicken coop.

Melissa didn't move from her place at the table. She sat reading the chapter on flower reproduction, stroking her stone while she discovered that the arrows in the diagram indicated parts named stamen, pistil, calyx. Socorro sat opposite her in the chair Daisy had vacated. She placed her hand on Melissa's to stop her from caressing the rock.

"Do you know, there's a trick so that you're never sad?"

Melissa looked at her teacher, into eyes surrounded by wrinkles so deep it seemed as if her face had survived more storms than the desert.

"A trick?"

"A very simple trick that anyone can do. It consists of being glad for what you've got instead of being unhappy about what you don't have."

"That's what Mom says."

"Because it's the best way to live."

Melissa shrugged, unsure she was able follow the advice.

"You're not the only girl who lives in such an isolated place," Socorro went on. "There're kids in other places who have real problems, things you'll never have to worry about."

"And what do I do with the things that do worry me? It worries me that you won't be coming all summer and that I won't see you for three months."

Socorro held her hand to her heart. "And you don't know what that means to me. But you should think about whether that's really a reason to be sad. If you use the trick I've given to you, you'll stop lamenting that you won't see me and that you don't have any other friends, and you'll be glad that you have two wonderful *hermanas*, and parents who love you very much, and a beautiful house in the wild. I, for one, would like to have a family as lovely as yours, or to still have my children at home with me. But I don't lament it. I'm glad I have a loyal husband to keep me company. Even if he has lost hope that his wife will ever pull a *cebolla* from the earth."

Melissa forced a smile. Socorro squeezed her hand.

"And when you really can't bear it anymore, when you feel alone and need to speak to someone, you can ask your father to drive you to the gas station and call me whenever you like." She opened the science book to the first page, where she'd written her number at the beginning of the term. "Or you can insist that your parents install a phone at long last. Almost everyone has one now."

Melissa ran a finger over the number.

"And now, up on your feet," Socorro said. "Let's get outside or we'll end up spending the whole day stuck in here."

Melissa closed the book with a smile and got up from the table. When she went to pick up the stone with eyes, Socorro stopped her. She gestured through the window at Iris and Daisy, engaged in a battle using fistfuls of earth.

"You have your sisters."

Rose returned from the garden with the basket filled with onions, tomatoes, eggs, and chilies of various colors. She set it on the table alongside the girls' closed books. She took off the gloves and, with them, wiped the sweat from her neck and forehead. Feathers fell to the floor. She saw Socorro and her daughters outside. As she washed the vegetables, she enjoyed the smell of life and nature that filled the kitchen every time she did this. She also cleaned the excrement from the eggs. As she sliced off a sunscalded part of the last tomato, it was just five minutes before the class would end.

She dried her hands on her apron and, standing on tiptoe, took a jar of money from the bookcase. Iris's books collapsed to one side on the shelf. She took a bill and the necessary coins from the container, recovered her hat from the hook on the door, and walked out to the teacher and the girls.

"Already?" Daisy asked, the shrillness of her voice as great as her disbelief that four hours had gone by. She held a necklace made with white flowers.

Sitting on a rock, Socorro looked at her watch, holding her wrist away from her eyes.

"How time flies when you're having fun, eh, Lily?" she said to Daisy. "See, Rose? It was too nice a day to be cooped up in the kitchen."

"Every day's nice here. The only thing that changes is how hot it is. And I intended to use this money"—she waved the note she held in her hand—"to have my daughters learn something important. I can teach them handicrafts myself all summer."

"We also learned the life cycle of flowers," Melissa said. "It was lesson twenty-three in the book."

"That's right, Mommy." Daisy came up to Rose's legs with a flower in her hands, pointing at two different parts in the center of the flower. "This is stamens, and this is the pastel."

"Pistil," Socorro corrected her.

"Pistil," the little girl repeated. "And I made you this necklace."

Rose bent down and Daisy hung from her neck a long blade of grass tied like a lasso, decorated with several flowers skewered by cactus spines. The older sisters wore similar ones.

"Thank you very much, Daisy." She hugged her daughter. "It's lovely."

When the little girl stamped on her foot, she realized she'd gotten the name wrong. She thought of a thousand answers to the question Socorro would ask, but the teacher must not have paid attention, because she just got up from the rock and brushed the dust from her skirt and bag.

"We may have learned a lot, but look what a state we're in," she said.

Rose and the girls played along with the teacher and brushed off their own clothes.

"And you"—Rose pointed at the plant remains on Daisy's arms, face, and hands—"the filthiest, as always."

Daisy smiled, proud.

"Go on, take her to the hose and get her washed," she said to Iris.

Her eldest daughter obeyed, taking Daisy by the hand.

"No goodbye for me?" asked Socorro.

Daisy ran to hug her teacher around the waist. "Goodbye, Socorro," she said.

The image sparked jealousy in Rose, who considered herself and her husband the only ones deserving of that show of affection so characteristic of the twins.

Iris kissed the teacher on the cheek.

"Don't stop reading," Socorro said. "A good collection of books can show you more than a thousand teachers ever could."

"I wasn't planning to. Even if my mother thinks they make me have my head in the clouds." Iris thanked Socorro for the advice with a spontaneous hug.

"To the hose," Rose said quickly, to interrupt it.

Melissa was the last one to say goodbye. Her embrace with Socorro was so heartfelt that Rose preferred to distract herself by watching Iris untangle the hose in the distance, beside the barbecue to one side of the porch.

"Don't forget the trick I taught you," Socorro said. "Be glad for what you've got . . ."

"I'll try," said Melissa. "I hope to see you again soon."

Rose was annoyed that they could talk without finishing their sentences, like great friends, considering how difficult she found it to communicate with Melissa.

"It'll be sooner than you think. Summers fly by," Socorro added.

Melissa headed to the porch, leaving trails more than footsteps in the sand. She looked down at the ground all the way there, searching for new rocks to give faces to.

"Look out for Melissa," the teacher said. "She's a really smart kid, but she seems unhappy."

"She inherited her mother's melancholy." Rose didn't need anyone to describe her daughters' personalities to her. "She's always been like that."

"Your daughter draws eyes on stones. She talks to cactuses."

"We've all had imaginary friends."

"At thirteen?"

Rose handed Socorro the money for the lessons. "We have to work hard for it. That's why I insisted you teach them a class. Don't think I don't like seeing my daughters enjoy themselves."

Socorro took her by the hands.

"You think I don't know that? Your love for those girls flows from every pore in your skin. You showed it when you got back on your feet the way you did after what happened with Edelweiss. For them. You faced the toughest challenge a mother can face, but you still have many to overcome. Iris is entering a . . . difficult age now."

The way she pronounced the word made it clear what she was referring to.

"She's still young for that," said Rose.

"Young? How old were you when you met your husband?"

Rose didn't answer.

"How old?"

"Fifteen."

Socorro's eyebrows almost reached her hairline. "Your daughter's older than that."

"But it was different. We lived in a city, surrounded by people."

"Believe me, your daughter's desire is no different from what you felt at her age. Or what I felt when I was young, a century ago. It's natural. Or what do you think those stamens and pistils the flowers have are for?

There's nothing wrong with your daughter's *despertar*." Though Socorro used the Spanish word, it was easy to imagine what it meant. "The problem is that she can't meet anyone to satisfy that desire. And as pretty as she is . . ."

Rose would have preferred to hug the thorn-covered cactus beside her than continue discussing her daughter's sexual desire. "When she's an adult, she'll be able to go with whoever she wants," she said—more loudly than she intended, the mere idea of Iris leaving home making her head spin—"and satisfy those desires you say she has. But right now she's a child who lives with her parents."

"Then don't be surprised by what she decides. And I tell you from experience. We live in a beautiful place to bring up a family. But young people want other things now. They want cars. They want to watch movies from their cars. They want to eat hamburgers while they watch movies from their cars. There's nothing here for them."

Socorro invited Rose to look around her. Only rocks, cacti, and various types of spiny shrub covered the landscape as far as the eye could see.

"Your daughters see no one outside of the family."

"Nonsense. They go with their father to the town once a month."

"One at a time," the teacher pointed out. "How many times has Melissa been in total? And who's she going to talk to if she doesn't speak Spanish?"

"They go to town more than I do. I never leave here. And I couldn't be happier."

"But you and your husband, you chose this way of life. They didn't."

"Do anyone's children choose their way of life?"

Socorro seemed ready to respond but in the end said nothing. She transformed whatever words she'd considered saying into a smile that unsettled Rose. It was the smile of someone remaining silent because they know that sometimes one must make one's own mistakes in order to learn the lessons. Rose gave her daughters that smile.

"Thank you for the class," Rose said.

They walked to the teacher's truck without saying anything else, hearing Daisy yell under the jet from the hose. When Socorro climbed into the vehicle, Rose wished her a pleasant summer.

"You, too," she replied. "Make the most of these summers. They'll be the best of your life."

With her hands on the wheel, she gestured at the girls. Rose saw Daisy in her underwear, spinning around in a puddle with her arms outstretched. Over her, a rainbow glistened in the atomized water coming from a split in the rubber of the hose. Iris was aiming for the little girl's face with the jet and laughed each time she hit her target, while Daisy tried to protect herself with her hands. Rose smiled at the scene until her eyes found Melissa, sitting alone in a kitchen that seemed so dark from outside. She was moving her mouth. Something caught Rose's attention on the second floor. The curtain in the twins' room had moved.

She banged twice on Socorro's hood to speed up their parting. "See you in September."

The truck moved off along the track, sending up a column of smoke and dust. Rose strode back to the house, ignoring Daisy's yells for attention. It was Dahlia who needed attention. She climbed the stairs two at a time and turned the key in the lock. When she opened the door, she found the little girl sitting on the floor, her head hidden between her legs. The jar of orange beads, also on the floor, was empty, some distance from her, the contents scattered all over the room.

"Honey . . ."

"That's not class."

More laughter reached them from Daisy and Iris outside.

"I always miss the best stuff."

"It was the last day. The teacher wanted to do something special with your sisters."

The little girl took her head out from between her knees, looking straight at Rose. Dahlia's jaw dropped when she saw her.

"You went to pick flowers without me?"

She swallowed as she finished asking the question, as indignant as the time she discovered that it was Mommy who made her toy rabbit talk. Rose touched the necklace hanging on her chest, as if she needed to check that it was still there.

"Dahlia, it was the teacher. I didn't—"

Rose was unable to finish the sentence before her daughter burst into tears. She sat on the floor opposite Dahlia, crossing her legs.

"Honey . . ."

Dahlia grabbed the necklace and pulled. The blade of grass broke without difficulty. The little girl left the bedroom. Rose followed her. On the stairs, they came across Melissa. Dahlia broke her necklace in the same way, scattering flowers all over the steps. Rose wouldn't have had time to offer an explanation to Melissa, who, at any rate, didn't ask for one. She continued up the stairs, whispering to her rock.

Dahlia ran outside. She stopped when she found her sisters playing with the hose. She looked at Rose as if she couldn't believe that she'd allowed her to miss out on so much fun. The little girl discovered her sister's necklace hanging on the hose's faucet, by the clothes she'd taken off before surrendering herself to the water. She broke it. Then she went up to Daisy and pushed her into the mud.

"You did it without me."

"It was my turn to take class today." Daisy wiped the wet earth from her face. "I don't complain when it's your turn."

Dahlia didn't reply but stripped down to her underwear, like Daisy. She sat with her in the puddle and replicated as accurately as possible the spots of earth her sister had on her body. She crossed her arms, angry with everything around her.

"I wanted to pick flowers, too," she sobbed.

Rose knelt beside her, trying to avoid the mud.

"Would you like us to pick some more? Tomorrow?"

Dahlia turned away.

"Tomorrow we can pick flowers again, all of us together."

She pinched Dahlia's elbow but the little girl snatched it away. Then Rose thought of something. She held out an arm to Iris, asking her to hand over her still-intact necklace. Iris gave it to her with a frown.

"Dahlia, listen to me."

The little girl resisted but finally turned around.

"Smell this necklace," said Rose.

Dahlia held her nose near the flowers. "It doesn't smell."

"Of course it doesn't. Because it's daytime. But do you know what we'll do tomorrow? Pick the flowers at dusk, which is when they smell good. Tomorrow we'll make much better necklaces than these ones."

Dahlia sniffed the flowers again. "They don't smell," she said with a smile. Then she turned to Daisy. "Your necklaces don't smell. We're gonna make better ones tomorrow. Necklaces that smell."

Daisy pulled a face.

"And I'm beating you with my sunset picture," Dahlia added. "I've already colored in the sky."

The twins got into one of their arguments, this time debating which of the two was the fastest at sticking on colored beads. Rose stood up without interrupting the dispute. She whispered to Iris, who aimed the hose at the little girls. Stealthily, she reached for the faucet and turned it on full blast. The jet of water hit Dahlia's face first, then Daisy's. The initial screams quickly became laughter, and the twins got up and jumped in the water, trying to splash Rose and Iris, who laughed from a safe distance.

Dahlia used some leaps to stamp on the flowers of the necklace that had fallen in the mud. "They don't smell!"

Rose asked Iris to finish washing the little girls and headed back into the house. Before she reached the porch, she turned around. She had Iris's necklace in her hands. She fingered it, feeling the texture of the flowers. Seeing her daughters so happy, she couldn't help thinking of Edelweiss.

She had an idea. She modified the necklace by bunching the flowers together in her fist, then gathered up the ones that had fallen from Melissa's necklace onto the steps. In the twins' room she recovered the flowers from her own necklace. As she did so, she heard Melissa talking in her bedroom.

"It's a good thing I have you," she was saying to the rocks.

Rose went down to the kitchen. There, she formed the flowers into a centerpiece, using some cactus spines to keep the arrangement together. She put it in a bowl filled with water. One of the petals tore, like a wound opening up. The fragility of that flower made her think of her girls, and she felt like crying. She also wanted to yell Edelweiss's name, to make her come back from wherever she was. She suppressed the urge to throw the bowl against a wall. She delicately knotted the long blade of grass from Iris's necklace and smiled as a tear slid down her cheek.

The puddle almost completely dried up before sunset. A late butterfly was sucking up the last of the liquid from the mud until the twins startled it with the tremor of their footsteps as they ran out to welcome Dad, arriving home on cue just as the sun fell. Daisy and Dahlia deafened him with their yelling while the butterfly, the cacti's shadows, and the moisture on the ground disappeared with the day. Only the shadows returned soon after, when a first-quarter moon appeared among the dark columns that the *cardones* had become, projecting their silhouettes across the earth. New shadows were also cast—by a beetle searching for food, by a bat finding the nectar of the flowers that seduced it with their nocturnal scent.

In the kitchen, Rose finished washing the dishes from dinner. She heard the stairs creak under her husband's weight as he came down from the bedrooms.

"They're all in bed," he said behind her.

She shook the water from the last piece of cutlery before leaving it to dry on top of the rest of the wet dishes. She cleaned the sink, wrung out the cloth, and turned off the faucet, turning around in time to receive Elmer with a kiss.

"I made something," she said. From the top of the refrigerator, she took the floral arrangement that she'd prepared in the morning. "It's for Edelweiss."

He smiled. He opened the back door and took his wife by the hand, inviting her to go out with him.

The cross with Edelweiss's name carved into the horizontal plank was to the right. It could be seen from the living room's large window. Though it was still hot enough that the sweat would evaporate on the skin rather than moisten it, the hair stood up on Rose's arms. She felt her stomach shrink, her heart expand—the mixture of love and anguish that visits to Edelweiss tended to spark in her. Together, they placed the centerpiece on a rectangle of earth marked by colored stones. Daisy and Dahlia had decorated them with beads to make the place where their eldest sister rested more cheerful. At night, the colors weren't visible. Everything was a dark, matte gray.

Rose rested a cheek against her husband's shoulder.

"Nothing's hurt me more than not seeing Edelweiss continue to grow"—she sniffed—"but now I don't want our daughters to get older anymore. Iris is so grown up . . . everything's gone so fast."

He squeezed her against his chest, kissed her hair.

"My daughters are going to want to leave this place," Rose said. "Why did we choose somewhere so lonely? So remote?"

Elmer didn't respond. There was no need. They both knew the answer to those questions. Her husband just rocked her with a slight sway of his body. He shushed softly in her ear to reassure her, but she made his shirt damp with tears.

They remained there, in front of Edelweiss's grave, while a shining gray moon climbed the sky. The screen door's hinges creaked. Dozens of insects rattled against the glass of the single bulb, alight on top of a post, that flickered due to some unevenness in the flow of electricity.

The pencil whistled against the paper as Melissa colored in the cacti's shadows. Sitting by the window in the kitchen, she was drawing Daisy and Dahlia, who were playing outside imitating the shapes of the cardones. They held their arms out, perpendicular to their bodies, and bent them with their hands pointing upward. Dahlia touched Daisy and pretended to hurt herself on the needles. Melissa laughed when she saw it.

"What're you laughing at?" Iris asked from near the stove. She was making *agua de Jamaica*, the cold tea they drank in the afternoons. When the water began to boil, she added four handfuls of dried hibiscus flowers. The liquid quickly turned dark red. "What are those two doing?"

Melissa invited her over to see for herself. The twins were now pointing at the horizon, using their hands as visors. Dahlia lay on the ground, her body lost in the shadow of one of the cactus branches.

"It's longer than it was before," Daisy said. "The shadow's bigger than you now."

Dahlia got up and together they celebrated the discovery with claps and little leaps.

"Mommy, the sun's going down fast!" they yelled at the same time. "It's not long now!"

Iris laughed over the shoulder of Melissa, who added a detail to her drawing. She pressed the pencil's tip down hard, making the cracks in the earth appear deeper.

"In the end, I'll be forced to admit you possess some talent," Iris said. "It's looking nice. I like the shape you've given the sun"—she pointed at it—"and I love the sense of movement the girls give off. They look happy even in pencil."

"Nice?" Melissa asked. "That depends on how you look at it. If you see two girls playing among the cactuses at sunset, then sure. But if you look at the parallel shadows of the cactuses, they're like the bars of a prison that keeps them locked up here."

Iris exhaled. "And Mom says *I'm* the melodramatic one, the one that makes stuff up."

Melissa closed the sketchbook.

"Hey, don't get angry," Iris said. "It's just you get so tragic, so melancholic and over the top sometimes. Do me a favor and just look at that landscape. Look where we live. Living here is the opposite to being locked up. If there's one thing we have enough of, it's space."

"That's not what I mean." Melissa looked around outside, hoping to find something different. A cactus she didn't recognize. A rock formation whose outline she hadn't seen every day of her life. She daydreamed of a building erected right there. Imagined other houses nearby. A person she didn't know. A street with people on it. A movie theater like the ones she saw in her magazines. "Sometimes I feel like I don't belong in this place. That I should be somewhere else."

"Oh, sis, that's what all humanity thinks. Almost every book you see there"—she gestured at her library on the bookcase—"reflects on that theme in one way or another. But where do you belong, if not here? Here you're with me, with them"—she touched the twins in the drawing—"and with Mom and Dad."

"Sure, as if you don't think about leaving."

"First off, I'm older than you, and that's why I have to start thinking about my future. And second, more than leaving, I'm thinking about how to meet a boy. If you bring one here for me, I'll stay in this house forever."

Melissa was about to complain that Iris always steered the conversation toward the same subject, but a hissing sound interrupted from the cooktop. The water had overflowed the saucepan. Iris went to deal with it. She strained the red liquid, filling a pitcher halfway up. The other half she filled with ice. She squeezed lemon into the mixture and stirred it with a wooden spoon.

Melissa turned her attention back to the twins. It took her a while to understand why they were going from cactus to cactus with their noses stuck out. Until they started yelling.

"Mommy! They smell! The flowers smell! Hurry, Mommy!"

Mom came into the kitchen through the back door. She was carrying a large wicker basket. Several pairs of gloves poked out from the edge. "That's them shouting, right?"

Melissa and Iris nodded.

"Boy, am I glad you made that," Mom said, indicating the drink. "I'm so thirsty. I feel as if I've been eating sand."

Iris went to serve her a glass, but Mom said it would be better outside. They only had an hour before it was dark. Melissa took the men's clothes that Dad had brought her from the town. She piled the shirt on top of the pants and put the cap on her head. She also picked up some scissors.

"Come on, let's go," Mom said.

Iris held a tower of glasses in one hand, the pitcher in the other. As soon as they went out onto the porch, Daisy and Dahlia ran to Mom. They snatched two pairs of gloves from the basket and laughed when they put them on. They were enormous on them. They whispered to each other before speaking.

"We've got giant hands!" they said. "We're gonna be able to pick millions of flowers!"

"OK, OK, hold on," Mom said. "How many necklaces are we going to make?"

Daisy spoke in Dahlia's ear. Dahlia answered her, also in her ear. They looked at Melissa, then Mom, then Iris. They pointed at the house, or something beyond it, probably Edelweiss's grave. They reached an agreement.

"Six," they said at the same time.

Melissa had the feeling Mom was going to say something—perhaps remind them that there were no longer six girls living in this house, or thank them for still thinking of Edelweiss—but the twins shot off toward the cacti, leaving her without the chance to speak. In midflight, Dahlia's gloves came off. When she stopped to pick them up, Daisy's came off. They decided to leave them lying there.

"I knew they wouldn't be any use."

Mom ran after the little girls when they went to move the folding ladder themselves. Dad had gotten it out at breakfast so they could reach the highest flowers. Iris and Melissa came down the porch stairs together, the tower of glasses clinking with each step. On the way they found a rock with an interesting shape. Melissa squatted to examine it up close.

"It has cheeks," she said to her sister. Then she addressed the stone: "I'll collect you later, I have my hands full." She showed the folded clothes to the rock.

"Where're you going to belong if not here?" Iris said with a smile. "Making the rocks and the cactuses come to life."

Melissa stuck out her tongue. She changed direction, separating from her sister, who continued toward Mom and the twins.

Daisy and Dahlia were fighting over the ladder when Iris arrived with the pitcher of agua de Jamaica. She offered a glass to the little girls.

"Can't you see we can't? We're very busy," Dahlia said.

"Can't you see we can't? We're very busy," Daisy repeated.

"All right, all right." Iris exchanged a teasing look with Mom.

"OK, you don't have to fight, you can both fit on here just fine." Mom touched the highest and broadest rung on the folding ladder. She let Dahlia climb up first, then showed Daisy where to put her feet. The two of them gained access to the tops of several flower-filled branches of the cactus. "You can start picking them, but watch out for those spines, please."

The girls sniffed the flowers.

"They smell so good!"

"They smell like melon!"

"They smell like melon!" they repeated in unison.

Mom asked Iris to pour her a glass. "Let lots of ice fall in."

She drank without letting go of the base of the ladder. Up top, the twins were laughing. They were counting off each plucked flower before letting it fall into the basket on the ground at the foot of the cactus.

When they'd finished the first one, they moved all the equipment to the neighboring cardón. On their return to land the twins took the chance to gulp down a glass of the homemade drink. As more flowers rained down on the basket, Iris observed Melissa, a few yards from them.

Sitting on a rock, she was cutting open the back of the shirt with the scissors, from the neck down. She also made a large cut on one side of the pants, from the waist to the bottom of the leg. Then she stood on the rock and dressed a cactus in the clothes. They stayed on perfectly, pinned onto the spines. Melissa adjusted the corners of the shirt collar and smoothed out the pants. She did up some of the buttons.

"Do *you* think she's too old for all that stuff?"

Mom's question surprised Iris. A couple of white flowers fell to the ground from the top of the ladder. The little girls' tally was approaching thirty. Iris shrugged and looked at Melissa, who was giving a little bow in front of the cactus.

"What're you going to call him?" Mom yelled.

Melissa turned around.

"I said what're you going to call him?" Mom repeated, even more loudly.

From there, Melissa showed them a flat stone on which she'd written *Thorns* in black tempera.

"Hi, Thorns." Mom raised a hand as if greeting a real person. "And hello to you, too, Needles and Pins. I hadn't said anything to you guys yet."

Beside the cactus that Melissa had just dressed were two others also wearing men's clothes. At their feet, their names were handwritten on stones. Melissa baptized the third cactus by placing the stone at its base. Then she approached Mom and Iris.

"Can I use the ladder to put this on him?" she asked, gesturing at the cap on her head.

Instead of answering Melissa, Mom yelled to the cactus. "Don't worry, Thorns, as soon as the twins have finished picking the flowers, we'll put your cap on for you."

Iris had to make an effort to stop herself from laughing.

"Mom . . ." Melissa looked down at the ground, nudging little stones with the toe of her shoe. "You don't need to speak to them . . . It's . . . it's my thing. They're just cactuses. They can't hear you."

Mom scratched the back of her neck and changed the subject by asking the twins how the picking was going. Three flowers fell into the basket, which was now almost full.

Iris picked it up and sniffed it. "They smell so good."

"They're ours!" shouted the little girls from up high.

"OK, but come on, you have plenty," said Mom. "It's time to stop."

Iris rounded the cactus to show the twins the contents of the basket. There were more than enough flowers to make six necklaces like the ones from yesterday.

"There's one left!"

"There's one left!"

They gestured at a large flower at the very top. Iris took a step back to see it clearly.

"I'm going to get it," Daisy said, stretching out on tiptoes on the ladder.

"No, I am." Dahlia leapt to get ahead of her sister.

Seeing the dangerous maneuver, Mom scolded them.

Daisy screamed.

"What is it?" Mom yelled. She gripped the ladder hard, her shoulders hunched as if she was expecting one of them to fall. "Iris, what is it?"

The large flower from the top of the cardón had come away but hadn't reached the ground. It was skewered on one of the cactus's spines.

"You pushed me!" Daisy burst into tears. "Look what you did!"

She showed Dahlia the consequences of her impatience.

Iris could see it, too. "She's scratched her arm on the cactus."

"Right, that's enough," Mom said. "Daisy, come down!"

The little girl obeyed. She climbed down crying, her chin wrinkled and pressed against her chest. Iris approached to get a better look at the wound. Daisy had a scratch on the inside of her forearm. Five red scores stood out on an irritated area that stretched from the wrist to the fold of the elbow.

"It's nothing." Mom blew on the marks. "Just a graze. There's not even any blood."

The little girl sobbed. "Dahlia pushed me."

Mom was so angry as she climbed the ladder that the contraption's legs ground against the earth every time she stepped on another rung. At the top, she grabbed Dahlia around the waist. The little girl resisted. She was stretching out an arm, trying to reach the detached flower.

Mom began to chide her.

But suddenly she broke off.

She fell silent.

She stood motionless, her eyes fixed on some point in the distance. The little girl was still stretching for the flower, twisting in her arms, but Mom didn't seem to care anymore.

"What is it?" asked Iris, who was still trying to console Daisy. "What can you see?"

Mom went on tiptoes at the top of the ladder. She narrowed her eyes, straining her sight.

"What can you see, Mom?"

Iris followed her gaze, but from the ground she could only see cacti and rocks.

Melissa came and stood beside her. "What is it?"

"I don't know," Iris whispered, "but Mom's seen something."

Their mother moved her lips, murmuring something to herself. She turned her head back toward the house. She looked at Melissa, at Iris, at Daisy. Her eyes inspected the contents of the basket. They stopped on the pitcher of agua de Jamaica. On the five glasses. She looked into the distance again. She let out a deep sigh as she bit her bottom lip. Thinking. Calculating.

"Mom, what's going on?" Iris said. "You're scaring the girls."

The anxiety in her voice alarmed even Dahlia, who paused her efforts to reach the flower to observe Mom.

Mom seemed more tense than angry. More nervous than annoyed.

Her breathing was audible.

"Mom, please," Iris repeated.

Then Mom reacted. She held Dahlia tight and climbed down the ladder in a hurry. She almost pushed the little girl to get her to stand beside Daisy, who was putting the fingers of a hand in her mouth and spreading saliva over her scratches.

"One of you, to your bedroom."

"Is Socorro coming?" asked Melissa.

Mom didn't answer.

"Come on, which of you two is going?"

The twins didn't even look at each other, angry as they were with one another.

"Why does one of them have to go?" Iris pressed her. "Who's coming?"

"It's Socorro," Melissa concluded with a smile, her hands gathered at her chest.

The look Mom gave her made it clear it wasn't.

"Dad?" Iris put forward, though the twins never hid for their father.

"If you don't decide between yourselves, you both go."

Iris didn't like the tone Mom was using with the twins.

"You go," Daisy said.

"No, you go," Dahlia replied.

"You go, because you did this to my arm."

"You go, because I went yesterday."

"But yesterday it was for class. This isn't class. This is because a stranger's coming. And the last time a stranger came, I hid."

"Liar! We both hid!"

"Well, it was years ago, so it doesn't count."

It hadn't actually been years, but Iris was glad that her sisters remembered Edelweiss's homemade funeral as something remote.

"Mom, if it's not Socorro who's coming," she asked over the twins' voices, "why do they have to hide?"

"Not you, too . . ." Mom answered. "Anyone who sees them could spread word around the houses, around the town." Her eyes flicked to one side. "Do we want Socorro to find out that she's been teaching class to four girls instead of three?"

"I'm not going!" yelled Dahlia.

"Well, neither am I!" yelled Daisy.

"Then you both go. Iris, take them to their room."

"Me? Why? Melissa can take them."

"Honey, please. You're not six years old."

Iris turned to Melissa to pass the task on to her, but her sister was no longer by her side. She'd climbed to the top of the ladder. On tiptoes, shading her eyes with her hand, she was looking into the distance as Mom had done. Her mouth was open.

Iris felt excitement in her stomach. "What is it?"

A smile was painted across Melissa's astonished face. Before she could reply, Mom turned Iris around by the shoulders and pushed her and the twins toward the house.

"Take them. Now. And you, Melissa, come down right away. Let's see if we can all start behaving ourselves."

Daisy sat on the ground. "I'm not going." She tried to cross her arms but separated them with a groan when her other arm made contact with her wound.

Iris went to pick her up. She wanted to take the twins away and get back as quickly as possible to find out what was happening.

The little girl lay down, twisting her body. Mom bent down for her. Daisy resisted.

Iris ended up just taking Dahlia. She ran, pulling her along by the hand, not bothered that the little girl's stride wasn't big enough to keep up with her. She heard Dahlia's shoes dragging over the dirt. She heard her yell and cry. They crossed the porch in just three paces. She picked Dahlia up to climb the stairs. When they reached the bedroom, Dahlia threw herself facedown on her bed and cried against the sheets.

Iris went over to the window.

She opened the curtains.

She had to blink several times to make sure what she was seeing on the road was real.

It couldn't be true.

She rushed out of the room and locked it from the outside, leaving Dahlia inside. She went down the stairs two at a time, three at a time. She opened the screen door with so much enthusiasm that the latch hit the wall. She could have floated over the porch.

She returned, her breathing labored, to the place where her sisters and mother were standing. She regretted rushing so much, because she'd broken into a sweat. Hair was stuck to her face, and she could feel moisture on the seam of her neckline. She separated the material from her skin and blew, feeling the coolness down to her belly. She combed her hair with her fingers, nervously, then adjusted her underwear through her dress, straightening the elastic. She rearranged her breasts in her bra. Seeing Mom's look of distaste, she stopped. Her mother was kneeling, loading everything she could into the wicker basket. Daisy asked her to be careful not to squash the flowers.

"I'm real angry at you," Mom said. And although she said it to the little one, she didn't take her eyes from her eldest daughter. Iris thought about saying something to justify her nervousness, but that was when she heard the boy's voice and everything was reduced to the sweet, deep sound of his words. Imagining the tongue that moved inside that mouth to utter them generated an electric current in Iris's body. She felt the heat from that energy concentrate in her chest, in her stomach, between her legs.

When she saw the stranger, Melissa thought of the photo of James Dean she'd cut the eyes out from two days before. The young man had the same thick lips, the same broad forehead with the hair combed back. His gaze was as intense as the one in the magazine image before she'd transplanted it to a stone. He wore a white T-shirt similar to the actor's, the sleeves rolled up to the top of his biceps. A line of dust marked the damp patches around his neck and under his arms. The knees of his jeans were so worn that the material, of a washed-out blue color, threatened to tear open on the next bend of his legs. He wore elaborate boots, with big soles and long laces. A backpack hung from his shoulders. Melissa saw Iris wet her lips and found it easy to trace the trajectory of her sister's eyes over the boy's body.

He observed them, too, and Melissa didn't know whether the intensity with which he inspected their faces was normal in encounters between people. The depth of his gaze, the way he studied the faces in front of him, reminded Melissa of the way she examined the rocks on the ground, searching for specific features.

His eyes lingered on Iris for so long that she finally blushed.

Mom pulled her back.

Melissa was overcome by an attack of shyness she was unable to control. She crouched on one side of Mom, like a small child. Even Daisy seemed more comfortable than she was, sitting by the basket and counting her flowers as if a visit from a stranger was a normal occurrence and not something that was happening for only the second time in Melissa's memory. And on the first occasion, only Mom and Dad had dealt with the priest who'd conducted the mass for Edelweiss in Spanish.

Melissa felt Mom straighten her back, facing the young man as if protecting her daughters from the unknown. The three of them formed a barrier. Despite the firmness of Mom's posture, her hand began to tremble. She hid it under her arm.

The boy held up a hand, showing the palm.

"*¿Ho . . . hola?*"

He spoke Spanish with an accent like Dad's when he talked to people in the town.

"*Hola,*" Mom replied.

"*Qué suerte enc—*"

"We speak English," Iris let slip.

Melissa heard Mom click her tongue.

The young man's expression changed noticeably. Furrows appeared on his forehead.

"Seriously? You're Americans, too?" His eyes widened, emphasizing his surprise. "Today must be my lucky day. I haven't seen anyone in four days. Not a single person. And when at last I do find someone, you speak my language. You don't know how happy I am. All I can say in Spanish is *más cerveza, por favor*, and *quiero otro taco*. That would've been a very boring conversation for everyone."

Melissa would have liked to respond to the comment, or laugh, but the force with which Mom squeezed her shoulder made her sense it was best to keep quiet. Iris didn't say anything, either. She just blinked at the boy, a foolish look on her face.

"I'm Rick," the young man added.

He took a step forward with his hand held out, offering it to Mom. She reacted with a flinch, moving away from him.

The boy retreated. He hooked his thumbs in the straps of his back-pack. "I'm sorry, I didn't mean to—"

"What're you looking for?"

Rick cleared his throat.

"I'm . . . I'm not looking for anything, to be honest. A little company, I guess. I've been walking for twenty-seven days and haven't seen anyone in four. I'm about to start talking to the rocks."

"To the rocks?" Melissa was openmouthed. The stranger was proving to be interesting. She could tell him a lot about the need to speak to stones. Mom squeezed her shoulder even harder, commanding her to be quiet.

"In fact," Rick went on, "I'm happy just to hear my own voice right now. What a relief! Let's see how I sound. One, two. One, two. Everything seems OK. Seriously, I was beginning to think I'd forgotten how to speak." He rounded off the remark with a lopsided smile.

Iris sighed.

"Well, you haven't forgotten," said Daisy from the ground, "because you haven't stopped talking since you arrived."

She had just blurted it out. There was a moment of surprise, of comical shock. Even Mom's eyes searched for her daughters'. It was Rick himself who started laughing, his half smile turning into a guffaw that showed the brilliant white of his teeth. The laughter then infected Iris, who laughed more loudly and in a higher pitch than she normally did. Melissa joined them soon after, without taking her eyes off Rick, whose T-shirt was now tight against his tensed abdomen. When he took in air, the muscles in his chest expanded so much that the garment seemed to shrink, revealing the buckle on his belt. Daisy was laughing, too. Mom needed a little shove from Melissa to get her going. When she did, she laughed heartily, the tension in her muscles disappearing. She eased her grip on Melissa.

"I like your honesty," Rick said to Daisy. "If only we adults were as honest as kids are, huh?"

He directed the question at Mom. Both Melissa and Iris fixed their eyes on her, hoping she would be friendlier.

Mom looked Rick up and down. "You're not wrong," she said. "The world would be a much better place."

She held out her hand to Rick, who wiped his own on his pants before accepting it.

"I'm Rose."

"Pleased to meet you, Rose. And you are?"

"They're Iris, Melissa, and Lily."

Mom used the twins' shared name, as she did with Socorro.

"You all have flower names. How nice."

Mom smiled. She seemed to like the fact that the young man had noticed the detail. Melissa was struck by the interest with which Rick listened, giving all his attention to Mom.

It was almost as if he was taking notes in his head.

While they made their introductions, Iris picked up the pitcher of agua de Jamaica. She filled a glass, intending to give it to Rick, but Mom stopped her from approaching, holding an arm out as a barrier.

The young man held up his hands.

"I'm harmless. I swear. And that drink looks fabulous. With all that ice. I don't know how many days it's been since I had a cold beverage."

"What're you doing wandering around here?"

"I ask myself that very question sometimes. So does my mother. She asks me endlessly whenever she sees me planning another trip. And you know what? I don't know the answer. I walk because I wouldn't know how not to walk, simple as that. And every time, I need a bigger challenge. The Pacific Crest Trail took me five months. Five months walking."

Iris let out a sigh of wonder.

"I've done the States to death, so I wanted to try Mexico, walk the length of the Baja California Peninsula, north to south. Almost a thousand miles. It's going to keep me busy for a while. We don't do this country justice up there, do we? We only mention it as a hiding place for fugitives, but it turns out to have all these wonders."

Rick gave a short pause, his eyes fixed on Mom.

"Well, what's the use in telling you if you've decided to live here? It must be for a reason. This landscape's incredible. I never get tired of looking at it, with all these cactuses, these imposing rocks. This solitude. I love deserts. And the smell—such clean air." Rick breathed in with gusto, looking around at the land with his arms outstretched, as if wanting to breathe in the entire landscape. "See what I mean? They'd have us believe that saguaros only exist in Arizona, symbol of the Wild West and all that. Turns out there are even more of them here than in our country. We're so ignorant up there. So ignorant."

"Those cactuses aren't saguaros," Daisy corrected him. "They're called cardones."

"Is that right?" said Rick. "And what's the difference?"

Daisy shrugged. She took two flowers from the basket. "See how nice they smell?"

"May I?" Rick asked Mom, who nodded after some deliberation.

The young man went down on one knee in front of Daisy and smelled the flower.

"And this?" He pointed at the scratches on the little girl's arm. "Did the cactus do it to you for trying to take away its flowers?"

"No, my sister did it."

Mom's back tensed.

Daisy held her hand over her mouth when she realized she'd said too much.

"Yeah, it was me," Melissa put in, to hide the truth. "But I didn't mean to do it, and I've already said sorry."

"That's true." Daisy nodded in an exaggerated way. "I forgive you."

Rick kept looking at the wound on her arm, oblivious to the lie.

"Well, it's no big deal. I don't think it will even scab over." He blew on the scratches. "It'll be gone in a week."

As he stood, the weight of his own backpack unbalanced him. He had to take two steps to one side to steady himself. He ended up facing the cacti that Melissa had clothed. He opened his mouth in surprise.

"They're my sister's," Iris hastened to explain. "She's the one who does those weird things."

Melissa gave her a reproachful look.

"No, well, they're just a silly thing, they're nothing, I don't—"

"Hey"—Rick turned his head—"I love them. They're very original. I've never seen anything like it. They're like desert scarecrows."

The display of acceptance filled Melissa's chest. She gave her sister a smile.

"They're named Needles, Pins, and Thorns?" Rick asked. "How apt."

Melissa nodded with a hint of shyness.

"You have lovely daughters," Rick said to Mom.

"My husband's about to arrive."

"I'm sorry, I didn't mean to . . . Oh hell, I keep putting my foot in my mouth."

"You didn't say anything wrong," Iris said.

"And it's true, we are lovely," added Daisy. "We're *three* lovely sisters."

She winked at Mom as she said the number.

"I can see that. One, two, and three." He pointed at Daisy, Melissa, and Iris. "You don't have any other sisters?"

The four of them answered at the same time: "No."

There was silence. Melissa sensed Mom's intention to end the conversation. Despite the laughs they'd shared, she still didn't seem to like the presence of this stranger at the house.

"And how old are you?" Rick suddenly asked.

"I'm six," Daisy quickly replied.

Mom shushed the little girl, but Melissa answered as well.

"I'm thirteen."

"And I'm sixteen," added Iris.

Rick repeated Iris's age in a murmur, as if making a note of it and filing it away. Iris played with a lock of hair. Melissa understood the meaning her sister was ascribing to the boy's attentions. She was always thinking about the same thing.

"So may I have that?" Rick gestured at the glass in Iris's hands. "I think I'm hiding it pretty well, but for five minutes I've thought of nothing but drinking down that cold water. I'd love to do it before the ice has finished melting."

Melissa and Iris laughed.

"You may," Mom said. "But then I'm going to ask you to leave. My husband's about to arrive."

"Can I give you some advice?" Rick invited Mom to come closer to him. He spoke in her ear so the others wouldn't know what he was saying, but Melissa managed to hear him. "Next time a stranger arrives on your land, best not tell him that your husband isn't home. You've told me twice now. Me, I'm just a harmless guy, but someone with worse intentions would've been thrilled to learn that you're here alone with your daughters."

Mom nodded as if she'd been told off. She took the glass from Iris's hands and gave it to Rick herself. He drank it in one go and expressed his satisfaction with a pant that made Daisy laugh.

"Well, thank you very much for that." He showed them the empty glass. "And for everything. You have a lovely family, really. A family of flowers. I'll go back the way I came."

This time, Mom thanked him for the compliment. Melissa and Iris communicated with her by raising their eyebrows over and over.

"Come on, Mom," Iris said out of the corner of her mouth. "He's a nice guy. Let him have dinner with us."

"Please . . ." Melissa whispered. "I want to talk to someone."

Mom looked at the clothed cacti.

"It's almost dark," Melissa added. "Please . . ."

"Don't worry," said Rick. "Being alone is part of my adventure. Sometimes I think I walk to get away from everyone. And if I'm going to leave, it's best if I go before the sun disappears completely."

The young man swallowed the ice from the bottom of the glass. Iris whispered in Mom's right ear. Melissa followed Rick's movements as he crouched at the foot of one of the cacti to leave his drink beside the pitcher and the rest of the glasses. Melissa saw him point at them, one by one.

Counting.

One, two, three, four, five.

In the same way he had counted the sisters before. He was pensive for a moment, with his elbow resting on his knee, his fingers pinching his bottom lip. Then he stood eagerly, as if driven by a new energy.

"Do you know what? I'll be honest. I could do with some real company. Having dinner with people would do me good. I think my brain's going to degenerate if I don't talk for a while. I've always believed in the kindness of strangers, and I think this is a good opportunity for the universe to show me that it exists."

"The kindness of strangers," Iris repeated. "That's from *A Streetcar Named Desire*."

"I love that play. Have you read it?"

"Have I read it?" Iris finished the question with her mouth open, a hand on her chest. It was several seconds before she closed it.

Rick turned to Mom again.

"I can cook my own food. I have a can of baked beans."

Mom took a while to decide. The sun hid itself behind the horizon. The light at that time of day was Melissa's favorite, because there was just enough of it to see the reality of things, without shadows or dazzle. A dust cloud was visible in the distance.

"There's my husband," Mom said. She seemed happy to be able to delegate the decision. "Let's go ask him."

Rick walked into the kitchen gripping the straps on his backpack. Right away he looked around the room for photographs. Or painted family portraits. He found none. He searched for information on the refrigerator door, but there were only children's drawings colored in with beads.

"You have a beautiful kitchen," he said to Rose. "Thanks for letting me stay, Elmer."

The man took a step forward. He faced Rick with his chest puffed out. "How do you know my name? I hadn't told you."

"From your coveralls." He gestured at the badge embroidered on the garment.

Elmer tilted his head to one side and frowned. "A very observant young man . . ."

Rick didn't know whether it was a compliment or a suspicion.

"Then try not to notice this mess," Rose intervened.

In a single flurry of activity, she removed a notebook from the table, took a pan from the stove, and threw the remains of a lemon in the trash can. With a cloth she wiped some red drops from the countertop and gathered crumbs in one hand.

She dusted off her hands. "You can leave that here."

She swooped on him to take his backpack, but Rick moved away from her. He didn't want her to touch it.

"You travel light," Elmer observed.

Once again, the intention of his words was difficult to decipher. Rick moved his backpack from his back to his belly and hugged it as if it were a traveling companion.

"It's the first thing you learn when you start walking long distances. You have to choose between taking things and being able to keep going," he said. "The more it weighs, the less chance you have of completing the route."

"And what do you take with you?" Melissa asked.

"It's rude to pry," Rose chided her.

"Just enough to survive," he replied. "A compass, a sweater, a raincoat . . ."

"You walk in this heat?" Elmer asked.

"To tell you the truth, it would have been better to come at another time of year." He pointed at the sweat stains around his neck. "Progress is real slow because of the heat. In fact, do you mind if I use the bathroom to change?"

Iris bit her bottom lip, waiting for her parents' response with wide eyes. Rose left the kitchen, went into a room that was probably the bathroom, and remained in there for almost a minute.

"All yours," she said as she came out, holding the door for Rick.

He thanked her with a smile, went into the bathroom, and locked it from the inside. The small space contained a toilet and a sink. The first thing he did was count the toothbrushes in a glass. There were three. He opened the mirror door above the faucet. He found several used razors. A dry bar of soap. A plastic bottle of perfumed water. Bobby pins and hairbands. Some tweezers. Another toothbrush with the bristles splayed, black from being used to clean the space between tiles. In the top section, he found various medications. Most were labeled in Spanish, but Rick recognized some of the active ingredients. *Salicex* had to be a painkiller, *Profineril*, an anti-inflammatory. And *Dormepam*, some kind of tranquilizer. Given the number of boxes of this last one, it was clear that one of the adults, or both, suffered from anxiety. Under the sink, a metal case contained gauze, surgical tape, Band-Aids, scissors, a thermometer. Rick looked around as if he might find something of interest on the walls, by the toilet bowl, on the ceiling. He clicked his tongue.

He opened his backpack.

First he took out the towel he'd used to pad it. He saw that his other T-shirt had ended up at the bottom. To retrieve it he had to remove all the other contents of the backpack: a Polaroid camera, a flashlight, a cassette recorder, a pocket notebook—its cover decorated with fake passport stamps—and a can of baked beans. He exchanged his T-shirt for another that was identical but clean and dry. He repacked the backpack, leaving the can out and using the towel to fill it out again and cover up its other contents. He left the camera on top.

Although he hadn't used the lavatory, he pulled the chain.

He went out drying his hands with the T-shirt he'd just taken off. Rose and her three daughters were still in the kitchen. The little girl was flitting around the legs of her mother, who was chopping vegetables on a board.

"My husband's gone up to get changed."

She invited him to take a seat. He left his dirty T-shirt on the back of the chair before sitting down. On the opposite side of the table were Iris and Melissa. He evaded their excessive attention by looking out the window.

The last trace of daylight, a purple line, was fading in the distance. Darkness was closing in on the cacti, the rocks, the trucks. There were two just outside the front door, in good condition. A little farther away he could make out the bodywork of three others, perhaps four. They appeared to be burned out, but with so little light it was difficult to be sure. Within a few minutes he wouldn't be able to see those. It would be as if there was nothing out there. Rick imagined the house seen from the sky, just a spot of orange light lost in an immense black desert.

"It's incredible how we human beings insist on living in the remotest places, don't you think?"

"It's incredible, yeah, yeah," Iris repeated.

"Are there streets where you live?" Melissa asked. "And people?"

Rose turned around. She upbraided her daughters by pointing a knife at them.

"How far is it to the nearest town?" Rick went on. "Seventy miles? A hundred? I can't even remember how many days ago it was when I passed the gas station. It must be a very long way."

"Dad works there," the little girl said.

Rose shushed her. "Or maybe the incredible thing is that we humans mass together in cities. That we live on top of each other, with no space. That everyone sticks their noses in everyone else's business when we have all this space available to us to live more freely and peacefully. Without having to explain anything to anyone."

"I know exactly what you mean," Rick said to reassure her. "Did you live in a city?"

"She did, not us," Iris said. "Does that seem fair?"

"A long time ago," Rose replied. "Before we had the girls. My husband and I got tired of living that kind of life and decided to give the girls something better. A life that's real. More earth and less asphalt."

"And separate us from other people," Melissa added.

"You were born here?"

"I already told you they were." Rose let a pitcher of water land with force on the table. "They were born right here."

"Like fillies," Iris whispered when her mother withdrew.

Rick gave her a smile and saw the girl's cheeks light up.

The intensity of Rose's knife blows against the board as she chopped increased.

"Do you like spicy food?" she asked.

"Don't worry." Rick took a multifunction knife from a side pocket of the backpack and positioned himself at the countertop beside her. "I don't want to be more trouble than necessary. I'll make my own food and you make yours. I can imagine how hard it must be to grow stuff here."

He drove the can opener into the metal and hacked his way around edge of the circular top until thick, rough fingers interrupted his movement. Rick smelled gasoline. Elmer spoke near his ear.

"If you eat in my house, you eat in my house." Elmer wrenched the can from his hands and threw it in the trash. "And you must be sick of canned and powdered food."

"I appreciate it, but—"

"But what?"

"There was no need to throw away the can. I could have eaten it tomorrow."

Iris laughed, covering her mouth. Elmer looked at him with his head tilted to one side, his hands inside the front pocket of the denim overalls he'd traded his work clothes for, weighing up whether to take offense. His deliberation ended in a guffaw.

"I can promise you, kid, you don't want to miss out on my wife's food. She's the best cook for a hundred miles around."

"She's the only cook," Melissa murmured at the table.

Her father took two beers out of the refrigerator and chucked one to Rick without warning. He managed to snatch the bottle from the air.

"Good catch. Do you like basketball?"

"I play baseball."

Elmer showed his disapproval with a snort. Rick shrugged while he opened the bottle with his knife.

"You know the good thing about being a man?" Elmer asked after his first sip. "That we can follow different sports—support different teams, even—but we'll always be able to enjoy a beer together."

The older man put his arm over Rick's shoulders and clinked his bottle against Rick's. Rick took advantage of the friendly gesture to propose something.

"Could I spend the night here?" he blurted out.

A chair scraped along the floor. Melissa and Iris held hands. Rose's knife hammered into the board. Even the little girl, who'd sat on the ground with the basket of flowers between her legs, looked up to hear the response.

"Here? In this house?" Elmer's tone had risen at least an octave. The proposal must have seemed so ridiculous to him that he could find no reason to be angry. "In your dreams, kid. Do you think I don't know how pretty my daughters are?"

Rick regretted having put the idea forward so soon. He thought of the five glasses he'd counted outside, by the pitcher. He needed more time in the house.

"Maybe he could sleep outside," Iris said.

Elmer looked him up and down. "If you want to sleep in one of the pickups, I won't say no. But the door to this house will be locked when you go out. You'll be alone out there. If you need a bathroom, you have the entire desert. And when the sun comes up you're going to roast, so you'd better get going before dawn."

"No problem," Rick said. It was better than nothing. "After twenty days sleeping on the ground, the seat of a truck will feel like a bed."

Rose peered out the window.

"Sleep in the Dodge. It's been in the shade all afternoon and it'll be cooler."

The little girl got up and showed the basket of flowers to her mother. "They're turning weird."

"It's the heat. Here."

The two of them knelt in front of the refrigerator, making space for the basket. They moved vegetables, bottles of milk, and packages of meat. Rick saw them whisper in each other's ears. The little girl tried to look at him, but her mother held her face to stop her.

"We're going upstairs for a second," Rose announced after putting away the basket. "We have to . . . I have to . . . I'm going to clean . . . Lily's scratches."

She pulled on the girl and they left the kitchen. Rick went to the sink and washed his hands with the sole intention of watching where they went. They had reached the bottom of the stairs.

"Mom, the onion's burning!" Iris yelled. She got up to deal with it herself, but when she shook the frying pan some oil blazed. She screamed.

Rose stopped. She explained something to the little girl, speaking very close to her face. She also gave her something she took from a pocket in her apron. Looking out of the corner of his eye, Rick couldn't be sure what he was seeing, but it appeared as if Rose was handing her daughter a block of butter and a slice of bread.

His breathing accelerated.

He looked away when Rose returned to the kitchen. While she dealt with the incident on the stove, Rick made himself relax by concentrating on how the foam dissolved under the water, between his fingers.

He thought of his mother.

He splashed soap in his eyes on purpose in case anyone asked him why they were watering.

Daisy climbed to the top of the stairs, dropping breadcrumbs as she went. She turned the key in the bedroom door, getting grease on it from the cheese she held in her hand. The movement stretched the skin on her scratched arm. She blew on the graze to ease the burning. Though the room was dark, she could make out her sister's form on the bed.

"Are you still angry?" she asked.

"You're mean."

"I brought you something to eat."

Dahlia sat up on the mattress and turned on the lamp on the bedside table they shared, between the two beds. Daisy gave her the cheese, the bread, and a napkin. She took it as if she'd gone days without eating.

"You never think about me." She took a bite of cheese. "I was stuck in here all morning yesterday. And again today."

"And you did this to me." Daisy showed her forearm.

Dahlia didn't look. "I didn't mean to do that. I was just trying to pick the flower." She chewed on a piece of bread, looking at the wall. As she always did when she was angry, she shied away from her sister's eyes. "What happened with the necklaces?"

"Mommy's put the flowers in the refrigerator so they stay fresh. We can't make them today because the boy's going to have dinner here."

Dahlia crossed her arms.

"I miss everything. Yesterday it was the last day of class. Today a visitor." She pouted with her bottom lip. "And it's all your fault."

Daisy was upset to see her so sad. "Do you forgive me?"

Dahlia didn't answer. Daisy tried to position her face in front of her sister's, but Dahlia avoided her by twisting her neck.

Daisy held her chin. "Do you want to go down now?"

Dahlia's eyes instantly sought hers. On her fingers Daisy felt folds appearing on her sister's cheek, forming a smile.

"Seriously?"

"I've already met him. And he's not that interesting."

Dahlia hugged her. "Thank you, thank you, thank you . . ."

"But the cheese is mine, then. Don't eat any more. It's going to be my dinner."

Dahlia put it on the bedside table, on the napkin. The bread, too. She leapt to the floor and hugged Daisy again. To celebrate, she started off the mirror game, counting with her fingers.

Facing each other, they began the learned sequence of gestures. Raise eyebrows. Stick out tongue. Lower eyebrows. Lift left corner of mouth. Lift right corner of mouth. Left corner of mouth. Right corner of mouth. Open mouth. Close mouth. Look left. Look right. Raise eyebrows. Stick out tongue. Puff up cheeks. Flatten cheeks. Wrinkle nose. Stick out tongue. Wink left eye. Wink right eye. Clap hands twice.

They leapt when they completed the sequence without error.

"We're a mirror! We're the same!"

Daisy straightened her sister's hair, which had become tangled from lying on the bed. She also positioned her bobby pins in a way more similar to her own.

"Let's see if Mommy and Daddy notice," she said. "I bet the guy doesn't."

"What's his name?" Dahlia asked.

"His name's Rick. And he talks a lot. He never stops. He's been walking for a year."

"Really?"

"Yeah. His shoes are all ruined. I think Iris likes him. She laughs like an idiot when he says something. Melissa's happy, too. Maybe she likes talking to someone other than her cactuses. But Mom's all worked up. She's being weird. And I don't think Dad likes him being here, but he's acting like he does. He's drinking beer with him, but I don't think he's his friend."

"OK. I wonder what I'll see. I was so bored up here. What're you going to do?"

"Beads. You're way ahead of me."

Daisy went with her sister to the door. "Go on, we've been forever."

Dahlia went to the top of the stairs. She turned her head and said bye to Daisy. As she went down, she heard the young man in the kitchen asking whether the sisters went to school. When she reached the first floor, she saw Mom there. She was cutting open a melon by the sink.

"Come on, dinner's on the table," she said. "What took you so long?"

When she saw her, she left the slices of fruit on the countertop and went to her, drying her hands on her apron.

"What're you doing?" she knelt and spoke to her close to her ear. "Why did you switch?"

"You noticed?"

"Honey, please."

"Daisy let me come down. Because yesterday it was me shut away and it's unfair."

"I know, but Daisy doesn't decide. Go up and tell her to come down. Don't be so silly, taking chances like this now."

"Mommy, it's OK, we're the same."

"Enough. Get up there right now."

Behind Mom, Dahlia saw Rick approach the refrigerator. He saw them.

"Hey, Lily, you're back?" he asked from there.

"I'm back," Dahlia answered.

Mom let out a sigh. The boy opened the door, knelt, and took out two of the green bottles that Dad drank. The rest of them clinked together on the shelf.

"Your flowers are doing great in here." Rick gestured at them with his chin. "It was a good idea to chill them. Want to come take a look?"

"See?" Dahlia whispered in her mother's ear. "He hasn't noticed."

Dahlia ran to the refrigerator. She peered inside, leaning on Rick's bent leg. He stroked the pile of flowers and remarked on how soft they still were. Together, they returned to the table. When Dahlia sat down, she noticed the quick exchange of looks between Dad, Melissa, and Iris. She winked at the three of them.

"I'm back."

Before sitting down, Rick handed the beer he'd collected from the refrigerator to the father. He waited for Rose to join them in the kitchen and pulled out a chair, gripping its back, inviting her to sit down.

"Thank you." She made a big show of lifting her apron, as if suddenly in attendance at a gala dinner. Then she winked at her husband and added, "I'm not used to such attentiveness."

Rick took the slices of melon that Rose had left on the countertop and deposited them on a plate in the center of the tablecloth.

"You've got everything covered," Iris said, the words coming out in a sigh.

"He's real nice. He stroked my flowers."

"Tell us about the big city," Melissa said.

"All right, all right," Dad interrupted. "Let the kid sit down and eat in peace."

Rick used the chair his dirty T-shirt still hung from. He put his backpack between his legs for safekeeping. The parents were at each end of the table and Iris had changed seats, so he had her to one side now. Opposite him were the youngest and Melissa, who had a stone with eyes resting beside her plate.

"What's that?" Rick gestured at the rock.

"It's nothing." Melissa looked down at her soup.

"Is it like your cactuses out there? Do you like bringing things to life?" She didn't reply.

"Does it have a name?"

A faint smile appeared on Melissa's face. "Yes."

"And what's it called?"

"This is Natalie."

"Hello, Natalie. What pretty eyes you have." Rick paused as if listening to some response from the stone. "Oh, well, thank you. It's nice to meet you."

He winked at Melissa. She smiled.

"Do you like the *sopa de tortilla*?" Rose asked.

"I like everything." Rick swallowed a spoonful to prove it. Though he would've liked a dish that wasn't so hot, he held a thumb up to show his approval. He'd almost forgotten how hungry he was.

"You haven't said what state you come from originally," he said after swallowing. "From the accent I'd say the Midwest. But I might be wrong."

Elmer busied his mouth with his bottle of beer. Rose corrected Iris's posture. Rick was beginning to dislike the time they took to answer his questions.

"We're from the United States!" yelled Lily.

"I know that. But I'm asking your mom and dad what—"

What he saw took away his ability to speak.

"... what ..."

He tried to regain his composure, but his throat was so tight he could barely utter a word. He struggled to keep talking. To overcome the shock.

"... what state ..."

He had to stop stammering.

"... what state they're from specifically."

He finished the sentence as if spitting it out.

"I don't know, Mexico?" the little girl said.

The stupid answer set off a volley of laughter.

For the rest of the dinner, Rick tried to appear calm. He smiled when the conversation required it, and showed understanding when the subject demanded it. He nodded frequently, and didn't comment on the fact that Iris's chair was moving ever closer to his. Rick served himself food, chewed, and swallowed. He praised the main course, complimenting the cook for her obvious command of Mexican cuisine. He engaged in small talk about how hot it still was even at that time of night, how tall the cactuses could grow in Baja California, and which had been the biggest scorpion they'd found on the land. His voice didn't fail him again, but while Rick laughed, passed dishes of shrimp tacos, or accepted a third beer, his eyes returned again and again to the forearm of the little girl in front of him. An unharmed forearm, with no trace of any grazes or scratches from the needles of a cactus. He had blown on the injury himself less than two hours ago. This Lily wasn't the same Lily as before.

Elmer returned from the living room with the liquor in his hand, fingers inserted in two shot glasses. Dinner was over and gnawed slices of melon decorated each plate.

"Think you can handle one of these for dessert?" he asked Rick. "It's too strong for my wife, so I never have anyone to share it with."

He pinched Rose's cheek so she wouldn't hold the comment against him, even though he knew she wouldn't.

"Hey. I'm talking to you." He waved the bottle in front of the young man, who was engrossed in his own thoughts. Elmer had noticed him looking distracted several times during dinner. Rick came out of his absorption and took the liquor. First he read the label. Then he inspected the inside of the bottle. The liquid projected a golden reflection onto the tablecloth.

"Is that a worm?" he asked.

"You bet, kid. It's mescal."

With his mouth open, Rick turned the bottle around. He shook it. The worm bobbed in the liquid, then returned to the bottom.

"It's a goddamn worm."

Elmer threw the glasses onto the table, as if they were dice.

"You game?"

"Am I game?"

Rick opened the bottle. Elmer moved Melissa aside to sit opposite him.

"I want some!" yelled Dahlia.

"Do you really want to drink a liquid with a dead thing in it?"

"It has a dead thing in it?"

Elmer nodded.

"Yuck. I don't want it, then."

"Can I?" Iris asked. "I'm game."

"How many glasses did I bring?" Elmer gestured at the pair on the table.

"I can drink from the same glass as him."

Elmer looked at his daughter. Almost for the first time he noticed the deep channel between her breasts, the rosiness her cheeks always displayed, the golden hair that had appeared on her arms, her skin suddenly fertile land. He observed the pimples on her chin and forehead, so similar to the ones his wife had at that age. It shocked him to realize that his daughter was a year older than his wife had been when he met her. Because he remembered the insatiable desire of that young woman.

"Don't even think about it." With his arm, he swept the two glasses aside to separate them from Iris. Then he turned to Rick. "And you, don't so much as look at her."

"Don't let him frighten you," Rose said to the young man. "He's harmless."

Rick filled the two shot glasses to the top.

"Do you drink it in one go?"

"You can drink it however you want."

"Does it taste like worm?"

"Try it and tell me."

Rick held the liquor to his lips. He left it there a few seconds, weighing how to drink it. He ended up tipping the glass all the way and drinking the mescal in one gulp. First, he opened his eyes wide. Then his face wrinkled up so much that his features seemed to disappear among the folds of his skin. He started coughing. He beat his chest.

"So?" Elmer asked. "Does it taste like worm?"

Rose offered the young man a glass of water. He pushed it aside and slid his chair backward. He rested his elbows on his knees, coughing face-down. One of the coughs turned into a retch, but he didn't vomit.

"Kid, you've just become a man."

Iris and Melissa each reproached him for the comment with a click of the tongue.

"Oh, please. It was just a drop of mescal. I didn't poison him."

Rick straightened. He blinked in quick succession to shake off the tears that surrounded his eyes.

"I want to share your pain," Iris said to him, "understand your suffering."

The second glass disappeared from Elmer's hands, and he watched Iris empty it into her mouth. As she swallowed, she covered her face with both hands. Her body shuddered, though her posture remained the same. When she uncovered her face again, it was red, her eyelashes moist.

"Now I understand what you've been through," she told Rick. "I've felt the fire in my soul, too."

Melissa rolled her eyes.

Elmer looked at his wife for some explanation of Iris's behavior.

"Our daughters are growing up," was her response.

Rick took the glass of water Rose had offered him. He gave a loud whoop. "Wow, that *was* strong." The suffering had disappeared from his face, which displayed the stupid smile of someone who'd just overcome a challenge. "Is that meant to be drunk for pleasure?"

"It sure is, kid. It's just the liquor from a cactus."

"Agave isn't a cactus," Melissa corrected him.

"Whatever. They're all plants with thorns."

Elmer recovered the glass that Iris had snatched from him. He filled it to the top, then drank it in one gulp.

"I could drink another one," Iris said.

Rose let out a laugh. "Don't push your luck. You're lucky we have a guest. I'm not going to tell you what my father did to me the first time he caught me drinking."

"Times change, Mom."

"Sure, that's what your teacher says."

Elmer interrupted the conversation. "Nobody's going to have another one." He screwed the lid back on the bottle. "You because you're sixteen, me because I have to work tomorrow, and you, kid, because I don't want you to die of dehydration on your hike tomorrow."

He gathered the glasses and put them in the sink. He left the bottle of mescal on the counter, next to the blender. Rick got up to help. He added the rest of the dirty dishes to the glasses, which he managed in just two trips. Without asking, he turned on the tap and started washing them. Elmer heard Iris let out a sigh, her chin resting on her interlocked hands. He also saw his wife's surprised smile.

"You don't have to do that," he said to Rick. "There're plenty of women in this house."

"A mother and *three* daughters," said Dahlia.

She winked in such a blatant way that Elmer was glad the young man had his back to the table.

"Are there no women in your house, or what?"

"Just my mother," Rick replied, his hands covered in lather. "I grew up an only child but helped in the house from a very young age."

Another sigh from Iris.

"So what's it like growing up without brothers or sisters?" Melissa asked.

Rick took a few seconds to respond. "Well, I don't know because I've never had any. But seeing families like yours, I think I've missed out on a lot."

Dahlia clapped her hands. Iris, Melissa, and Rose looked at one another, touched. The young man dried his nose with his wrist, without letting go of the scrubber. Elmer gave him two slaps on the back.

"How about you stay and listen to some music with us before going to sleep?"

Rick nodded.

"Yippee!" shouted Dahlia.

Elmer went to the living room to get the record player ready. When he reached the window at the rear of the house, he heard his wife's footsteps approach.

"I was coming to do exactly that," Rose whispered. "I don't want him asking questions. I don't want to have to talk about it."

Elmer sent a kiss out into the darkness, through the glass.

"Me neither."

He turned the handle that closed the slats of the venetian blinds, hiding Edelweiss's cross from view. He unhooked the guitar from the wall and hid it behind an armchair, then put an arm over his wife's shoulder as they returned to the kitchen. When they passed the stairs, Rose whispered to him that she'd go up and pay Daisy a visit, so she wouldn't be mad.

Husband and wife danced in the middle of the room. The little girl copied them, holding an invisible partner. Melissa was in charge of changing the records. Her stone with eyes was beside the player. Iris occupied one end of the sofa, her feet up on the seat and her elbows resting on the arm. She kept looking at Rick, who was sitting in an armchair, his backpack between his legs.

The little girl slipped when she stepped on a rug. While her mother helped her to her feet, addressing her as Lily, Rick noticed the uninjured arm again.

"Careful, Lily. You know how slippery it is."

Rick wanted to be rid of the effects of the beers and the worm liquor so he could think more clearly. He concentrated on the sound of his fingers drumming on the arm of the chair. What he really needed to do was to go back over his cuttings.

"Would you like to dance?" Iris asked from the sofa. "I'm a really good partner."

"Iris!" her father scolded her.

"I can't dance," Rick answered.

He could dance, but he didn't intend to do anything that would complicate matters with Elmer.

"But it's easy!" Lily, or whatever the girl with the unharmed arm was called, spun around until she was dizzy.

Rick picked up the backpack from between his legs.

"What I'd like to do is take a photo of you all." He took out the Polaroid. "I make an album of all the people I meet on my travels."

The force of Elmer's footsteps sent the needle on the record player off course, and a screeching noise interrupted the song. Before Rick could react, he had the father in front of him.

"Put that away."

Elmer's frame, as wide as a truck's cab, filled Rick's field of vision.

"The camera?"

"Put it back in your bag, will you?"

"But I—"

"Don't make me say it again," Elmer cut in. "Put it away."

Rick felt the man's beer breath on his face. He obeyed the order.

"Are you Mennonites?" he asked as he returned the camera to the backpack. "I've heard there're lots in Mexico. But I thought you didn't use electricity or dress like everyone else."

"We're nothing like that, kid. But we don't like photos. Have you seen any in this room?"

Rick pretended not to have noticed that detail. He looked around the room as if for the first time, as if he hadn't spent three entire songs inspecting it.

"I draw pictures of us," Melissa said.

She ran to the kitchen and returned with a sketchbook. She showed one of the pages to her father. When he gave his permission with a nod, she showed it to Rick.

"See? This is my parents last month."

A pencil portrait reproduced the couple's faces to perfection, their features lifelike thanks to a skillful use of shadows. The work on the eyes, which were full of personality, was exceptional.

"Hey, this is really good. I'm not surprised you don't want to have photos."

"The trouble is that I'm in almost none of them, as if I wasn't part of the family," Melissa said.

Rick tried to turn the page to see another portrait, but Elmer stopped him.

"I think it's time for you to go now."

"But I've barely had a chance to speak to him," Melissa complained.

"I want to dance some more!" yelled the little girl.

"We're all going to bed."

Iris left the living room.

"Aren't you going to say goodbye?" Elmer asked his daughter. Receiving no answer, he turned back to the young man. "Come on, I'll show you to the pickup."

Rick got up from the armchair and slung the backpack over his shoulder. Melissa said goodbye, her rock in her hands.

"Good luck on your travels."

"Thanks. If I get bored"—he gestured at Natalie—"I see now that I can talk to all those rocks and cactuses that are out there."

"Or talk to people," she said. "I'm sure it's more interesting."

Rick didn't know how to interpret the mixture of feelings Melissa's words conveyed.

"Thanks for washing the dishes." Rose held out her hand.

"Thank you for dinner."

"Goodbye, sir," said the little girl.

"Goodbye . . . Lily." He struggled to vocalize the name because he no longer believed in it. "It's been a pleasure."

Iris returned from the kitchen. She was carrying a book. She stopped in front of Rick.

"Look, it's *A Streetcar Named Desire*." She showed him the cover. "I'm going to read it again."

Elmer exhaled deeply as he opened the screen door. Iris stayed leaning on the banister. She bit her thumbnail with a smile.

"Can I put on another song?" Melissa asked from the living room.

"Just until I get back," said Elmer.

They left the house as the music filled the living room again. In the dark, it was as if the porch steps disappeared into nothing. Rick heard the wind whistle between the boards. Dry bushes crackled in the breeze. In the background, just a single bulb glowed on top of a post. A defective current turned it on and off, made it palpitate, as if the desert had a pulse.

Elmer put an arm over his shoulder. They walked, without saying anything, to one of the two trucks, the Dodge that Rose had suggested.

Elmer leaned on the side mirror, looking back at the living room. In the orangey square of the window, Rose and his daughters appeared and disappeared, dancing to the rhythm of the music.

"Do you have children, kid?"

"It's getting a bit late for that. I'm twenty-five and there's no girl in sight."

"Late? I didn't have my eldest till I was thirty."

Rick looked at Iris through the glass. He didn't think she could see him from there, but her movements changed. They became more sensual.

"People who don't have any children miss a lot of pleasures," said Rick, "but they also avoid a lot of suffering."

Despite the lack of light surrounding them, he could see Elmer frowning.

"Balzac," he explained.

"You're a reader. Like my daughter."

Rick nodded.

"Well, do you know something? A man without a family"—Elmer wrote in the air, as if remembering another famous quotation—"is a desert without cactuses."

"Who was that?"

"Me, kid. I just made it up."

Rick forced a smile.

"Take it from me, son. A man without a family ain't a man. He ain't anything. What's the point in a life without children? What was I going to do? Work hard every day for me and my wife to dine alone at night? Without the laughter of a little girl?" He opened his arms as if unable to fathom the sheer stupidity of the idea. "Humanity's going to have a tough time if youngsters like you start giving up on the idea of making a family. Without those girls dancing in there, I'm worth less than a coyote skull drying in the sun."

"You have a very beautiful family," Rick said. "All girls."

"Nature does what it wants with us." His voice was toneless, as if affected by some somber thought. "I devote my life to those women. It's the only thing that gives it meaning."

Elmer stood watching the window. Rose was spinning around in the living room in a whirl of white fabric, her broad smile gleaming. To bring her dance to an end, she stretched out her arms and unfolded her fingers like a fan. Her laughter could be heard at the truck.

"It all started with wanting to make the most wonderful woman in the world happy." Elmer closed his eyes. "I'd do anything to hear her laugh like that all the time."

He was silent for so long, savoring his memories, that Rick felt uncomfortable. A coyote howled in the distance.

"I sincerely hope you're lucky enough to feel the happiness I feel"— Elmer slowly opened his eyes, returning from some pleasant memory— "and that you make your own family soon. You said before you would've liked to have had brothers and sisters. You can still make that happen for your children. Except"—he lowered his voice to a whisper—"don't have five, it's too many."

Rick stopped breathing.

"You have three."

"I'm including my wife, I mean the women in my family."

"That's four, isn't it?"

"Family of five, kid. Or am I not part of this family? Family of five. Four women. Are you trying to mess with my head or something?"

It was Elmer who was twisting his words to make them mean something different from what he'd initially said.

"Some muddle you've got yourself into, kid. That shot of mescal's left you weak in the head. I think it's time for you to get some sleep." Elmer opened the vehicle door. Discovering the keys in the ignition, he took them out. He put them in the front pocket of his denim overalls, clearing his throat. "Don't be offended."

"Of course not. Take them. That way I won't be tempted to start up the truck and finish my route in two days instead of three months."

Elmer gave the seat a slap.

"All yours. If you lie like this across it, you'll be comfortable. You're not tall, so you'll fit easily. I don't fit in this one even sitting—my knees touch the steering wheel. That's why my wife uses it. If you prefer, you can sleep in the cargo area, but I see you don't even have a mat."

"I"—he thought of an excuse as quickly as he could—"I lost it yesterday."

"Good night, kid. And what I said about frying as soon as the sun comes up: best not to find out for yourself. Get walking before it happens. I'll tell my wife to put a bag out on the porch so you can have something for breakfast."

"Don't worry, there's no—"

"I'm not worried, I just feel bad about throwing your can in the trash. Good luck, kid."

Elmer went back to the house.

"Leave the windows open!" he yelled from the porch.

Rick heard him close the screen door and bolt it. He also shut and then locked the main door.

"You don't want me coming in?" he asked the darkness.

The breeze shook the dry bushes.

The sound was like rattlesnakes.

At Mom's request, Iris went to return Edelweiss's guitar to its nail on the wall. She had to dodge Dahlia, who was spinning all around the room with her arms outstretched. Dad got back from showing Rick to the truck. He locked the door with the key from the inside.

"Is he dangerous?" Mom asked.

"He's a stranger."

"How's he going to be dangerous when he's that good-looking?"

On tiptoes, Iris struggled to hook the wire around the instrument's headstock. Dad snatched the guitar from her hands. He looked at her with his lips pressed together.

"Can't I say he's good-looking?"

He snorted. He hitched the wire at the first attempt and centered the instrument with little taps on each side of the sound box. "I said just one more song."

"You were talking to him for so long . . ." Melissa lifted the needle to interrupt the music, put the record back in its cover, and closed the device's lid. "I would've liked to talk to him some more. He could have told me lots more things. I had so many questions for him."

"You've asked him plenty already," said Mom.

"Truth be told"—Dad scraped two fingers against his chin—"the only one asking a lot of questions was him, don't you think?"

Iris caught her parents exchanging a series of looks. They went from worry to calm, from calm to concern, from concern to serenity. It was impossible to interpret their meaning.

"Can I go get Daisy?" asked Dahlia.

"Go see her, but stay up there. Don't come down here, because of the window."

Iris picked up her copy of *A Streetcar Named Desire* to take it back to the kitchen. She stood and gripped the doorjamb before she went in.

Rick had left his dirty T-shirt on the back of the chair.

Something resembling an electric shock ignited in her stomach again. She turned to make sure the rest of the family was still in the living room. Nobody could see her. She left the book on the shelf without bothering to put it back in its place. She took the T-shirt, feeling an urge to smell it. She filled her chest with Rick's scent. A tingling ran through her, from her knees to her belly button. She didn't feel it on her skin, but inside.

"Iris?" Dad called.

She swiveled, looking for a place to hide the T-shirt. Her mother could find it in any drawer, cupboard, or shelf. She put it under her dress. The damp feel of the material between her legs made her shiver. She used the elastic on her bra and panties to keep the garment pressed to one side of her body. She smoothed down the outside of the dress, flattening the lump.

Dad appeared in the door.

Iris breathed in.

"I thought you were in the bathroom," he said.

She shook her head.

"Can I use it?"

Iris nodded without saying a word. When Dad went into the bathroom, she checked the back door in the kitchen, the one Mom used to go out to the vegetable garden. They hadn't locked it. She smiled. She escaped upstairs without anyone seeing her.

In her bedroom, lying face up on the bed, she pulled out the T-shirt. She covered her face with it and felt Rick's warm sweat on her forehead, her nose, her lips. She took deep breaths under the moist garment.

Sitting on the truck's passenger side, Rick saw the living room light go out. And the one in the kitchen. Then the upstairs windows lit up, revealing the family's movements inside. He inspected the dashboard and sun visors, rummaged through the glove box, put his hands in all the compartments he found. Nothing. In the space behind the backrest his fingers felt tools, coarse rags, some kind of cleaning product, and a long metal cylinder. Two long metal cylinders. He ran his hand along them until he found a trigger, a butt. It was a shotgun. He snatched back his hand as if it had been burned.

Rick dipped his hand in his backpack, on the driver's side. He recognized the feel of his wallet and his flashlight, which he turned on, keeping the light close to his body to avoid attracting attention. The cab was illuminated with a faint blue glow. In the notebook he wrote the names Iris, Melissa, Lily, Rose, and Elmer. He noted their physical descriptions, their ages, his supposition that they were from the Midwest. He also wrote details of the kitchen, the living room, the medications he'd seen in the bathroom. Their refusal to have their pictures taken. From the name Lily, he drew an arrow to the words 6-YEAR-OLD TWINS. He underlined them and added a question mark.

His hand was moving at a furious rate.

On the last page of the notebook, protected by the back cover, was a map. He unfolded it with a rustling of paper. It showed all of North America. A thick line marked the route he was following, a winding path down the southwestern United States that would end at the very bottom of the Baja California Peninsula, Mexico. On the way were fifteen destinations circled in pen. Twelve of them were crossed out. Of the three remaining circles, one indicated the area where he now found himself. The other two, farther south, were the last places left to visit.

He took a deep breath, exhausted from looking at the distance he had traveled, remembering the suffering that was behind that simple line cutting through part of the United States and Mexico.

He folded the map, closed the notebook.

There was still light in one of the bedrooms.

"Ain't it about time you went to sleep?"

He turned off the flashlight, rested his head on the window frame.

He closed his eyes just for a second.

Laughter woke him up.

It was still dark, with no trace of light on the horizon. He was unable to calculate how long he'd been asleep, but the saliva that had gathered at one corner of his mouth confirmed he had been. He wiped it off with the back of his hand. He hadn't let go of the notebook.

There was laughter again.

It wasn't coming from inside the house, but from outside, from among the rocks. Rick stuck his head out the window. In the darkness, the cacti seemed to him like beings that roamed the desert, ghostly shadows that groaned whenever the wind howled.

More giggling.

Rick moved over to the driver's side and leaned out that window. He saw a cloud of orangey light in the same place where he'd found the family for the first time. The glow quivered, as if produced by a candle. He thought he could see some pants floating in the air. The shine of blonde hair. A face in the night. It was Melissa, sitting on the ground in front of her clothed cactuses. The pants weren't floating, they were stuck to the spines. Rick heard whispers, more laughter. The girl was gesticulating, turning her hand, opening and closing it, the gestures typical of a conversation. There were more whispers. Another contained giggle.

Rick brought his head back in.

"Sure, living in cities is unnatural."

He sighed, rubbing his eyes. Now he'd have to wait for Melissa to finish talking and go back to the house. He looked at the notebook on the passenger's side.

The handle on that door shook.

"What the hell?"

He checked that Melissa was still in the same place. There she was, in her bubble of orange light. The handle moved again. Someone was pulling on it from the outside. The attempts stopped suddenly. Until a hand slipped through the window, searching for the lock. It released the mechanism. Rick had just enough time to grab his notebook before the door opened.

He hid it under his seat.

As he looked up, he found Iris climbing into the pickup. She closed the door, careful not to make noise.

"We don't want Dad to catch us," she whispered.

Rick thought of the shotgun.

Iris sat looking ahead, rubbing her hands together between her legs. She took a deep breath.

"It already smells like you." Her eyes sought his. "The truck. It's impregnated with your scent."

He didn't know how to respond. "Er, thanks?"

Iris slid along the seat, moving closer. She was wearing a nightgown the color of her name. She even smelled like the flower she was named after. Rick tried to make eye contact, but his attention was drawn to her exposed shoulders, her broad neckline, her cleavage. He realized she'd noticed his gaze because her cheeks flushed red. Rick pressed his back against the door, distancing himself as much as possible.

"You make me feel like the heroine in one of the best books."

"Iris, I don't . . ."

Their thighs brushed against each other. She rested a hand on his knee, under the steering wheel. It was light, as if a moth had flown into the truck and perched there. She seemed surprised by her own daring, because she looked at her hand, as stunned as he was.

"Till this moment, I never knew myself," she whispered.

She said the words as if she already knew them, as if she'd wished for the moment to arrive when she could make them hers. Rick guessed she'd taken them from one of her books. The moth climbed from his knee to halfway up his thigh.

"Iris, please."

Rick trapped the curious insect. Her fingers interlocked with his. Iris held both of their hands to her own lap. She used her free hand to stroke them where they met.

"Oh, I'm all nerves. I've never held a boy's hand like this. I've dreamed endlessly about the day I'd finally have my chance, and suddenly it's happening. Tonight. I haven't known many boys, I haven't even *seen* many boys. But look at me now, holding the hand of a guy who looks like a movie star."

Iris's eyes glistened. For an instant, Rick was touched by the purity of her smile, the innocence of her words, the simplicity of the feelings she described.

"We can ask the night to keep a secret for us," she added.

Rick retrieved his hand from Iris's lap, as if suddenly discovering it was there.

"I don't think your father would be too happy."

"Only the moon and the stars will be witnesses."

She moved nearer. Iris's face was so close to his that Rick was breathing the air she exhaled. It aroused a feeling in him that was like biting into a piece of fruit in summer.

"I'm ready."

"I, this, I don't—"

It may have been fatigue, or some mysterious nocturnal enchantment of the desert, or simply Iris's beauty, but her lips rested on his without him doing anything to prevent it. They both stopped breathing.

Melissa's laughter broke the spell.

"No, no, no." Rick moved Iris away, pushing gently on her shoulders.

Still offering her lips, she was keeping her eyes closed. She opened them slowly and looked Rick in the eyes.

"I counted to ten, to give you time to disappear if you were a dream," Iris said. "And you're still here."

He was unable to look away.

Until they heard footsteps outside the truck.

"Is Melissa talking to her cactuses?" Iris asked.

Rick nodded. She bent down to hide, and he pretended to be asleep. The crackle of the sand under Melissa's slippers traced a route that skirted around the vehicle before moving off in the direction of the house. The two of them looked up when the porch boards creaked, the sound far away. Melissa was carrying a candle in a lantern.

"And how does she intend to get back in?" Iris whispered.

Her sister didn't even approach the door. She headed to one side of the porch and climbed onto the handrail. Then she scaled one of the posts with ease.

Iris let out a little gasp. "I didn't know that trick."

Melissa walked along the roof to one of the three windows on the exterior wall, the one on the far left. When she was back in her bedroom, the candle went out.

"That Melissa's full of secrets," said Iris.

"It must be a family thing."

Rick's thought escaped as words. He regretted it immediately. When Iris frowned at him, he diverted her attention to the furtive nature of her visit to the truck, making her see that it also counted as a secret.

"What I feel isn't a secret," she said. "It's forbidden."

Rick didn't know how to answer. He coughed without needing to, just to break the silence.

The kitchen light startled them when it came on.

They heard a key turning inside in the front door.

Iris looked at Rick with her eyes wide. "My dad?"

The bolt on the screen door was pulled across.

"I'm going," she said.

"No, no, he'll see you, don't—"

Iris ducked out the door. She whispered to him to please stay another day, that it couldn't end like this. Then she made off, bent over. Rather than going toward the porch, she went around the house to one side, heading for some back door.

When the porch light came on, Rick wiped his lips with his hand, as if Elmer might detect a trace of the kiss his daughter had given.

An arm poked out through the door.

Rick stopped breathing until, narrowing his eyes, he saw that it was Rose's hand. She left a paper bag on a little table outside the front door. From the vehicle he could make out a pointed shape. The corner of a sandwich, maybe. He breathed with relief. He felt stupid. Just as Elmer had promised him, his wife was leaving out some food so he could have breakfast before he set off. She must have remembered in their bedroom, in bed perhaps, and she had taken the trouble to go down to the kitchen to make something and put it out on the porch for him.

Rose closed the doors again, locking both. Rick thought of the notebook under the seat. The map. The fifteen circles marked on the route. Suddenly, seeing the breakfast Rose had prepared for him in the middle of the night, he was sure he would also end up crossing out the circle that marked this house on the map.

A light came on two windows from Melissa's, on the far right of the exterior. Iris's form appeared behind the glass. Though she wouldn't have been able to see anything in the darkness outside, she blew a kiss in the direction of the truck.

The window went dark as if the house had closed an eye.

Rick waited another half hour before climbing out of the cab.

He left the property following the path the pickup's wheels had marked among the cacti. His first footsteps along the parallel furrows in the sand were slow, stealthy. He held his backpack so that nothing inside it would make noise. He carried the flashlight in his hand, but didn't turn it on until he was sure that nobody would see the light from the house. When the crunch of the grit couldn't give him away either, Rick ran.

He ran along the edge of the dirt track, raising dust as he went, concentrating hard on the circle of light the flashlight projected, expecting to find the marker. Tiredness forced him to slow his pace. After catching his breath for a minute, he picked up speed. When a stitch jabbed him in the abdomen, he worried that he'd left the marker behind. He'd been running for longer than he'd estimated it would take. His uncertainty grew until the only rational option was to turn around, but it was at the precise moment when he decided to that the mound of stones appeared to one side of the road. Positioned on top of one another, they resembled a circular pyramid, a formation that wouldn't occur naturally. Rick stopped. He breathed violently through his mouth. His throat burned, his ears were ringing, his chest hurt. The saliva in his mouth was like glue. He dried the sweat on his forehead with the hair on his forearms.

The mound of stones marked the place where he had to leave the road and head into the desert. He walked among cacti and rocks, guided by the flashlight beam. A scorpion passed through the luminous circle on the ground, coming out of the darkness before taking refuge in it again. It crossed with its sting coiled over its back, its pincers high. After five minutes of walking perpendicularly to the dirt track, Rick reached the ridge. He sat on the edge with his feet hanging down and let himself fall. He quickly touched the ground. It was a short drop.

The flashlight illuminated his car's Colorado license plate, and a warm feeling filled him with peace. In the middle of the night, lost in that desert, his house seemed as unreachable as the moon that shone in the sky, but his 1959 Lincoln was there, and in some way it was like being home.

Rick opened the trunk with the keys he'd hidden in the exhaust pipe. He took out the thick brown folder he had concealed under a toolbox. A red pen was secured under one of the elastic bands. The seat of his car received him as if hugging him, the opposite of how he had felt in Elmer's pickup. His heart, which had finally recovered its normal pace after the run, accelerated again when he stood the folder on his knees, resting it against the steering wheel. He kept the flashlight on, positioning it on the dashboard.

He opened the folder with trembling hands.

It contained dozens of cuttings, original documents, and copies of newspaper articles. Rick had read them all, but there was too much information, too many dates, too many names to commit to memory. He hadn't retained every detail, but studying the collection of papers so many times, he'd ended up classifying it all in some way in his head, and he knew roughly where to start searching. When he wanted to find a document, his fingers would take him directly to the top or the bottom of the pile. He also usually knew in advance whether the information he needed to find was in one of the copies or one of the original documents, whether the article he thought he remembered was accompanied by a photograph, and even what part of the page the information was on, once he found it.

He dipped his hand into his backpack in search of his notebook. His fingers felt the objects inside three times before it dawned on him that he'd hidden it under the seat when Iris got into the truck, and he'd left it there.

"Goddamn it . . ."

He strained to remember his notes. With pen in hand, he navigated the documents in the folder. He compared papers. He selected some, bringing them to the top of the pile. He discarded the ones he didn't think were relevant. He unfolded papers, then folded them back up again. He clicked his tongue several times, whenever he feared his search would come to nothing. As it always had. He began to believe that the document he was looking for didn't exist, that he'd fabricated it in his imagination while he ate shrimp tacos with the family. He shook his head as he read many of the articles. His hands and eyes coordinated to perfection, checking the information. Emotion began to stir in his stomach as some of the documents passed various tests. The smile on his face widened with each red cross he used to mark a document.

Until the one he was really searching for appeared.

The one he'd thought of as soon as he saw the uninjured arm of a little girl passing herself off as her twin sister.

It wasn't a product of his imagination.

It was real.

Rick shut the folder. He pulled on the elastic band with such force that it snapped. The elastic whipped him, stinging like a small burn. He returned the file to the trunk. When he moved the toolbox, a bottle of Coca-Cola rolled toward him. He opened it on the bumper and drank it without caring that it was as hot as coffee. Sticky. He needed fluid so he could run again. A bird sang to the dying night. The horizon was no longer black but dark blue, and he had to be back at the house, lying in the pickup, before the sun came up. He slammed the trunk shut with such violence that some unseen creature fled in fright, slithering through the bushes.

Elmer came out of the upstairs bathroom, adjusting his work coveralls. The twins received him by wrapping their arms around his waist. His neck still burned from his aftershave. From the kitchen, the smells of breakfast and the sound of the pans reached them upstairs. Rose had gone down when he was getting into the shower. Elmer opened the door to Melissa's room.

He found her talking to her rocks.

"Can't you smell the eggs? Don't keep Mom waiting."

"I'm coming." She turned to the stones. "So whose turn is it to come down today? No, Clark, not you. And Natalie came down yesterday. It's . . . Gregory's turn."

She picked up her chosen rock and walked out with it, dodging around him and the twins at the door. At that time of morning, the sun's rays lit up the wall in Melissa's room where she hung her family portraits. Elmer ran his eyes over them, allowing himself a few seconds to revisit all the good memories he had shared with his wife, with his daughters.

Next he opened Iris's bedroom door.

"Can't you knock?" she asked, covering herself up to her head with the sheet.

"We're all downstairs having breakfast already."

"No, we're not, we're here, Daddy," the twins said.

"She knows what I mean. Come on."

Iris took a while to get up. When she did, she dragged the sheet with her, using it as a dressing gown to cover herself.

"Do you sleep in the nude or what?"

Iris let out a sigh of irritation. "Can I get dressed in peace, or do I have to do it in front of all of you?"

Elmer ushered away the twins, who went down the stairs ahead of him holding hands, their steps synchronized. When they reached the bottom, Mom yelled to them from the kitchen that there was only enough cocoa for one of them, and they sped forward to squabble over it. Rose gave him a wink, making him complicit in the trick that never failed to get the twins to come to her.

"Open up over there, will you?" she asked. "Let some air in."

Elmer unlocked the front door. Through the screen's green mesh, he saw the breakfast bag on the little table outside. He recognized the way his wife rolled up the top of the paper. He was so annoyed by the kid's rudeness, the bad manners he showed by rejecting the food Rose had made for him in the middle of the night, that he thought about hiding the bag so his wife wouldn't see it. But she appeared beside him before he could do anything.

"What're you looking at?" she asked, a slotted spoon in her hand. Seeing the bag, she came to a different conclusion. "He hasn't left yet?"

His wife's words contained just a hint of alarm.

"How can he still be in there?" Elmer gestured at the Dodge, its cab fully in the sun. "It must be two hundred degrees in that truck."

A frenetic clatter broke out above them. It came down the stairs until it reached the door. Iris tried to look over Elmer's shoulders.

"Is he still there?" she asked. "He hasn't gone?"

Melissa joined them, carrying her rock.

"Take one of the twins away," Elmer said to Rose.

She went back into the kitchen and left it pulling on Dahlia, who advanced without taking her eye from the glass of chocolate milk she carried in her other hand. Before reaching the stairs, Rose gave the slotted spoon to Iris, telling her to watch the stove.

Elmer went out, closing the screen door in his daughters' faces.

"He stayed for me," Iris whispered behind him.

Elmer picked up the paper bag and looked up and down the porch. It seemed more logical that Rick would have sought refuge somewhere in the shade. As he went down the steps, his suspicions about the kid, the ones he'd finally dismissed overnight, returned with intensity. Of course the kid wouldn't be sitting in the shade chewing on a blade of grass, resting before continuing his hike. The kid would have used the confusion to slip in through the back door, and he would already be upstairs jumping on his wife's back. Attacking his girls. Elmer turned toward the front of the house. For an instant, he imagined the young man in the twins' window, threatening Rose with a knife at her throat. Asking them if they hadn't known, deep down, that sooner or later they would receive the punishment that . . . he shook his head to expel the vision. In the window there was only his wife, anxious like him.

Elmer walked on toward the truck. The two windows were open. He remembered the conversation he'd had with the kid the night before, leaning against the mirror. It suddenly struck him as ridiculous that the youngster who couldn't even drink a shot of mescal without coughing like a child should harbor dark intentions.

"Hey, kid, are you in there?"

Elmer took another couple of steps forward. Before peering into the vehicle, he knocked on the door with his knuckles.

There was no response.

He knocked again.

Rick's head suddenly appeared. The kid looked from side to side, disoriented. His face was lined, his hair tangled. He blinked behind hair that had collapsed over his eyes. A swirl of it made him look like a child. If there was one inoffensive young man anywhere in the immensity of that desert, this was him. Elmer felt relieved. And angry with himself for letting fear fabricate bad omens after all this time.

"Did I wake you?"

"Wake me?" Rick asked. "What time is it?"

Elmer had to let go of the handle several times before he could open the door. It burned. The youngster came out of the truck enveloped in an asphyxiating swell of air that smelled of hot metal. His T-shirt was stuck to his body.

"Man, don't tell me you've slept till now. In this heat."

"All night. Like a log." Drips of sweat slid down the kid's sideburns, yet he grunted with pleasure as he stretched. "I hope you don't mind me staying so late. I'd spent so many nights sleeping on the ground, lying in there was like heaven."

Rick noticed the paper bag. "What's that?"

"My wife left you some breakfast on the porch, like I said she would. In case you went before the sun came up." He pressed the bag against the young man's chest. "It's yours. You can take it with you or eat it in the truck you're so fond of. That way the bread will toast a little."

Rick gave a half smile.

"We're having breakfast, and I have to get to work."

Melissa yelled from the house. "He can stay and have breakfast with us!"

Iris opened the screen door and came out onto the porch. Hugging one of the structure's posts, she waved the slotted spoon in the air. "I've already made eggs for him!"

Rick left his boots on the floor, his socks in a ball inside. He placed the backpack protectively between his legs when he sat at the table. The first thing he noticed was the little girl's arm. It was the twin with the scratches, not the one who'd had dinner with them the night before. His heart accelerated when he remembered the document in his folder. Melissa ate cereal while she stroked one of her rocks, grinding the occasional flake against the mouth painted on the stone.

"It's Gregory today," she whispered to Rick.

The twin with the scratched arm was watching the rest of the family with her mouth slotted onto the edge of her glass, blowing bubbles in the milk every time something made her laugh. Iris kept seeking out Rick with her gaze, giving him conspiratorial smiles every time their eyes met. He tried to avoid her looks so her father wouldn't intercept them. He didn't ask about the dirty T-shirt he'd left hanging on the back of a chair. He sensed that Iris had something to do with its disappearance, and he preferred not to risk the rest of the family finding out. He did his best to overcome the desire to take off the one he was wearing, which was soaked in sweat. Staying inside the truck until they came looking for him had been tough. When the sun reached the cab soon after dawn, not long after Rick returned, the temperature had risen until it was difficult to breathe.

He'd made himself hold on because the pretext of having overslept would be more believable than any other he could come up with. It was the excuse most likely to enable him to remain at the house after Elmer had told him, twice, to leave the place before daybreak.

The father ate quickly, his fork scraping on the plate every time he skewered his scrambled eggs. He alternated each forkful with sips of coffee as black as the scorpion that had crossed in front of Rick's flashlight in the night. With the quantity of *salsa verde* he'd poured over his breakfast, each mouthful must have burned more than that scorpion's sting. A foot brushed against Rick's. Iris's flushed cheeks gave her away.

"What soft feet you have," she whispered.

He moved his chair backward.

"Come on, kid, eat," the father said. "We're leaving in five minutes."

"We're leaving?"

"You're coming with me to the gas station. That way you can save yourself a ninety-mile hike."

Rick took a sip of coffee to give himself time to think.

"But that would be cheating," he improvised. "I've come to walk, and walking's what I have to do."

"Nice try, kid"—Elmer let out a guffaw—"but I'm not going to leave you alone in the house with my daughters."

"Dad, he's still got lots of food left to eat," Iris broke in.

Elmer stood and picked up the boots from the floor.

"You have five minutes to get it down, or it stays on the plate." He dropped the footwear on the table, making the teaspoons tinkle in the cups. "Five minutes."

"Are you seriously going to leave that pair of boots where we eat?" Rose scolded her husband. "Just look how worn and filthy they are."

He removed them right away, picking them up using a finger and thumb as pincers.

The ball of socks fell out. It rolled along the tablecloth among the cups, the plates, the box of cereal. Rick watched it move in slow motion, his mind working at full speed trying to come up with the excuse that would enable him to prolong his stay.

"They stink!" yelled the little girl, who laughed into the liquid in her glass, splashing her face with chocolate milk.

Rick trapped the ball as if catching an animal. The little girl's comment had given him an idea.

"You're right, Lily, they reek. So do I." He wrinkled his nose to keep the youngest daughter laughing. Then he asked Elmer, "Do you mind if I take a shower? I think the little one has said out loud what we were all thinking. I'll only be five minutes."

Elmer opened his mouth but closed it without saying anything, as if he'd tried to find a reason to refuse him the shower but hadn't found one. "Five minutes, not a second longer," he finally said. "And only because I don't feel like driving ninety miles with a guy who smells like a run-over coyote, not because I feel sorry for you."

"You don't smell bad," Iris whispered. "You smell like you."

Rick pretended he hadn't heard her. He drank the rest of his coffee in one gulp, stuffed the ball of socks into his boots, and got up, holding his backpack.

"I guess the bathtub's upstairs, right?" He managed to suppress the trembling in his voice prompted by the possibility of investigating upstairs. "The bathroom down here didn't have one."

The father snorted.

"Our shower's upstairs, all right," he said. "You come with me."

Rick followed him. When they passed the half bath near the front door, Elmer asked him if he needed a towel or soap.

"Both."

"You really don't have much in that backpack." Elmer took a towel and a bar of soap from the bathroom. "Please tell me you at least have a toothbrush."

Rick nodded, though it was a lie. His stomach began to contract when they approached the foot of the stairs. Then Elmer strayed off toward the front door. He guided him outside, across the porch. Rick felt the heat from the boards on the soles of his feet. They went down the steps and around the house to the left. Rick stepped on some stones, which hurt his bare feet. On the side wall stood a narrow pipe with an opening at the height of Rick's chin.

"No man's going to take his clothes off in the same house as my wife and daughters, kid, so you'll have to make do with this faucet," Elmer said. "And don't pull that face. I wash here myself whenever I work outside on the trucks."

He handed Rick the bar of soap, then stuck the towel on the spines of one of the cacti.

"As you can see, there're plenty of places to hang your clothes. Just mind you don't prick your balls. Come on, hurry up, you've got five minutes." Elmer turned the valve before leaving, and a powerful jet hit the ground. As he turned the corner where the porch was, he yelled, "Four minutes."

Rick took a while to react. The idea of using the shower to gain access to the top floor hadn't panned out as he'd hoped. He needed more time. He couldn't let Elmer take him to the gas station.

He swiveled around as if he could find the solution on the ground. The spurt of water spattered him with mud. He left his backpack to one side and started undressing because it was what he was supposed to be doing.

"Think, think, think . . ."

As Elmer had with the towel, he hung up his T-shirt using the cactus spines. He folded his pants on top of the backpack. When he took off his underpants, hooking them onto another spine, his nudity made him feel defenseless. He bent his knees to go under the jet, hoping the water would deliver an idea, and rubbed the bar of soap against his chest.

"Two minutes, kid!"

Elmer's voice from inside the house reverberated off the wall. Rick spread the soap over his body, hoping for an epiphany. The revelation arrived as he rinsed his hair. He came out from under the stream of water, leaving the faucet running. He didn't even wash away all the lather. Without giving the idea time to ripen, he grabbed the towel hanging on the cactus.

"One minute!" shouted Elmer.

Rick bit the towel, pushing the fabric inside his mouth. He began breathing more heavily. The sound of the air as it entered and left his nose was louder than the jet of water hitting the ground. He moved closer to the cactus. He was right-handed, so he chose the left arm.

He had to do it.

He had to do it now.

He took one last breath.

He hammered the inner side of his arm into the cactus.

The spines pierced his skin like dozens of injections administered at once, hypodermic needles extracting blood from his wrist to his biceps. The needles in his muscle burned most of all. Rick screamed into the towel. He breathed in again before moving his arm downward without separating it from the cactus. The spines tore at his flesh like an enraged cat. When he retracted his arm, the spines still stuck to it were the ones that hurt the least. The ones that clung to the cactus exited the flesh as if the nurses administering the injections were digging around with the needles, intent on torturing him.

He used the towel to muffle another scream.

He hammered his arm into the cactus again.

This time, the pain made him light-headed. The smell of blood and cactus sap turned his stomach.

He swung his arm once more.

His body went cold. He observed the damage through tears. Blood covered his entire forearm, it dripped onto the ground and his feet. Spines sprouted from his flesh at the most unexpected angles. The image of shaving them like hair made him laugh insanely, causing him to choke.

He lay on the ground and took the towel from his mouth, struggling to contain a scream. He used it to cover himself in case the girls came out. Lying in the sand, covered in his own blood and spattered with mud by the jet of water, he cried out. First they were generic howls of pain to attract attention, screams he didn't need to feign. Then he called for aid.

"Help!"

The entire structure of the house creaked with the movement that broke out inside.

Rose shuddered when she heard the first scream. The soapy cup she was washing slipped from her hands. The girls' chairs scraped against the kitchen floor. She left the dishes.

"What's happened to him?" Iris asked after the second howl.

Rose hadn't seen her so pale since she told her what happened to Edelweiss. Daisy tried to take refuge between her legs, but Rose got her out of the way and ran to the door. The girls followed.

Elmer was already outside, on the porch.

"What is it?" asked Rose.

"I don't know. You all stay here."

"He needs my help," Iris sobbed.

Rose clicked her tongue at Iris's excessive interest in the young man. She knew the fantasies her daughter would be creating in her head. "I'm coming with you." She opened the screen door despite her husband's resistance. From outside, she ordered her daughters not to move. Daisy was crying in Melissa's arms. "Don't be frightened, Daisy, it's all right."

Another scream from the boy made her jump.

"Has a snake bitten him?" Iris's voice faltered.

"Stay here."

Rose gripped Elmer's arm. They rounded the house toward the faucet. She let out a cry when they found the boy lying on the ground, near one of the cacti, covered in earth and blood. It flowed from one of his arms, diluting itself in the water and soaking into the towel he had bundled up on his crotch, his pubic hair visible. He struggled to speak.

"I . . . I slipped when I came out." He coughed. "I wanted to get the towel, but I fell on the cactus. Right on the cactus with this arm. Because of the soap."

With his eyes, he indicated the bar of soap floating in a puddle of lather on the ground. Then he showed them his arm.

Rose held her hands to her chest with a gasp. "It hurts just looking at it." She sucked air through her teeth. "That's a lot of spines."

She knelt next to Rick to assess the damage. The blood made it impossible to see the depth of the wounds, but the dozens of needles made his flesh look like a pincushion.

"Some mess you've got yourself into, kid." Elmer held his hands to his head, the truck keys hooked on his thumb. "And I was already late."

"Please, Elmer. Just look at the poor boy," Rose reproached him. "Help me lift him up."

Between the two of them they managed to get him on his feet. Rose washed away the blood with handfuls of water until she had a better view of the injury.

"It's not so bad," she finally said.

"It's not?" Oddly, the boy didn't seem pleased at the observation. "The pain's making me dizzy." He held his hand to his forehead.

"The skin and flesh are broken, but it doesn't look like you've damaged any nerves. And I can't see the bone," explained Rose. "It's the spines you want to worry about. There're a lot of them and they could get infected. I'll have to get them out for you."

"All of them?" Elmer asked with an impatient snort.

Rose didn't bother answering him.

"Come on, let's get you to the kitchen."

Without giving her husband the chance to complain, she led Rick back to the house, keeping his arm as straight as possible.

"Kid, make sure that towel's on properly," Elmer yelled behind them. "I don't want it falling off in front of my daughters."

Carefully, they climbed the porch steps. Rose didn't take her eyes off the wound, though Rick was looking away. Elmer ran to catch up with them and reached the door before they did. On the other side of the screen, the girls burst into questions.

"Oh, no. What happened? Why's the towel red?"

"I'm scared, Mommy."

"Are you all right, Rick? Tell me you're all right. I need to know you're all right."

Rose asked them to get out of the way, and Elmer helped clear a path. As they came in, Daisy ran upstairs, Melissa asked if it was very painful, and Iris's eyes welled up. Iris tried to approach the young man, but Elmer stopped her.

"If you want to help, bring the first-aid kit."

"And the tweezers," Rose added. She sat Rick down in the kitchen, his arm stretched out on the table.

"What happened?" Melissa asked, holding the doorjamb.

"I slipped and fell on a cactus. If only it'd had clothes on like yours."

"Thorns, Needles, and Pins would never have done that to you."

Iris strode into the kitchen like an emergency-room nurse and bit her bottom lip when she saw the injury. She emptied the contents of a metal case on the table and deposited a pair of tweezers there as well.

"Your wounds hurt me as much as they do you," she whispered to Rick.

Rose elbowed her out of the way.

Daisy returned from wherever she'd been and picked up the thermometer. "Do I have a fever, Mommy?"

Rose raised her arms in the air.

"OK, everyone out!" Elmer said. "You're getting in the way!"

Iris took Daisy by the hand. Melissa joined them in the doorway.

Before leaving the kitchen, Iris turned back. "When pain is over, the remembrance of it often becomes a pleasure."

Elmer sighed. Rose shook her head.

The first thing she picked up was a bottle of iodine.

"This is going to sting," she warned.

She soaked the wound in the dark, metallic-smelling solution. Rick clenched his fist and closed his eyes. He bared his teeth.

"Come on, kid, don't be a crybaby." Elmer was pacing the length of the kitchen, shaking the keys to the truck.

Rose blew on the wound to dry it and picked up the tweezers. They were the ones she used for her eyebrows. She felt woozy looking at the field of needles on his arm. Selecting one of the thicker ones first, she pulled on it suddenly, without warning. She deposited it on one of the bandages, leaving a dark red blot on the material. Then she extracted another one.

"Is this going to take long?"

Rose let her shoulders drop.

"This is the second one." She showed her husband the tweezers clasping the spine. "Look at his arm and work it out."

"What am I supposed to do? I can't show up two hours late."

She left another blot on the bandage.

"Don't move," she told the young man.

Rose got up and invited her husband out through the back door.

"I think you can go," she whispered once they were outside.

She could smell the garden's vegetables warming in the sun.

"Are you crazy?"

"Look at him."

Rose guided Elmer's gaze toward the boy. His hair was stuck to his face, the towel was wrapped around his waist like a skirt that was too small for him. He was shivering.

"He's harmless," said Rose. "He tried to hide it, but he jumped with each spine I pulled out."

"He is pretty pathetic, I'll give you that."

"And if he tries anything, it's five against one."

Elmer smiled.

"Patch him up and then he goes." He held his wife's face. "Patch him up. And then he goes. And he doesn't go near Iris."

"I want him out, too. But if that boy has a mother, she'll thank me for not letting him walk off with an infected arm."

"You're too good."

"No, I'm a mother. It's easy to feel compassion when you understand that everyone's the child of a woman like you."

Elmer kissed her on the lips. They returned to the kitchen.

"Kid, you're lucky that my wife's a better person than I am. I'm going, she's going to take care of you. As soon as she's gotten the last spine out, you leave the way you came. Got it?"

The young man nodded.

"No eating, no resting, no drinking, no saying goodbye to my daughters. You leave. And if it's through that back door, all the better."

"I appreciate it."

"And you're going to do me a favor right now and get dressed, however much it hurts."

Iris appeared in the kitchen. She had Rick's backpack and clothes. The boy snatched them from her hands, his healthy arm fast as a whip. Rose attributed it to shyness at seeing his underwear exposed.

"We're going to leave you for a minute so you can get dressed," Elmer said.

Before leaving the kitchen with him and Iris, Rose took the basket of flowers from the refrigerator. They found Melissa sitting on the stairs, Daisy using her legs as a backrest.

"All of you outside," Elmer said. "This place is a hospital now and no visitors are allowed."

The girls went out to the porch.

"Why don't you make the necklaces?" Rose handed the basket to Daisy. "It'll keep you busy."

The little girl leapt with excitement, but Iris and Melissa slumped into the porch swing, showing no interest in the flowers.

Rick managed to put on the T-shirt without bending his arm too much. He marked the material with spots of iodine and blood. Through the window, he saw Rose saying goodbye to her husband.

"That's it, go . . ." he whispered, buttoning up his pants.

The truck moved off down the dirt track. He could hear the girls talking on the porch. When he saw Rose return to the house, Rick positioned himself on the chair again, his arm outstretched on the table, beside the tweezers.

"Are you dressed yet?" she asked from the living room.

"Yes, unless a pair of bare feet frighten you."

Rose walked into the kitchen and resumed her work. With the tweezers, she selected each needle she thought the most isolated, or the least tilted, and pulled on it with confidence. She collected them on a bandage that grew redder as she worked.

Rick didn't show the pain he felt from each extraction. "You're good at this."

"Living here with so many daughters, you can imagine it's not the first time I've removed spines from an arm."

"I saw the accident the little girl had yesterday."

Rick regretted his words when Rose's tweezers stopped in the air. Perhaps she was recalling how the girl's arm had miraculously healed during dinner, in full view of a stranger. She took longer than usual to select the next needle. When she pulled it out, it hurt more than the previous ones. Rose began removing them with greater speed. She stopped bothering to find the spines in the best position or move aside the shreds of skin and just plucked them one by one in order of proximity.

"We're going to get this over and done with so you can leave the way you came," she murmured.

She pulled out another spine, then found two that were close to each other and plucked them both with one tug. Before long she needed another bandage to collect them on. She ended up with quite a large pile.

She passed the tweezers over the arm one last time. "I can't see any more."

She applied another layer of iodine to the wound before covering it with several bandages she secured with surgical tape to complete the dressing.

"I really appreciate it," Rick said.

She returned the iodine, surgical tape, thermometer, and other utensils to the metal case.

"At least it won't get infected now, but you should see a doctor in the next village." She closed the lid. "All I've done is what any mother would do."

"Is there any better care than that?"

Rose didn't respond. She stood up, threw the bloody spines and dirty bandages in the trash, and pushed her chair under the table.

"You heard my husband." She gestured at the kitchen's back door. "You can leave through there. If you want to take the breakfast bag, it's still on the porch."

Rose moved aside to let him past. Rick needed a few seconds to work out his next move.

"Come on, I have to see to the garden and hens," she said.

Rick relaxed his legs and fell against the sink. He slid down the cabinet with his back against it until he was sitting on the floor. He saw his boots by a leg of the table.

"Whoa, I feel a little dizzy." He exaggerated the sensation, laying himself down where he was.

He heard Rose click her tongue. Her feet moved in a circle, away and then back again.

"It must be the blood," he went on. "I guess I lost more than you'd think."

A teaspoon clinked inside a glass. Rose knelt and offered it to him, lifting his head.

"It's water with sugar. It'll make you feel better."

Rick took a few sips of the sweet mixture and forced a cough.

"All right, come on. Can you get up? Go lie on the sofa for a few minutes."

"I don't know if I can."

He deliberately slowed his movements. Rose offered support and picked up his boots from the floor. On the way to the living room, they passed the screen door.

"What is it?" Melissa asked.

"He had a bit of a spell. It's fine."

"Do you need anything from me?" asked Iris. "Anything at all . . ."

"He doesn't need anything."

Rose guided Rick to the sofa and dropped his boots to one side. She plumped up a couple of cushions and positioned them under his head and knees.

"You have ten minutes to recover."

She sat in the armchair to wait. She appeared to have no intention of leaving him alone.

Iris's voice reached them from the porch. "Mom?"

"No, he doesn't need your help—at all."

"It's Lily."

"What's the matter with Lily?"

"She's not here."

"What do you mean, she's not there?"

"She was here with her flowers, but now we can't see her."

"Melissa, tell me what's going on. I don't trust your sister," Rose yelled without moving from her chair, watching Rick the whole time.

"It's true, Mom," Melissa confirmed. "We were here on the porch swing and Lily was in the sun with her necklaces. Now there's just the basket."

"All right, then go look for her."

The sisters shouted the little girl's name. They repeated it again and again, each time screaming louder, without moving from the porch. They started laughing after each yell. They seemed more concerned with winning some kind of prize for the loudest shriek than finding their sister.

With a snort, Rose got up from the chair.

"Don't move," she said to Rick.

When she went out onto the porch, the screen door hit the frame hard.

Rick leapt up from the sofa.

Iris stopped yelling when she saw how angry Mom was as she came out.

"Are you for real?"

Melissa stifled a laugh.

"Where's"—Mom looked to one side, as if calculating whether Rick could hear her, to know which name to use—"Lily?"

"She'll be around, Mom. She'll turn up."

"Around?" She waved a hand at the desert. "Climbing on the rocks and falling on a cactus? Or lifting up stones until she finds a scorpion like last time?"

Iris was about to say sorry when the honk of a horn made the three of them jump.

"Look, there she is," she said.

Daisy was inside the truck, standing on the seat. She was moving her hands around the steering wheel as if driving. She yelled something unintelligible.

Mom pointed at the Dodge's door.

"Who left it open?" She maintained the alarm in her tone. "The boy, of course. Who else could it be?"

"What does it matter, anyway?" Iris said. "Lily's safe. It's not as if she's going to start the thing and smash into the house."

A few words escaped Mom's lips as she remembered something.

"The shotgun . . ." she whispered.

She ran out to the little girl.

"Did she say shotgun?" Melissa asked.

Iris nodded while she took advantage of the situation to sneak into the house. She was longing to see Rick alone.

"Shouldn't we wait?"

"Oh, please. Mom worries about everything. That girl's not going to pick up a gun and start shooting. You wait here if you want."

But Melissa followed her in.

They found Rick in the living room. On two feet, he was unhooking the guitar from the wall. When he noticed that they'd come in, he cleared his throat. He tried to return the instrument to its place but missed the nail. He left it resting against the sofa before lying down.

"Feeling better?" Iris asked.

"A little, yes."

She approached the sofa as nervous as she had been the night before. She wanted to talk to him, to discuss her memories of their forbidden encounter, but with Melissa there it was impossible.

"Weren't you going to help Mom?" she asked Melissa.

"I want to speak to him, too."

"Where is she?" Rick asked. "Your mother."

"Telling Lily off out there."

From outside they could hear the truck's horn hooting over and over. Rick sat up, suddenly recovered. Iris sat on one side of him. Melissa sat on the other, moving the guitar aside.

"That guitar wasn't here yesterday, was it?" he asked.

Melissa shrugged.

"Who plays it?"

"I do, a little." Iris moved closer to Rick. "Do you want me to sing something for you?"

"Ignore her," Melissa said. "She hasn't got a clue."

Iris felt like shoving her sister against the wall.

"Only Dad knows how to play it now, but he almost never does," Melissa continued. "It was our eldest sister's."

Rick gestured at Iris. "Hers?"

Having his eyes on her rekindled the heat in Iris's stomach, heat that rose to her cheeks. She blinked without looking away.

"No, our eldest sister." Melissa picked up the guitar, showing Rick the side of the sound box with the name carved into it. "Her name was Edelweiss."

Rick's neck cracked due to some sudden tension. His eyes opened wider than normal. He swallowed so hard that Iris could hear it.

"Another sister?" His voice was no more than a sigh. "Older than you?"

"Two years older," Iris said. "She would be eighteen now. She died last year."

Rick's eyes welled up until they looked like glass. He let out a sob.

"What is it? Don't suffer for us. We're getting through it, slowly."

Rick stroked the name engraved on the guitar. His fingers were trembling.

"What's wrong?" Iris asked.

He turned to Melissa. "Do you have a drawing of her?" he whispered.

Melissa nodded and got up to look for a sketchbook.

"Why're you so sad?" Iris asked.

Rick was running his finger over each curve of the name carved into the wood. She noticed him trying to contain his words, as if he was afraid his voice would fail when he tried to speak.

"You don't need to feel embarrassed with me," Iris said. "Knowing you completely is what I long to do."

Melissa returned with the sketchbook. She passed it to Rick, showing him a page with one of her last portraits of Edelweiss.

"I didn't draw so well. It could've been a lot better."

"You didn't draw that well then or now," Iris said, sticking her tongue out at her.

But it wasn't true. The portrait was beautiful. Seeing it, Iris remembered the afternoon on the porch when Melissa had drawn it. The smell of honey that Edelweiss gave off after taking a bath. The golden glow of the sun on her hair, gathered in a side bunch with a cactus flower over the ear.

Peering at the portrait, Rick's voice fractured when he started crying. "No . . ."

Iris had seen a man cry only once: her father. She wanted to console Rick but didn't know how. Melissa was no help. A tear fell onto the flower drawn in the portrait, making it wilt. Blotting Edelweiss.

Elmer stopped the pickup on one side of the road. Arriving on time at the gas station no longer mattered to him. He'd been dazzled as he drove past an unidentified gleam coming from somewhere in the middle of the desert, a flash of sun reflecting off something he had never seen before at that time of day. Then he'd discovered a lot of footprints on the dirt track, the ones the kid must've left with his boots the previous day, before he came across Rose and the girls. The strange thing was that at a certain point the footprints suddenly disappeared.

Elmer got out of the truck. The sun was hot on the back of his neck as he inspected the end of the trail, trying to understand the kid's movements. He found a mound of stones. A marker. He turned around to scan the landscape. The flash that had dazzled him before caught his eye among the cacti. He set off toward it, trying to silence the bad thoughts.

Over a ridge, covered in rooted-up dry bushes by way of camouflage, he found a car. A Lincoln with Colorado license plates. The sweat on his back turned cold. Elmer searched it for any evidence that it belonged to Rick, his heart thundering in his ears. He found the keys hidden in the exhaust pipe. When he opened the trunk, an empty Coca-Cola bottle rolled toward him. His worst fears were confirmed when he found a brown folder.

Rose rounded the back of the Dodge while Daisy yelled imaginary directions at the steering wheel. The little girl stopped when she saw her mother in the window.

"I can drive, Mommy. It's really easy."

"And how do you drive without this?" From her apron, she produced her key.

"By moving this round thing." The girl started play-driving again, her hands sliding around the wheel.

Rose took the chance to have a look behind the seat. As she'd feared, the shotgun was still there, along with a box of shells, but Daisy hadn't noticed it.

The horn honked twice. "There was a dog on the road," Daisy explained. "I didn't want to run it over."

"Come on, that's enough. Out now. I've left the boy on his own."

"No, I want to get to Daddy's gas station." Daisy concentrated on the landscape she was picturing in front of her.

"Come on, get out."

The girl ignored her.

"I won't say it again." Rose opened the door.

Daisy honked the horn.

"Now!"

Daisy hunched her shoulders, frightened by the volume of her mother's voice. She counterattacked by honking the horn again. And again. She honked it nonstop over Rose's yelling. When her mother swooped to grab her, Daisy fled to the passenger's seat, out of her reach.

"Bet you can't catch me . . ."

Rose tried to reach into the cab, but the steering wheel thwarted her attempt.

"Please, honey, I have to get back to the house. The boy's on his own."

Daisy laughed. She jumped up and down. She evaded her mother's hands. When the girl sang a little song to taunt her, Rose exploded.

"Get out!"

She struck the driver's seat. Something fell onto the floor, under the steering wheel. Daisy opened the passenger-side door and leapt to the ground without saying another word.

Rose saw what had fallen under the wheel. It was a notepad, a little book she'd never seen. Its cover was decorated with false passport stamps.

"I'm sorry, Mommy," said Daisy, behind her now.

"It's OK," she replied, without turning around.

All of Rose's attention was on the notebook. She picked it up, and it opened by itself. It contained a folded piece of paper, thicker than the rest of the pages. Rose unfolded what turned out to be a map. A line showed a route through the states of Colorado, Utah, Nevada, Arizona, New Mexico, and California. It continued into Mexico, down Baja California. Several waypoints were marked, some of them crossed out. One of the waypoints was in the area of this house.

"What is it, Mommy?"

The little girl's voice was distant.

Rose's hands began to tremble.

She tried to fold the paper back up but was incapable of doing so. She ended up screwing it into a ball, which she threw onto the seat. She flicked through the notebook. Details written in ballpoint pen filled its pages. Names, dates, towns. On the last written page, Rose found her own name. And those of Iris, Melissa, Lily, and Elmer. When her eyes followed an arrow pointing to the words 6-YEAR-OLD TWINS, a deep groan came from her throat.

"What is it, Mommy?"

Rose hid the notebook in the front pocket of her apron. Without stopping to think, she picked up the shotgun. She inserted two shells. Her hands no longer trembled.

"Is there a coyote?" the little girl asked when she saw the gun.

"Stay behind me. Keep close."

Daisy obeyed the order, walking right up against her. Grit shot out under Rose's firm strides. She marched even harder when she discovered that Iris and Melissa weren't on the porch. The entire wooden structure creaked when she climbed onto it. She opened the screen door as if trying to tear it from its hinges. Once inside, she asked Daisy to lock herself in her room with Dahlia, confirming the story about the coyote that the little girl had herself invented. Daisy went upstairs without complaint.

Rose arrived at the living room, hiding the shotgun to one side of the door frame. Sitting on the sofa, Iris, Melissa, and Rick looked up. The boy had red eyes, like he'd been crying. On his knees lay Melissa's sketchbook, open to a portrait of Edelweiss.

"Melissa, Iris: out," said Rose. "Now."

"What is it? The whole house shook when you came in."

"Your father told you not to talk to the stranger."

"He's not a stranger, his name's Rick." Iris rested her chin on his shoulder.

Rose's back went as rigid as the barrels of the weapon she was concealing.

"Go up to the twins' room right away." Her voice was stern. "Lock yourselves in with them."

Rick's frown eased.

"What twins?" Melissa winked, trying to warn her that she'd put her foot in her mouth, like they did sometimes with Socorro.

"Go." The severity of Rose's tone and the fact that she didn't care about mentioning the twins in front of Rick conveyed the seriousness of the message. "Up to the girls' room. And lock the door."

Her daughters got up.

"Mom, tell us what's happening. You're sweating." Iris turned to the young man. "Don't go without saying goodbye."

Rose took Iris by the shoulder and pushed her out of the living room. "Go!"

"You spiked me with your nails!"

Melissa tried to placate her sister, who huffed with indignation. She led Iris upstairs, whispering something in her ear. Before reaching the upper floor, Iris gave Rose a bitter look, her brow knitted. Rose kept the shotgun hidden, concealing it with her body, until her daughters were out of sight.

In the living room, Rick was leafing through the sketchbook. A grimace disfigured his features. He wiped his tears and nose with the bandage on his forearm. Rose's stomach turned at her seeing a stranger observe her family like that.

"Put that down."

She entered the living room with the shotgun to one side, down her leg. Rick blinked, not sure of what he was seeing. He gripped the sofa, his shoulders tense.

"My mother said you can tell a lot about a man from his shoes. She even used it as an argument to explain why she never liked my husband. His were too clean, she said, too shiny. As if it was something bad, as if she thought it was more honest to show the dirt and couldn't understand why Elmer was intent on hiding it. My mother might've liked your shoes, with all that dirt. But there you have it: there's nothing honest about yours. Yours lie." Rose gestured at them beside the sofa. "Those boots back up your story, you must've prepared them well. Dirty as they are, with the soles almost coming off, the laces frayed . . . They're a hiker's boots, no doubt about it. Did you buy them off someone? Or take them from a garbage dump at the last stop on your route?"

Rick didn't answer. Rose enjoyed his agitation.

"Your boots lie," she said again, "but your feet don't. I've had them in front of me all morning, and I almost missed it. Clearly you didn't quite go far enough to make your story believable. Look at them. Look at your feet."

Rick lowered his head. He moved his toes.

"Not a scratch, not a single black or broken nail, not even a blister. Not even a long toenail," Rose went on. "Those feet haven't walked for twenty-seven days straight. I bet they haven't even walked for one."

Rick looked at her with glassy, rage-filled eyes. A shock jolted his body, activating his muscles. He leapt toward her.

"Don't even try it." Rose wielded the shotgun, aiming it at his face.

Rick halted. His eyes flicked around the room: window, floor, shotgun, door, ceiling, other window.

"Don't try anything." Rose caressed the trigger. "I welcomed you into my home. I tended that arm as if it belonged to one of my daughters. But I won't hesitate to shoot you in the head, twice, if I consider it necessary."

The young man swallowed.

"Tell me who you are," Rose demanded. "What are you doing here?"

Rick didn't answer.

"Tell me who you are!"

"I'm just a hiker who was looking for some company."

Rose took a step forward, treading on the rug.

"Stop lying." The shotgun's barrels were now just a few inches from Rick's forehead. "You're not just a hiker."

His face tensed, his expression sharpened.

"And you're not the mother of those girls."

Rose flushed red in front of him, her features contorted. Her eyes filled with tears. The words had been like a slap in the face.

Her finger tensed over the trigger.

Rick grabbed the weapon. He flung it aside, unbalancing Rose. The rug she was standing on made her slip. A gunshot exploded near Rick's head. He saw the hole in the ceiling as a deafening boom penetrated his ear. Plaster rained onto his shoulders and over Rose, who was stamping her feet on the floor trying to get up. Her body's violent jerking expelled her apron pockets' contents. When he saw his notebook, Rick understood what had happened. Rose opened and closed her mouth, yelling something that was silent to him. He could hear nothing other than the ringing. He scoured the floor in search of the shotgun. He saw it under the armchair.

Rose's hand landed close to the butt. Rick stepped on it. He got hold of the shotgun, jumped over her body, and fled the living room. From the front door, he saw his backpack in the kitchen, as well as his boots by the sofa. He thought about retrieving them, but Rose was regaining her balance. The trembling in his hands prevented him from even operating the bolt on the screen door. He slid it from side to side, unable to make it work. The ringing in his ears began to subside.

"Mom!" Iris yelled from upstairs. "What's going on?"

"He shot at me!" Rose said.

Rick broke open the screen door with the butt of the weapon and split the frame's crosspiece in two with his knee. He pushed himself through the metallic mesh onto the porch, scraping his arms. His bandage tore. He leapt down the steps. Landing on the sand scraped his feet. Something dug into his heel. The shotgun found its way between his legs, making him trip. He managed to brace himself with his hands to stop his fall. The wound under the dressing reopened from the effort. The bandages turned red. He cast the shotgun aside. When it hit the ground, it went off. Rick protected his head, but the shot hit glass behind him, a window on the house. Without slowing down, he looked over his shoulder. Rose was coming down the porch steps, trying to reach him. He trod on a spine-covered shrub and screamed. He changed direction toward the dirt track that he'd used the night before, to avoid sharp stones and cacti. He followed the wheel marks, trailing bloody footprints.

He wasn't going to let himself get caught.

The second time he looked over his shoulder, the distance between him and Rose was much greater. He let out a deranged laugh: he was going to make it. He was going to reach his car with his feet ruined, but he would press hard on the gas to escape from there. And he'd call Mom from the next village. At the speed he was running, the tears that appeared at the corners of his eyes when he imagined speaking to her were flung backward.

Rick looked behind him again.

Rose was just a distant smudge.

Relief, excitement, impatience filled his lungs.

All at once they emptied when in front of him he discovered Elmer's pickup.

Elmer squeezed the steering wheel, his fingers white from the pressure.

Rick was there in front of him, barefoot. He was breathing with difficulty, grimacing with pain as he opened his mouth. His arm was bleeding the way it had been when they found him lying under the faucet, near the cactus. A terrifying thought struck Elmer—that the blood wasn't the kid's.

He revved the engine to make it roar.

Rick escaped off to one side of the dirt track. He ran, dodging cacti, jumping rocks. Elmer followed him in the truck. The cab shook from side to side, jolting his body. He hit the roof with his head, the steering wheel with his knees. Metal screeched when rocks scraped the undercarriage. Sparks flew from the truck body. He avoided the cardones with sudden turns that made the wheels skid. A blow bent the side mirror toward the window.

Rick began to stumble. It took him several attempts to jump over a grouping of rocks in his path. The irregular arrangement of the cacti seemed to be disorienting him, because he was turning around and backtracking, as if lost in a maze. Elmer overtook him to the left, cornering him against a wall of cardones as thick as pillars. Penned in, Rick tried to escape by scaling a rock formation taller than himself, but his feet slipped on the stone. He turned to face the truck, his eyes frenzied. His forehead was knitted with panic, his mouth twisted with pain. When the engine roared under the command of Elmer's foot, Rick begged for mercy. He showed his empty hands, a sign of his defenselessness.

"Please, I just want to get away from here." He held his palms together in front of his mouth as if praying. "Please . . ."

Elmer squeezed the steering wheel. If only he *could* just let the kid escape. He'd drive to the gas station like he did every morning and be back by sunset so the twins could welcome him with arms around his legs. If he could, he would travel back in time so that this day never had to happen. So that he never opened his home to a stranger. So that the brown folder that he had on the passenger's seat never existed. And so that he was not here now, his foot on the accelerator of his pickup, charged with stopping this boy from destroying the most important thing he'd built in his life.

Rick walked sideways toward the only free space between two cacti. With each little step the relief on his face grew, as though he was gradually confirming the reprieve he hoped Elmer would give him. As though the truck were a wild animal that had decided not to eat him. If he reached the opening, he could escape. He took another step.

The tension in Elmer's arms made a muscle pull in his back. He was going to let the kid go. He managed to convince himself that it was what had to happen. He and Rose had feared this moment since they'd started a family, and they had to be prepared to face the consequences of their actions.

Now it was time for them to pay.

Rick had just three steps to go to reach his way out of there. He moved his hands and made a hushing sound, as if soothing a rabid dog.

Elmer closed his eyes.

He stepped on the gas.

The young man's high-pitched scream ended in a guttural groan. Elmer didn't let up on the pedal. There were mechanical noises as the engine revved. Tire rubber burned, glass shattered. He wanted to attribute the organic sounds to the cardones breaking up as they gave way. The truck shuddered as it drove over the obstacles, until it crashed into something. Elmer could smell gasoline and steam. He'd hit another cactus. He sat there for a few seconds with his head resting against the steering wheel. He breathed. While he tried to muster the courage to get out, he saw Rose appear in the rearview mirror. She was carrying the shotgun.

Elmer climbed out with the brown folder. Together they observed the aftermath of the collision. Several cacti had collapsed. On top of them, impaled on their needles, lay Rick's body, the limbs bent like those of an articulated cutout. Elmer bit his fist. Then he vomited. Rose stroked his back until he recovered.

"It was all a lie. He had a car four miles away." Elmer wiped his lips. "I found this."

He showed the folder to his wife.

"More information on us?" she asked.

"More?"

Rose took the notebook out from her apron.

"I found it in my truck. He was onto us."

"Did he hurt you?" Elmer studied his wife's face as if conducting a medical examination. "Are the girls OK?"

"They're all fine. But he told me something terrible, he said something terrible to me." Rose hunched her shoulders, covering her ears as if trying to block out the echo of some bad memory. Then she fixed her eyes on Elmer's. "What if you hadn't come back? If you hadn't discovered his car? You saw how far ahead of me he was, he was about to get away. He could've gotten away and ended every—"

Rose burst into tears.

"It's all right, it's all right." Elmer kissed his wife's sweaty temple. "He didn't get away, he's right here, dead. And we have the documents. He can't do anything now, nothing's going to happen." He looked over Rick's battered body and lowered his voice to a whisper. "Now we have to think about what we're going to do. We have to think really hard about what we'll do."

In the twins' bedroom, Iris poked one eye above the bottom corner of the window. That was how she witnessed Rick fleeing with the shotgun, unable to find an explanation for it. She saw him throw it on the ground, how it went off—the twins screamed when the glass smashed in Melissa's room. She saw Mom pick up the gun and run after him. Iris spotted the dust cloud that approached along the road before Rick came face-to-face with Dad's pickup. She also watched Rick escape. And she saw Dad corner him against some cacti and then run him down.

She made for the door.

"Where're you going?" asked Daisy.

"Where're you going?" asked Dahlia.

The twins were clutching Melissa, the three of them cowering in a corner of the room.

"I can't see anything from the window," Iris lied. "I'm going to find out what's happening. It's OK, stay here."

"Be careful," Melissa said.

Iris ran down the stairs as if her feet were wheeled. She found the screen door in pieces. In the kitchen, she saw Rick's backpack and felt an urge to inspect it, to know more about him, but she went out onto the porch without stopping. She felt every little stone through the soles of her slippers, as well as the heat from the ground. That night she'd slept in Rick's T-shirt, but when Dad appeared in her room in the morning, she'd used the sheet to cover it up before changing into her usual nightgown. That nightgown now got caught on a cactus. She just pulled on it, tearing the material. She dodged around more of the spiny plants and more rocks, guided by the plume of smoke and steam that marked her parents' location.

When she spotted them from behind through the forest of cacti, she ran toward them. The sound of her footsteps alerted Mom, who turned around just before she reached them. Her mother stopped her with an arm at belly height.

"Get out of here."

Mom pushed her back—away from Dad, from the truck, and from Rick. It was the first time she'd used such force against Iris, which worried her even more.

"What happened, Mom? Tell me what happened."

Iris dug her heels in, putting up resistance. She struggled to hold her grip in such flimsy slippers.

"You get out of here, or I'll drag you to your room by your hair."

Mom spat the words out through clenched teeth, spraying saliva. Her mother had never spoken to her like this before. An attack of rage made Iris's blood boil, and she gathered all her fury in her stomach and shoved Mom to one side, making her stumble. Free of her, she ran to the scene of the collision, dodging around Dad, who could do nothing to prevent her from seeing the catastrophe.

"Honey, don't . . ."

Iris knew from her books that the most powerful love stories usually end in tragedy, but not even all the words Shakespeare wrote in his entire life could describe the pain that shattered her soul when she saw Rick's body. Over the stink of gasoline and burned rubber, Iris recognized the smell of his T-shirt.

"What have you done to him?" Her voice was no more than a whisper, almost a death rattle.

"I protected my daughters," Dad replied. "That's what I've done."

Iris cried against the mask of fingers with which she now covered her mouth and nose.

"He was dangerous, he had a shotgun."

"He threw it away." Iris choked on her tears, and her mouth tasted of salt. "When you ran him down he didn't have it anymore."

Mom swooped in on her. Iris fell to her knees, letting herself be caught. She had no strength left to resist.

"What have you done to him?" she sobbed.

She let Mom lift her up. She even cried on her shoulder while her mother took her away from there.

"Stop being silly now," Mom said. "A day ago, you didn't even know him."

Then Iris heard Rick's voice.

At first she thought it was her mind reproducing a memory, but the way Mom stopped, with her spine erect, made it clear that she had heard it, too.

Iris turned around.

"Help," Rick spluttered.

Seeing him move his head rebuilt her shattered soul at once.

"He's alive!" she screamed. "We have to help him!"

Rick raised a hand. He also tried to stand up, but the change in his weight distribution made the bed of cacti under him collapse. He groaned with pain when the fall jolted his body.

Iris tried to approach. The lasso formed by her mother's arms tightened around her ribs, suffocating her.

"Let go of me!" Iris yelled with compressed lungs.

This time her slippers suddenly lost their grip. Mom dragged her, taking her away, at times carrying her, spitting Iris's hair out when it went in her mouth. Her mother ignored her screams, maintained the pressure with her arms. She didn't hesitate, either, to push her with her knees, or to immobilize her head by trapping her chin in her hand. She took her back to the house in a single burst of energy. Iris tried to grab on to the porch posts, the screen door, the living room doorway, but Mom stopped her with powerful tugs. She kept going even when Iris broke a nail trying to hang on to the banister.

Mom pushed her into the twins' room. She landed barefooted—she'd lost both slippers along the way. The tear in her nightgown had ridden higher. Melissa, Daisy, and Dahlia gasped.

Mom slammed the door shut without saying a word.

The key turned in the lock outside.

Iris leapt to the door. She shook the handle, unable to open it.

"Help him!" she shouted with her mouth against the wood. "He's not dead!"

He fought to open his eyes, disappointed to find himself in such a blurred world. After each blink, roots of pain sprouted from his pupils toward the inside of his head, but one after the other they helped him bring the reality in front of him into focus. A stone with eyes was the first thing he made out. He had the feeling he'd met a girl who spoke to cactuses—who stuck eyes on rocks, who gave them names. It was a vivid feeling, like a memory, but he was unable to figure out in what context of real life such an encounter would have taken place. It must have been a dream. That was it: he was waking up from a bad dream. A nightmare about cactuses that attacked him, needles sticking out of his skin, liquor with worms in it, being chased over burning earth, two identical little girls, and a basket of flowers. Cactus flowers. But also an iris. A melissa. A lily. A rose. Rose. The flower with thorns. His arm burned when he thought of thorns. His pulse accelerated. He remembered an injury, tweezers, fingers, a face. Rose. A gunshot. He heard glass break in some corner of his memory.

But it wasn't in his memory.

Crouching, a woman was picking up pieces of glass from the floor that broke into smaller fragments when she dropped them in a bucket. The pieces belonged to a window that was above the woman. Outside, the sky was purple, and the air entered the room as hot as the desert sand. The wall opposite the bed was covered in pencil drawings depicting a large family. A happy family. The woman collecting the glass appeared in many of those drawings. Among the girls' faces, there was one that returned Rick to the reality of the situation.

He remembered everything.

The portrait he'd seen in the living room hadn't been a dream. Nor had the identical girls, or being run over by a truck, or waking up among cactuses, or the way they had dragged him over the ground and up the stairs to put him in this room. He was in a bed. The stone with eyes observed him from a bedside table. Next to it was a glass, a pitcher of water, medicine boxes. He looked at the ceiling, then at his body, covered by a sheet. He wanted to get up, but neither his legs nor his arms obeyed his orders. They just squirmed, obstructed by one another, connected in some strange way.

The sound of the mattress springs alerted Rose, who was the woman picking up the glass, that he was awake. She left the bucket on the floor and went out of the room. She returned with her husband. Whose name was Elmer.

"Who are you?" Rose asked. "Why are you here?"

Rick peeled his tongue from the roof of his mouth as if it were made of Velcro.

"Water . . ."

"Tell us who you are."

". . . I need water."

The bitterness of the saliva he swallowed made him retch. It tasted of dry blood. His entire body hurt from the convulsion.

"When you tell us why you're here." Elmer sat on the bed, his hands on either side of the mattress, his head over Rick's face. "And why you had those documents in your car. Who are you?"

Rick's breath escaped in a sigh. Elmer's face moved away. He reached for the glass of water on the bedside table and, without holding it to Rick's lips, poured the contents over his mouth. Rick opened it to capture as much liquid as possible. His tongue regained volume, elasticity. His skin seemed to come back to life, to come loose from the muscle.

"Who are you?"

Rick wriggled about under the sheet, unable to understand his limbs' behavior.

"Am I tied up?"

Rose was watching him from the foot of the bed. She touched her husband's shoulder so that he would get up. She lifted the sheet, offering

Rick the chance to look at himself. There were more patches of purple or yellowing skin on his naked body than pinkish ones. The bulges on his legs raised the possible number of knees to five. Though he couldn't reposition them, he checked that he hadn't lost mobility by bending his toes. His arms were straight, immobilized at his sides. Rope was knotted around his wrists. They'd secured it under the bed, making movement impossible. The self-inflicted injury on his arm burned at each point where Rose had extracted a needle. Identical points were spread all over his body from when the truck hit him.

"The ones I removed from your arm were a handful compared to the ones I had to take out now." She gestured at the most affected area on one side. "Some are still in there—in your back, especially."

Rose dropped the sheet. She tucked the edges under the mattress, as if making the bed, binding Rick even more tightly. She covered him to the chin with the taut fabric.

"Are you going to tell us who you are?" she asked.

Elmer took the brown folder from the desk and dropped it on Rick's abdomen, setting off a blaze of pain in his ribs.

"Police? Detective? FBI?"

"Po . . . po . . ."—he tried not to stammer so he would sound convincing but was unable to stop himself—"police."

Elmer turned his face toward his wife, shielding his mouth with his hand. He whispered something unintelligible.

"You're lying," she said, looking Rick in the eyes. She sat on the bed, tightening the straitjacket that held him even further. "You are lying. An officer doesn't injure himself on purpose. Or do you want me to believe that you really just fell against that cactus?" When she bent forward, the sheet suffocated him. "What've you been searching for in the places marked on your map? What have you been searching for here?"

Rick extended his neck in an attempt to get more air through to his chest.

"Tell us who you are!" Elmer yelled.

"What do you know?" whispered Rose.

She lay her hand on the bed in such a way that the material pressed down on Rick even more. He swallowed, and his Adam's apple rose. It didn't go back down. He felt his face redden. The pain in his head intensified with each heartbeat. The springs squeaked when he writhed.

Rose lifted her hand, freeing part of the sheet. Rick breathed so hard it hurt his throat.

"Who are you?" she persisted. She brought her face so close to Rick's that their noses almost touched. "What do you know?"

Rick narrowed his eyes. "I know you're not the mother of those girls."

Rose slapped him. It hurt from his jaw to his eyebrow. She pointed at him with a finger that she then drove into his cheek. Her eyes glistened.

"Of course I am."

Rick wet his lips, preparing himself for what he was about to say.

"My sister's, too?"

He saw the immediate realization in Rose's eyes. The spark that must have gone off inside her head irradiated light through her pupils. Her features tightened, before relaxing. Her mouth opened.

"Of course," she breathed, "I should've known it as soon as I saw you. You have her eyes."

The same hand that had slapped him now rested on his face. It stroked it with the thumb. It felt his cheeks. It traced the line of his eyebrows. Rose's fingers ran over his features as if she already knew them. She'd stopped blinking, hypnotized by what she saw.

"Edelweiss . . ." she whispered.

There was a maternal gentleness in her touch that disgusted Rick. He shook his head to escape from the fingers that caressed him as if saying goodbye to a corpse. He bit the air.

"That wasn't her name," Rick muttered. "She was called Elizabeth."

Rose shook her head as if he'd said something stupid.

"Edelweiss," she repeated. "She was a flower. Like all of my girls."

"Eliz—"

Rose's hands covered his mouth.

"Edelweiss," she whispered, increasing the pressure.

Rick caught the flesh of a finger in his teeth. He bit down with all the might of his jaw. Rose leapt up from the bed with a howl. Elmer leaned over the bed and squeezed Rick's throat with one hand.

"Did you . . ." Blood-flavored saliva bubbled in Rick's throat. He had just enough air to finish the question. "Did you kill her?"

Rose groaned with pain, as if she'd been punched in the stomach. Elmer released Rick's throat to hold his wife, who had burst into tears. He consoled her, whispering words in her ear, rocking her.

"Answer me," Rick growled. "Yes or no."

"You have no idea how much that question hurts." Rose sniffed and wiped the moisture from under her eyes, from above her lip. "Losing a daughter is the most painful thing that can happen to a mother."

"She wasn't your daughter." Rick's voice broke up. "And the most painful thing that can happen to a mother isn't her daughter dying. It's her daughter disappearing. Her daughter being stolen from a park one morning, and never knowing anything about her again." A tear made a wound on his temple sting. "Not knowing hurts more than death. I know it because I've seen that pain every day in my mother's eyes. And it's much worse than what I see in yours now."

"You told us you were an only child."

"You made me an only child when I was two. You stole Elizabeth from me. My little sister . . ."

Rick closed his eyes. He saw Elizabeth's little face in his mind. The face in the only black-and-white photograph that Mom still had, taken a month after she was born. That little face now merged with the pencil drawing Melissa had shown him, in the living room, of the beautiful woman that his sister had become. Small variations transformed the image until it became his mother's face.

"She was just like our mother." Rick kept his eyes closed so the illusion wouldn't vanish. "She had the exact same face as my mother."

"You're wrong," Rose said. "*I* was her mother."

"She was not your daughter!" Rick kicked his legs in spite of his condition. The indignation hurt more than a few dislocated bones. He felt something inside him tear. "She was not!"

Cramps made his body arch. He writhed under the sheet while the hybrid image of the baby, the portrait, and his mother distorted in front of him. When his muscles reached maximum tension, they gave way. The sudden relaxation made him slump onto the mattress. He regained his breath with deep gasps as the folder slid off his abdomen to one side. Elmer retrieved it and realigned the edges of the documents.

If he'd had any strength left, Rick would have thrashed about on the bed again. The physical pain was easier to endure than the horror of the acts committed by the couple in front of him. He spoke without looking at them.

"She wasn't even enough for you. Losing her daughter destroyed my mother forever, but for you, my little sister wasn't enough. You needed more." He directed the accusation at Elmer, who looked away, at the documents. Then Rick turned to Rose. "How many mothers have you done it to? How many of those girls have brothers or sisters like me?"

"I think you already have an idea." Elmer found the documents Rick had marked with a red pen in his car. He waved them in the air. They were the papers noting disappearances that fit the girls' profiles. "And here you are." He held up a newspaper article with Rick's photo.

"How can you live like this? How many families have you destroyed to make yours?"

Rose avoided eye contact, looking down at the floor, her arms crossed over her chest.

"Make him stop," she said to her husband.

"What kind of family have you created? It's . . . you're . . ." Rick couldn't find suitable words. "It's sickening."

"Make him be quiet."

"And you say you live here to escape the city, to build a family closer to nature, away from the concrete. But you didn't have to come this far to do that. Not to such an isolated place. This house isn't a lifestyle choice. It's a hideout."

"You don't know anything," Rose said.

"I know you hid a twin from me. Thousands of girls disappear, but pairs of twins, not so many. *I'd like to have some little twins as well*, you must have said when three daughters were still not enough. Something like that, huh? But those girls are still appearing in the newspapers. It'd be very dangerous for you if anyone saw them together."

Rose looked out the window.

"Well, you were right, because for me they were the final clue. If you had those twins, you could also have my sister. Someone who snatched a pair of girls could easily have snatched another." Rick lifted his head up despite the pain. "Or even three others."

"Make him stop, please, make him stop."

"If I hadn't discovered them I would've gone after dinner. I would have visited the two houses I had left, then given up once and for all and gone back to Colorado." The tightness spread halfway down his back, the muscle cramped. "Even my mother was asking me to forget about it, to get on with my life. I couldn't even tell her that I was still searching for Elizabeth, because it just made her worse." The pain in his neck blinded him, and he let his head fall back on the pillow with his eyes closed. "She'd already given up. Eighteen years is a long time. And in the end you have to give up, accept that disappearing is a form of dying. A time comes when the only thing that consoles a mother is hoping her daughter is dead. That's how much you hurt her." He turned his head to Rose, soaking the pillow with tears. "But I guess you don't care about that."

"Be quiet!"

Rose reached the bed, grabbed his left foot, and twisted it. The pain condensed in his ankle as if a stake were being driven through it. A scream emerged from his gut and burst out of his throat. He repeated it to distract his mind from the pain. He screamed once more.

"Stop yelling," Elmer ordered.

This time Rose didn't just cover his mouth with her hands. She pressed her entire chest against his face, suffocating him with her flesh, with her clothes. He shook his head until the searing throb in his ankle began to subside. The stake disintegrated, and continuing to scream required too much effort. The peace that the absence of pain brought sedated him, and his body cried out for rest. When Rose freed his face, Rick took in a mouthful of air as soothing as the water Elmer had thrown over his lips. He looked her in the eyes before whispering a question.

"Was she happy here?"

Rose dried his eyelids. She brushed aside his hair.

"Very." She gently smoothed the sheet over his chest, her gaze lost in some fond memory. "She was very happy."

Elmer kneaded his wife's shoulder. They exchanged a nostalgic smile that saddened Rick.

"Did she never know that—?"

"Of course not," Rose answered without letting him finish. "We were her parents. And she had four sisters."

"None of them know anything?"

Rose shook her head with her eyes closed, as if it bothered her to have to reply to such an absurd question. She was stroking her husband's fingers on her shoulder, fiddling with his ring.

"You disgust me," Rick said.

From outside, Melissa's voice reached them. "Dad?"

Elmer went to the window. Rose threatened Rick by grabbing the same foot she'd twisted before. She placed an index finger over her lips.

"Can we come in? We've hosed down the whole truck. It's getting dark."

"Where are your sisters?"

"They're coming."

The twins' screams and laughter sounded close.

"How is he?" Melissa asked. "We heard him scream."

"We'll be right down."

Rose let go of Rick's foot but preserved the threat by turning her hand in the air.

"What're you going to do with me?" he asked.

Elmer placed the folder on a shelf above the headboard. When he tried to close the folder he found that its elastic band was broken.

"Cover it with the stones," said Rose. "Put it underneath."

"Nobody's going to come in."

Rose took the rock with eyes from the bedside table. Rick heard heavy objects, other stones, moving along the shelf. The wood creaked as it bowed.

"That's better," she said.

"What're you going to do with me?" Rick repeated.

They looked at each other but didn't respond. Rose tucked the sheet under the mattress.

"At least let me breathe."

Elmer waited for his wife at the door.

"Some water . . ."

"You're going to have more medicine in an hour," Rose said. "You can wait."

They left the room and locked the door from the outside. Rick thought of his mother. Until it was too dark, he lay looking at his sister's face in the drawings on the wall.

At the front door, before going out, Rose rearranged her dress, adjusting the shoulders. From her husband's forehead she wiped a drop of blood that had survived his bath. She took his hand and they sighed together. They opened the door.

Iris was standing on the porch, on the other side of the battered screen door, twisting a hairband in her fingers. Over her head, the mosquitoes swirled around the light on the porch ceiling. Sitting on the steps, Daisy and Dahlia whispered into each other's ears. Melissa was stroking one of her rocks with eyes.

"How is he?" asked Iris.

"Get yourselves ready, we're having dinner."

"Aren't you going to answer me?"

Rose took her by the arm and led her to one corner of the porch.

"Honey, I'm sorry for dragging you like that to your sisters' room," she whispered. "But I had to get you away from that boy. He's dangerous."

"What was he going to do to me after being run over like that?"

"You can never be too safe."

"How is he?"

Met with silence, Iris inspected her mother's face, searching for some reaction in her features that could serve as an answer. She found nothing. She yanked her arm free and escaped into the house. She had to struggle with the screen door to get in—the hinges had come loose and the frame got in her way. Elmer went after her.

Melissa stood up.

"Did you have to put him in my room?" She brushed off the backside of her skirt. "How am I going to put Gregory back? It's Marlon's turn to sleep in the bed with me tonight."

"We have bigger problems right now," Rose said.

"Sure, mine are never important." Melissa went into the house, muttering to her stone.

Rose told the twins to go in with her, but they didn't move. They sat huddled with each other on their step, Dahlia gripping the handrail post.

"What's wrong? Don't you want dinner?"

Daisy whispered something in her sister's ear.

"We're afraid to go in," they said at the same time.

Rose asked them to make space for her. She sat between them, gathering the excess material of her dress between her legs. She took their hands and placed them on her knees after kissing the palms.

"What're you afraid of?"

"The man. He used the shotgun."

The little girls nestled closer, seeking refuge. Rose enjoyed the way their hair smelled the day after a bath, when the soapy aroma intermingled with the scent of the sun and their light perspiration.

"There's no need to be afraid. Your father and I have taken care of him. We won't let anything bad happen to you. Not ever."

"Are you sure he won't do anything?" Daisy asked.

"He screamed really loud," Dahlia said.

"He's not going to do anything to you." She kissed their crowns. "Anyway, if it's about screaming, we know all about screaming. Don't we?"

The little girls' eyes lit up in the unique way they did when Rose encouraged them to be naughty. It was Rose who screamed first. The girls laughed. Then Dahlia screamed. And Daisy joined in before she'd finished. Rose joined the chorus. They screamed one after the other, all at the same time, in pairs. Dahlia tried screaming with different vowels, and Daisy copied her. Somewhere in the desert a coyote responded with a howl. The little girls shrieked with laughter in Rose's arms.

"See? In a screaming battle, we win. So you don't need to be afraid to come in."

The twins kissed her on the cheeks.

"Does one of us have to hide?"

"No, girls. He won't see you."

"But what if he sees us both together? Maybe he'll be the one who's scared!"

"Exactly. Let *him* be scared," Rose said.

She let the girls laugh a little longer. She savored their happiness, the warmth of their bodies. Then she clapped her hands in the air.

"Right, come on. Inside."

The twins ran into the house, making the boards vibrate all along the porch.

"Wash your hands!" Rose yelled.

She propelled herself up with her heels against the step. She tried to hang the door back on its hinges, but it was impossible. In the end, she moved the entire frame aside. She left it resting against one side of the porch swing where Edelweiss had so often sat to play her guitar at sundown. The basket of cactus flowers the twins had collected yesterday was now resting on the seat. It seemed as though that had happened a long time ago. She thought about returning them to the refrigerator, but when she inspected the flowers under the porch light, she found that they'd withered. She smelled them. They reeked.

Iris was pacing from one side of the kitchen to the other, her footsteps tracing a figure eight. Each time she passed in front of the oven, she was enveloped in a cloud of heat that smelled like toast, cheese, and beans.

"Would you stop?" Dad asked.

He pulled out two chairs for the twins to sit on. Melissa and her stone occupied their usual position at the table. Mom came into the kitchen carrying the basket of flowers. She tipped it into the trash can, hitting it on the side to make sure all the contents went in.

"Nooo!" yelled Daisy and Dahlia.

"They've gone bad. We'll pick more another day."

"Tomorrow!"

"Will you tell me whether Rick's OK?" Iris searched out the face of her mother, who peered inside the oven without replying. Dad also avoided eye contact, rummaging for something in the fridge. "Is he going to die?"

Mom slammed the oven door shut. "You're going to frighten your sisters." She used the volume of a whisper, but the tone was as if she were shouting.

"We'd rather he was dead," Dahlia said.

"We'd rather he was dead," Daisy repeated. "He frightens us."

"He frightens us."

Iris took a fistful of flowers from the trash. She spread them over the table, in front of the little girls.

"Your flowers are dead."

Mom elbowed her aside and swept the petals off the table with the side of her hand.

Dad took Iris to the kitchen doorway. "That boy's none of your business."

"Who are you to decide what's my business and what isn't?"

"We're your parents." Mom joined the conversation. "Doesn't that count for anything?"

Iris didn't like the exchange of looks between them. She held a hand to her throat to contain her anguish.

"He's dead," she sobbed. "I saw it in your eyes, he's dead."

"How can he be dead? Didn't you just hear him scream?"

The twins spoke from the table.

"The vultures are going to eat him."

"The vultures are going to eat him."

"He's not dead! Melissa, do me a favor. Entertain those girls," Dad ordered. Then he grabbed Iris by the wrist and spoke very close to her face. "But he deserves to be. That bastard attacked your mother." He gestured at her with his thumb. "He fired at her with the shotgun he took from our own truck. The truck we let him sleep in. That's what we got for being good to him."

"So you had to run him over?"

Dad's nostrils opened wider than usual.

"What did you want me to do?" he snorted. "Tell me, what should I do when I see a stranger running away from my house, where my daughters are, carrying a shotgun?"

"He wasn't carrying it, Dad. When you arrived he'd thrown it away."

He squeezed her wrist with more force. "All right, well, next time a stranger attacks your mother, I'll let him go. Even better, I'll give him all our money." Dad raised the volume of his voice with each syllable. "He can take whatever he wants. My daughters, if necessary. I'll give him the key to the truck and load the shotgun myself so he can shoot us all if it's what he wants!"

Iris was motionless. She didn't even dare wipe the droplets of saliva from her face. The twins burst into tears. Mom swatted at Dad before going to them.

"Don't worry, girls, it's all right. No one's going to hurt you."

From the table Mom turned her head, giving Dad and Iris a scolding look that disarmed him.

"I'm sorry," he mumbled. "All of you, I'm sorry. But I was scared, too. You can't imagine the things that ran through my mind when I saw him running like that. Covered in blood."

"Why were you coming back?" Iris asked.

"Huh?" Dad blinked several times.

"Why were you coming back? You'd gone to work."

"Why was I coming back?"

Iris nodded. Her question was clear.

"Because . . ." Dad looked toward the table. "Because of your mother. She told me to . . ."

"He forgot some money he had to take to Socorro." Mom separated herself from the twins. She took the jar of money from the shelf and removed a bill. She handed it to Dad. "Don't you forget it tomorrow."

Dad put it in his pocket without looking at Iris.

"Shouldn't we call the police?" Iris asked. "Someone. An ambulance."

He held his arms out to the sides, indicating the whole kitchen. "With what telephone?"

"And what if we take him? We'll reach the hospital before midnight."

"Honey"—he took her by the shoulders—"your mother and I have the situation under control. When I get to the gas station tomorrow, I'll call from there. The police, ambulance, or whoever will come and take him away. It's not an emergency. Your mother's done everything she can for him. The kid's OK. Hurt, but OK. It's not like we want a young man to die in our home."

Mom let a hand drop onto the table.

"Can you all stop?"

The twins trembled, gripping her.

"He doesn't scare me," Melissa said. "But I want my bedroom. I have to organize my stones."

"Melissa, please . . ."

Mom gave a deep sigh. The kitchen fell silent. The refrigerator motor kicked in. Melissa whispered in her rock's ear.

The scream came from above as if a thunderbolt had hit the kitchen.

"Help!"

Iris's heart stopped when she heard Rick's voice. Then it thumped wildly.

"Help!"

The twins gave a start in their chairs, then held on to Mom. She started yelling as if it were a game. She smiled at the girls, encouraging them to join in. The three of them yelled over Rick's screams for help. Melissa hunched her shoulders at the outburst. Iris tried to run to him, but Dad stopped her, making a barrier with his arms.

"You stay here."

"Come yell with us," said Mom, encouraging the twins to shout even louder.

Iris covered her face with her hands and shook her head. She resumed her pacing.

"Please!" Rick's voice sounded broken. "Help!"

Daisy and Dahlia screamed a letter *u*.

Elmer needed just three steps to climb the staircase.

"Help!"

He took the bedroom key from his pocket.

The draft coming in through the room's window was not enough to eliminate the smell of Rick's wounds, of his bruised flesh. Rick took the opportunity while the door was open to scream louder.

"Help!"

"Shut up."

The boy was breathing through clenched teeth, saliva bubbling at the corners of his lips.

"Do not scream again." Elmer aimed a finger at him that was so tense he could have driven it into him.

Rick narrowed his eyes. He clenched his jaw. "Help!"

The scream ended in a snort that sounded painful. Elmer let his fist fall on the kid's stomach. The crunch repulsed him. He shook his hand to free himself of the feeling.

"Don't make me do these things," he said. "I don't know how to do these things."

Rick coughed. He was choking on blood or saliva.

"But don't mess with my daughters." Elmer wiped the kid's mouth with a bandage. "Don't try to do stupid things like call for help when we're in the kitchen with them. There are two very young girls down there. Think about them."

"What're you going to do with me?"

"I don't know." He threw the dirty bandage into the bucket, on top of the broken glass. "I honestly don't know."

Rick closed his eyes. The springs squeaked under his body with each spasm.

Elmer dried his tears. "Try not to cry," he said. "Be a man."

But Rick didn't hold back. He cried in silence, sucking in snot that he had no other way to remove. His suffering moved Elmer to pity, it reminded him of the moments in his life when he had cried in the same way. He rummaged through the boxes of medication on the bedside table, by the bandages and pitcher of water. He found the Dormepam that Rose took at certain times and took out two. Rick didn't cooperate when he tried to administer them, continuing to sob while Elmer forced his fingers between his lips until he felt a tongue rough like the skin of an elbow.

"They'll help you stop thinking."

When Elmer held the rim of the glass to his mouth, Rick eagerly trapped it in his teeth. He absorbed more than drank the water.

"Let's see if they stop you from wanting to scream and scare my girls."

Elmer tried to return the glass to the bedside table, but there was no space among the jumble of medicine leaflets and boxes that he'd created. He ended up leaving it on the shelf where the rocks were, on the brown folder. Then he left the room.

Before closing the door, Rick said something from the bed.

"I just want to tell my mother . . ." he whispered into the darkness. "So she knows I found her baby."

Melissa knew how each floorboard in her room creaked. Even sitting at the kitchen table, she could visualize Dad's movements over their heads, inside the bedroom. She knew that he'd positioned himself next to the bed, that he'd searched for things on the bedside table. She also deduced that he'd stopped at the door for a few seconds as he left, because there was a pause in the usual prolonged creak of a board in the threshold.

Mom took a tray out from the oven.

"*¡Molletes!*" the twins squealed when they saw the toasted rolls with beans and cheese. Sitting opposite Melissa, they touched her hand to share the good news with her.

Iris was biting her thumbnail, waiting for Dad to return to the kitchen.

"What's wrong?" she asked when she saw him appear.

"Nothing, his leg was hurting," he said. "He needed a little more medicine."

He sat down, avoiding more questions from Iris. He rubbed his hands while Mom placed the hot tray on the table, on top of a folded cloth. "Delicious, huh?"

"Very!" the twins said.

"How's my bedroom?" Melissa asked.

"Fine, honey, fine."

"And my rocks?"

"Your rocks are rocks." Dad burned himself on the cheese when he bit into his mollete. "How are they going to be?"

Melissa consoled Gregory with a stroke. "And where am I going to sleep?"

"I got the sofa ready for you," Mom said. "You'll be very comfortable."

"I know, but I'm supposed to sleep with Marlon tonight. Gregory's been with me all day, so it's his turn on the shelf overnight. And Marlon knows it's his turn in the bed. There's an order, Mom."

"Well, honey, you'll have to skip the order for a day." She chose a mollete from the tray. "They're rocks. Rocks. They don't know anything." She offered her daughter the toast she'd taken.

"I don't want any." Melissa slumped back into the chair, her arms crossed.

When Mom tried to leave the mollete on her plate, Melissa batted it away, making her mother brush her elbow against the hot baking tray. The bread fell on the table, and Mom clutched her arm with a groan.

"OK, that's enough!" Dad yelled.

Mom used ice to soothe the burn.

"Nobody goes near the door to that bedroom. Understood?" Dad fixed his eyes on Melissa, then Iris. "No-bo-dy. Not within a yard of that door."

The twins shook their heads, several times.

"We don't want to. He frightens us." Daisy breathed in sharply, alarmed at something. She shared whatever her worry was with her sister. "Is he going to steal our bead drawings?" they asked at the same time.

"Of course he's not," said Mom.

"But they're works of art, worth a lot."

"I know"—Mom smiled—"but that boy's not going to go into your room."

The twins wiped their foreheads and sighed. They bit into their molletes, relieved. Melissa ate hers after all, but she did so looking out the window, ignoring her family as she gazed at the darkness outside. She was longing to tell Needles, Pins, and Thorns what had happened.

Rose washed the last fork and left it to dry. She returned the clean tray to the oven, then undid the knot at the back of her apron. Folding it, she put it down beside the stove. She turned off the light and left the kitchen.

In the living room she saw Melissa peering out the window onto the porch, with one hand on the glass. Rose approached her daughter from behind, without disturbing her. She had always wanted to be able to enjoy moments of peace with her middle daughter the way she did the smell of the twins' hair the day after their bath. But Melissa's melancholic mood worried her too much for that to be possible. She didn't like Melissa's nostalgia for things she'd never seen.

"Will you be OK in here?"

Melissa closed the blinds as if her mother's voice had broken the fascination the night landscape held for her. What a second earlier seemed to be a source of serenity, immersing her in those thoughts Rose had never been able to decipher, had become irrelevant in her presence. Melissa turned and replied with a nod, going around her to reach the sofa.

"It's not for long," Rose said. "You'll be back in your room soon, and then you can sleep with whichever rock you want."

Melissa held her stone close to her mouth. "Now she says it's not for long," she whispered.

She tucked in the sheet before lying down. She left a space for the stone between her body and the backrest.

"Good night, Gregory," she said. "Good night, Mom."

Rose kissed her on the temple. "Good night, honey," she whispered in Melissa's ear. "I love you so much."

Before leaving, she stopped at the window at the back of the house. The cross standing in the earth filled her with anguish, with love. She thought of Rick tied up in the bed, of his eyes.

"Shall I close these blinds for you as well?"

"No, leave it open," Melissa replied without opening her eyes. "So Edelweiss feels closer."

Rose let go of the rod. She sent a kiss beyond the glass before leaving the living room. On the floor upstairs, she found the bill she'd taken out of the jar. She put it away, ashamed at how she'd lied to Iris.

Elmer came out of Melissa's bedroom and locked the door. Rose asked him about the boy.

"The pills have kicked in." Her husband pressed his hands together and positioned them at the underside of his tilted head.

Iris came out of the bathroom. "How is he?" She looked at Rose, then at Elmer. "Is he better?"

Her father nodded.

Rose opened the twins' door to make sure they were sleeping. They were breathing in unison in their beds, in the dark, the room a space of total calm. Rose closed the door, and Elmer locked it from the outside.

Iris made a face. "What's that about?"

"That's peace of mind," Elmer said.

"And you lock your door from the inside, too. Unless you want us to do it for you."

Iris went into her bedroom and closed the door.

Rose waited a few seconds.

"I can't hear the lock," she said. She waited a while longer. "I can't hear it."

There was a metallic click on the other side of the handle. She pictured her daughter turning the key grumpily to make a louder sound.

"That's better," Rose said into the wood. "We're doing it to protect you."

With her husband, she went into their bedroom as they did any other night. Like any other night, they brushed their teeth at the same time, the two of them in front of the mirror. They each undressed on their own side of the bed. They said nothing to one another throughout the process, but that could happen on any night. Elmer went over to the switch to turn off the light, making sure the bedroom door was open, the handle touching the wall.

As she did every night, Rose sat on the edge of the mattress, took some lotion from the bedside table drawer, and spread it over her forearms. That was the moment she burst into tears.

Elmer slid over the bed. He took the bottle from her hands and made her lie down, with her back to him. He made a nest with his arms into which she curled up.

"They're my daughters," she said.

"Of course they are," he whispered in her ear.

A gecko on the ceiling of the porch caught a mosquito with its tongue. On the ground, a mouse fled from the menacing rustle of a bush, scampering along the sand, dodging cacti and other spiny plants. The moonlight gave the rocks a silvery quality and the sand a metallic color that transformed the desert into a galactic landscape.

Iris pulled Rick's dirty T-shirt out from under the mattress. She breathed through it. Mom had just asked her to lock her door from the inside. She lay on the bed hugging the garment, which had dried completely but preserved his smell. She stroked the wall with the tips of her fingers, imagining herself closer to him. Between this room and Melissa's was the twins' bedroom, but she could ignore it in her mind and dream that she was touching a wall that Rick could touch on the other side. He would feel her energy through the partition, and it would ease his pain. She was certain that if they both placed their hands on the wall, without seeing each other they could superimpose their fingers precisely, guiding themselves only by the attraction of their skin.

The line of light under the bedroom door disappeared. Mom and Dad must've turned off the light in their bedroom. Iris waited. With her eyes closed, she enjoyed the feel of the wall, imagining it was Rick's body. She prolonged the fantasy for fifteen minutes. Twenty. Then she got up and hid the T-shirt under the sheet. She pressed her ear against the door.

Silence.

She turned the lock, avoiding the slightest click. As she opened the door, every tiny squeak of the hinges seemed to her like a clangor that would wake the whole family, but her parents' breathing remained constant. If she got a little closer to Melissa's bedroom she would also hear Rick breathing, perhaps smell his aroma escaping through the cracks around the door. She opened the door just enough to squeeze out, pressing her breasts against the edge of the wood. She stood with just the tips of her toes on the floor, keeping contact to a minimum. The third floorboard she trod on creaked harshly.

"Iris?" Dad's voice sounded as firm as it did at any other time of day. "Iris, is that you?"

She hunched her shoulders, motionless, not knowing what to do. She kept her balance on tiptoes, her toes tense against the floor.

"Iris," Mom said.

Hearing her parents' mattress springs, she reacted. "I was going to the bathroom."

"Well go, then. And come right back."

She dropped her heels and took firm steps, not caring now if the floor shook. She went into the bathroom but didn't use it. She looked in the mirror, grimacing when she discovered a new pimple on her chin. She tried to improve her messy hair by combing it with four fingers. Then she smoothed down her eyebrows with a pinkie wet with saliva. After a while, she pulled the chain.

When she came out of the bathroom, Dad spoke from his bed. "Back to your room."

She looked at Melissa's door. She knew she couldn't get in because her parents had locked it, but she'd make do with lying there, on the floor. Resting her cheek against the wood, listening to Rick sleep. Keeping him company like a domestic animal until they took him to the hospital tomorrow.

She took a step toward him.

"I said to your room."

Iris let her shoulders drop. She returned to her bedroom with heavy footsteps, tears brimming over her lower eyelids. She'd wanted to slam the door but stopped herself so as not to wake Rick, if in fact he could sleep given the pain he was in. Retrieving his T-shirt from under the sheets, she wore it around her neck like a scarf. She paced around her room, trapped in her powerlessness. She toyed with the threads that hung from the torn stitching down the side of her nightgown.

She stopped at the window.

She peered outside. The three adjoining bedrooms looked out from the front of the house. Iris remembered Melissa scaling one of the posts the night before, walking across that same roof to her room. The window next to her own was the twins' room, but through the one beyond that she would be able to see Rick. The sound of glass breaking repeated in her mind, the noise she'd heard after the gunshot. Not only would she be able to see in, but she could also enter through the broken window. A gecko appeared on the tiles, and Iris imagined herself doing the same, using the roof as a walkway to take her to Rick.

She held her hands to her heart. She crossed the room and listened through the door, but she couldn't hear her parents' heavy breathing. They hadn't gone back to sleep yet. She sat at her dressing table, where she opened *Pride and Prejudice* to page 17. Resting it against a bottle of perfume and a powder compact, she read until she folded the corner of page 93.

She didn't need to go to the door to hear her father's snoring.

She hid the T-shirt under her sheet. Standing at the window, she took a breath so deep that it startled the gecko. The animal disappeared behind a ledge. Iris climbed out onto the roof with bare feet. The breeze that found its way under her nightgown dried the sweat her nerves had brought on. Among the cacti, or under the stones, some crickets chirped. The moon had painted the landscape gray. She stooped as she walked past the twins' room, willing them not to wake up. Not just so they wouldn't give her away, but also because of the fright it would give them to see a figure in floating cloth through the window.

Anticipation filled her chest before she reached the next bedroom. She was only a step away from seeing Rick again. She thought to herself that in this story it was Juliet who was going to find Romeo, not on a balcony but through a window. She fantasized about listening to him from her hiding place as he revealed his love for her in a soliloquy, but her Romeo was badly wounded and wouldn't have the strength to speak.

She peered in, holding her breath.

The white sheet reflected the moonlight, illuminating the only clear form in a room immersed in shadows. A smile spread across Iris's face as she began to make out the contours of his feet, his knees, his chest. Her heart beating in her ears drowned out the crickets. She ran a finger over the empty window frame until she pricked herself on a fang of glass. To avoid snagging her nightgown, she gathered it up to her belly, leaving her legs and underwear uncovered. She went through the nonexistent pane, stepping onto Melissa's magazine-covered desk. Holding on to the toothed window frame, she reached the floor without difficulty. With her night-gown still above her waist, her stomach contracted when she found herself almost naked so close to Rick. She let the garment fall over her knees, enjoying the brush of the material against her skin.

Iris recognized the smell from Rick's T-shirt. It reawakened in her the sensations of her nocturnal visit to the truck. His breathing was uniform. After each inhalation, there was silence for a few seconds before he exhaled. Iris imagined herself nestled up against him on the porch swing as they fell asleep together at sunset. In her fantasy, she also heard the chords of Edelweiss's guitar. Somehow, her sister was still alive and sat on the porch steps and played for them. Iris approached the bed, straining her eyes in the dark to avoid the furniture, taking care not to knock anything over that would make a noise.

The sheet covered Rick to the neck, his body hidden under cotton. It dawned on Iris that he would be naked, and the muscles in her abdomen tensed, setting off a tingling in the lower part of her body. She had to open her mouth to breathe. She wet her lips. The same excitement that had made her want to touch James Dean's pants in the photograph was now impelling her to pull back the sheet, fold the material from the chin to the chest, from the chest to the belly, from the belly to . . . the knees. Her thoughts embarrassed her. She covered her flushed face with her hair even though nobody could see her. That kind of behavior was not becoming of a lady. No love story worth its salt would begin with a woman taking advantage of a wounded man. Instead of uncovering him, and to prove to herself the purity of her intentions, she adjusted the sheet under Rick's chin, pulling it up a little farther.

"The Fates have something much better in store for us." Her words were little more than an outbreath, inaudible thoughts. "How are you?"

The faint light from outside allowed Iris to discern some of his features. He had a swollen eye, a split eyebrow. The dark patches on his face that weren't shadows turned out to be bruises. A groan escaped from between his lips. A rattle. Iris held her ear to his mouth, from which warm breath emanated. There was no second groan, but she heard his tongue scrape against the dry skin of his lips, unable to moisten them.

"Wait," she whispered.

A glint floated over the bedside table, a moonbeam's reflection on the water in a pitcher. Iris felt around for a glass among the medication boxes, bottles, and leaflets. The rustle of the paper was deafening. She found nothing. She looked at the other bedside table, at the darkness that surrounded it. Another floating glint revealed the glass. It was farther up, on the shelving where Melissa kept her rocks. When she went to take it, Iris scratched her wrists on something that protruded from the shelf. A cardboard edge. She recognized the thick cardboard of a folder. She ran her finger over the stack of paper it contained, as if counting the pages of a book.

They must be drawings of Melissa's.

Iris reached the glass. With her free hand, she lifted Rick's head. He held out his tongue when he felt the edge of the glass between his lips, searching for the liquid. He moaned when he couldn't locate it. Iris tilted the glass so that water went into his mouth. He received it with a gurgle. A slight upturn appeared at the corner of his lips, a trace of a smile that filled Iris with tenderness. She felt as if she were nursing him, giving him life with a liquid that sprang from her.

He choked on the final drops. The coughing joined the noise of the shaking mattress and the creaks of the bedframe. Iris returned his head to the pillow. She made a shushing sound near his face until he was calm. The house remained silent—the coughing fit hadn't alarmed her parents. Rick's lips were shiny after regaining their moisture.

Iris wondered what they tasted like.

Her breathing grew labored.

With her lips apart, she covered Rick's. She caressed them with the tip of her tongue. The contact set off an explosion of pleasure that made her head spin. She gripped the headboard.

"Last night when I kissed you in the truck I wasn't brave enough to open my mouth," she whispered onto his lips. "What a fool I was."

Without realizing it she'd rested a hand on his chest. She felt his muscles through the material, the grooves of his abdomen. The heat that his body gave off set her on fire inside. She wanted to keep touching, to feel all of his body, to taste his flavors.

Another coughing fit shook Rick, interrupting her fantasy. Iris hushed him again, but this time it didn't have the same calming effect. His coughing spattered her face with saliva. He ended each cough with a groan, as if the convulsions hurt him inside. The headboard hit the wall as the intensity of the spasms grew.

She heard the floor in her parents' room creak under Dad's weight.

A light shone into the room from under the door.

Iris ran to the window. She climbed out onto the roof without lifting her nightgown, which got caught on the glass fang in the frame. She gathered it with a tug and sat down on the tiles, her back against the wall. Despite the danger to her, she wanted Dad to come in as soon as possible to tend to Rick's coughing, to relieve the suffering that the convulsions caused and that also hurt her.

She heard Dad open the door. She stopped breathing. The coughing fit ended at that very moment, before Dad could even turn on the bedroom light. Rick's breathing regained its normal rhythm as if the coughing had never happened. Dad waited a few seconds before leaving.

Iris let out a sigh.

A voice made her jump.

". . . if it's Marlon's turn to sleep in the bed with me, then I'll have to make sure he does, whatever that guy's . . ."

It was Melissa, down on the ground.

She was speaking to her stone, walking away from the house. She walked among the cacti, following a memorized route in the darkness. Iris saw her stop in front of a row of bluish sparkles, the moon reflecting on one of the clothed cardones' shirt buttons.

"I'd better get back," Iris whispered to Rick through the window. "We'll see each other again tomorrow, before they come for you."

Back in her bedroom, Iris slumped onto the bed on her back, her arms outstretched, and gave a deep sigh. She spread Rick's T-shirt over her face.

The wind blew Melissa's hair over her face. The gusts began to arrive just as she sat down in front of Needles, Pins, and Thorns, and they continued throughout the conversation. At first she'd been annoyed that she couldn't fetch the lantern and candle from her room, but it would have gone out anyway.

"So, from what I can see, we all feel the same." She removed the hair from her face with her little fingers. "Nobody's going to know, and I'm not scared of the man. I can do it."

The three cacti and Gregory agreed.

"Then let's go." She got up with the stone. "Thanks, guys. I'll tell you all about it tomorrow."

The wind had brought with it narrow clouds that striped the moon. Melissa pointed Gregory's eyes at the sky so he could see it. The effect was also reflected on her bedroom window, at least on the pane that remained intact. The broken side was a black square of total darkness.

She aimed the stone's face at the front of the house. "Look, you can see it there, too."

Melissa climbed the porch post without letting go of Gregory, even when a gecko forced her to change her handhold. She reached the roof and walked along it as she had on so many nights, taking care not to make the tiles crunch outside her sisters' windows. She kept hold of the stone when she climbed into the room as well. She knew what to grip on to, where to support herself, when to jump.

The smell in the room reminded her of the Band-Aid she'd removed from her finger a few days after she'd cut it dressing Needles.

Melissa went up to the young man in her bed. She touched his shoulder with a finger.

"You asleep?" She prodded him twice more. "Are you sleeping?"

There was no change to his breathing, and his eyelids were motionless. He was covered up to the chin with the sheet, as if he was cold despite the heat.

"The one time I have someone to talk to . . ."

She wanted to put Gregory on the bedside table, where she also thought she'd left Marlon, but she found it covered with things for the injured man. Medicine, a glass. In the dark she counted the shapes on the shelf. All the rocks were there. She would have to find Marlon by touch. She ran her hand along the shelf. She recognized James, the newcomer, by his pronounced nose and masculine forehead. She also felt Clark and Cary.

Her arm encountered an obstacle.

A folder that wasn't hers.

On top of it, like a paperweight that kept it closed, was Marlon. She identified him from the rough texture, especially on his cheeks, though she could barely touch them with the tips of her fingers. The papers were in the way, preventing her from picking up Marlon even on tiptoes. She decided to lift down the entire folder, with the stone on top. The thick stack of paper held the rock's weight. She put the whole thing down on the floor and said hello to Marlon in a low voice. She said good night to Gregory as she returned him to the shelf.

"What a day for it to be your turn to come down from there, huh?" she whispered.

She tried to wake Rick again.

Nothing.

She shrugged.

Gathering up Marlon, she went to put the folder back where she'd found it. She didn't want Dad to discover that someone had been in the room. But the stone asked her a question.

"I don't know," she replied. "It's not mine."

She listened to Marlon.

"But we can barely see." She gestured at the darkness that surrounded them.

Marlon said something else.

"Oh, of course it's here."

She found the lantern in the room and lit the candle with a match. The light was weak, so it didn't reach the bedroom door. Only someone out on the land would have been able to see it, and the whole family was asleep. She sat on the floor with the folder on her knees, Marlon on her lap, and the lantern to one side.

"Let's see," she said to the stone.

She opened the cover without moving the elastic band, which was broken. A newspaper clipping slid between her crossed legs. The masthead of the paper it was taken from was stapled to it: the *Rocky Mountain News*. The date, in September 1952, sounded very remote to Melissa, since it was a few years before she was born. The article was about a missing baby, a little girl someone had snatched from her crib in the night while her parents slept in the adjoining room. Then Melissa took out a full page from another newspaper, this time from Arizona and dated 1963. It was folded in such a way that it showed only the report on some parents accusing a hospital of losing their newborn. Behind it she found a cutting from a newspaper called the *Deseret News*: a piece from 1964 on another missing baby in Murray, Utah.

"What is all of this?" Melissa asked Marlon.

She went through more clippings, more documents, more newspaper pages. She leafed through dozens of cases, perhaps almost a hundred. There were cuttings from 1949, 1959, 1951, 1967, 1962. They were from the *Santa Fe New Mexican*, the *Tucson Citizen*, the *El Paso Times*, the *Denver Post*. Masses of mastheads with the names of cities. They all told stories of lost babies, missing girls, abducted girls. Others announced the discovery of a body in a river, remains of clothing found in a forest, and even the confessions of mothers who had admitted to murdering their children. A shiver washed over Melissa's shoulders. The candle flickered beside her, illuminating the horror and suffering contained in those reports with its quivering orange light.

Melissa slowly leafed through them, wanting to stop but unable to do so, trying to fathom the unfathomable. A deep sadness gradually took hold of her with each new clipping. The trick that Socorro had taught her, the one where she focused on the good things she had in her life, now made complete sense. She wanted to wake her parents, her whole family, to thank them for being who they were, for loving her, for taking care of her so well, and for giving her a home to be happy in, even if there were little things she didn't like and despite sometimes feeling like a stranger in her own home. She wanted to thank them for protecting her from strangers like Rick, who abused the kindness of others and might harbor intentions as terrible as whoever was responsible for the acts described in the documents. Melissa felt lucky. The folder on her legs contained a horrifying world of which she, to her good fortune, was not part. For the first time, she felt truly happy that they lived in such an isolated place, far from all that horror.

Until she flicked to the next page.

It was a Nevada newspaper, from six years before. The headline announced the recent disappearance of two girls. The text of the article explained how the mother had left them in the car as she returned a cart to the supermarket where she'd just done her shopping. The woman heard the screech of brakes in the parking lot, followed by the roar of powerful acceleration, but she didn't connect it to her little girls. She even stopped at a flower stand at the supermarket entrance and chatted for a few minutes with the salesperson, trying to choose the right bunch for a family dinner she was hosting that evening. When she got back to her vehicle, her twins were no longer in the rear seat.

Melissa's eyes stopped blinking. The writing in front of her disappeared, turning the cutting into a gray piece of paper with just one word printed on it. *Twins.* It was repeated several times in the article, forming a horrifying constellation amid the invisible text. Her eyes moved to one corner of the clipping, where someone had traced an *x* in red pen. The mark was repeated on subsequent documents.

Seeing the black-and-white image, Melissa screamed.

She covered her mouth with both hands.

The sheet of paper fell to the floor, sliding over the wood to the feet of the bedside table.

Her eyes burned. Marlon's weight on her lap was suddenly suffocating. It stopped her from taking in the air she needed. She pushed the stone. It fell with a heavy thump.

Rick moaned.

Melissa froze.

The house was silent.

Little by little, she regained control of her breathing. She left the folder on the floor and dragged herself along on her backside, around the lantern, until she reached the photocopy.

The date on the article was the most recent. From seven months ago. BROTHER FIGHTS ON TO KEEP MISSING-BABY CASE OPEN AFTER 18 YEARS. Melissa struggled to read the headline despite the capitals. The tears in her eyes blurred the letters. Though the photograph was also out of focus, she knew the young man in it was Rick. She had only met him yesterday, but not even the most intense desire to disbelieve her own eyes could refute the evidence.

It was him.

The image revealed something that horrified Melissa even more. She recognized his eyes, the bone structure that surrounded them. His brow. She stood with the lantern and held the page near the face on the pillow. Then she went to the wall covered in her best drawings. She found a portrait in which Edelweiss wore Mom's straw hat, her smile as delicious as the vegetables she held to her chest. Melissa had sketched it one spring in the garden.

She held the newspaper article next to it.

The candle's warm glow illuminated both faces.

At once the flame went out, unable to survive the shaking of Melissa's trembling hand.

Rick began coughing.

She didn't react. She couldn't even think. She knew she was standing somewhere. That she'd discovered something terrible. That a light had gone out. She experienced that knowledge as a collection of abstract feelings she was unable to process.

She heard a hammering.

It was her bed's headboard banging against the wall. She had the absurd idea that Edelweiss's brother was coughing between the sheets, but that wasn't possible. Edelweiss didn't have any brothers, just four younger sisters who missed being in her arms as much as the guitar hanging in the living room did. This man was choking behind her. An arc of light entered through the crack under the door. She heard footsteps in her parents' room and Iris coming out of her bedroom.

"Stay inside." It was Dad, speaking to Iris.

The severity in his voice tore Melissa from her trance.

She returned the lantern to its place, blowing to dissipate the smoke that still floated from the wick. She picked up the folder from the floor. When she was about to put it up on the shelf, she stopped. She took out several of the documents marked with red pen and put them under her arm. She pushed the folder under the stones, as she'd found it.

Outside the room, Iris spoke. "He's suffocating."

"I'll take care of it." Dad's shadow crossed the arc of light on the floor.

Melissa climbed onto the desk and mounted the window frame. Out on the roof, she realized she'd left Marlon on the floor, near the bed.

The key entered the lock.

There was no time to think. She leapt back over the desk into the room, treading only on the points of the floor that didn't creak. She recovered her stone, returned to the window, and bounded through it.

The bedroom door opened just as she managed to hide to one side of the frame, her back against the wall. A square of light was projected onto the porch roof, brushing against the tip of one of her slippers. Melissa jerked her foot back as if it had been burned. She heard Iris begging Dad to let her in. She also heard the commotion when Mom came out to deal with her sister, telling her that she was going to wake the twins, that Melissa was sleeping on the sofa. Mom made Iris go back to her bedroom. That room projected another searchlight onto the porch roof. Melissa held her breath, hugging Marlon. Feeling threatened by the two windows, she closed her eyes, as if not seeing would make her invisible. She heard Dad approaching the bed, where Rick was fighting against his constricted throat. She heard the bubble of water as he filled the glass, the rustle of medicine leaflets, the plastic crackle of a blister pack as he extracted a pill. Dad tended to Rick until the coughing stopped. Melissa's pulse accelerated when she heard him nosing around the shelf where the rocks were, where she'd left the folder. Perhaps she'd put it back the other way around, or with the sheets of paper uneven. Dad might look through the documents and discover that the ones marked with red pen were missing.

"The easiest thing would be to let you die," he whispered there inside.

Thick saliva blocked Melissa's throat.

She struggled to swallow.

She sat there, clenching her teeth, until Dad left the room. When she opened her eyes, the two squares of light on the roof had disappeared. To avoid passing Iris's window, she went down the post on the other side, the one with the parched paint, the one she never used because it was more splintered and scratched her hands. She let Marlon drop as though he were just a stone.

Melissa went in through the back door. She completed her journey to the sofa with a blank stare, prohibiting her eyes from falling on any of the details that defined the family life of this home. She didn't want to see the identical yellow bowls from which the twins ate their breakfast cereals in the morning. Or any of the jars of beads they used to color in her drawings. Nor did she want to see Iris's books. Or the apron that Mom left folded beside the stove each night after washing the dishes from dinner.

All of a sudden, the true meaning of those objects was unknown to her.

She sat on the sofa and covered herself with the sheet, brushing the hair from her face with her pinkies. She unfolded the papers on her knees. Melissa spent the night reading about the four cases recounted in the documents marked with an *x* in red pen. She had to stop several times to dry her tears.

Elmer did not sleep again after tending to the kid. Lying face up, he watched the room grow brighter as the sun rose. With his hands on his stomach, he waited until it was time to get up. Lying beside him, Rose was silent, but Elmer knew she was awake, too. She barely made a sound as she breathed, and her arm wasn't stretched out under the pillow.

A raspy voice broke the silence of the house.

"Water . . ."

Elmer leapt out of bed. Rose sat up, alert. Iris came out of her bedroom.

"Does nobody sleep around here?" he asked.

He crossed the hallway in the direction of the voice.

"Water . . ."

"He needs water, Dad," said Iris.

"I *can* hear him."

He unlocked the door and went in. Rick tried to yell, taking advantage of the open door, but what came out of his throat was an off-key croak. Elmer relocked the door.

"Don't start."

"Give me water . . ."

"I gave you some last night, don't you remember?"

"Water . . ." Rick flailed about under the sheets.

"Don't make so much noise, please. My daughters are waking up."

The springs squeaked as Rick thrashed again. Elmer placed a hand on the kid's chest.

"Please."

He searched for the glass on the shelf with the rocks on it. He thought he'd left it half full on top of the folder, but he found it empty on the bedside table. He shrugged. His memory was becoming less reliable with age. So that he wouldn't forget to take the folder away, he left it at the foot of the bed. He offered the glass to Rick, who sipped the water.

"Am I going to die in this bed?" A drip slid down from the corner of his mouth until it was channeled through a cut on his jaw.

Elmer didn't respond to the question. He tipped the glass so that Rick would drink faster and evaded his glazed eyes by turning his head toward the wall of portraits. When the kid had finished, he returned the glass to the bedside table without looking him in the face.

Rick kicked his legs. He groaned with pain. He continued to thrash about. Elmer frowned.

"What're you doing?"

The folder at the foot of the bed fell onto the floor. The documents flew out, spreading across the wood. One slid to the door, the corner of the page slipping under it. A film of dust that covered the boards was shining in the morning sun.

"What're you playing at?" Elmer asked.

Rick breathed in, filling his lungs. His nostrils bubbled.

"Iris!" he screamed. "Iris!"

Elmer covered the kid's mouth with his hands. He kept them there even when Rick stuck out his tongue. To keep him from biting, he squeezed Rick's jaw with his fingers. Iris's footsteps running toward the room shook the cans of pencils.

Rose joined her daughter on the other side of the door. "You can't go in there," she said. On the floor, very near their feet, lay news of a girl who had disappeared in California. The corner of the paper was poking under the door. Rick's eyes moved from side to side, above Elmer's hand.

Elmer spoke close to the kid's ear. "Don't try anything."

The door handle shook.

"Don't even think about opening that door," said Rose.

Rick writhed on the bed, making the frame and springs creak.

"He wants to see me!" cried Iris.

The handle rattled, but the lock held fast. Rick's chest deflated under Elmer's weight, and he felt the kid's tensed muscles relax.

"That's enough now, honey," Rose said.

"But he called my name. He wants to speak to me."

"Who knows what he really wants? He also said he wanted somewhere to sleep and ended up shooting at me."

Iris sighed.

"Help me get breakfast ready. Before the twins wake up."

Rick groaned, but neither Iris nor Rose seemed to hear him. They were already on their way down the stairs. Elmer waited for them to reach the kitchen.

"Don't try anything like that with my daughters again," he said. "Don't even try it."

"Anything like what? Letting them know the truth?"

A plastic cracking sound detonated between Elmer's fingers as he took out a pill.

"The only truth is that we're their parents."

"Those papers on the floor prove otherwise."

"Those papers might have some value to you. To me, the pieces of paper on the wall mean much more." He lifted Rick's head to make him look at Melissa's drawings. "What you see there is a family. A thousand newspaper articles like yours couldn't change what my wife and I have built. Where were you during Edelweiss's happiest times?"

"Searching for her."

"You weren't there. Her sisters were. Her parents were."

"You—"

"You're going to sleep till I get back." He let the kid's head fall onto the pillow, interrupting his words. "I'd rather you weren't awake near my daughters."

He put the pill in Rick's mouth. Rick spat it out, and it rolled along the floor. Elmer took out two more. He pushed them to the back of the kid's throat, fighting against Rick's attempts to bite his fingers. He smothered the kid's nose and mouth.

"Don't make this difficult."

Rick held on until his face turned red. When his Adam's apple moved up, then down, Elmer released the gag. He filled the glass and held it to

Rick's lips. The kid drank, looking him in the eyes. Elmer picked up the pill he'd spat out.

"You have to sleep till I get back."

He inserted the third pill between Rick's lips. The kid swallowed without resistance. Elmer returned the glass to the bedside table. Squatting, he picked the papers up from the floor, starting with the one under the door. The kid's breathing began to steady as Elmer stacked the crumpled documents in a pile that turned out thicker than before. He put them back in the folder.

"Eliza . . . beth . . ." Rick whispered.

Elmer slammed the folder shut.

He went back to his bedroom. From under the bed, he took out the notebook that Rose had found in the truck. Securing both under the elastic of his underpants, he covered them with his T-shirt. He went downstairs. The refrigerator door opened. A frying pan was on the stove. Rose and Iris were making breakfast in the kitchen. Water was running in the bathroom by the front door. Melissa had already gotten up.

He went out onto the porch without being seen and walked barefoot to the barbecue beside the hose. He placed the folder containing all of the documents on the grill. From a bucket he took a metal bottle and a matchbox. Dousing the papers in flammable liquid, he dropped a match on top of them. The edges of the folder curled up, and the brown cardboard soon caught fire. The notebook's cover, reinforced with some kind of varnish, took a little longer. The flames devoured faces, words, lies. Elmer poked the fire, reducing the past to ashes.

Rose flinched when the kitchen ceiling vibrated. Rick must have made the bed shake again.

"See?" She opened the box of cereal she'd just gotten down from the cupboard. "He's aggressive and dangerous."

"Will he be OK?" Iris asked from the refrigerator. "Will the ambulance come in time? When's Dad leaving?"

Rose heard the toilet tank emptying. She saw Melissa come out of the bathroom and head to the living room. She went after her.

"Serve up the cereal," she said to Iris from the doorway. "And stop worrying so much about a stranger."

The force with which Iris slammed the refrigerator door made the bottles of beer inside jingle. Rose found Melissa unmaking her bed on the sofa.

"Morning."

Her daughter shook the sheet, folded it, and piled up the cushions.

"Was it so bad sleeping down here?"

Melissa plumped up the backrest, the cushions. She plucked fluff from the upholstery.

"What's the matter?" Rose snatched away the pillowcase Melissa had just taken off a pillow and invited her to sit down on the sofa with her.

"Melissa, please, look at me." She tried to lift Melissa's chin with a finger, but her daughter resisted. "We needed a bed for the boy. And this sofa isn't so bad." She bounced on the seat to prove it. "Don't be like this. You'll be back in your room in no time."

Melissa looked at her.

"That's better."

But there was a tension in her daughter's brow that hardened her gaze, making it darker, as if the color of her eyes had dropped a shade overnight.

"What?" Rose traced a line on her own cheek with her finger. "Do I have a sheet mark on my face?"

Melissa shook her head.

"Why're you looking at me like that, then?"

Her daughter's hair fell over her face when she looked down at the floor again.

"Talk to me, sweetheart." Rose squeezed her hand. "Are you worried about having a dangerous man in the house?"

Rose noticed Melissa's slippers to one side of the sofa. The toes were covered in a reddish dust, and spiny seeds were stuck to the rubber soles.

"You won't say anything to me, but I see you went out last night to talk to someone."

Melissa lifted her head all of a sudden, her eyes wide open. Rose pointed at the evidence.

"I got you!"

Her daughter's hand tensed under hers.

"But don't worry, we won't tell your father. If it was hard to sleep in here, I can see why you wanted to go out and speak to your cactuses. Did they tell you anything interesting?"

The girl let her head fall again. She shrugged.

"Sorry. The cactuses are your thing, and I don't have to play along. In that case, I won't ask your rock if it was so bad sleeping down here when it was his turn to sleep on the shelf." She lay a hand on the stone. "I'm sure . . . Gregory? . . . was glad he got to spend the night with you."

Rose waited for an answer.

"Really, you scare me with your adolescence." She repeated a phrase she used with increasing frequency. "But just one thing, honey. Put some proper shoes on if you're going to go walking at night, don't go out in those terry cloth slippers. Out there everything stings, everything burns, everything attacks. Well, like life itself."

The front door opened. Elmer was coming in from outside. Rose realized he was barefoot, contradicting the advice she'd just given Melissa.

"Thanks for ruining what would've been a great maternal lesson," she said to her husband.

"What've I done?" He raised his hands, protesting his innocence.

"You smell like smoke," Melissa observed.

Rose held her hands to her chest. "Finally, she opens her mouth."

Iris came out of the kitchen pouring milk into a bowl as if she couldn't wait to serve it.

"When're you leaving?" she asked her father. "You have to call the ambulance from the gas station. Are you going now?"

Rose got up.

"All right, leave your father in peace." She stopped Iris from pouring the milk before the bowl overflowed. Iris seemed to have detached herself from her actions while she waited for Elmer to respond. "He's going to take a shower"—she slapped her husband on the shoulder to let him know that he smelled like bonfire—"I'm going to fetch the twins, and you two are going to finish getting breakfast ready."

She pulled Melissa up off the sofa and pushed her into the kitchen along with Iris, who turned her head back over her shoulder.

"Hurry, Dad, please."

Rose and Elmer climbed the stairs. The smell of smoke on her husband's T-shirt reassured her, because it meant all those documents no longer existed.

"He won't wake up," Elmer said about the boy. "I gave him three. He may well sleep till tomorrow."

"And then what?" she asked. "What do we do then?"

Elmer went into the bathroom without speaking, the screech of the shower faucet as he turned it his only reply.

Rose held her ear to Melissa's door. When she heard the boy breathing, she thought of Edelweiss.

In the twins' room, she walked over the yellow carpet of sunlight that spread across the floor at that time of day and would disappear without a trace by midmorning. She sat on Daisy's bed and shook the mattress with her backside, pushing herself with her feet on the floor. The little girl stirred between the sheets with a moan.

"The Breakfast Express is preparing to depart," Rose announced, making the bedframe clatter. "All diners aboard the train!"

Dahlia, in the other bed, reacted first. She got down from her mattress and climbed onto Daisy's to sit next to Rose. She hugged her with her eyes closed, her hair tangled.

"I'll get on the train but I'll sleep till we arrive." She rested her head on Rose's lap.

The chuckle Rose let out finally woke Daisy, who sat up with her head tilted, her eyelids still stuck together with sleepiness.

"What's going on?"

"The breakfast train's about to leave." Rose intensified the clattering and Daisy changed her neck's incline, searching for balance. "Up to you if you want to come."

Daisy opened her left eye, squeezing the right one even more tightly shut. She smiled when she saw Rose driving a train her sister had already boarded. She took her seat on the other side, hanging on to Rose's arm, ready to enjoy the scenery through the windows.

"But it has to be fast. I'm hungry," Daisy said.

Rose laughed again. She pulled twice on an imaginary cord, imitating the sound of a whistle. She maintained the bed's clattering and held her daughters. She wished they really could board a train and travel a thousand times around the world. So that the journey would never end.

Iris set a pile of silverware on the tablecloth. She sat opposite Melissa, who'd remained silent, with her hands on either side of her plate, while Iris finished making breakfast. She served herself a cup of coffee, added two spoonfuls of sugar, and stirred it as if ringing a handbell.

"Did you hear?" she asked. "He said my name. Rick, this morning. He wanted to talk to me."

She took Melissa's hand to share her excitement with her. A tear appeared over her sister's lower eyelid. It fell onto the table, propelled by the pronounced ramp of her cheekbone, leaving a damp mark on the cloth that was soon lost among the traces of milk, water, and coffee.

"Is it classes again?" Iris asked. "I won't lie, I struggle to comprehend why Socorro's visits mean so much to you."

Melissa caught her bottom lip between her teeth. She looked to one side. Then to the other.

"What? What is it?" Iris could see in her sister's face when she was fighting with herself not to reveal a secret. "You can tell me, whatever it is. Have you found out something about Rick? Have you looked in his backpack? I don't know where they've put it, but I'd love to take a peek inside."

Melissa released her lip.

She breathed.

She fixed her eyes on Iris's.

"What?" Iris pressed her, dragging her chair nearer the table with her feet.

Melissa let her shoulders drop.

"It's Socorro," she sighed.

Iris pushed her sister's hand away as if discarding a book that no longer interested her.

"I thought it was something important." She sipped her coffee, trapping the teaspoon with her finger. "Why's Dad taking so long?"

The ceiling shook. The twins were running up there. Their screams reached the kitchen, mimicking a train's whistle as they came down the stairs.

"No more peace and quiet," said Iris. "The Breakfast Express has arrived."

Melissa sniffed and dried her eyes.

Mom walked in just in time to see the gesture.

"Honey, you can't spend the whole summer like this." She inspected the table and nodded at Iris to give her approval. "It's the only summer of your life when you'll be thirteen years old. Don't waste it."

Melissa held her head with her knuckles at her temples, her elbows on the table, and cried over her plate. Mom shrugged, appealing to Iris for help, but Iris ignored her. Mom knelt down to greet the twins.

"End of the line." She showed a palm as if it were a railway signal. "Please alight from the train and enter the restaurant."

The little girls went to sit down, but when they discovered that Melissa was crying, they positioned themselves on either side of her chair.

"She's still sad about the classes," Iris explained. "She misses Socorro."

Daisy separated Melissa's hair from her face, hooking it behind her ears. Dahlia stroked her arm, walking her fingertips from Melissa's wrist to her shoulder.

"They're little ants," Daisy said into her ear.

Melissa wiped her nose.

"How can you be sad when the cactuses are covered in flowers?" Daisy let her elder sister's hair fall over her back and smoothed it down. "Just think how nice they're going to smell tonight."

Melissa leaned back in her chair and stretched out her arms with a smile. The twins accepted her invitation for a hug. They kissed their sister on each cheek, drying her eyes.

"You can't complain about your sisters, that's for sure," Mom said. "They're the sweetest little girls in all the state."

"The only little girls!" they said at the same time.

Iris looked at the kitchen clock.

"Is Dad leaving or not?" she asked, arms crossed.

Elmer zipped up his coveralls. From his chin he plucked a square of toilet paper that was stuck to the skin with dried blood. He never cut himself shaving, but today the razor had nicked him five times. Now he was by Rick's bed, assessing his condition. The sedatives had slowed the rhythm of his breathing so much that the pause between each breath was worrying. Rick's lips were so dry that they'd lost their color and were barely distinguishable from the rest of his skin. His black eye looked worse than yesterday, it could continue to swell.

Elmer was glad he didn't have to see anything from the chin down. The sheet covered the bruises, the protruding bones, the rope with which he himself had bound the kid's wrists. He felt the urge to vomit. Not because of the wounded flesh in front of him, but because of his actions. He overcame the wave of nausea by imagining Rick's body uninjured under the sheet. The white material covered his entire anatomy, and Elmer could persuade himself that it hid smooth, healthy skin. Defined, intact muscles. The need to throw up began to subside. Elmer was an expert at spreading white sheets over reality.

"You're going to stay like this till I get back." He inhaled deeply to rid himself of the last remnants of nausea.

On the reassuring clean white of the material appeared a stain—a yellowish wet patch that expanded its circumference over Rick's pelvis. A chemical smell filled the room.

"Oh no." Elmer held his hands out toward the stain as if he could stop its progress, but he didn't even touch the sheet. "No, no, no."

He left the room.

He went downstairs, hearing the twins whistle like trains in the kitchen. Cutlery scraped against a plate.

Seeing him come down, his wife walked up to him. "You're not having breakfast?" She dried her hands on her apron.

"You think I'm hungry?"

"I can see the state you're in." She peeled the toilet paper from the cuts on his face. "I can't eat, either. And Melissa hasn't touched her food. I wish I understood that girl, there's no getting through to her."

They walked to the front door together.

"He's wet the bed," Elmer whispered into Rose's ear.

"Just wet it?" She wrinkled her nose.

"I think so."

"I'll go up in a second, when the girls have finished. And you." She rested a hand on his face. "Come back soon."

"I don't know what they're going to think of me after I didn't show up yesterday."

"Make something up, anything. I don't want us to be alone with him."

"You're five against one," he said, repeating the argument she had used the morning before.

"That's what I said before I knew who he was."

"He won't wake up. He's barely breathing."

He opened the front door. When he went to open the screen door, his hand was left in the air. The confusion lasted a few seconds, until he remembered that the kid had ruined it. Chairs in the kitchen scraped against the floor. The twins ran after him.

"You're going already?"

"You're going already?"

Iris appeared behind them. "Call the ambulance first." She grabbed the sleeve of his coveralls and shook it. "As soon as you arrive."

"I will." Elmer tried to hold her gaze but looked away, at Rose.

His wife pulled Iris's hand away, smoothing down the creases she'd left on the fabric.

"Melissa!" Rose yelled. "Melissa, aren't you going to say goodbye to your father?"

There was silence.

"Goodbye, Dad," she said from the kitchen, a halfhearted murmur.

"Goodbye, honey," he called.

On the porch, Rose kissed him on one corner of his mouth. "Come back soon," she whispered.

"Come back soon!" cried the twins.

They wanted to follow him out, but Rose held them by their shoulders. "You can't keep him today."

Elmer walked down the three steps while the girls kicked against the floor, trying to free themselves from the trap. Before reaching the pickup, he turned and waved.

"Please, Dad!" Iris yelled, perching on the handrail. "Call right away."

He turned without responding so he wouldn't have to lie. Before climbing into the truck, he extracted pieces of glass from a headlight. From the grille he removed a lump of cactus that had survived his cleaning of the truck. Other signs of the collision, like the bent side mirror, were camouflaged by the general disrepair of a truck beaten up by weather and time. With his hands on the steering wheel, he discovered Melissa observing him from the kitchen window. She was moving her lips, speaking to one of her rocks. Elmer put the truck into reverse, turned the wheel, and set off up the road. He stepped on the gas. In the rearview mirror, Rose and the little girls were still waving goodbye from the porch.

Elmer drove with his eyes fixed on one side of the road until he found the mound of stones that marked the position of Rick's car. He got out of the pickup. Among the cactuses he saw the same glint he'd seen yesterday: the sun reflecting off the Lincoln's bodywork. From behind his seat, Elmer pulled out the kid's backpack. The boots, with a ball of socks inside, hung from the straps. He picked up a can of gasoline from behind the seat, one of the ones he filled without permission at the end of his shift at the gas station to reduce the cost of running the generator at home. He selected a screwdriver from among the tools scattered around the truck's cargo area. The matches he carried in the pocket of his coveralls shook in their box with each step he took toward the car. First he unscrewed the license plates. Then he let the air out of the tires. He splashed the upholstery with gasoline and started the fire on the driver's seat. He waited for the flames to spread. Returning to the pickup, he felt the heat on the back of his neck, across his back.

Rose took a key out from her apron and opened the bedroom door. She was carrying a stack of clean sheets, holding them against her hip. When she put them down on Melissa's desk, magazine cuttings fell to the floor. It was a few minutes before she was able to lay her eyes on Rick. She held her hand to her mouth when she saw the bruises on his face, the damp circle on the sheet. When she freed the edges from under the mattress, she was surprised at how tight she had made the sheet, at the pressure it exerted on the boy's body. She rested a hand on his chest by way of an apology. She removed the dirty sheet by rolling it down from his chin to his feet, sucking in air through her teeth several times as she uncovered the injured body. She left the roll of wet material on the floor and slid the bottom sheet from under Rick. He groaned when her actions moved his limbs.

"Nearly done, nearly done."

She gave a final tug to pull out a corner of fabric trapped under the heel of his twisted foot. She piled that sheet on top of the other one. From the top of the stack on the desk she took a towel she'd moistened in the bathroom. She cleaned Rick's skin, avoiding the most damaged areas. The rope had made new wounds. She tended to Rick's genital area unabashedly, as a mother would. When she covered the mattress with the clean bottom sheet, she knew she was hurting him again, but it was impossible not to move him. Then she let the second sheet fall onto his body. She thought about making it less tight than before, but remembering the accusations Rick had leveled at her, she tucked it under the mattress as far as her hand would reach.

She sat on the bed. She stroked the contours of his eyes, that part of him that reminded her so much of Edelweiss.

"What're we going to do with you, huh?" she whispered. "If only you'd never come."

She chose three locks of hair on his forehead and shaped them before brushing them to one side, then ran a fingertip over his eyebrows.

"I'd have liked to have had a son." She felt the angle of his jaw as she wished that she could have witnessed a boy grow up. Seen a face widen, heard the voice of a child transform into a man's. Elmer would've taught him to shave, would have played basketball with him with the hoop and the backboard that they ended up using one summer to light the barbecue. "Shall I tell you something? My husband thought the twins were boys. We only realized when he got home."

She smiled to herself, moving her finger down to Rick's Adam's apple, then up along his hairline, stopping at the corners where his hair receded, corners none of her daughters would have.

"It would have been nice to have had a boy."

The sound of the twins' laughter came in through the window, as if they'd wanted to distracted her from her thoughts. She saw Daisy and Dahlia running around outside, chasing each other in turns that seemed random. Farther away, almost on the horizon, a plume of black smoke rose up from among the cacti.

"I'm sorry." Rose stroked Rick's face. "I'm so sorry. If only you'd never come."

Melissa poked at the remnants of ash on top of the still-warm metal of the barbecue. They consisted of a pile of black sheets that broke up when touched, turning into a black powder that fell through the cracks in the grill. She pulled out the tray. The rusty screech of the rails set her teeth on edge. With a finger, she bored through the mountain of ash until she hit the edge of a page. She dragged it to one side of the tray. It was a little triangle. She picked it up between two fingers and blew hard to remove the soot, revealing a piece of brown card. The corner of the folder that had contained the documents.

"What's that fire?" Iris asked from the porch.

Melissa pushed the tray back under the grill, biting her tongue to fend off the shivers. She expected to find Iris leaning on the handrail, right above the barbecue, asking about the pile of ash to which her father had reduced the suffering of so many families. But Iris was standing on the porch steps. With her hand at her forehead, she was looking at something in the distance.

"What could that fire be?" she said again. "Turn around. See?"

She indicated to Melissa the direction in which she should look. As soon as she turned, Melissa saw a plume of smoke originating somewhere in the desert. It climbed into the sky, forming a black cloud. Melissa moved the triangle of card between her fingers, pricking herself with the sharpest point. She wondered what her father was burning now.

"What're you looking at?"

"What're you looking at?"

The twins ran up to them. They climbed onto the porch and let out a sigh of wonder when they discovered the black cloud. Mom came out of the house, carrying a ball of sheets.

"What's that smoke, Mommy?"

"What's that smoke, Mommy?"

"It's nothing, girls, the sun must've set fire to a dead cactus."

Melissa didn't like the ease with which her mother lied to the twins. She took a few steps to distance herself from the barbecue.

"Is our house going to burn down?" the twins asked.

"Of course not." Their mother came down the stairs, going around Iris. "The fire will consume the cactus, and then it'll have nowhere to go with all this sand and rock."

Mom looked at Melissa. "Feeling better?"

Melissa clenched her fist, driving the corner of the card into her palm. She nodded, though it was a lie.

"Good."

Iris put *Pride and Prejudice* down on the bottom step. She went and stood in front of Mom with her arms outstretched.

"Give them to me." She offered to take the sheets. "I'll carry them."

"Please, Iris"—Mom turned her torso to separate them from her—"they're dirty sheets."

"I don't care. They're his."

Her mother objected to her comment with a snort.

"How is he?" Iris asked. "Is he improving? Do you need me to help you with anything? Do you want me to wash him before the ambulance arrives?"

Mom shook her head as though she couldn't believe what she was hearing. "I'm taking care of it." She moved her daughter out of the way with her arm. "It's nothing for you to worry about. Play with your sisters."

"I'm going to wait here. The ambulance won't be long," said Iris. "Dad reached the gas station a while ago, and he'll have called right away. It'll be here any minute."

Iris looked out at the road as if medical assistance was about to arrive, as if her eyes could already see the emergency vehicle approaching the house through the cloud of dust that its wheels would raise, taking the bends at full speed to urgently attend to Rick. She smiled at Melissa.

"He'll be OK."

She threw her hair over her right shoulder, tugging on it with her hands as she began pacing a figure eight in front of the house. She traced it twice, going over her own footprints. When she began the third lap, Melissa stopped counting.

Following the twins, Melissa went in search of Mom. After going around one side of the house, they found her at the washing machine. She poured a quantity of detergent on the sheets that to Melissa seemed excessive. Then she closed the lid so hard that the whole contraption shook. She leaned against it, hiding her head in her hands.

"Mommy?" said Dahlia. "What's wrong?"

Mom gave a start, straightening up.

"With me?" She sniffed and forced a smile while she removed the hair from her face. "Nothing. Why?"

Rose pinned a corner of a wet sheet to the clothesline. She stretched out the material before adding the second clothespin. Then she clipped two more on at intermediate points to make it more secure. The wind that swept past the rear of the house dried the laundry faster but could easily blow it from the line. Standing between the two hanging sheets, hidden in a refuge of damp fabric, Rose raised her arms to try to enjoy the freshness that enveloped her, to relax with the clean smell.

"A tunnel!"

"A tunnel!"

Before she'd lowered her arms, the twins raided her refuge, running through the corridor of sheets from one end to the other. They went around her on either side.

"Quit running or you'll kick up the dust and it'll all stick to the sheets."

Daisy and Dahlia stopped. They went through the tunnel in the opposite direction, this time on tiptoes. They touched the wet sheets with their palms as if they were the walls of a secret passage. One of Daisy's hands was printed in dust on the bottom sheet.

"Come on, out," Rose grumbled. "Running or no running, you're banned from entering."

She blocked the twins' path, making them walk back. The little girls sniffed the air, their noses held up to the sky.

"They smell so good," Daisy said.

"We want to live in there!" Dahlia breathed in with such relish that her arms stretched backward. "They smell of flowers, they smell like dahlias."

"They smell like daisies." Daisy filled her chest. "They smell like my flowers."

"Dahlias!"

"Daisies!"

"Dahlias!"

While the twins yelled, Rose saw Melissa sitting on the ground, in front of Edelweiss's grave, a hand on the earth.

"Actually," said Rose, interrupting the argument, "actually they smell like jasmine . . . and melissa." She waited for a reaction from her middle daughter. She raised her voice. "And melissa!"

Melissa didn't hear her, or wasn't paying attention. Rose saw the flower arrangement that she and Elmer had left on the grave a few days before, now withered. The desert did not favor life.

"I said the sheets smell like melissa!"

Daisy and Dahlia whispered to each other beside her before running to their sister. They sat down around the grave, playing with the stones that they themselves had covered in colored beads. Rose went after them, she scored a basket with a clothespin in the wicker container on top of the washing machine.

"Mom says the sheets smell like you," said Daisy.

"They smell like jasmine and you," Dahlia added.

"It's detergent with melissa," Rose explained, "and it smells great."

"It smells great!" yelled the twins. "We want to live in a house of wet sheets!"

Melissa gave her sisters one of the sad smiles she'd learned to force to show gratitude to others. Then she returned her attention to the cross. Rose wanted to grab her by the shoulders and shake her until she explained what was going on.

"Weren't you feeling better?" she asked.

Melissa lifted her bottom lip. The twins walked around the grave, inspecting the state of the rocks, indicating the ones that needed fixing. Melissa hugged her knees. She swayed, biting the skin on her wrist. She looked at the cross and then at Rose. At the grave and then at Rose.

"Mom," she said after several seconds.

"What, honey?" Rose knelt to listen to her.

Melissa hid her mouth behind her knees, and her swaying grew more intense. Her eyes returned to the grave, but her gaze seemed lost beyond it, underground.

"Mom . . ."

"What is it?" Rose stopped the swaying by resting a hand on the back of her daughter's neck. "You can talk to me."

Melissa looked at her. She took a deep breath. For an instant, she looked as if she was about to share a confession, but then she let her shoulders fall with a sigh.

"I don't know, Mom," she said. "I don't know what's wrong with me."

But Rose could guess what was wrong. What was wrong was that she missed the teacher she could talk to without finishing her sentences, who gave her advice on how to be happy, and who taught her exotic words in Spanish. She bit her tongue to stop herself from screaming at Melissa that if she missed Socorro that much, maybe she should go live with her.

"There's lots missing from this one!" Daisy showed Dahlia a stone from which most of the beads, blue ones, had fallen off.

"And even more from this one!"

"We have to fix them." they said.

Rose regretted her thoughts. She stroked Melissa's hair by way of an apology.

"When you're ready," she said to her.

A bell rang in the kitchen.

"Lunch is ready, come on." She pulled Melissa up by the elbow. "You two, leave those stones. You can come back later if you want."

The twins put the rocks back, moving them to hide the husked areas. They ran to the back door that led into the kitchen. Rose put an arm over Melissa's shoulders. Her daughter looked at the cross one last time before setting off with her.

Rose laid out plates for her four daughters and placed a dish, still hot from the oven, in the middle of the table. Through the window, she saw that Iris was still outside, pacing up and down. She was looking to the horizon.

"Iris!" she yelled, leaning out onto the porch. "Iris! Lunch!"

Her daughter turned around but didn't answer. She resumed her circular march with her hands hooked around her neck. As they ate their lunch, Rose watched Iris's movements from the kitchen. She saw her go on tiptoes a number of times, forming a visor with her hand, hoping to see the ambulance appear in the distance. She saw her cross her arms and uncross them. Sit down and stand up. Stand on tiptoes again. At the table, the twins were discussing flowers and colored beads. Melissa was whispering things to her rock. When they finished eating, Rose used tinfoil to cover the plate Iris hadn't touched and a fork to scrape the remains of her own meal and the girls' into the trash.

They all went out onto the porch. Daisy and Dahlia occupied the porch swing, its mechanism squeaking to the rhythm of their laughter. Melissa announced that she was going to talk to Needles, Pins, and Thorns. She picked up Iris's book from the bottom step and handed it to Rose, who used her apron to clean off the dust that had covered it.

"Iris!" she shouted, her hands cupped around her mouth. "Come on, Iris, you have to eat!"

This time her daughter heeded her summons. Iris walked back to the house, kicking up dirt with each stride. She stopped at the bottom of the steps. Her face, shoulders, and neckline were as covered in dust as her book.

"Why hasn't the ambulance come?" A film of tears covered her narrowed eyes. "Why hasn't Dad called?"

Rose handed her *Pride and Prejudice*, as if by doing so she could evade the question.

Iris snatched it from her. "Why has nobody come?"

Receiving no response, Iris huffed. She held her hand to her forehead. Her chest rose and fell in time with her accelerated breathing. When she turned around to face the horizon again, Rose noticed how pointed her shoulder blades were. Iris let herself drop onto the second step. And there she remained, slumped against the handrail.

As the sun fell, the letters grew illegible on the page. It didn't matter—Iris couldn't read anyway. Sitting on the porch steps for hours with the book open on her knees, she hadn't even managed to finish one chapter, paying more attention to the horizon than to the novel. The plume of black smoke in the distance had gradually faded until it disappeared. The brilliant blue of the sky had turned purple.

"Hang in there," she said with her chin lifted toward Melissa's window, sending her words up to Rick. "They'll be here soon."

From the kitchen came the sounds of the knife against the cutting board, a pot being filled from the faucet. Mom had started making dinner.

Iris wondered what was causing the annoying tapping against wood she heard. She discovered it was the heel of her own restless foot.

"Hang in there," she said again.

A cloud of dust was floating over the road, far off. Iris straightened her back. She followed its course to make sure it wasn't just another whirl of dirt like the ones that had fooled her throughout the day. The dust cloud remained constant, moving in a straight line. Iris closed her book. She stood up. She blinked without taking her eyes off the track.

"See?" she whispered. "They're coming for you. You're going to be all right."

Iris heard the handle of a knife being put down on the counter. The faucet being turned off. She heard Mom's footsteps coming from the kitchen.

"What is it?"

"They're coming, Mom." She pointed at the mass of dust moving ever nearer. "Do we have to bring him down?"

"Iris . . ."

She ran to the entrance to the road without listening to what Mom had to say. The smile on her face relaxed her jaw muscles, which had grown stiff with tension. She was suddenly aware of the hunger she felt. Her stomach grumbled when she remembered how she'd turned down the meal that Mom had offered her so many times in the afternoon—she'd even left the plate on the porch step, until Daisy and Dahlia's constant running had covered the tinfoil in sand.

She went on tiptoes, feeling a sharp pain in her calf muscles. The dust cloud now reached the tall cactus, the place where it would have to turn onto the track that led to the house. Iris wet her lips. She stretched her neck. When the source of the moving dirt cloud was visible, she sighed.

It was Dad's pickup.

She rested her heels back on the ground with her mouth open and her stomach contracting, crushing any hint of appetite once more. The truck passed by her, covering her in dust before she could react. She wanted to scream at her father, but she choked on grit. She coughed. She ran after the vehicle, waving her arms. The dust cloud made her invisible.

"Dad!"

The pickup stopped a few yards from the porch, where the twins had just appeared. They ran at Dad from the front, while Iris ran at him from behind. They reached him first, hugging his waist. Iris caught up with them, almost breathless, but she used the little breath she had left to yell.

"Why haven't you called?" Each gulp of air scraped her throat. "What about the ambulance?"

"Hello to you, too."

"Why hasn't anyone come?" Iris felt the saliva sputtering from the corners of her mouth. "It's almost nighttime. Why haven't you called? Why didn't—?"

"I called," Dad cut in, raising his voice. "I called."

Iris threw her head back, frowning.

"Don't make that face, of course I called."

"And?"

"I called this morning. They asked me a lot of questions. Where's he hurting, what's wrong with him, whether he can breathe. They didn't consider his condition an emergency."

Iris tried to say something, but she choked on her words. Dad glanced to one side before going on.

"He's not bad enough for them to send us an ambulance. We're a long way away, honey. It's over four hours here and back from the hospital. They can't use the vehicle and ignore other emergencies, real emergencies. The kid doesn't need urgent attention."

"What?" Iris breathed through her teeth, her hands on her waist.

Dad tried to take her by the shoulder, but she stepped back.

"He can recover here with the right care."

"In a girl's bed?"

"We're taking care of him." Mom appeared next to Dad. "If the hospital themselves don't consider it an emergency, well, they know more than we do. And more than you do."

Iris looked up at the sky and let out all the air she had left. She covered her face with her hands and shook her head.

"I hope the vultures eat him," said Dahlia.

"Yeah, that way he won't steal our pictures," Daisy added.

Tears moistened Iris's palms. She took them away, revealing her face. The twins held hands when they saw it.

"What have we said?"

"Iris, do us a favor," Mom said. "We're the grownups, and we're taking care of the situation."

"Your mother's caring for a man who fired a gun at her, don't forget."

Iris screamed with her teeth clamped together, her fists clenched over her belly. Continuing to look at her parents, and even at the twins after what they had said, made her chest hurt. She paced, sobbing, retracing the footprints she'd made when she still thought someone would come to tend to Rick. Her parents yelled her name from some indeterminate place, their voices changing position. Dad appeared in front of her, his arms outstretched. She managed to dodge him. She ran without direction until she saw Melissa in front of her cacti, in the distance. She fled toward her, away from the others. She sat on the ground beside her.

"I love him," she sobbed with her head on her sister's shoulder. "I love him."

Melissa hugged her. She made a hushing sound in her ear. She wiped Iris's tears with her fingers, the dust scraping her cheeks.

When Iris looked at her sister, she was surprised. "And why're *you* crying?"

Melissa shook her head, making nothing of it.

The moon was red that night, like a wound on the sky. Elmer observed it from the broken window in Melissa's room. The weak glow of that lesion did little to illuminate the landscape, turning the forest of cacti into a mystery of dark and spines. On the land near the house, boulders stood out in the blackness, the dying light of some star reflecting on their surfaces. Beyond them, an animal's skull was bright among the remains of four burned-out trucks.

A black smudge fluttered in front of Elmer's eyes. An insect perched on the intact windowpane, its wings unfolding against the glass. It was a dark moth, as big as the palm of a hand. When one of these appeared at the gas station, his workmates yelled and swatted at it to scare it away. They called it the *Mariposa de la Muerte*, the Butterfly of Death, and swore that it was a harbinger of death. Elmer didn't believe in local superstitions, but he banged on the windowpane to make it leave. The moth remained motionless on the other side of the glass, big as a bat. He had to stick his hand outside to frighten it off.

"It's beautiful . . ." Rick whispered behind him.

Elmer turned around. The kid spoke with the side of his face resting on the pillow, looking out through the window. He barely moved his lips, and he was fighting to keep his eyelids open.

"The moon . . ."—a string of saliva spilled from the corner of his mouth—"so red. So lovely . . . Is it nighttime already?"

"I'm going to have to make you go to sleep again."

"No . . . please. I had a nightmare . . . I was tied up and . . ." He abandoned the sentence with a groan.

The blister pack crackled between Elmer's fingers, which trembled at the idea of continuing to sedate the kid. He took out a pill. He positioned his thumb over the next one along, wondering whether to administer such a strong dose again. He made the plastic click, but left the pill in the packaging. He placed just one Dormepam in Rick's mouth, separating the kid's teeth with his fingers. He let it drop into Rick's throat before pouring half a glass of water on top of it. A cough spattered his face. He had to tip the kid's head back so that the liquid and the medication were pulled in.

Rick opened his eyes, just a crack. "All I want is to tell my mom . . . so she knows Elizabeth was happy here . . ." he murmured. "The moon . . . it's so red . . ."

Elmer left the room. Iris was waiting in her doorway. When he looked at her, she slammed the door shut and turned the lock angrily. Elmer checked the twins' bedroom. They were both asleep on the edges of their beds, as close as possible to each other. They were breathing in unison. Elmer closed the door without making a sound and locked it from the outside. Downstairs, in the living room, a light was still on.

"Good night, Melissa," he said, holding on to the banister.

He heard his daughter shake a pillow, plumping it. She put a rock down on the table, or on the floor. She didn't respond.

"I said good night."

Her slippers dragged along the floor.

"Honey, good night."

"Good night," Melissa said in the end, ". . . Dad."

"Sleep well."

As he entered his bedroom, Elmer recognized a large wooden box on the bed, with hinges. He hadn't seen it for six years, since the twins arrived. Rose was standing in front of the mirror. She was looking at her reflection from the side, giving shape to a bump that had appeared under her nightgown, at stomach height. He positioned himself behind her. They interlocked their hands over the round belly, massaging it as if something was really growing in there.

"I've been so happy making this family," she said.

Elmer rested his chin on her shoulder. "It's the best thing we've done."

Rose twisted her neck to escape his tickling breath. They both stroked the fake pregnancy, smiling at the image from the past that the mirror offered them.

Just then a loud bang in the living room reverberated through the house. Rose flinched in his arms. She turned to face him, wedging the false belly between them with maternal gentleness.

"What was that?" Her eyes took up half of her face.

Elmer let go of Rose and went to poke his head out the door.

"Melissa?"

"I dropped my stone," she shouted from downstairs. "Nothing's broken."

Rose undid a clasp under her nightgown. She did it without looking, with the deftness of someone who has repeated an action many times. Her stomach was left empty. The pregnancy vanished, reduced to an uncomfortable jumble of silicone, orthopedic straps, and aluminum buckles. Lifeless items that in their lives had been substitutes for blood, the placenta, amniotic fluid. The unpleasant reminder made Elmer shudder. She put the prosthesis back in the box, then closed the lid as if it were a jewel case, fastening a golden clasp. She stroked the grooves in the wood, an engraving of a stork. On tiptoes, she put it away at the top of her wardrobe, hiding the box behind a bag of old clothes.

"I'll go see how she is," said Rose.

"Speak to Iris, too. She slammed her door in my face."

Melissa retrieved Marlon from the floor. He'd slipped from her hand because she'd wanted to pick him up without letting go of her sketchbook. Though she'd just told Dad that nothing was broken, she discovered a deep notch in the wood flooring.

"That chin of yours . . ." she said to Marlon.

She left him on the table, reminding him that she'd have to return him to the shelf later, that it wasn't his night to sleep with her, it was Clark's. Sitting on the sofa, she opened the sketchbook on her lap, to the page where she'd hidden the documents she'd taken from Rick's folder. The ceiling creaked over her head. She pricked her ears to identify who was responsible, to hear which direction the feet were traveling. It was Mom, and she was coming down the stairs.

Melissa slammed the sketchbook shut. She looked around. The footsteps drew closer. She tried to hide it under the pillow, but the corners jutted out from one side. Mom was now at the bottom step. Melissa dropped the sketchbook behind the back of the sofa. A corner of the spine hit the floor.

"Now what've you dropped?" her mother asked as she walked into the living room.

"I banged myself on the wall"—she rubbed an elbow—"making this bed that isn't a bed."

"You don't do it right, that's the problem. Up you get."

"What for?"

"If we pull the sofa out we can tuck the sheet in behind the backrest. That way you won't have it twisted up like you do now."

"It doesn't matter, Mom."

Mom approached the sofa. She spanned it with her arms, one hand on the back, the other on Melissa's seat.

"Lift your feet up and I'll move it."

"I said no, Mom. There's no need."

But she pulled it anyway. When she separated it from the wall, another corner of the sketchbook struck the floor.

"I said don't move it." Melissa kicked her heels, disguising the sound with the blows. "I like it as it is."

"So you admit you like sleeping down here?" Mom looked up with a half smile, without letting go of the sofa.

Melissa crossed her arms. She slumped into the backrest with such force that the sofa was pushed back toward the wall. Mom sat down next to her.

"Honey"—she rested a hand on Melissa's knee—"I just want you to be OK."

For a second, Melissa wanted to break into tears. To tell Mom what she'd read and ask her why all those newspapers lied. Why the stranger who slept in her bed had come to this house searching for a sister who couldn't be his, however much his eyes resembled Edelweiss's. But she said nothing. She just removed Mom's hand from her knee and sat up to stretch for Marlon. She placed him beside her pillow.

"We're going to sleep."

"You can talk to me." Mom continued to look at her. "Tell me you know that."

Melissa nodded.

"But tell me."

"I know I can talk to you," she repeated without enthusiasm.

"Like you can with Socorro. Better than with Socorro. I'm your mother. There's nobody in the world who loves you more than I do."

Melissa gathered her legs in and lay down in the same space in which she had sat.

"Do you want me to change the rock? Two nights is a long time to skip your order. And that Gregory has sad eyes. I don't think he's the best company for you."

"No need." She covered Marlon to hide him, though it was clear that to her mother all the stones looked the same. "I'm happy with Gregory. I'll apologize to the rest when I can speak to them."

When Mom stood, Melissa stretched her legs along the sofa. She didn't sit up to receive the good-night kiss her mother offered but, without moving, let her plant it on her cheek.

"I just want you to be OK," Rose said again.

Melissa stretched out her arm, feeling the wall until she found the switch.

"I'm turning it off," she warned, before doing so.

In the dark, Mom gave her another kiss. Then she crossed the living room and climbed the stairs. Melissa moved her mouth close to Marlon's ear.

"Don't let me fall asleep," she whispered. "We have to stay awake."

The rock said something.

"Good idea."

Melissa got up from the sofa. Through the window onto the porch, the moon caught her attention with its orange glow. In the kitchen she drank three glasses of water, one after the other. She went back and lay beside Marlon.

"Done."

Lying on her back in bed with Rick's T-shirt over her face, Iris took deep breaths. She imagined Rick lying there, next to her, the two of them covered by the sheet, whispering to each other the many things they still had to say. She could feel the warm breath of his secrets on her ear, and the hairs on the back of her neck stood on end.

Knocks on the door made her jump.

"Can I come in?" Mom whispered from the other side.

Iris sat up as if waking from a trance, dazed by the intensity of her fantasies. The door handle shook.

"Iris"—knuckles struck the wood—"I want to speak to you."

She got up and hid the T-shirt under the mattress, pushing it as far as her hand reached. She scanned the rest of the room. She smelled her hands, the shoulders of her nightgown. Although Rick's aroma intoxicated her, Mom wouldn't detect it. She opened the door just enough for her face to fit in the gap.

"What do you want?"

"Let me in, honey." Mom stuck an arm in, then a leg, pushing her way through. Inside, she shook out her hair, clicking her tongue. "You girls sure are making it hard for me to talk to you today."

She rearranged Iris's nightgown. Iris wiggled her shoulders to reject the adjustment.

"And that needs sewing." She gestured at the tear down the side.

"*You* did it."

Mom sat down on the bed, right above where Iris had just hidden the T-shirt. When she pushed it under, she must also have dragged part of the sheet in with it, because the fabric disappeared in a suspicious way under the mattress. Iris looked away from that spot and combed her hair with her fingers to draw attention from it. Mom rubbed the bed, the space beside her. She waited for Iris to sit down.

"Why're you mad at your father?" She tried to tidy her daughter's neckline again. "With us?"

Iris stopped her mother's hand in the air.

"Rick needs an ambulance. Or a doctor." She held the hand between hers. "Please, Mom, he needs urgent medical attention."

"He's a lot better." Mom scratched the back of her neck. "You haven't seen him."

"I saw what Dad did to him with the truck."

"That's why Dad called the ambulance this morning. And they said there was no need for them to come—"

"That he's too far away, you mean."

"—that they couldn't come, whatever." Mom raised her voice, then paused. She continued in a whisper. "We're doing all we can for him."

"You're not doing anything."

"Honey"—Mom moved even closer to her—"do you really think we'd let a boy die in our house without helping him? Why would we want to do that?" She hunched her shoulders, as if it was an absurd question to even ask.

Iris couldn't imagine an answer. She observed the wrinkles that emerged from her mother's eyes in the direction of her temples, three on one side and two on the other. She once heard Mom say to Socorro that she had one for each of her daughters, actual marks on her skin from the effort and sacrifice she'd made for each of them.

"I'm taking care of him," Mom said.

"Shouldn't we call his family? Someone?"

"That's what we want. For him to speak and give us a name, a telephone number. But he still hasn't woken up since . . ." She didn't finish the sentence.

"Since he was hit by a truck."

"Since your father acted in self-defense."

Mom tried to hold a hand to Iris's cheek. Though Iris's first instinct was to move away, she ended up resting her face against the warmth of that palm. She nuzzled against it, remembering times when just contact with her mother's skin had been enough to make her feel better.

"Can I see him? I want to see him, Mom."

Her mother took away her hand, leaving a cold patch on Iris's face.

"Honey, I'm taking good care of him. Because we weren't going to let him die in the sun. But that boy fired a gun at me. He shot at me and ran off. I'm not going to let my daughters near him."

"What did he want? To rob us?"

"How do I know?" Mom exhaled. "He spent the night in the truck, maybe he liked what he saw and thought he'd help himself. Or maybe he thought there was more money in that jar than there is."

Iris found it difficult to believe.

"Or maybe"—she smiled with half of her mouth—"maybe your sisters are right and he wanted to make off with their pictures."

Iris didn't respond to the joke.

"He seemed so nice . . ."

"Honey"—Mom lifted her chin with a finger, until their eyes met—"people are almost never what they seem."

The five wrinkles at her eyes now seemed deeper.

"Will he be OK?"

"We're doing what we can."

"And Dad?"

"All your dad wants is for him to get back on his feet, pick up his backpack, and leave the way he came. To get as far as possible from this family."

Iris toyed with a thread that hung from the side of her nightgown.

"He really did seem like a nice boy . . ."

She rolled the thread around her finger and unrolled it.

"Don't give it another thought." Mom kissed her on the forehead. "Let's see what tomorrow brings."

"Thanks, Mom."

"I just want you all to be OK."

Iris plucked the thread with a tug. "I know."

Mom left the room. Iris turned the key and waited to hear her parents' door close as well before inserting her arm under the mattress. She sat on the floor, using the bed as a backrest, and pressed Rick's crumpled T-shirt against her face.

Rose appeared in the bedroom. She slumped onto the floor, her back against the closed door. Elmer leapt up from the bed.

"What happened?"

"I can't lie to my daughters like this." Rose buried her face in her hands and shook her head. "I can't."

Elmer pulled her elbows apart, revealing her face. Her chin began to tremble. Her eyes were filled with tears.

"What're we going to do, Elmer? Wait? Keep the boy until . . ." Her voice broke down.

"We don't have to decide anything now," Elmer whispered in her ear.

"And what about tomorrow? Or the next day?"

Rose blinked, waiting for an answer that he was unable to give.

Iris sat at her dressing table. Last night's pimple had improved, and it was barely visible now. She stretched the material at her neckline, smoothing out the creases. She opened her book to the page where she'd gotten stuck that afternoon. She weighted down the corners with her perfume and powder compact.

She read thirty pages.

She completed a hundred strokes with the hairbrush.

When she finished, the house was in complete silence. She'd heard murmurs in her parents' bedroom until late, but a good while ago they'd stopped. She pressed on the atomizer to release a cloud of perfume that rained on her chest. She patted her face with the powder compact.

Then she straightened her back and squared her shoulders.

She smiled at her reflection.

Before climbing out onto the roof, she made sure Melissa wasn't talking to her cactuses. The moon glowed yellow, the same color as the sparkles coming from Thorns's shirt buttons. As far as she could make out, there was no silhouette in front of him that could belong to her sister. Walking barefoot over the tiles, she passed the twins' window in one stride. She entered Melissa's room with a foot on the desk, taking care to avoid the teeth of broken glass as she went through the frame. Her lungs filled when she recognized Rick's form under the sheet. Her breathing was as labored as the night before.

"It's Iris," she said in his ear. "You cried out for me this morning. You were yearning to see me."

In the dark, the skin on his face seemed bluish. She inspected it with her fingers, hoping for some kind of reaction. There was none. His eyelids were motionless, his breathing constant. His facial muscles remained flaccid.

"Do you want water?"

His closed lips appeared less dry than the previous night, but she filled a glass and held it near his mouth.

"You have to drink."

She rubbed the edge of the glass against his lips. She wanted to relive the pleasure of quenching Rick's thirst, of alleviating his physical needs. The glass clinked against his teeth without him responding to the stimulus.

Iris had an idea.

She drank the water but didn't swallow it. She left the glass on the bedside table. Resting her lips on Rick's, she searched for the opening with her tongue and let the liquid escape, little by little, into his mouth. The feeling was even more intense than what she'd experienced the day before. It was a kiss more romantic than the ones in her books that had made her sigh as she read. In the end, the water spilled from the corners of Rick's mouth onto the pillow. Iris sat up. She could feel her heart beating in an unfamiliar rhythm. Her head rocked, a pleasant swaying. All of a sudden, she grasped why flowers displayed such pretty colors, why there were stars in the sky, why Edelweiss's guitar produced such a beautiful sound. She understood why Dad kissed Mom at every opportunity. The words spilled from her lips like the water that had just spilled between Rick's.

"I love you," she whispered.

She leaned over him, holding him through the sheet. She slotted her face into the space between his jaw and his shoulder. It felt like the most welcoming place she had ever known.

"You're going to be OK. Mom's taking care of you. They're going to kick you out as soon as you're better, but maybe I can go with you. We can walk together as far as our feet can carry us. My soul sees the purity of yours. I know you never meant to do anything bad to us."

She lay one side of her face on his chest. She smiled when she heard his heart. With her eyes closed, she could feel her heartbeats synchronizing with his. When she pressed her ear down to listen more, Rick groaned.

"You feel it, too?" She looked at his bluish face. "Our hearts are dancing to the same rhythm."

Wrinkles formed on Rick's forehead, but he didn't respond. Iris used his chest as a pillow again. She ignored the groan.

"I feel like Juliet waiting for Romeo to awake." She bit the insides of her lips.

She stroked Rick's hair, her other hand resting on his belly. She touched the hard, undulating surface of his abdomen with her fingers, and felt the temperature of her body rise. Her fingertips ran over the muscles' parallel grooves, letting themselves be guided by the deep valley that traversed them through the middle. That valley led her fingers downward. Iris's breathing accelerated, her heart now beating at a much faster rate than Rick's.

She granted her hand total freedom.

It headed down until it came to rest on the soft part between the muscles.

Its fingers investigated that area, discovering shapes and textures unknown to her.

Her labored breathing moistened the sheet with its heat. She felt another dampness in her underwear. Her whole body trembled. She pressed herself harder against Rick and had an urge to bite the sheet. To scream. She closed her hand. The shudders culminated in an intense contraction of every muscle. Her toes scratched the floor as they curled. The unfamiliar pleasure repeated in successive spasms that blinded her. When they subsided, Iris removed her hand from where she had it. She hid it behind her back. Straightening up, she wiped her cheek. She tidied her hair and adjusted her nightgown as if she were getting dressed.

"I . . . this . . . it was . . ."

She didn't know what words to use to express herself. She kissed Rick's lips once more.

"I love you." The feeling was now a physical reality that had changed her body forever. "You're going to be OK."

She went back to her bedroom feeling so ethereal that her feet might not have touched the roof. She landed between her sheets as if returning from a magical nocturnal flight.

Melissa opened her eyes. She'd fallen asleep. She turned her face toward the window, her stomach tense. The darkness on the horizon was total—it was still the middle of the night. She sighed with relief and felt a tingling in her urethra.

"It worked," she whispered to Marlon.

She walked with her legs together to the toilet, her thighs rubbing against each other. She peed out the three glasses of water she'd drunk as an alarm system. On her way back to the living room, she stopped at the foot of the stairs. She pricked her ears. The silence was the same as it always was in the early hours. Melissa retrieved Marlon and went outside, through the back door in the kitchen. She walked around the house to the porch. She climbed up the post with the dried-up paint, the one that scratched her hands but led straight to her window. She entered her bedroom through the broken pane.

The room still smelled like used Band-Aids. As it had the previous night, the sheet covered Rick to the chin. His position was almost identical.

"And to think how much I move around in that bed when I sleep . . ."

Melissa left Marlon on the shelf, where there was no longer a folder. On tiptoes, she felt around for Clark. She recognized him by the distinctive hole in one ear. Moving the stones around, the changes of weight on the shelving, made it creak. Melissa tightened the nut that always came loose.

"Till next time, Marlon," she whispered. "Good evening, Clark."

Then she turned to Rick.

"I need to speak to you. It's important."

She touched his shoulder, but he didn't wake up. Melissa held her mouth near his ear. She raised the volume of her voice as far as she considered prudent.

"Wake up, I have to speak to you."

She waited a few seconds. There was no response. She pinched his nose. She thought he'd wake, desperate for a breath of air, but his lips opened a crack and he breathed through his mouth. Melissa scanned her room, inspecting her belongings. In a drawer, she kept some paintbrushes, old jars of tempera, watercolor sets, and tubes of oil paint. She rummaged through the contents until she found a bottle of turpentine, a paint thinner she'd only used once, to erase the mouth from a rock that looked too sad. When she unscrewed the lid, she had to tilt her head to one side to escape the pungent smell. She held the opening to Rick's nose, then waved the bottle in front of his face. She blew at the liquid to make it easier for him to inhale its fumes.

"Wake up." She shook him by the shoulder again. "How can you sleep like this?"

The thinner had no effect. Melissa put it back. She found the lantern, lit the candle with a match. She investigated the medication on the bedside table. Salicex. Profineril. Dormepam. She knew Mom used those last ones when she was struggling. She said they helped her sleep. Melissa held the box to the lantern, illuminating the text on the back. Although it was in Spanish, she understood the meaning of *6 horas*. She looked out at the dark sky speckled with stars. She tried to calculate how long ago Dad would've gone to bed.

"I'm going to wait," she whispered to Rick. "Please wake up before dawn."

From the same chest of drawers that contained the tempera, Melissa took a sketchbook. She flicked through the pages until she came to a blank one. From a can of pencils on her desk, she selected the sharpest. Then she moved the chair next to the bed. Sitting in front of Rick, in the orangey light of the lantern, she removed the hair from her face with her pinkies and began to draw him. The angle of his jaw was her first stroke. She kept true to the position he was in—lying flat, covered in the sheet up to the chin, his head resting on the pillow. But she ignored the wounds on his forehead, the cut on his nose, the bruises on his cheeks. In her drawing, Rick was a healthy guy sleeping peacefully on a bed that could've been his own.

The final detail she added to the portrait was his eyelashes.

The pencil's tip was blunt from so many strokes.

Melissa turned her head.

A yellowish radiance told her that day was about to break, as if the horizon were a corner the sun was about to turn.

"Come on. Please." She pinched Rick's cheek. "I'm running out of time. We need to talk."

Rick felt a tingling on his cheek—a sudden focus of sensation in a body that could have been made of stone. In his state of sedation, he imagined that he was a statue of white marble. And that a pink spot had appeared on his cheek. A scale of human skin. A cluster of living cells that began to infect the surrounding mineral material, spreading throughout the anatomy until it covered the statue in organic tissue.

And that statue coated in life was him.

He woke with a spasm.

When he opened his eyes, his optic nerve smarted all the way to the back of his neck. The pain in each joint made it clear he was no statue. Stone didn't hurt like that. He recognized the room he was in. He remembered what had happened. He tried to move his wrists, but he was still tied up. Pinching fingers were causing the sensation that had brought him back to life.

"You're awake."

Alarmed, he turned his face toward the girl's voice, feeling a stab of pain from his neck to the middle of his back. He saw a nightgown. A midlength head of hair. A stone with eyes.

"I need to speak to you."

It was the middle sister. Marguerite. No, Melissa. Rick scanned the room. He was afraid he'd find Elmer at the foot of the bed, crouched in a corner, perching on a shelf, hanging from the ceiling. That man could come out from between the sheets at any moment and stick his gasoline-flavored fingers in Rick's mouth. Fingers that dulled his senses. He writhed, trying to escape the threat that wasn't there. He ignored the crunches within his flesh, the crackle in the tissues. His body's twisting made cramps spread to his buttocks.

"Quit it, Dad will hear you."

Rick stopped. "Are you alone?"

She nodded.

"Help me." He spat the words out through his teeth, dizzy from the pain that the motion of his eyes had detonated in his head. "Melissa, please, help me."

"Don't worry, you're OK." She rested a hand on his chest. "My parents are taking care of you."

"Melissa, your parents . . ." Rick looked at the face of the girl who spoke to him as if lulling a restless baby to sleep. As if instead of his having broken bones, lying on a rope that bound his hands together, and being riddled with cactus spines, his stomach had merely been upset by some bad food. Melissa's face was a bubble of innocence, ignorant to the truth.

Rick felt incapable of touching her with his dirty, reality-covered fingers, of destroying something so fragile with the information he possessed. "I need a hospital . . . Please, Melissa, tell someone I'm here."

The morning light that began to illuminate the room helped Rick read the girl's eyes for the first time. There was an incongruous maturity in her look.

Melissa removed her hand from his chest. She took a deep breath.

"Are you Edelweiss's brother?"

The bubble exploded in front of Rick's eyes without him touching it. "You know?"

"I was here last night." A film of tears clouded her eyes. "I saw your folder. My parents did all of that?"

If the rope that bound him had suddenly disappeared, Rick would have used his freedom not to tend his injuries but to hold Melissa. The sadness he saw in those eyes hurt him more than his two fractured knees. He squirmed, as if he could somehow halt the loss of innocence, plug the leak with his hands.

"I'm sorry," Rick said, as if it were his fault.

He had too often seen the void that hope leaves when it abandons someone. How dull the eyes become after losing the light of expectation. He'd seen it go out in his mother's eyes. His father's. Sometimes even in the ones he saw in the mirror. But seeing it happen in the eyes of a young girl was heartbreaking.

"I'm so sorry," he repeated.

Melissa stroked her stone and pressed it against her belly.

"My parents did all of that?"

Her eyes traveled around the room, filling with tears as they paused on certain locations. Family memories that no longer had the same meaning, Rick guessed. Maybe she was looking at pen marks on the door frame that recorded her growth. Or some old toy that her parents had given her years ago.

"I'm the baby from the orphanage, right?" she blurted out. "In your articles. Those ones are the stories about me."

Rick nodded.

The way she lowered her head and looked at her feet moved him.

"They didn't steal me from a family," she said to the floor.

"But they did your sisters. Like Edelweiss, my sister. Her name was Elizabeth."

Melissa wiped her tears.

"I read about it. It's a very pretty name." She sniffed. "Though I like Edelweiss more."

He conceded with a nod.

"She was a great sister," she whispered. "The best."

"She was?" The pain disappeared from his body, numbed by a warm feeling of happiness.

"It was her that gave me the idea to put eyes on my stones. And on the cactuses. She knew that I felt lonely here, so far away from everything, that I wanted to talk to other people. One day she showed up in my room, right here, with four rocks and an old movie magazine. Between the two of us we found the nicest eyes from all the pictures and brought the stones to life. We did the mouths with a paintbrush." Melissa traced a smile on her own face. "Dad brought the magazines for her, and now he brings them for me. Edelweiss liked the photos of the actors. See that drawing of her with the guitar and a towel on her head?" She pointed at one of the portraits on the wall. "We were copying a photograph of an actress. She never saw the movie, or heard the song she played, but she loved the picture."

Rick recognized a scene featuring Audrey Hepburn. He remembered how his mother had cried watching the movie at the theater, unaware there was a drawing of her missing daughter imitating that image. When the melody his mother had whistled for days, the tune the actress played on her guitar in the movie, played in his head, the anesthesia of happiness stopped working. The pain returned, to the joints and to the muscles, but it was a pain so deep he wasn't sure it was just physical.

"You don't know how much I'd have liked to have known her . . ."

As he had just done, Melissa said sorry, even if what had happened had nothing to do with her. From a chair beside the bed she retrieved a sketchbook. She left the pencil on the bedside table.

"I did this."

She turned the book around. He saw himself reproduced on the paper, his face repeated on the page as if it were a mirror. Although he hadn't seen himself since the truck hit him, he knew Melissa had left out his injuries. The burning sensation on his forehead and the palpitations in his right eyebrow couldn't belong to that unscathed face drawn in pencil.

"Your eyes are like Edelweiss's," Melissa noted.

"They're our mother's eyes." The whistled melody returned to his mind. "That's how I recognized Elizabeth in the drawing you showed me in the living room."

Melissa tried to take his hand, but trapped as it was under the sheet, she ended up resting hers on his chest.

"Why've you covered yourself up like this? Aren't you hot?"

"Melissa . . ." He hesitated, reluctant to pop the bubble with his fingers. "Your parents have me tied up."

"Tied up?"

She took a step back.

"I need your help, Melissa. Can you make a call?"

"We don't have a phone."

"Walk to another house, the nearest one."

"There aren't any near here."

"Drive? Do you know how to drive?"

"I'm thirteen."

"Then tell someone, your sister. Tell Iris. Have you told her . . . ?"

She shook her head.

"Tell her I'm tied up. That your parents aren't making me better. That I need help."

Melissa held her hands to her face. She moved them to her ears as though toying with the possibility of covering them so she couldn't hear. As if she wanted to stop hearing.

"What will happen to my parents? And to us?"

Rick opened his mouth to say something, but closed it without uttering a word. He didn't want to lie, nor was it wise for him to tell the truth. He fell silent while the furrows on her forehead changed shape and anguished whimpers emerged from her throat. She scraped the palms of her hands against her stone. The girl in front of him had to decide whether to help a stranger—and in doing so, destroy her parents, break up her family, and end the life she knew—or do nothing so that everything would stay the same.

Rick was gripped by the certainty that he would die in that bed.

"I've often felt I don't belong in this place." Melissa looked up at the ceiling. "Sometimes my family don't understand me. I can't talk about my stuff with Mom. I've wished I could live somewhere else. With more people. In a city. To have friends other than my sisters, some rocks, and a few cactuses."

"You can have all of that," Rick whispered.

"I could?" A flicker of a smile lit up her face for an instant.

"You could. A new life. Somewhere else."

The first rays of sun poured in through the window and lit up the wall of portraits. The appearance of the band of light caught Melissa's attention, as it did Rick's. The flecks of dust shining in the amber glow of dawn created a veil of sparkles that gave the portraits a magical quality. Like memories floating in a golden consciousness, in a perfect past.

"They're my parents," Melissa said.

The affection with which she looked at the pictures tightened the grip of terror on Rick.

"You have to help me." His voice took on a pitiful tone. "Please, Melissa, you have to do something."

A floorboard creaked outside the room.

Melissa looked at the door.

"It's Dad."

"Untie me," Rick pleaded. "At least untie me."

Melissa searched for the edge of the sheet at the side of the mattress.

"It's tucked under."

She tugged on it, making the bed shake with each attempt. Rick clenched his teeth, confronting the pain that each jolt caused. The headboard banged against the wall.

"He's going to come in," Melissa whispered. "I have to go."

"Please, do something. You have to help me."

"He's going to see me . . ."

Melissa moved away with an arm stretched out toward him, as if struggling to separate herself from the bed, to leave him there. She closed the sketchbook and returned it to the shelf. She put the lantern back and moved the chair.

Through the crack under the door, she could make out Dad's feet.

The key entered the lock.

Melissa climbed onto the desk.

The handle turned.

From the other side of the window, standing on the porch roof, Melissa gave Rick a look in which it was impossible to read whether fear, sadness, guilt, or affection carried the most weight.

Elmer walked into the room.

The desk was still rocking.

The gasoline smell that accompanied him was weaker than at other times, but Rick could still taste it on his palate. He began coughing to distract Elmer from the empty frame through which Melissa had just disappeared.

Elmer didn't bother tending to him. He went straight to the window.

He leaned out and grunted in suspicion.

Rick closed his eyes, held his breath.

He feared the worst.

"Hi, Dad," he heard Melissa yell.

Her voice sounded far away, as if she was wandering the land.

"Up already?"

"I couldn't sleep. It's so hot in the living room as soon as the sun hits it." Her casual tone was believable. "I'm going to speak to my cactuses."

Rick breathed out. He opened his eyes a crack.

"The dawn's so beautiful from your bedrooms," Elmer yelled. "The whole desert, just for you girls."

"The best thing is that the first place the sun shines is on the portraits."

He turned toward the wall. Then he gave his daughter a thumbs-up, sticking his arm out through the broken pane.

That was when Rick saw Melissa's pencil on the bedside table.

She'd left it among the medicine boxes.

His body made an instinctive attempt to grab it, but his wrists were still tied, however much his nervous system refused to accept it. He considered blowing at the pencil but gave up on the idea when he imagined it rolling along the floor to Elmer's feet.

Elmer turned around.

Rick closed his eyes. He slowed his breathing to pretend to be sleeping, though his heart rate demanded otherwise. In the darkness of his mind, a single thought twinkled.

That Elmer must not see the pencil.

The bedframe moved slightly to the left when Elmer leaned against the other side. Perhaps he was observing Rick, deciding what to do with him. Or with his corpse.

"What're we going to do with you?"

Rick slowed his breathing. He could hear the floorboards dip under Elmer's weight. He was at the bedside table. Moving medicine boxes around. Paper rustled. The water bubbled in the glass as it filled. Elmer folded some cardboard. There was a metallic tear, a plastic cracking sound. The sequence was repeated twice more. He was taking out the pills.

The fingers invaded Rick's mouth. The taste of gasoline turned his stomach. After a fingernail scraped the roof of his mouth, the edge of the glass touched his lips. He felt the tablets roll on his tongue. He received the water with such eagerness, the dry tissues of his throat hurt as they crackled.

But forcing himself not to swallow hurt even more.

He let the liquid escape slowly from the corners of his mouth, as if it were a meaningless trickle, so that Elmer wouldn't suspect that he wasn't swallowing the medicine. The lack of air made Rick feel like his head was inflating. It burned. He couldn't hold on much longer.

Elmer left the glass on the bedside table.

He walked to the door.

He locked it from the outside.

Rick spat out the water as he regained his breath. He choked. The coughing hurt his ribs and every muscle down to his ankles. Even so, he smiled when he spat the three pills onto the pillow. One rolled off the pillow and fell onto the floor. Rick sucked the wet sheet to quench his thirst.

Melissa sat in front of her cacti with Clark between her legs. The sand scraped her backside through her nightgown.

"I'm going to need a lot of help," she said to them. "I have to make a decision."

The warm breeze had dried her tears on the walk here. The sun was shining on her face, offering a pleasant warmth. She wanted to enjoy the sensation, but new tears emerged onto her cheeks. She swallowed salty saliva while she told Needles, Pins, and Thorns what had happened.

Pins was the first to ask her a question.

"Tied up," Melissa replied. "He can't move."

Melissa listened to the opinions of each of them, turning her face toward whoever was speaking.

"Of course not," she responded to Thorns. "I want us to stay together."

Needles said something.

"Yeah, I know."

She nodded while he explained himself. Pins added something.

"So what do I do?"

Needles vehemently defended his position, but Thorns took the opposite view. Pins, like Melissa, was unable to make up his mind.

"I could call Socorro."

The idea reignited the debate. Thorns got angry.

"I don't want that!" Melissa answered. "They're my parents!"

Needles counterattacked.

"Iris? I don't know," Melissa said. "Edelweiss?"

She took note of Thorns's opinion. Pins asked a question.

"To have never found out," she responded.

Melissa kept listening to their arguments until the three cacti began to blur. The green of their bodies blended with the colors of their clothes. Melissa covered her face so they wouldn't see her cry.

"I don't know what I should do," she sobbed. "I honestly don't know."

Pins made a joke about hugging her despite his spines, but Melissa wasn't in the mood to smile.

Someone yelled her name in the distance. She turned her head, moving her hair aside with her little fingers. Iris was calling her from the porch. She was gesturing at her to come.

"I'll be back later," she said to the cacti.

She returned to the house with Clark, who hadn't said a word during the conversation. In the kitchen, she found Iris at the stove.

"Morning," Iris said, and broke an egg on the edge of the pan.

She intoned the greeting like a melody and accompanied it with a broad smile. A pinkish radiance colored her cheeks. All of her skin, her shoulders, her chest, seemed brighter, more full of life.

"I said good morning." She looked at Melissa with her hair to one side, her neck stretched as long as Mom's. Even her breasts seemed more voluminous—they wobbled when she stirred the eggs with a wooden spatula. "Why that countenance?"

"And why are you so cheerful?" Melissa retorted.

Iris raised her eyebrows. Her eyes were shining in a way similar to when she was reading her romantic novels. The curve of her lips was the one that having a secret gave them.

"Tell me why," Melissa insisted.

Iris took a while to respond.

"Do I need a reason?" She breathed in as she shrugged. "It's summer, the cactuses are flowering. I'm reading a fabulous book by my favorite author. I'm young. I'm pretty . . ."

Melissa stopped paying attention. She fled to the refrigerator. Iris came up behind her.

". . . and I have a wonderful sister. How could I not be happy?"

Iris planted a wet kiss on her cheek. While Melissa was trying to wriggle out of an asphyxiating hug, the twins appeared in the kitchen wearing their red pajamas. Seeing the display of affection, they joined with their arms open.

"Sorry, I have *three* wonderful sisters," Iris said.

The twins laughed. They buried their heads in the middle of the huddle, as if that demonstrated their love even more. All of a sudden, Daisy pulled hers out, her hair in a mess.

"You actually have four."

"Four wonderful sisters!" Iris yelled, aiming her mouth at the back door. "Sorry, Edelweiss!"

Mom walked into the kitchen. "If only they were like this every morning."

Melissa sensed that Mom intended to join them in the group hug. She broke away before her mother had a chance, separating from her sisters with her elbows.

"Darn, too late." Rose knotted an apron to her waist.

"Is he any better?" Iris indicated the ceiling with her eyes, referring to Rick.

"Getting there."

Glass bottles clinked in the refrigerator when Melissa slammed it shut.

"Somebody woke up in a bad mood," Mom observed.

Melissa sat at the table without responding. She watched her family while she served herself some cereal.

Mom spoke to Iris. "You slept better, huh?" She removed a lock of hair from her daughter's face. "You're radiant."

The pink of Iris's cheeks deepened until a toasted smell emanated from the frying pan. Iris ran to take the eggs off the heat. Daisy and Dahlia pulled on Mom's apron.

"We slept well, too."

"We slept very well."

Their mother knelt down and let the twins cuddle her.

"Are you hungry?"

"Really hungry!"

"Really, really hungry!"

The three of them touched noses in a gesture of animal affection, a mother sniffing her cubs' muzzles.

"It seems to be Melissa who hasn't got used to her new bed." Mom sat opposite her. "You look like you've had a terrible night. And Dad told me you were already up at dawn, wandering around out there. I hope you were wearing proper shoes."

Melissa pressed her tongue against the roof of her mouth so that tears wouldn't give her away. Mom leaned forward. Resting on her elbows, she brought her face closer. She looked from side to side to make sure Melissa's sisters weren't listening.

"Do you want us to put Iris down on the sofa tonight? And you sleep in her bed?"

Behind Mom, where Melissa could see her, Iris held her hands together in a plea, the spatula pointing to the ceiling.

"There's no need, Mom."

"Sure there is, you've spent two nights down here."

Iris intensified the entreaty, interlocking her fingers.

"She's taller. It'd be a tighter squeeze for her."

"You sure?"

"Honestly, Mom, there's no need."

"Sure you're sure?"

"I'm getting used to it now."

Mom glanced behind Melissa, to where the twins must have been.

"Is Iris pleading with you behind my back?"

Melissa turned around. In Mom's view, Daisy and Dahlia were copying Iris's imploring gesture. Seeing them, she let out a guffaw. Even Iris burst into laughter. The twins joined in, bringing Mom with them.

"Well, as long as you two agree," she said to Iris and Melissa, "as far as I'm concerned, you can sleep where you want."

"Where you want!"

"On the moon!"

"On a cactus!"

The twins' silly comments rekindled the others' laughter, but Melissa suddenly lost enthusiasm.

"Honey, don't be so serious." Mom rested a hand on hers. "It won't be for long."

To those words Melissa could now ascribe a terrible meaning.

Dad walked into the kitchen, doing up the zipper on his coveralls.

"How I love hearing you all laugh like that."

Iris went up to him. "Sorry for getting the way I did yesterday." On tiptoes, she kissed him on the cheek. "Mom explained everything."

Her mother got up, placed a tender hand on Iris's shoulder, and kissed Dad on his cheek.

"What have I done to deserve such a lovely wife and kids?" he asked.

Daisy and Dahlia joined the group.

"Now all I need to be the happiest man on earth is for my middle daughter to stop making that sad face," Dad said. "I just need one smile from my middle daughter."

Melissa observed the family tableau in front of her. A few days ago she would've felt inspired to immortalize the moment in her sketchbook, but now she wasn't so sure what the image meant. She pressed her tongue against the roof of her mouth again. This time she wasn't going to be able to contain the tears. Then she saw the twins stretching their lips. They did it in such an exaggerated way that their eyes closed. Then they opened them, puckering their mouths. It was as if they were teaching her to smile and checking how effective their lesson was.

Melissa broke into a smile.

"Done." Dad raised his arms. "I'm the happiest man in the world."

After breakfast, the family went out to say goodbye to Dad. Melissa stayed in the kitchen. From the shelves where Iris kept some of her novels and Mom kept the jar of money, she picked up the science book she'd used for the last time three days ago, when Socorro took them outside to illustrate the lesson on plant reproduction.

She took the book to the living room and sat on the sheet that was still tangled up on the sofa.

She opened it to the first page.

Where Socorro had written down her telephone number.

Melissa looked at the teacher's handwriting. She went over the numbers one by one, imagining how she'd dial them on the telephone at Dad's gas station, to tell Socorro what she'd discovered.

From outside, the twins' laughter reached her. The pickup's engine started, and that was followed by the drag of tires on the dirt. The porch creaked.

"Let's see if Dad can fix this screen door soon," she heard Mom say.

Daisy sped through the front door, aboard an imaginary airplane. Dahlia pursued her with her arms stretched out on either side. They landed in the kitchen. Before Mom or Iris came into the living room, Melissa turned to another page in the book. A schematic diagram on lepidopteran metamorphosis appeared in front of her.

"You're unbelievable," Iris said when she saw her. "Studying on your vacation?"

Melissa didn't bother to look up.

"Leave her be, will you?" Mom intervened. "Go see what the girls are doing. I don't think they're clearing up breakfast."

Mom sat on the sofa next to her. "Honey, the vacation's for relaxing."

She tried to close the book, but Melissa kept it open.

"Socorro told me I could call her if I felt like talking to someone."

Mom's back tensed. "And you can't talk to me? Isn't your mother enough?"

"To someone from outside." She looked away. "To talk about other stuff."

"And bother a teacher in her free time? The classes have finished for her, too, remember."

Iris spoke from the kitchen. She had Daisy on her back. "Calling the teacher in the summer," she snorted. "I've never heard anything like it."

"Never heard anything like it! Gee-up!"

Mom shushed them, waving her hand so that they'd leave her and Melissa in peace. They broke into another trot in front of the refrigerator.

"But if I wanted to call her," Melissa went on, "what would I need to do?"

"I don't think a teacher—"

"She's more than a teacher to me, Mom. She's my friend."

"You'd have to go to the gas station with Dad"—Mom's lips hardened—"and that's a headache for everyone. Nobody's going to bring you back, so you'd have to spend the whole day there."

Melissa bit the inside of her lip. She wasn't even sure she wanted to call Socorro. She thought of Rick's eyes pleading for help from the bed. She looked at the window, at the land outside. She remembered the conversation with Needles, Pins, and Thorns.

"Can we ask Dad later?"

Mom took a while to respond.

"All right." Her face relaxed. "If it means that much to you, we'll ask him later. But you can forget that book. You're on vacation."

She snatched it from Melissa's hands without giving her the chance to argue and went off to the kitchen. The book made a clapping sound as she dropped it onto the dining table.

"Melissa wants to talk to the teeeacher," the twins taunted her from there. "Melissa wants to talk to the teeeacher . . ."

Melissa didn't respond to the provocation. She gathered up the sheets, folded them, and shook the cushions.

Rick heard Elmer's truck starting up. Through the window he saw the plume of dust moving away along the dirt track.

For the first time, he was awake after Elmer had left.

He began to squirm under the sheet. The pills that he'd spat onto the pillow rolled onto the mattress.

He screamed through clenched teeth after every twist.

After an agonizing minute, he no longer knew why he was moving around, or whether the suffering was worth it. He knew that letting himself be sedated again would have gotten him nowhere. As would remaining immobile. But struggling under the sheet with no chance of freeing his wrists or escaping seemed like an act of masochism.

Suicide.

Repeated lifting of his shoulders finished the work that Melissa had begun at dawn, when she tried to free the sheet from under the mattress before her father came in. Feeling the tightness of the material ease, Rick smiled. The skin of his cracked lips smarted as it split. He rocked himself from side to side, biting his tongue to distract himself from the pain in his legs. By swaying side to side, he managed to tip the sheet off, leaving himself uncovered.

"And now what?" he asked out loud.

A deep sigh deflated him when he looked at his naked body. Not just because of his injuries, but because of how obvious it was that any attempt to escape would be futile. His dislocated legs couldn't hold him up—he could barely even move them. His hands were no use, tied up as they were.

Seeing the pencil on the bedside table reminded him of Melissa.

His only chance of salvation rested with that girl.

He tried to blow it off. A pencil on the floor would be less suspicious than one placed on the bedside table. With a little luck, it would roll under the bed and disappear from sight. Propelled by Rick's puff, the pencil swiveled, pivoting on a single point on the tabletop.

Rick blew again. His lungs burned.

The pencil turned like a propeller, without moving from its place. The tip brushed against a crumpled medicine leaflet.

"Come on."

When Rick blew again it provoked a coughing fit that made his ribs ache. He jerked his body against the bed in an attempt to knock the pencil off. The headboard battered the wall and the vibration was transmitted to the bedside table. The pencil moved toward the edge. He jerked again. It rolled closer. He gave another jerk. And another.

The pencil rolled off.

There was also a creaking sound above the headboard.

Rick saw the pronounced bend in the shelf located directly above him. It was the one where he'd seen Elmer put the folder containing his documents. He tried banging the headboard against the wall once more. A loose nut danced on the bolt that must be holding up the shelf. Another blow almost forced the bolt from the wall. Releasing the fixture would make the entire unit come down.

Through the window, Rick heard footsteps outside.

"Iris!" Rose yelled from the porch. "Come here and help me fold this!"

"Is it yesterday's laundry?" the twins asked.

"Yup, but get out of the way. We need space, they're big sheets."

"They smell like jasmine!"

"They smell like jasmine!"

Rick couldn't understand what they said next.

"What, Mom?" Iris asked.

He considered shouting, calling for help. But then Rose would know that he wasn't asleep and would come up to sedate him again. And any information that he screamed to the girls would sound like the rantings of a sick man.

"Take those corners," said Rose.

"Are they his sheets?"

Rose didn't answer, or did so in a low voice, because Rick heard no response. The twins were chanting something about Melissa and their teacher.

"Do you want me to help you change the bed for him?" Iris asked.

"Don't be ridiculous." He heard Rose shake the material. "Come on, give me that. All right, done. I'm going up. You take the twins somewhere to play."

Rick tensed on the bed.

"You can go see Melissa, she's with her cactuses. She can quit talking to them and pay a little more attention to her sisters."

"We're her sisters!"

"We're her sisters!"

Rick heard lots of sand peppering the wood of the porch. The twins must have gone running.

"Come on, go with them."

"Are you sure you don't need help?" Iris persisted. "It'll be much quicker if we change the sheets together . . ."

Rose said something that was unclear from the bedroom, but the wooden porch stairs creaked under the weight of angry footsteps that must've been Iris's. Then Rose went into the house.

She was coming to remake the bed.

And she was going to find him uncovered.

Rick edged to the far left of the mattress, the side to which the sheet had moved. He stretched his bound hand and managed to pinch the material.

Rose was coming up the stairs.

He pulled with all the strength he was able to concentrate in two fingers. The grip he had proved insufficient to pull the sheet onto him. Rick's wriggling moved the headboard. The bolt scraped the wall, spitting out plaster.

Seeing the young man uncovered, Rose shielded her face with her arms. She guessed he'd freed himself from the sheet. And from the rope. And that he'd lain in wait to leap on her like a coyote. She relaxed her defensive posture when she understood how ridiculous the idea was. With his injuries, Rick wouldn't even be able to sit up on the mattress. Nor could he have moved the sheet by himself, sedated as he was. Rose traced the trajectory a current of air would take from the broken window to the bed. Elmer must have loosened the sheet in the night, and the draft must have blown it off Rick.

Rose went and stood beside him.

His breathing was slow and steady. The pills had taken effect. His bruised body was sinking into the mattress as if he'd fallen from a great height. Rose picked up the sheet from the floor and discarded it in a ball near the bed. With the palm of her hand, she checked the state of the bottom sheet, feeling around the body, the waist, between his legs. He hadn't wet it or soiled it. No need to change it. The appearance of some of the bandages that covered his wounds had worsened. Some of his injuries hurt just looking at them. Rose unfolded one of the sheets she'd brought. She spread it out, clean and perfumed, over Rick's body. Even over his face. It was a relief to see the bruises and fractures disappear under the fabric.

"Forgive me," she whispered to herself.

She proceeded to tuck in the sheet, going around the bed from one bedside table to the other. Then she folded the end covering his face down over his chest. She stretched the sheet as much as possible before securing it under the mattress.

That was when she saw the pills.

Two intact Dormepams trapped under the pillow. Just then, a third one crunched under the sole of her shoes.

Rose screamed even before Rick jerked his body in the bed. The sheet escaped from between her fingers, as if it had been snatched from her. The headboard hit the wall. She heard a loud bang followed by a crash as something collapsed. Rose didn't understand what was happening until a rock hit her shoulder.

Melissa's shelf was coming down.

On top of her.

The board hit her head, and a screw was driven into her back. The corner of a stone struck her on the back of the head. The pain made her dizzy, and she collapsed beside the bed. On her knees, she hunched her shoulders to protect herself from the rocks that rained down on her. The lampshade crumpled. A lightbulb exploded. Medicine boxes were crushed.

When the pitcher fell onto the floor, the water soaked her feet, but the glass didn't break.

"I don't know what you're trying to do," Rose sputtered.

She shook her head, trying to clear her mind. The blow to the back of her skull had made her entire spine vibrate. It felt slack, like the strings on Edelweiss's guitar when she loosened the tuning pegs. She couldn't get up. She rested her hands on the floor. In that animal pose she fixed her eyes on Rick, who was looking at her from the bed, spitting as he breathed. He was laughing and then screaming. Screaming and then laughing. The rocks had fallen on him as well. One of the biggest ones was balancing on the edge of the mattress, above Rose.

"Don't you dare."

Rick stretched the fingers of his right hand.

He made just enough contact with the stone to knock it off.

It fell on one of Rose's vertebrae. A gelatinous crunch traveled down her spine. Her legs went numb. Her pelvis reeled until her hip collapsed to one side. Rose massaged her thighs, her calves, her knees.

"No, no, no, no, no . . ." She saw her fingers knead the flesh, but felt nothing.

On the bed, Rick's eyes, and his mouth, opened wide. He seemed as shocked as he was satisfied at the outcome of his attack. He twisted his neck, writhed on the mattress. Rose grabbed hold of the bedframe and pulled herself up until she reached his foot.

When she used it as a handgrip to sit up, his ankle made a crunching sound.

Rick's scream reverberated against the windowpane. A distant echo reproduced it among the rocks out on the land.

"Be quiet," Rose said.

But she knew her daughters would've heard it. Even if they were near Melissa's cacti. Iris's voice confirmed they had.

"Mom!"

She still sounded far away. Rose let go of Rick's foot. Lying on the floor, she dug her fingers into her thighs. They provoked a flash of pain. A warm tingling sensation spread through her legs, restoring feeling in them.

"Mom!"

The voice was approaching fast. Rose lifted the weight of her body, gripping the mattress. She pounced on Rick, who was still screaming. She tried to shut him up with her hands, but he bit her. Rose took the two pills from under the pillow and sneaked them between his open lips. When he choked, she took the opportunity to cover his mouth. He spattered her with snot when he coughed through his nose. But finally, he swallowed.

"Mom! What is it?"

Iris asked the question from the porch, but didn't stop to wait for an answer. She came into the house. Her footsteps grew louder as she climbed the stairs. Her fists pounded the door.

"Mom? Mom!"

Rose squeezed Rick's jaw. She smothered his face with her chest.

"Everything's fine, honey."

"Rick?"

He convulsed, and the springs squeaked. Rose lay on top of him, crushing torn tissue.

"I'm changing the sheets," Rose improvised. "He has some pain, that's why he yelled."

The handle shook but the door remained closed. Rick's jerking began to subside. The pain or the tranquilizer was subduing him.

"Are you OK?"

"Yes, honey."

"Let me in? Can I see him?"

Rick's resistance waned until it disappeared completely.

"What did I tell you yesterday? Get back to the twins."

Iris stayed at the door for a few seconds before leaving. When she got herself off him, Rose checked that Rick was still breathing. She wasn't sure which alternative she preferred.

He was alive.

The rest of the girls reached the porch.

"Mommy!"

"Mommy!"

"It's OK," Iris said.

Rose sat on the bed, waiting for the pins and needles to leave her legs. She looked at the destruction around her with a hand on her forehead. With her hair wet with sweat and stuck to her face, she left the room. She locked the door and put the key in her apron pocket.

Mom came out onto the porch, gathering her hair in a ponytail that she then released. Melissa noticed rings of sweat at the neck of her blouse and under her arms.

"This heat, it's making me sweat," she said when she realized her daughter was looking at her.

One of her shoulders seemed lower than the other. A recent graze, as red as her cheeks were, ran down her arm. She hid it behind her back. "Why're you staring at me like that?"

Sitting on the steps, her back against the handrail, Melissa shrugged. Mom also had bruises on her legs.

"What's the matter with Rick?" Iris asked.

Daisy and Dahlia were clinging to her waist, taking refuge behind her legs.

"We're scared," they said.

"Everything's fine, girls." Mom sought out the twins' hands and pulled to get them out from behind their shield. "He has some pain. And I needed to move him to change the sheets. I would've been more worried if he hadn't screamed."

"But is he all right?" Concern furrowed Iris's face, disfiguring it. "Is he conscious?"

Mom wet her lips.

"He hasn't woken up yet." She looked to the horizon, shaking her head. "He hasn't said anything since he's been in that bed."

Melissa felt an urge to escape, to run up the road until her shoes disintegrated. To pop up anywhere else, at any other moment. To go back in time by three days, to when Mom didn't lie like she did now. Or at least when Melissa wasn't aware of it. She hugged her knees and bit her forearm.

"But is he getting better?" Iris was insistent.

"I'm doing my best."

With a deep sigh, Melissa looked at the silhouettes of Needles, Pins, and Thorns. She needed to speak to them.

"He's going to end up stealing our pictures," Daisy said.

"He's going to end up stealing our pictures," said Dahlia.

"Nobody's going to steal anything." Mom pinched their noses. "Do you know what it's the perfect day for?"

The twins held hands, anticipating the suggestion that Mom was going to make.

"It's the perfect day for having a picnic, in the shade of those big rocks out there."

Daisy and Dahlia jumped up and down to celebrate Mom's idea. They repeated a memorized sequence of gestures in perfect synchrony.

Melissa made her pencil move faster. She wanted to finish drawing the lizard before it escaped. She'd outlined the head, the body's arc, the position of the legs. When she looked down to reproduce the curve of the tail on paper, she heard the reptile run off into the bushes. It didn't matter, she could finish the rest from memory. She brought the pencil tip to the bottom of the page, where the corner of the picnic blanket was. She shaded the red checks and touched up the contours of the stacked paper plates, the remains of the chicken. She brought out the shine on the pitcher of agua de Jamaica. She perfected the texture of the used napkins, the chewed bones. She added detail to the Aztec sun embroidered on the apron Mom had taken off before they ate. She also improved the brim of the hat her mother wore over her face as she lay in the sun taking a nap. She ignored the bruises on her legs.

She depicted the twins climbing the rock, as they were doing now. They were scaling it and then jumping down as if they were flying. Melissa made the most of another leap to capture the shape of their hair. Next she moved the pencil to the figure of Iris, who'd resumed her reading after lunch. She'd sketched her sitting against a rock, using the knee of a bent leg as a lectern for her book. She looked at her again now, to give more expression to the intensity of her features as she concentrated on the page, but Iris was getting up. She was coming toward her. Melissa made sure the documents from Rick's folder were well hidden among the back pages of the sketchbook.

"Hey." Iris gathered up her skirt before sitting down. "How's it looking?"

Melissa moved her hand away and blew off graphite dust. Her sister let out a sigh of wonder.

"I'm not even going to bother joking that you can't draw. This is amazing." She peered at the drawing with a finger in her mouth. "Shame I got up before you finished. If I'd known I cut such a beautiful and captivating figure, I wouldn't have moved."

"I just need to add that pimple on your chin . . ."

Iris elbowed her. "Don't you dare." She grabbed the butt end of the pencil. "Can you finish me from memory?"

Melissa quickly added the profile of Iris's nose to the sketch.

"You know me to a T," said Iris. "It looks lovely. Anyone would almost wish they could live in the drawing, play with those little girls, lie next to the woman in the hat and take a nap. Or flirt with that refined lady who's enjoying her book so much, I bet she's a very smart young woman."

She paused, waiting for a laugh. Not receiving it, she pointed at the place in the drawing that Melissa would've occupied during lunch.

"But it's a shame you're missing."

"It doesn't matter." Melissa screwed up her face, shrugged her shoulders. "I'm always missing."

"There you go again. Please don't start with one of those depressing interpretations of your drawings. Don't tell me the desert represents the void of the soul, or that the rocks are really monsters that keep the girls imprisoned."

Hearing that, Melissa drove the pencil into the paper with such force that the tip snapped.

"All right, all right. Don't get mad. Your drawings are your drawings. But I wish you were able to enjoy their beauty. And not just because of how they look on paper but because of the reality they portray." Iris lifted Melissa's chin, forcing her to look at what was in front of her and not down at her drawing. "Sometimes I don't know why I'm in such a hurry to grow up, why I daydream about escaping from here in Rick's arms. I wonder whether there really will be a moment in life that's better than this one. Edelweiss dying has taught me that nothing is eternal, and I'm afraid that time will separate the rest of us, too, that we're going to start losing one another . . ." Iris smiled, her gaze lost among the cacti. "Maybe the best thing would be to stop time and stay in a perfect afternoon like this forever, become one of your drawings."

Melissa turned the pages toward the front of the sketchbook, taking care not to let Rick's cuttings fall out.

"Then I'd rather time had stopped here." She showed her sister an old drawing.

"When Edelweiss was here." Iris understood. "Me, too."

Melissa went to correct a detail on Edelweiss's dress. When she held the broken tip of the pencil near the paper, Iris snatched it from her.

"Leave it. It's perfect as it is. Don't change anything."

Iris was still holding Melissa's pencil when Daisy's scream startled them both. Iris saw Dahlia stumble as she leapt from the top of a rock. Trying to find her balance, she trod on Mom's belly and fell to one side on the checkered picnic blanket, knocking over the stack of plates. Chicken bones went flying across the fabric. The pitcher spilled its contents, soaking everything with red liquid, including Mom's apron. Dahlia skidded through the dirt on her hands before coming to a stop.

Iris ran to tend to her, but Mom was there first.

"Let's see, open your hands."

Dahlia was sitting on the ground, crying.

"Open them," Mom insisted, kneeling beside her.

Daisy joined the group the moment her twin sister unfolded her fingers. Mom blew at the sand on her palms. Some grit remained stuck to the bright pink skinned parts.

"It's nothing."

"That's what happens when you think you're a lizard." Iris ruffled her hair. "Do you really think you can run around among the rocks like they do?"

"You're not a lizard," Daisy said, wagging her index finger.

Dahlia sobbed.

"Leave her be," Mom said.

Iris tried to tidy up the mess on the blanket. She got her hands and knees wet as she crawled over the material. A piece of chicken skin stuck to her elbow. She made a face as she picked it off.

"We'll need to soak that blanket right away," said Mom, still blowing on Dahlia's hand. "Take it to the sink. And bring me the iodine when you come back. It's in the downstairs bathroom."

"No!" Dahlia kicked, trying to get free. "Iodine stings!"

"It stings because it cures." Mom kissed her hand.

Iris brought the corners of the wet blanket together in its center. She lifted it, forming a sack. The cutlery clinked against the pitcher as she hung it over her back. She arched her spine when the wetness passed through the material of her dress to her skin.

"Who in their right mind . . . ?" Mom said.

Iris stuck out her tongue.

Then she turned to Melissa. "Don't draw me like this. I'd rather be the sensual young woman reading a book."

She walked back to the house, quickening her pace as the wetness spread over the back of her dress. She dumped the sack near the kitchen sink with a final thrust of her lower back. She regained her breath leaning against the counter, her hands at her chest. She wasn't sure whether her heart was beating so hard because of the effort or because she'd realized she was alone in the house with Rick. She could stand at the door to his room, hear him breathing, even if only for a minute. Say something to him through the crack to see if she could wake him.

She opened up the picnic blanket and took out the pitcher. She removed the plates. The sooner she left this to soak, the longer she could spend at the door. She waved the blanket in the air to shake off the chicken remains. Several bones, a whole wing, fell onto the floor.

And so did Mom's apron.

The Aztec sun looked up at Iris from between her feet.

Unable to believe what it could mean, she checked its pocket with the toe of her shoe. She felt something hard. She made the blanket into a ball, put it in the sink, and turned on the water. She knelt over the apron and, with her fingers, confirmed that the hard object in the pocket was a key. Iris took it out. She inspected it, her mouth open.

And she ran upstairs with it.

Being able to kiss Rick in the light of the day would be like announcing their love to the world, leaving the shadowy realm of secrets to nurture their romance like a flower in the open air. She even felt a sense of loss for the nocturnal liaisons that would no longer be theirs.

Outside the locked door, she tidied her hair, curved the material at her neckline. She was embarrassed to let him see her like this, her dress all stained at the back, but Rick would understand the urgency of her visit. She couldn't stay long because she had to take the iodine out to Dahlia.

She inserted the key in the lock.

She went into the room.

The first thing she saw was Melissa's stones scattered across the floor, their eyes looking up at her at strange angles. Some of the eyes had come unstuck. Then she noticed the shelf, collapsed on one side. It had scraped the wall on the way down and destroyed whatever had been on the bedside table. She recognized pieces of curved glass from a lightbulb, and the lamp's cracked base. The pitcher was on the floor.

Finally, Iris's eyes came to rest on Rick.

Her hands acted on their own, covering her face, her eyes, as if someone else, or the most sensible part of herself, wanted to protect her from the horror. She breathed against the darkness of her moist palms, her breath warming her face. It suffocated her. She parted her fingers, opening them a crack through which she could peek at what she had in front of her.

The tangled sheet barely covered Rick's body. It wound around his legs like a cloth reptile. Iris saw bruises on his chest, wounds on his abdomen, yellowish lumps by his knees. One of the bandages, the one that covered the arm he'd hurt while showering, was brown. On several parts of his anatomy she could make out cactus spines still buried in his flesh. Seeing the angle of his right ankle compared to the leg, she felt pain in her own. She let out a grunt.

"What've they done to you?"

She took a step toward the bed. The floor creaked beneath her. She found a whitish powder stuck to the sole of her shoe. She picked up the crushed blister pack. Dormepam. More boxes of the same tranquilizer were squashed under the collapsed shelf on the bedside table.

"What are they doing to you?"

Iris swooped on Rick. She kissed him on his mouth, his forehead, his cheeks. She discovered the dozens of wounds that the darkness had stopped her from seeing the previous night. She stroked the roughness of his stubble. A fevered trembling took hold of him. She held the glass of water to his lips. He didn't react. She gave him a drink from her own mouth. She searched for his hand under the tangled sheet.

At first she didn't know what the bumpy texture she found could be. She followed it with her fingers. It went around Rick's wrist.

Rope.

But it couldn't be rope.

Mom and Dad would never do anything like that.

She lifted the sheet.

Mom yelled outside. "Honey! Come on, I need that iodine!"

Iris barely understood what Mom was saying. Her eyes were fixed on the rope that bound Rick's wrists.

"Iris!"

She knew a voice was yelling outside, but she didn't care what it was saying. It was the voice of the person who'd tied up the hands of her wounded lover.

"They're not taking care of you," she whispered. "What are they doing to you, my darling? Are they trying to keep us apart?"

She asked the question very close to his face.

"Iris!" The yelling continued outside.

"But they will not defeat us." Iris's enraged declaration spattered Rick with saliva. "I'll go for help. You're going to be OK."

"Iris!"

The voice sounded closer. She heard Dahlia crying. Through the window, Iris saw that Mom was walking back to the house, pulling the little girl along behind her. Her strides quickened.

Iris had to move.

She considered spreading the sheet out to cover Rick, to alleviate his shivering, but it would betray her visit.

"Forgive me."

She left the sheet as it was. She checked the collapsed shelf, the bedside table, the floor. With her foot she pushed the trampled blister pack under the bed. She brushed the powder off her sole.

Mom's footsteps sounded close.

Iris left the room and locked the door. She ran downstairs, skipping steps as she went. She passed the front door the moment Mom reached the porch, and collected the bottle of iodine from the bathroom. In one leap, she reached the kitchen. She slipped on the water that had overflowed from the sink. She gripped the counter to stop herself from falling. She'd left the faucet on. She turned it off.

Mom was inside the house.

"Iris!"

Iris had the key in her hand. The apron was in the middle of the puddle of water. She crouched down and returned it to the pocket. She looked around, searching for some excuse for her delay. Opening the bottle of iodine, she poured it on the table, as well as on her dress. She turned around just as Mom arrived in the kitchen doorway.

Iris saw Mom's eyes inspecting the room. They didn't stop on the puddle on the floor. Or on the dark stain on her daughter's dress. They kept scanning until they located the apron. She crouched down to reach it, resting the toe of her foot in the water. She felt its contents. Her shoulders relaxed when she recognized the shape of the key. She tied the apron to her waist as if it wasn't wet.

"What happened?" she asked. "What took you so long?"

Dahlia was whimpering beside her.

"I don't know what happened with the sink, it overflowed. And to top it off this opened on me." Iris showed her the iodine bottle. "Who knows how I'll get this stain out now."

She rubbed a cloth against the mark on her dress, fighting against the stain the way she wanted to fight her mother.

"It's no big deal," Mom said. "We'll put it in the washing machine later."

Iris scrubbed with such energy that the material burned her knuckles. Mom grabbed her wrist.

"Stop."

She picked up the iodine bottle and shook it near her ear to check whether any of the solution was left in it.

"Clean that up before it soaks into the wood." She gestured at the orangey puddle on the table. "I'm going to the bathroom with Dahlia."

"Not iodine!" the little girl yelled on the way. "It stings!"

Iris tried to control her breathing while she wiped the table with the cloth. The liquid had reached Melissa's science book. Mom had left it there in the morning. She picked it up by a corner and shook it, spattering her dress. She dried the cover and opened it to deal with the wet pages. On the first page appeared a name, along with a number.

Socorro's telephone number.

Iris looked through the kitchen window.

Her eyes fell on the Dodge parked outside.

Screams came from the bathroom. "Ow, ow, ow, ow, ow . . ."

"Keep still now, I have to dab it with the cotton ball."

"Ow, ow, ow, ow, ow!"

Mom reappeared in the kitchen.

"I'll trade you taking care of your sister for cleaning up this mess." She held out her arms, offering Iris the cotton balls and the bottle of antiseptic. "At least I know the mop isn't going to kick and scream."

Iris glanced sidelong at the truck and dropped the cloth on top of the iodine spill.

"All yours."

Before leaving the room, Iris put the science book on its shelf. She dodged Mom on her way to the bathroom. She didn't want to so much as touch her.

"Some mood you're all in today," her mother murmured in the kitchen. "And I was so relaxed, taking a nap."

Iris disinfected Dahlia's graze, dabbing hard with the cotton. The little girl began to complain, but soon realized that her sister was in no mood for a tantrum. Daisy and Melissa came into the house when Iris was throwing the cotton balls in the trash.

"Are you OK?" Daisy asked.

Dahlia nodded doubtfully, exaggerating her condition.

"Are you going to be able to keep playing?"

"Sure she is," Iris replied, "it's nothing, let's go outside."

As they left the bathroom, Mom spoke to them from the kitchen.

"That's it, you just relax, your mother's here to do everything." She was wringing out the mop with her hands. "Honey, don't look like that, it was a joke."

Iris tried to force a smile, but it came out as a weird tic that barely lifted the corner of her mouth.

"You're not going to change your dress?"

"When I get back"—she pushed her sisters toward the porch—"I'm going to get it dirtier at any rate."

Outside, Melissa settled into the porch swing with her sketchbook. Daisy and Dahlia sat on the steps. Iris looked at the Dodge, biting the inside of her cheek. She encouraged the twins to play on the land, gesturing at the area near the truck. They whispered to each other.

"We've been in the sun too long," they said at the same time. "We feel like staying in the shade."

"Are you really going to pass up a visit to the House of Crazy Mirrors?"

The twins looked at each other. The dents in the vehicle's body-work caused distorted reflections that always made them laugh. After whispering something in each other's ear, they shot off in that direction. Melissa snorted. The whole family used that trick any time they wanted some peace and quiet on the porch.

"It's not that." Iris turned around. "I'm going with them. So I can make sure Dahlia's careful with her hand."

Melissa raised her eyebrows.

"All for me, then." She stretched her legs out on the swing.

Iris went after the twins.

Daisy and Dahlia were looking at themselves in the truck doors, in the grille, in the bumper. They were blowing up their cheeks or curving their arms to one side of their body to accentuate the distortion. They laughed at each reflection, seeing themselves very tall, very fat, or very thin.

Iris climbed into the vehicle, on the passenger's side. She sat there side-on, her legs hanging out. If Mom looked from the kitchen, she'd think she really was watching the twins. She laughed louder to blend in with the scene, while checking with a quick glance to see if the key was in the ignition. It wasn't. She sent the twins to the rear of the Dodge, telling them that the license plate made a great mirror. She took the opportunity to fold down the sun visor.

The key fell onto the seat.

Daisy and Dahlia laughed when they saw the crazy shapes that their sister's body took on when she joined the game. But Iris didn't stop looking up at Rick's window, mentally pleading with him to hang on, to wait. Between her legs she felt the heat of the key she'd hidden in her underwear.

Rose returned to Rick's room when the orange sun was just perching on the horizon. At that time of the evening, the stones scattered around the room projected elongated shadows on the floor. From the broken window, Rose saw Melissa talking to her cacti. She was waving her arms in a heated way, which was rare in her conversations with them. She spotted the twins lying on their backs on the ground near the truck. They were opening their arms and legs, making angels in sand turned purple by the dusk. She knew Iris was on the porch, reading. The swing's rhythmic squeak reached the bedroom.

Rick was snoring with his head twisted on the pillow, the sheet entangled with his legs. His dislocated foot had swollen until it hid the ankle. Rose looked away. The aftermath of their struggle was still fresh in the room, and on her body. Her right shoulder still hurt, and cleaning the kitchen had only made it worse. The strange sensation that her spine was out of place hadn't subsided. She counted three bruises on her legs.

Rose gathered up Melissa's stones and piled them in a corner, making sure the faces were the right way up. Two of them had lost their eyes yet smiled even in their blindness. She also tried to straighten the shelf, but the side still screwed to the wall restricted her movements. She tidied the bedside table by rebuilding the crushed medicine boxes, standing the lamp up. She threw the remains of the lightbulb in the wastebasket and picked up the pitcher. On the floor she found some crushed pills she swept with her foot.

There was a trampled blister pack under the bed—she must have kicked it under while they struggled. When she returned it to its box and saw all the sedatives together, an idea cast a shadow over Rose's thoughts. Her eyes fell on the pitcher, then the glass. They strayed to Rick's face and back to the pills.

She disentangled the sheet from between the boy's legs. When she walked around the bed to cover him, she caught a glimpse of a golden sparkle on his face. A shining filament seemed to be floating above his mouth, bobbing on his breath. Rose took a closer look. Hooked on his stubble was a hair. A blonde hair. It ran down part of his cheek to the chin before continuing down the neck and finally tangling with the hair on his chest. Rose pulled it off. She pinched an end in each hand, establishing its length. It was as long as Iris's.

"*What?*"

The word escaped her lips like a pant. A weight heavier than all of Melissa's stones crushed her chest, making it hard to breathe. The breeze that came in through the window made the hair flutter. She looked at the broken glass. She walked to the window frame and leaned out. Her eyes followed the roof to Iris's bedroom. She imagined her daughter's feet treading those tiles in the night.

"She couldn't have."

Her heart was beating hard in her constricted chest. She left the room, locking the door. She went into Iris's bedroom and searched the book-lined shelves, the wardrobe, the dressing table. She rummaged among the powder compact, the hairbrush, the perfume. She spun around, scanning the room, with no clear idea of what she expected to find.

She looked under the bed.

As she crouched, her own hair fell in front of her eyes, and the sun's rays landed on it as they had on Iris's. Could it be that the hair she found on Rick's face hadn't belonged to Iris? It was Rose herself who'd fought with him. And it was also she who'd lain on top of him. One of her hairs could easily have gotten caught in his stubble. One of the strands that was as long as her daughter's.

Rose breathed out, kneeling beside the bed.

"You're being paranoid," she told herself.

She let go of the sample of hair she still held in her fingers. She used the mattress to lift herself up, which caused it to shift on the box spring. The corner of some unknown material poked out from underneath.

Rose pulled on it.

She found herself holding a dusty ball of white cloth.

Her jaw dropped when she stretched out the T-shirt.

Outside, in the distance, the usual plume of dust announced Elmer's arrival. The sun had just hidden behind the horizon.

Elmer waved his hand through the window to greet Melissa, who seemed to be arguing with her cactuses. The twins appeared off to one side of the truck and ran through the cloud of dust after him. When he stopped the vehicle outside the house, he saw Rose on the porch, her arms crossed. She was yelling at Iris, who was reading on the swing. Elmer ran to them.

"What is it? What's wrong?" He leapt up the steps to reach his wife. "Calm down."

He went to touch the bruise he saw on Rose's neck, but she stopped him, apparently not wanting to talk about it in front of Iris.

"Daddy!"

"Daddy!"

The twins reached the porch. Elmer held out an open hand to make them stop and keep quiet.

"Have you been in?" Rose growled the question at Iris.

Iris took her feet down from the seat and hugged her book as if it were a shield.

"Been in?" Elmer asked. "Where?"

His daughter couldn't hold his gaze—she kept her eyes to the floor.

Rose took a step toward the porch swing and pointed at Iris with a tensed finger. "Have you been in to see the boy?"

The sweat that covered Elmer's back went cold.

Iris hooked her hair behind her ears. "I don't know what you're talking about, Mom. I haven't been in anywhere."

"You've been in the boy's room. Melissa's bedroom. Through the broken window, over the roof."

"No, Mom. What window?"

"In her room." Rose gestured at Melissa, who was arriving at the porch.

"Her window's broken?" Iris didn't blink. "I don't know what you mean. I haven't been in any room."

"You went in there. You've spoken to him."

Elmer took his wife by the shoulders. "Relax." He raised his eyebrows to get her to mind what he said. "She says she hasn't been in."

"What've you seen?"

"I haven't been in there."

"What have you seen?" Rose's voice had turned into a sob.

Elmer shook her to make her stop. Some pain in her shoulder made her groan.

"She's seen something . . ."

"She says she hasn't gone in there. Let's stay calm and hear her out."

"I haven't been in, Dad. I don't know what she's talking about."

Rose snorted and fixed her eyes on Iris. "I found a hair—this long—on the boy's face."

"A hair?" Iris screwed up her nose. "And why would it be mine? It could be Melissa's. Or yours. Even the twins'."

Elmer noticed that Melissa was listening to the conversation with her eyes on the ground, watching the argument from behind a curtain of her own hair. She was pressing one of her rocks against her belly.

"Please, Iris, show me that you're honest, at least."

"I haven't been in that bedroom, Mom."

Rose shrugged with a deep sigh. She pulled something out from behind her back, where it had been hanging from the apron strings.

"And this?" She unfolded Rick's dirty T-shirt. "I found it under your mattress. Where did you get it from if you haven't been in the bedroom? Are you still going to deny it?"

Iris got up from the porch swing.

"I took this T-shirt the first day he arrived. He left it in the kitchen when he got changed." She snatched the garment from her mother. When Elmer tried to separate them, she spoke to him. "You ruined his other one when you ran over him."

Elmer caught the accusatory finger Iris pointed at him. Rose pinched him in the side, gestured at the twins with her eyebrows. He let go.

"Why're you doing this to me?" asked Iris. "It wasn't me."

"It was your hair. I know my daughters."

"I haven't been in there!"

"It was your hair!"

Rose raised her voice. So did Iris. Elmer joined in the argument and the twins began hitting the porch handrail to add to the racket.

"It was me!"

Melissa's cry made everyone fall silent. Elmer couldn't remember ever hearing her speak like that. Rose held her hand to her mouth.

"Melissa . . ." she whispered through her fingers.

"I climbed up there." She pointed at the porch structure. "I do it some nights when I go out to talk to the cactuses. I went in to switch my stones around. I have to sleep with a different one every day."

"I asked you if you wanted me to switch them—"

Elmer covered his wife's mouth to stop her from starting another argument. Rose went down off the porch, hugged Melissa, brushed the hair from her face.

"Honey, why would you do something like that? Put your life in danger for some rocks?"

"I wasn't in any danger."

"Did you see anything?"

"I was in and out. It was dark."

"Did he try to do anything to you?"

Melissa shook her head and pressed her chin against her chest. A tear fell onto the dirt. Elmer thought about approaching, consoling his daughter the way he had when she was younger, holding her face against his chest and stroking it, but he let Rose do it.

"Don't cry, don't be afraid." She dried her daughter's cheeks with her thumbs. "You can't go in that bedroom, you hear me?" She turned her head to include all the sisters in her warning. "If I have to I'll stand guard myself inside the room. You have to understand, that boy's dangerous."

Melissa's crying intensified, her shoulders trembling.

"What is it, honey?" asked Rose. "What've I said?"

Melissa didn't answer. Elmer caught Iris holding Rick's T-shirt to her nose. She closed her eyes as she smelled it.

"What're you doing?" He tore the garment from her hands with a tug. "What kind of a girl am I bringing up?"

The rage that had flushed Iris's cheeks red during her clash with Rose now hardened the angles of her face.

"I'm no girl, Dad. I'm a woman. And I have every right to fall in love with a man."

"Hang on, hang on." He shook his head. "What?"

"Yes, fall in love with a boy."

"This boy?" He held up the T-shirt as if it were roadkill.

"Iris, please, don't be ridiculous," Rose cut in. "You've known him for a day."

Iris moved closer to the steps. "And how long did Marius need to know that he loved Cosette?"

Elmer didn't understand the reference, but Rose was left openmouthed.

"Loved?"

"Yes, Mom. Love."

Rose ignored Melissa's crying. She went into the house and paced around the kitchen. She returned with something in her hand.

"Love a boy who fired a gun at your mother?"

Rose showed her the remains of a shotgun shell. She held it so close to Iris's face that she had to turn away so it wouldn't touch her nose.

Elmer snorted. "I think I've been buying you too many romantic novels . . ."

Iris fled into the house and scampered up the stairs. She slammed her bedroom door so hard that the porch shook. Elmer went after her, but only climbed the first step. Much the way he hadn't known how to go to Melissa to console her, he had no idea what he could say to Iris to make her feel better.

The wind flapped Melissa's nightgown as she stood at Edelweiss's grave. A shiver ran through the skin on her arms. She looked at the cross, using a pinkie to remove the hair the current of air had thrown onto her face. The moon cast shadows in the grooves of each letter engraved in the wood, misshaping Dad's writing. A gust of wind carried off the wilted flower arrangement before she could react, scattering lifeless flowers across the land. Some of them were caught between the rocks that marked out the grave, the ones the twins had decorated with colored beads. Most of them rolled off into the darkness. Melissa watched them fly toward the shadows.

"I don't know whether I'm doing the right thing," she whispered to her sister. "I just hope you understand."

Although she could hear the voices of her cacti and stones with ease, Melissa had never heard her sister's again except in her memories—words that she'd said when she was alive. Now she listened with her face tilted to one side, an ear aimed at the grave. In the distance, she heard the agitated murmurs of Needles, Pins, and Thorns, who must have been carrying on the heated debate from earlier in the day. Clark, whom she held in her hands, wanted to say something, too, but Melissa hushed him. The only person she wanted to hear was Edelweiss. She pleaded inwardly for her to respond, to please tell her what she thought about the decision Melissa had made. She closed her eyes and visualized her sister approaching with her everlasting smile, enveloped in the honey smell of her hair. Edelweiss took her by a shoulder, and she moved her lips, yet Melissa could hear nothing but the howl of the night wind. It roared in her ears, muting the world. When she opened her eyes again, her sister was just a wooden cross with a name written on it in shadows.

"I hope you understand," she said again. "Rick's a good guy."

The hinges on the back door squeaked. Mom poked her head out.

"You still there? It's time to come in, there's a lot of wind."

Crouching, Melissa patted the earth, saying goodbye to Edelweiss.

In the kitchen, Mom was clearing away the final remains of dinner. She scraped a fork against a plate, throwing the food Iris hadn't touched into the trash. She hadn't come out of her room since the fight. Dad was going up to put the twins to bed.

Melissa left Clark on the living room table, on top of the science book that Iris had somehow stained with iodine. She heard Mom turn on the tap, squeeze the dish-soap bottle, scrub something with the scourer. She retrieved her sketchbook from its hiding place behind the sofa and opened it to the last page, where she was keeping Rick's clippings. She'd studied them so many times that she had almost learned them by heart, though she tried hard to ignore the real names her sisters had possessed in their first months, or days, of life. It was also strange for her to read the names of the towns they'd come from, far-off places where they had never really set foot. Those names, those towns, seemed like strange words from a foreign vocabulary, a language invented to tell the gigantic lie that was the other reality the newspapers spoke of. Or maybe the lie was this reality, in which Mom had given flower names to five girls hidden away in a house among the cactuses. Much of Melissa's discussion with Needles, Pins, and Thorns had revolved around figuring out what was more real: the families the sisters had never been a part of, or the one Mom and Dad had created for them.

Melissa turned a page in the sketchbook and fixed her eyes on the drawing she'd been looking at with Iris after lunch. A snapshot in which Edelweiss still appeared, and where Melissa herself could be seen—she seldom added herself to her drawings. It was an image from a family's perfect past. Melissa repeated in a mumble the words Iris had said to her when she'd tried to change a detail in the portrait.

"Don't change anything," she murmured in the living room.

"What's that?"

Mom's voice made her jump. She was looking at her from the entrance to the living room, drying her hands on her clothes. Melissa closed the sketchbook.

"Were you talking to your rock?" Mom sat on the sofa next to her. "Do you want me to switch it for another one?"

Melissa moved the sketchbook over to the side away from Mom, between her body and the arm of the sofa.

"I promise I'm going to do my part to make sure we communicate better," Mom said. "It's pretty clear to me now how important it is for you to follow the order with your stones, and I'm going to try to attach the same importance to things as you do. If I'd listened to you when you told me the first time, you wouldn't have done what you did."

Melissa sighed. She preferred not to hear Mom talk about Rick.

"Are you all right, honey?"

She nodded, even though it wasn't true.

"I want to start proving it to you, so I'm going to ask Dad to take you to the gas station so you can speak to your teacher, if that's what you really want." She pinched Melissa's cheek. "Do you still want to talk to Socorro?"

Melissa hugged the sketchbook that contained news of destroyed families among the drawings of a happy family built on their suffering. They were two realities that could not coexist, and it was up to Melissa to decide which one prevailed. She looked at the science book where Socorro had written her telephone number. Then she closed her eyes. Her mind rang with Needles, Pins, and Thorns's arguments. She also visualized Edelweiss, floating in front of her as she'd just done at her grave. Melissa gave her one last chance to speak her mind, but on her translucent face all she could see was a smile.

"No, it's all right, Mom." Melissa opened her eyes. "I don't have to speak to my teacher."

"Good," said Mom, unaware of the true implications of the decision her daughter had just made. "We're going to have a great summer."

Melissa squeezed the sketchbook hard, silencing the imaginary cries of the people in the articles' photographs—people whose pain she couldn't allow herself to hear, even if Rick was among them.

Mom brushed aside her bangs as if she were a little girl. "You'll have your bed back soon."

Melissa preferred not to ascribe a specific meaning to those words. She pressed her tongue against the roof of her mouth to hold back her tears.

Rose said good night to Melissa with a kiss on the cheek. She went to the window to say good night to Edelweiss. Upstairs she found Elmer, who was coming out of the twins' room, taking care not to make any noise as he closed the door.

"Can you explain to me now why you're covered in bruises?" he whispered when he saw her.

They hadn't had a moment alone since he'd returned. Rose gestured with her head that they should go into Rick's room. She opened it with the key she'd taken from her apron. When she turned on the light, Elmer's eyes doubled in size as he saw the fallen shelf, the rocks stacked in the corner.

"Was it him?" His initial anger turned to disbelief. "Was it?"

Rose nodded. She told him about the pills that Rick had spat out, the loose bolt, and the rocks raining down on her back. The muscles in her husband's jaw grew tenser as she told him how the struggle had unfolded.

"But you're all right?"

"It hurts, a bit"—Rose massaged her shoulder, making light of it—"but we can't keep him here. Not after what he did to me. I swear, just thinking that Melissa's been here, that he could've . . ." Her voice failed her.

She let her husband comfort her, rub her back.

"And what Iris said . . . In *love*?" Rose uttered the word as if it tasted bad in her mouth. She shook her head, biting her bottom lip, remembering Socorro's warnings about the needs of a young woman her daughter's age. "We can't keep this boy here. Not anymore. How long do you think it'll be before Iris tries to sneak in through the window now that I've told her how to do it?"

In the bed, Rick went into spasm. He groaned, shaking his head as if about to wake, but his body relaxed again. His breathing steadied its rhythm.

"We have to do something," said Rose.

Elmer understood. He paced around the room, from one wall to another, with his hands on his hips. His fingers went white from the pressure they exerted. Then he grabbed his chin and squeezed it hard.

"I was about to let him go," he said. "When I stopped in front of him with the truck, there was a moment when I thought about letting him get away, letting him run off through the cactuses. I didn't think I was capable of running him down. I never thought I could do something like that. I didn't want us to be that kind of people. I squeezed the steering wheel"— now he clenched his fists in the air—"accepting that the time had come to face up to the consequences of what we've done."

"What we've done is bring up a beautiful family." Rose stroked his face. "Love our daughters more than anything in the world."

"That's why I hit the gas." Elmer guided her hand to his heart. "And I think I'll hit it again if I have to. Maybe we *are* that kind of people."

"We wouldn't be if he hadn't come," Rose whispered. "If only he hadn't come . . ."

She rested her cheek against her husband's chest. When she noticed his efforts to hide that he was crying, she hugged him around the waist. She didn't ask him why he sniffed, or why he dried his eyes with his wrists. She didn't look him in the face until she knew he'd recomposed himself.

"How do we do it?" he asked.

Rose broke away and went to the bedside table. She spread all the blister packs of Dormepam over the bed and looked at her husband.

Elmer lowered his head, accepting the suggestion. He pushed aside the movie magazines and cans of pencils on Melissa's desk, placing the glass in the space he'd made. He tilted the pitcher in front of his eyes and found it empty.

"I'll go." Rose took it from his hands.

Elmer transferred the blister packs to the desk. He sat on the chair with a sigh with which part of his soul seemed to escape. He began popping out the pills. Rose was hypnotized, watching them fall onto the table with each plastic crackle her husband's thumbs produced.

She didn't even realize that Iris had come to the door.

"I don't care that you're there," she said through the crack. "Rick, hold on, you're going to be OK. My heart is and will always be yours."

The handle shook. Elmer covered the pile of tablets as if Iris had come into the room, though they both knew the door was locked. Rose showed him the pitcher, indicating that she was going to fetch water. She told Iris to take a step back before opening the door. As soon as she went out, her daughter leapt into the doorway, trying to see something. Rose closed the door in her face.

"I'll fill it." Iris took hold of the pitcher's base. "Please, Mom, I'll fill it. I'll bring it up to him."

Rose moved her aside with an arm. "I don't know what else has to happen before you all understand that this boy's dangerous. We're taking care of him. There's nothing you girls can do."

A sudden calm relaxed Iris's face.

"Good night, Rick." She spoke straight to the door, as if Rose no longer existed. "Hold on."

"That's enough. Get back to your room." Rose gestured at it with her chin. "Your sisters are sleeping."

Iris turned away and returned to her bedroom. Rose expected her to slam the door shut, but she closed it gently. She locked it from the inside, as they'd insisted she do these last few days.

"Sleep well, honey," Rose whispered.

She went down to the kitchen without making much noise in case Melissa was already asleep. She left the empty pitcher on the counter. She took the water from the refrigerator, but stopped before filling it. She'd seen something next to the blender.

She went back to the bedroom without the pitcher.

Elmer was crushing the heap of tablets with the glass. After that he rolled its thick base over the pieces, reducing them to powder. He ended up with a pile large enough to fill a salt shaker.

"The water?" he asked when he saw her.

Rose showed him the bottle of mescal she'd brought. The one Rick had drunk from on the first night. With his fingernail, Elmer tapped the glass to dislodge the powdered pills stuck to it.

Iris sat at her dressing table.

From the powder compact, she dug out the hidden truck key. She shook it, blew on it. She fanned the air to disperse the cloud of makeup.

She looked out the window without leaning through it, her back pressed against the wall beside the frame.

Mom had gone back to Rick's bedroom after filling the water pitcher in the kitchen. The light from the room projected a luminous square on the porch roof. Vague shadows betrayed her parents' movements inside.

"Come on, come on."

She was going to set off when they were asleep. She'd tested where to tread so that the boards didn't creak. Made sure the back door in the kitchen was open.

"Go back to your room."

She opened her book on the dressing table. She was unable to concentrate on what she was reading. The letters on the page seemed to rearrange themselves to spell out her thoughts.

She brushed her hair, counting the strokes back from one hundred. She did so with such force that the brushing hurt her scalp. The teeth of the brush caught dozens of hairs like the one Mom had discovered on Rick's face.

"Hold on," she whispered at her reflection. "Just a little longer."

Melissa was looking up at the ceiling. Though she'd been lying on the sofa for a while, she still hadn't closed her eyes. Above her head, hanging from the wall, she could see Edelweiss's guitar, her name engraved on one side of the sound box. She thought of her sister's other name. Elizabeth. She thought of Rick.

She tried to change position, moving onto her side to face the backrest. On the other side of it, between the sofa and the wall, was the sketchbook containing the articles. The people in the photographs, Rick among them, whispered things in her ear. She turned her back on them. In front of her she saw the science textbook on the table. The ink with which Socorro had written her telephone number seemed to be glowing through the pages, making itself visible in the darkness.

Melissa turned back again.

The people in the news stories began to scream at her.

She changed sides.

The luminous number pulsed.

She lay face up.

She read the grooves in the wood that spelled Edelweiss.

There was no way to escape her thoughts.

Melissa sat up.

She separated the sofa from the wall. She took the documents from among the drawings and inserted them in the science book. The sketchbook she left on the table, open to the portrait of the perfect past. Her rock asked her if she was going to take him back to the bedroom, because it was his turn to sleep on the shelf tonight.

"Not right now, Clark. Wait for me here."

Melissa went to the kitchen. From the second drawer, she took out a box of matches.

She went out through the back door.

Elmer handed her the glass. Rose's hand trembled as she took it. She positioned it under the edge of the desk. With her pinkie extended, she swept the pile of whitish powder into it. She could feel her heart beating in her temples.

Elmer unscrewed the lid on the mescal bottle.

"Don't do it . . ."

At first, Rose assumed she was hearing a thought. That her conscience had adopted the injured boy's rasping voice to sound more convincing. But Elmer must have heard it, too, because he looked at her, holding his breath.

"Please, don't do it . . ."

They both turned their heads toward the bed. Rick was observing them with eyes so wide that it seemed he had no eyelids. It was as if the effect of the sleeping pills had not just disappeared but reversed. He seemed focused, alert.

"Please."

Rose lowered her head. She preferred not to see him, or hear him. Elmer squeezed her knee, kissed her on the forehead.

"You don't have to do it," Rick added. The dryness of his mouth was making him click his tongue in unexpected consonants. "I won't say anything. I promise. I came here looking for my sister, and my sister's gone. I don't care about anything else. I'll go away as if nothing happened. I swear. You can carry on living here with the rest of them as if they were your daughters."

"They *are* our daughters."

"Your daughters. You can carry on living here with them. But let me go. You don't have to do that." His body convulsed in a failed attempt to indicate the glass. "Please, don't do it."

Rick's voice was improving as his throat regained elasticity. To Rose it seemed as if he spoke at a deafening volume. She looked at the glass in her hand, the crushed pills. She passed it to her husband before approaching the bed.

"I know you couldn't do that," she said to Rick. "You see your sister in all of my daughters. You think of yourself, of your mother. And you'd like to be able to help those other women."

"Their mothers?"

"I am their mother." Rose gestured at her own heart with such force that her fingers drummed on her sternum. "All those other ones have is blood."

Rick's lidless eyes grew in size, as if inflating.

"My mother was more a mother to Elizabeth than you will ever be."

"You think so?" The remark didn't even offend Rose. A lie couldn't hurt her. "For starters, her name was Edelweiss. And your mother wasn't holding her hand when she took her first steps, right there on the porch. Your mother doesn't know how much she loved melon, or how scared she was of scorpions. She doesn't know how her face wrinkled up when she cried, or how many teeth she showed when she smiled. It wasn't your mother she stole sticks of cinnamon from when she was cooking, or gave a bunch of cactus flowers to as a gift. Your mother didn't know that she turned into a mermaid in the bathtub. She didn't put up with tuneless guitar chords for weeks until Edelweiss managed to put her fingers in the right place. Nor will she ever see the incredible color that her hair took on when the sun went down over this desert. Your mother never had to wash her nightgowns when they stank of sickness. Nor was she by her side, holding the same hand that she'd held that day when she'd taught her to walk, when she smiled for the last time at her bedroom ceiling." Rose dried her tears before they'd even appeared. "It doesn't matter what your mother feels, or if she believes flesh and blood means something. Edelweiss only had one mother. And that was me."

Elmer put the bottle and glass down on the desk. He rubbed Rose's shoulder with a warm hand and kissed her on the back of the neck.

"A real mother doesn't need to hide her daughters," Rick said. "She's proud to show them to the world."

"There's no mother prouder of her girls than I am."

"You even gave them flower names."

"Sure I did." Rose frowned, not understanding. "Because they're beautiful."

"Or because you collected them?"

Rose screwed up her face.

"That's horrible." His dirty interpretation of her daughters' names disgusted her. "Take it back, it's horrible."

"Horrible is what the two of you have done."

"Give our daughters great parents?" Rose looked at Elmer. "A good family? They've had everything they need, everything they—"

"Your daughter talks to stones," Rick cut in.

"We've given them a good life."

"A life that isn't theirs."

Rose shook her head. There was no point in explaining something to someone who refused to understand.

"You're bad people." Rick spoke through clenched teeth.

"And you're so good," she said. "That's why you'd turn us in if we let you go. Or would you have me believe you won't tell your mother? You'd tell her and the rest of them. You'd need to reunite all those other women with their girls, to imagine that it's Edelweiss—"

"Elizabeth."

"—being reunited with your mother. You wouldn't care about destroying this family. Separating my daughters from their parents."

"You're the one who separated them from their real pare—"

Elmer covered his mouth. Rick jerked his body, making the mattress springs squeak. Then he twisted his neck, pressing his head against the pillow, and thrashed his whole body under the sheets, as if an intense pain ran through him.

"If only you hadn't come."

Rose took the bottle of mescal from the desk and filled the glass halfway. She stirred the contents with one of Melissa's pencils. She had to add more liquor to get the powder to dissolve.

Iris had completed the hundred strokes an eternity ago. The light in Rick's bedroom was still on. Her parents' voices reached her from there now and again, syllables that occasionally stuck out in an unintelligible conversation.

"Come on," she said into the air. "Go back to your room."

She switched the cheek she was biting on—the inside of the other one had begun to taste of blood. She wandered her room, tracing one of the infinity symbols in which she'd tended to become trapped these last few days. In one hand she waggled the truck key, the key ring hooked onto her ring finger as if she'd already married Rick.

She imagined the Dodge's headlights looking at her from the ground.

Waiting for her.

"I'm coming . . ."

The winding course of the loop her feet traced reminded her of a skein of wool. She thought of rope. And remembered the way Rick's wrists had been tied.

Iris stopped.

She couldn't wait any longer.

She'd have to change her escape plan.

She looked at the window.

As she'd done the two previous nights, she climbed out onto the roof. In her hand she carried a pair of slippers. She had an urge to peek into Rick's room and resume the nocturnal liaison with her lover, but in there with him were the archenemies of their romance.

The wind whistling among the cactus spines and the rustling bushes disguised the crackle of the tiles under Iris's bare feet. She held her breath until she reached the edge of the roof. First she let her slippers drop, so light that the wind blew them against the front wall of the house. Then she waited for another gust to climb down the post. The creaks of the porch could have been caused by the wind.

Grit dug into the sole of her foot before she'd recovered her footwear. The whirl of air that breached her nightgown cooled the nervous sweat that covered her body. The living room was dark—Melissa must be asleep. Rather than head straight to the truck, crossing the land in view of her parents, Iris skirted around the yard. She disappeared among the night shadows.

Melissa reached the barbecue.

She set the box of matches and the science book on the grill.

From among the book's pages she took out the documents that, in the end, were going to be burned like the rest. Melissa was going to finish the job that Dad had begun, reducing to ashes the unreal names of her sisters, their far-off places of origin, the photographs of the people who belonged to other families.

The first match went right out.

The second didn't even light. It just fizzled, consuming the match head.

Nor could she light the third, the fourth, or the fifth.

The wind seemed to blow harder each time she tried, as if a presence near her wanted to put them out.

Rose made her eyes go out of focus so she wouldn't see her husband hold the glass to Rick's lips. It reduced what was happening in front of her to blurry smudges, like the vague images of a nightmare.

"You're doing this to my mother for the second time," Rick said.

Sitting on the bed, Rose tried to take his hand, an offer of affection that he rejected. He twisted his bound wrist to hide his fingers under his leg.

"Don't touch me."

The blurry smudge that was Rick turned its face away on the pillow, escaping the glass. From Melissa's pencil can, Rose took a ballpoint pen. Using her teeth, she pulled out the tube of ink from inside. She passed the empty outer cylinder to Elmer to use as a straw.

"I'm going to need you to help me," he said.

Rose took a deep breath, and brought reality into focus.

"Hold his head," Elmer instructed.

She went to the other side of the bed, to where Rick was facing. With a hand, she straightened his jaw, the one that had rekindled in her the desire to have a son. With the other, she lifted his head the way she would have with that boy to treat a sore throat with some syrup. Rose wanted to hide her tears, but one rolled down her cheek. It fell onto Rick's face.

"You don't want to do this," he whispered. "Please, don't do it."

Rose looked at the wall of drawings.

"You're doing this to my mother for the second time." Rick spoke quickly now, firing off words as if he knew his time was running out. "She was just starting to get over what happened with Elizabeth. Please, think of my mother."

"I'm a mother, too."

"Don't do it. It's not fair, this happening to her."

Rose felt her brow tighten over her eyes, and her lips went tense. She fixed her gaze on Rick.

"Fairness doesn't exist. Things just happen to people." She let go of Rick's head, discarding it on the pillow. "Every day, all over the place, terrible things happen to people. People kill one another in their cars. Others fall down the stairs in their own homes. Can you imagine?" Rose closed her eyes as she recalled it. "Something bad happened to those women, to your mother, too, like it does to so many people. What happened to them was that they lost a baby."

"You took the babies from them."

"Those women lost their babies." She stopped after each word, as if teaching him a lesson. "Because they're things that happen. There're mothers who give birth to babies that don't live two days. Others, their children are killed in war. There are also mothers who kill their children themselves or abandon them on the sidewalk. Some, their babies go missing. Whether we did it or not, it would still happen. Or am I to blame for everything bad in the world?" She paused, even if she didn't expect a response. "Some terrible things have happened to us, too, believe me. Receiving the news that you can't have children, when being a mother was your life's dream . . . trust me, it's not easy. But did I let it destroy me? No. Did I complain, did I cry about it? No. Alongside the most wonderful man in the world"—she took Elmer's hand, stroked it with her thumb—"I found a solution to my problem. We found a way to move forward. And those women . . . those women have to find a solution to their problems, too. To what's happened to them in their lives."

Rick looked from her to Elmer, from Elmer to her. He was frowning with such force that the scab over a wound on his eyebrow cracked. Strings of white, sticky saliva sewed together his dehydrated lips.

The stitching of sputum broke open when he spoke. "*You* are what happened to those women . . ."

Rick pushed his head against the pillow, as if trying to get away from them. Rose gripped his jaw again. She lifted his head.

"If only you hadn't come," Rose said. "This wouldn't have to be happening."

"We don't want this, either," Elmer added.

He held the glass near Rick's mouth, aiming the makeshift straw at his lips. Rose could smell the mescal. She also recognized the Dormepam, that sticky taste that clung to the roof of the mouth even hours after taking it. The mixture was so concentrated that a whitish sediment swirled at the bottom of the liquor.

Rick pressed his lips together until they whitened.

Elmer tried to push his way in with his fingers. He attempted to lever the kid's mouth open by wedging the pen between Rick's teeth.

"I can't do it," he said.

Rose pulled Rick's chin to open his jaw, but Rick's bite was so strong that his molars ground together. So she pushed his chin in the opposite direction, closing his mouth. She covered his lips with a hand. Her husband gave her a confused look.

"Up his nose," she said.

Rick whined like a crying dog.

With a movement of her head, Rose urged Elmer to proceed. He held one end of the pen between his thumb and forefinger and guided it to Rick's nose, looking away, his face turned toward the window. He was inhaling through his teeth, repulsed by the idea.

"You hold him," said Rose.

Elmer handed her the glass and immobilized Rick in the same way that she had, trapping his jaw. Rose inserted the end of the tube in Rick's right nostril. Rick opened his eyes wide, his breathing accelerating.

Rose sealed off his nose.

She could feel the pen through the cartilage.

Rick stopped breathing. He held on until his face turned purple, but then he breathed in. The liquid climbed up the tube.

It entered Rick's body.

Some of the mescal returned to the glass, but then it climbed up the tube again as if in a closed circuit of tubes with no escape valve.

Rick choked with his mouth closed.

Retches and spasms broke out inside his chest.

When the convulsions stopped, Rose freed his nose. Substances of various densities and temperatures spattered her, expelled at high pressure from Rick's nostrils. Rick's horrified eyes were flooded with something that didn't look like tears. The glass was empty except for some sediment from the pills. Rose took Rick's hand out from under his leg, where he'd trapped it so that she wouldn't touch him. She stroked it until his fingers went floppy.

His whole body relaxed.

"Have we . . . have we . . . ?" Elmer asked the question without letting go of Rick's jaw, his forehead resting on the chest that had just deflated.

Rose searched for a pulse on Rick's neck.

She felt a gentle throb under the tips of her fingers.

"Not yet," she informed her husband. "But you can let go of him. It won't be long."

Elmer released the muzzle.

A barely audible rattle came from between Rick's lips.

"I just want to tell my mother . . ." He moved his head to one side. "I found her . . . Mom . . ."

Rose dried her eyes with the back of her hand. She sought refuge on her husband's chest, letting herself be held.

She needed to hear his firm heartbeat.

But what she heard was an engine starting.

Two spots of light were projected onto the bedroom ceiling. A truck's headlights.

Elmer leapt to the window, throwing Rose against the bed. Leaning out, he held a hand in front of his face to shield himself from the blinding beams. His body was a dark silhouette against the light.

"It's Iris," he said.

"Iris?" Rose's hand flew to her heart.

"She's goi—"

Elmer ran downstairs with half the word still in his mouth.

Rose went after him.

She slammed the door behind her, without stopping.

Melissa was watching the front of an orphanage disappear among the flames when she heard an engine start behind her. She shook the grill to get the fire going, so that the final scraps of paper would burn away before Dad found out what she was doing. Rick's face was the last thing to blacken—it floated up toward the sky as a flake of burning soot that she put out with a swipe of her hand.

The truck maneuvered erratically on the land, the engine's mechanical noises like broken cogs. Melissa identified it as the Dodge.

"Mom?" she wondered out loud.

But Mom didn't drive this badly. The vehicle suddenly accelerated toward the house. It braked when the headlights were almost touching the porch, forming well-defined circles of light on the timber. A frightened shriek came from the cab.

"Iris?"

Melissa recognized her sister at the wheel, fighting with it and with the gearshift. Her hair flapped with every turn of her head.

Dad appeared on the porch.

"Iris! No!"

A metallic screech came from under the hood. He leapt down the steps and grabbed ahold of the mirror on Iris's side.

"Stop!"

"He needs help!" Iris screamed. "I love him!"

A loud roar from the engine propelled the truck backward, dragging Dad with it. His feet lifted up clouds of dust.

"Iris!" yelled Mom, climbing the porch handrail. "You don't understand! Don't do anything!"

The truck spun, threatening to throw Dad off.

"Brake!"

The centrifugal force of the circular skid finally launched Dad onto the ground, where he rolled, bellowing with pain. Mom ran to his aid. The Dodge moved away from the house, forming a swirl of dust among the cacti on the dirt road.

Melissa whispered a question into the air. "Where're you going?"

Then she remembered the iodine marks on the book. She opened it to the first page, knowing what she was going to find. She ran her finger along the torn edge where a piece of the page was missing.

She looked up at the plume of dust that clouded the moon.

She visualized her home burning in the rearview mirror of that truck. When Iris was far enough away, the house would finally disappear.

The truck's jolting as it went over some potholes lifted Iris from her seat. She hit the roof with her head without letting go of the steering wheel. Despite the blows, she stepped hard on the gas. On the passenger's seat was the piece of paper with Socorro's telephone number on it. Bouncing up and down beside that was the key to Dad's pickup.

Elmer folded down the sun visors. He lifted up the mats. He ran his hand along the space between the windshield and the dashboard. He heard Rose go around the outside of the Ford, kneeling in the dirt in case the key had fallen under the vehicle.

"Nothing. It's not here," she said through the open window on the passenger's side. "She's taken it."

Elmer covered his face with his hands, his elbows resting on the steering wheel. He slapped himself. He hit himself on the head, forcing himself to think. He got out of the pickup and climbed into the cargo area. He rummaged through it until he found the large screwdriver. The hammer. Back in the cab, he used them to break open the steering column.

He pulled two wires down.

"Dad?"

"Not now, Melissa."

He searched for a knife in the mess behind the seat.

"What do you want, honey?" Rose asked. "What're you doing here?"

The girl said nothing.

"Why're you giving me this?"

"It was Socorro's telephone number."

Elmer couldn't see what was happening outside the vehicle. His attention was on the wires.

"What's going to happen, Mom?" Melissa asked.

"Nothing's going to happen, everything's fine," Rose answered. "We're just worried about her driving on her own. She hasn't learned properly yet."

Elmer stripped the wires and twisted the bare copper threads together.

"Go back to the living room," Rose said. "I don't like you coming out at night to talk to those cactuses."

Elmer heard Melissa go back to the house. He burned his fingers on the sparks that flew when he connected the wires. Through the open window, Rose showed him the first page of a textbook. She pointed at a torn corner.

"She's taken the teacher's telephone number."

Elmer touched the wires together again, and more sparks flew. He kept trying even when the electric smell began to mix with the smell of burned flesh.

The sketchbook remained on the sofa where Melissa had left it. It was open to the family portrait with Edelweiss. She felt a nostalgia for the past contained in those pages, but also fear in the face of a future holding no more family moments to depict in pencil. In the end, it would be Iris who changed everything, though it had been Iris who'd asked Melissa during the picnic to leave things as they were in the drawing. Melissa felt stupid for thinking the family's future depended on her decision alone. Perhaps the truth always found a way.

Her stone spoke from the table.

"Clark, please, it's not a good time."

The rock insisted.

"I can't take you now." She pointed at her parents out on the land. Orange flashes illuminated the inside of the truck. "They'd see me climb onto the roof."

Clark said something.

"Open?" Melissa blew out. "I don't think they would've forgotten, no matter how quickly they came down."

But the stone persisted until he'd persuaded her.

Halfway up the stairs, she could already hear groans from Rick. Closer to the door, Melissa discovered that they were in fact words. He was mumbling them, as if talking in his sleep.

Melissa gripped the handle.

"It won't open," she informed the stone.

But the door swung open. She hugged Clark as she walked in, pressing his face against her belly so that he wouldn't see the chaos in front of them, the fallen shelf. Melissa knelt in front of her rocks, stacked in a corner. She held her hands to her mouth when she discovered that Natalie and Marlon had lost their eyes. She searched for them on the desk. There were empty blister packs on top of the magazines, a whitish powder all over the sheets of paper. A wet pencil was moistening a sketch, blotting it.

"What happened?"

"Melissa . . ." Rick whispered, "it was me, the shelf, I did it . . . I'm sorry . . . your parents . . ."

He was looking at her with eyes that were all pupil, as if black was their color. Melissa went to him. On the bedside table was a glass with the casing of a ballpoint pen in it. The end was resting on the remains of a substance similar to the one that was crusting around Rick's nose.

"What've they done to you?"

She knew when she saw the empty Dormepam boxes by the broken lamp. When she looked at the used blister packs on the desk. When she felt the powder that had stuck to her fingers after she moved the sheets of paper. She wiped them on her nightgown to remove any trace of her parents' actions from her body.

"Iris has gone for help," she said to him. "She's taken Mom's truck."

A grimace screwed up Rick's face.

"And you? You didn't say anything." He closed his eyes, then opened them again. "You decided to keep your home."

"I'm sorry."

Melissa lowered her head. She expected Rick to berate her. To yell all the awful things at her that she'd imagined the people in the newspaper photographs shouting at her.

"I don't blame you," he said. "I would've done the same . . . This is your home . . . your family . . ."

Melissa wiped away the tears that slid down her cheeks. She sniffed.

"It was Edelweiss's home, too," she said, looking up. And then she repeated the sentence in a different way, even though it was hard to say the other name. "It was Elizabeth's home, too."

Rick's distorted face regained its familiar shape when he smiled.

"Elizabeth . . . Tell me about her . . . tell me about my sister . . . your sister."

His eyes quivered in quick, uncontrolled movements, as if he were sleeping with his eyelids open.

"Hold on. Iris has gone for help."

But Melissa saw the glass on the table. She imagined how big the dose must have been to leave that much sediment. He didn't have long. With her elbows sinking into the mattress, she took Rick's hands.

"Tell me about her . . ." he said.

"Can you look at the wall with the drawings?"

"I don't think so . . . I can't see . . ." he whispered. "Are my eyes open?"

He asked the question with his eyes wide open, his giant pupils focused on the distance. Melissa didn't answer. She'd wanted to show him the drawing at the bottom of the wall, the one of Edelweiss's grave at the back of the house.

"She's here," she said. "Elizabeth, she's very close to you."

A broader smile than the previous one reset his features once more.

"She's here? In the room?" Rick moved his head from side to side on the pillow. He was reacting to stimuli that didn't exist, seeing things that weren't there. "Elizabeth?"

Melissa pressed her tongue against the roof of her mouth, fighting tears that she shed nonetheless.

"Yes, she's here," she said, "in the room."

Rick's eyes stopped on an arbitrary point.

"Right there, beside you," Melissa said. "She's wearing her hair the way she liked most, gathered over her shoulder. With a cactus flower over her ear. Can you smell the honey? It's her shampoo. She used to make it herself. She knew how to do so many things . . ."

Rick took a deep breath of air.

"That dress she's wearing was her favorite," Melissa went on. "She said it came out of the washing machine so white because it was made of real edelweiss petals. And that the four flowers embroidered on the skirt reminded her of her sisters. She's smiling, like she always did. Can you see her?"

Rick nodded at nobody.

"I see her . . ." he said, closing his eyes. "At last . . . Elizabeth, it's so good to meet you, at last."

"She's holding your hand."

"I can feel it." He squeezed Melissa's. "I can feel your hand, Elizabeth. You're just like Mom, you're just like her when she was young."

"She says thank you for coming to find her."

"Of course I came. You're my little sister . . ."

Melissa let the tears flow, allowed them to soak her face as Rick's soaked the pillow.

"Elizabeth . . ."

"Thank you for coming to find me," Melissa said, standing in for Edelweiss, for Elizabeth. "I'm so glad you came."

He smiled as far as his lips would reach.

"I'm glad I came, too," he said. "It was worth it just to see you."

Rick's fingers lost their strength.

"Now we have to go to see Mom . . ."

His hand went limp.

His whole body relaxed.

A sob washed over Melissa. She cried with her forehead resting on Rick's chest. His breathing slowed until it stopped completely.

Rose saw the blood on Elmer's blackened fingers. Repeated rubbing against the copper wires had blistered his skin.

"Come on!" he yelled.

Sparks flew from under the steering wheel, and the engine reacted with a slight murmur that promptly died out. Rose was outside the truck, standing next to him, the door open. The smell of electricity, of hot flesh, was making her sick.

"Leave it."

But Elmer connected the two wires again.

"We wouldn't catch her now, anyway." Rose rested a hand on her husband's. "It's been too long since she left."

Elmer let go of the wires. He collapsed against the back of the seat.

"It's over." He raised his arms, accepting defeat.

"No. We're not going to give up now."

"We have a kid tied up in a bed." Elmer gestured at Melissa's window, then at the road. "And our daughter's gone to tell the world."

Rose paced up and down the land, her eyes on the ground. She walked from one end of a straight line to the other, in both directions. She rubbed out some of the footsteps Iris had left on the day she waited for the ambulance to come. On her fifth lap, Rose lifted her head to suggest an idea, but she remained silent. It was unfeasible. On the ninth loop, she caught a glimpse of the empty sofa in the living room out of the corner of her eye.

"Melissa?"

"What about Melissa?" Elmer asked from the truck.

Rose went up to the porch to peer in through that window. On the sofa, there was only a sketchbook.

"She's not there."

Elmer got out of the pickup. He looked up at Melissa's illuminated bedroom.

"Did you lock the door when you came out?"

Rose felt her face lose its color. She held her hands to her cheeks. Elmer opened his mouth. They both yelled at the same time.

"Melissa!"

They ran inside. From the foot of the stairs they could already see the glow emanating from Rick's room.

"It's open . . ."

Rose was left paralyzed, unable to let go of the newel post she gripped. She didn't want to go up and find Melissa in the middle of her ruined bedroom. Demanding to know why the shelf of stones had collapsed. Why they'd tied up the young man they were supposed to be taking care of in her bed. Why there was a glass on her bedside table containing the remains of sleeping pills dissolved in alcohol.

"Melissa!" Elmer reached the top of the stairs in three strides.

Rose squeezed her eyes shut. She hunched her shoulders as if preparing to hear an explosion.

"Mom?"

She thought the voice had come from upstairs. She pictured Melissa waving the glass at her from there. She even thought she could hear the jingle of the pen against the glass.

"What is it?"

The second question enabled her to determine that the voice came from one side. Rose opened her eyes. Her daughter was coming out of the bathroom with a rock in her hand.

"Nothing, we thought that . . . we thought . . . Elmer!" she yelled up the stairs. "She's here!"

A door banging shut on the second floor extinguished the light that had alarmed them.

"Where else was I going to be?"

Rose shook her head while her daughter went around her and into the living room.

"Have you been crying?" Rose asked. "Your eyes are red."

"I was washing my face."

She heard Melissa slump onto the sofa.

A cloud of mosquitoes flitted around the truck's headlights. The hot air coming in through the window had dried Iris's skin, her tears. The illuminated area in front of the vehicle revealed the dirt track, the cacti that flanked it on either side, the mice crossing in front. Insects exploded against the windshield, detonating with more or less force depending on the thickness of their bodies. The biggest one left a brownish mark in a corner of the glass.

Iris began to think she'd taken a wrong turn, or gone in the wrong direction. She'd been driving for too long. Her foot gradually eased off the accelerator as her uncertainty grew. She pressed hard on the pedal again when, on the right-hand side of the road, a wooden sign appeared. It was nailed to the trunk of a cardón, handwritten in black paint. It informed her that the gas station was nine miles away.

Rose went into the room. She found Elmer by the bed, pressing his fingers against Rick's neck. Though her husband's face made it obvious what had happened, she questioned him with her eyes.

He nodded.

A pain that wasn't physical gripped Rose's chest, or her stomach. She didn't want to connect Rick's death to Edelweiss's, but she couldn't help thinking of her daughter, of how, after a final exhalation, the smile she'd been giving the ceiling had faded away.

Elmer withdrew his hand from Rick's neck. He lifted his arms as he had after he failed to hotwire the truck, accepting defeat.

"And now what?"

"Now we still don't give up," said Rose. "Help me with the shelf."

They pulled on it until they managed to tear it from the wall. The bolts came straight out without the nuts loosening. Rose left it to one side as if they were making some everyday alterations.

"We have to straighten this up as much as possible." She gestured all around the room. "You tidy the desk."

Elmer shook the magazines, dried the splashes. Rose took the glass to the bathroom. Under the faucet, she washed it with hand soap. Remnants of medicine and mescal disappeared down the drain. She returned it, filled with clean water, to the bedside table, placing it next to the pitcher. She made the lamp stand up by resting it against the wall, turning the shade to hide the torn part. She left the boxes of medication in view, except for the Dormepam. She threw those in the trash, along with the blister packs Elmer had removed from the desk and the empty pen they'd used as a straw. Crouching, she tied up the trash bag, then pulled it out of the can. A piece of glass was poking out of the bottom, tearing the plastic. She thought it was a fragment of lightbulb, but it was thicker.

It was a shard from the window the gunshot had shattered.

Rose stared at it.

She was resting an elbow on her bent leg, her forefinger on her lips. A grunt of realization escaped her throat.

"What're you thinking?" asked Elmer.

She leapt up.

"Help me untie him."

Elmer frowned.

"Help me," she said again.

She removed the sheet covering Rick without allowing herself to be affected by the sight of his injuries. Elmer flinched just looking at them. She began to untie the knots on Rick's left hand, and her husband did the same with the right.

"If your idea is to hide him," Elmer said while he fought with the rope, "it'll be easier to carry him, wherever it is, if he's tied up."

"It's not that."

"What, then?"

Rose stopped working on the knots.

"Finish up," she instructed Elmer.

She left the room, taking the trash bag with her. When she passed the door to the twins' room, the handle shook.

"Mommy? What's all the noise?" Daisy asked from inside.

"Are you all awake?" Dahlia asked.

"Let us out," they both said.

Rose swallowed.

"Go back to bed, it's nothing. The stranger had a turn."

"Is he going to steal our pictures?"

"Is he going to steal our pictures?"

"Not if you keep your door closed, no."

Rose continued to her bedroom, carrying the bag full of bloody bandages, remnants of medication, and broken glass. She hid the bag in the wardrobe. From one side, from behind the one long overcoat she owned, she took something out. She returned to Melissa's room, where Elmer was finishing the task of untying the hand she'd left half-done.

"So?" he asked.

Rose showed him the shotgun.

She loaded it with two shells.

The telephone booth at the gas station projected a diagonal shadow onto the ground. Its angle had changed as the moon moved along its trajectory. Iris was waiting with her hands in the pockets of her nightgown. Her right hand toyed with the coin she had left over after making the call. The wind messed up her hair. It also shook the door on the Dodge that she'd left open when she got out.

She could hear the sound of an engine in the distance. A vehicle's headlights pierced the darkness. Iris went out onto the road and waved her arms until the truck stopped in front of her. She climbed, panting, into the passenger's side.

"I don't like being scared like this at all, Iris." Socorro spoke with one hand on her chest, the other on the steering wheel. "Who is this boy? Are you all OK?"

"Let's go."

"Did you drive here on your own?"

"Come on, go." Iris banged on the dashboard.

Elmer looked out through the broken window. The wind was blowing so hard that the crickets had stopped chirping. A black moth, big as a bat, perched with its wings spread on the roof tiles. Elmer didn't bother frightening it away.

He crossed his arms.

Each time he changed the distribution of his weight, a floorboard creaked under his feet. Sitting on the bed, Rose was biting her thumbnail.

They remained in silence.

Until Rose got up. She went and stood next to Elmer.

"They're coming."

"How do you know?"

A purple haze floated over the road, dust clouds colored by the moon and the night. At the tall cactus, the vehicle making them turned down the track that led to the house.

"Let's go," said Rose, tapping him on the shoulder.

She picked up the shotgun that was resting on Melissa's desk. Elmer inserted his arms under Rick's and pulled him up from the bed by the armpits. He bit his tongue to counteract the unpleasant sensation that the crunch of broken bone induced in him.

"Open it," he instructed his wife—his lower back wouldn't take the weight for long. "Come on."

Elmer's knees began to give way, and his legs trembled. The plume of dust had become a storm cloud that threatened to unleash itself on the house.

"Hurry."

Rose opened the door. She headed with the weapon to the marital bedroom. Elmer followed her. Rick's head flopped from side to side in front of his face. The hanging feet entangled with Elmer's legs. He almost tripped in the hallway.

Melissa looked up at the living room ceiling. Her parents' footsteps reverberated above. They moved from the bedroom where Rick was to their own. Her rock asked her a question.

"I don't know, Doris."

Outside, the headlights of a vehicle approaching flashed among the cacti, between the rocks. Standing at the window, Melissa saw her own elongated shadow climb the living room wall and crawl along the ceiling. Socorro's truck stopped, braking hard. Grit rained against the porch.

Iris got out from one side and helped the teacher get out on the other. Melissa had never seen Socorro with her hair down. Holding hands, they climbed the porch steps. The truck's lights were still on, its doors open.

"Come on!" Iris shouted. "They have him tied up!"

Before they reached the door, a gunshot went off upstairs. Socorro covered her head and retreated, dragging Iris with her. Melissa dropped her rock on the floor.

"Riiick!" Iris yelled.

She pulled on Socorro's hand, fighting to go in the house, but the teacher resisted. She held Iris back against her will.

"I have to go! It's Rick!"

Through the front door, Melissa saw them arguing. Socorro grabbed hold of a porch post to pull Iris back with more force. Upstairs, there was a loud bang. Mom screamed. The ceiling shook when something heavy landed on the floor. A body. Then glass shattered. There was the sound of wood breaking. The teacher's face contorted with each noise.

There was a second gunshot.

"I need to go up!" A painful howl tore Iris's voice.

She freed her hand with a jerk that sent Socorro back against the porch handrail. Then she went through the front door and ran upstairs. Outside, the teacher panted as she steadied herself again. After a deep breath, she followed Iris up to the top floor. Neither of them noticed Melissa, who picked up Doris from the floor and went up after them.

She found them huddled in the doorway of her parents' bedroom, looking into the room at whatever had happened in there. Iris turned around, covering her mouth with her hands. Socorro knelt, with difficulty, beside two blood-soaked bodies.

"*Dios mío*, Rose."

Melissa couldn't make sense of the scene she found in the bedroom. Mom's arm was poking out from under Rick's naked body, which was crushing her against the floor. Dad was writhing in one corner, sprawled on top of the wreckage of a bedside table. He was holding his head.

"Rose, *por favor*, answer me." Socorro spoke with her cheek pressed against the floor. "Rose. Rose."

Mom let out a deep groan, pushing Rick from on top of her. He fell to one side, into the pool of blood. Between them there was a shotgun.

"I'm all right," said Mom, regaining her breath. "The blood's his. I'm all right. I had to shoot him. He just appeared in our room. All of a sudden."

"Ay, Rose." Socorro wiped the splashes from Mom's face. "I've just had the scare of my life."

Dad fought with the splintered wood to get to his feet. He planted a hand on the wall to regain his balance.

"What happened?" Iris spoke without uncovering her face. "Rick . . . he's . . . he's . . ." She sobbed into her hands, her shoulders shaking. "I can't look. What have you done to him?"

"Look at your mother. Look at me!" Dad showed her his stained, torn clothes. "With the little performance you put on, we forgot to lock the door, and now look what happened." He gestured at the floor. "Try telling me now that the kid wasn't dangerous."

Iris's eyes were wide open, her eyelashes wet, her jaw hanging. She wasn't blinking.

"Lucky I managed to defend myself better this time." Mom used the shotgun as a cane to pull herself up. "I knew I was right to keep it under the bed."

With her dress, she wiped the blood from a cut on her arm.

"Mom . . . I'm sorry . . ." Iris sputtered. "But it . . . it can't be . . . He was tied up."

"Tied up?" Dad asked.

"That's what she told me." Socorro gestured at Iris. "She called me from the gas station, told me that there was"—she screwed up her face as if about to say something strange—"that there was a boy tied up in her sister's bed."

Melissa looked at Rick's wrists. The blood masked the chafe marks the rope would have made.

"And did she also tell you that she was in love with him? With a boy she doesn't know? Who we offered shelter for a night and who shot at my wife so he could rob us?"

"No." The teacher spoke through clenched teeth. "She didn't tell me that."

"I . . . it's just that . . ." Iris couldn't find the words. "This . . ."

"We were taking care of him, Socorro." Mom gave herself a few seconds to take in air. "They didn't want to send us an ambulance here, so far away, and we looked after him as best we could. Elmer only hit him in self-defense, with the truck, a few days ago, when he saw him escaping from the house with a shotgun, after he fired at me . . . and now he shows up here, in the bedroom, like an animal, in the middle of the night." Mom sat on the bed, fighting to breathe. "And my daughter thinks she's in love with him, and that we're against them being together."

"All very Romeo and Juliet," added Dad. "It's because of all those books she reads."

"Iris . . ." Socorro whispered. She held out a hand to touch her, but she moved away. The teacher turned to Mom. "Did I or didn't I warn you?"

Mom lowered her head, accepting the blame for something she had been warned about.

"But . . . but it can't be," Iris said. "His ankle was broken, his leg was bent. He couldn't have made it here, it's impossible."

Mom's hands squeezed the mattress hard. Socorro tilted her head to one side, observing Rick's body from top to bottom.

"They look bad," she said. "Did he come from the other bedroom to here? With those legs?"

From behind Iris, Melissa didn't manage to see her parents' faces, or whether they were exchanging looks, but she did hear them rush to respond, stumbling over each other.

"He appeared all of a sudden . . ."

"It was at the door . . ."

"Yes, that's right, when we were coming in . . ."

"No, he was coming out . . ."

Socorro let out a grunt of suspicion. Melissa hugged Doris, pressed her against her belly. Wordlessly, she asked Rick to forgive her for what she was going to say. She covered her rock's ears so that she wouldn't hear her lie.

"It's true, he did," she said. "I saw him."

All the faces turned to her. Melissa looked only at Mom's. At how her eyes widened in surprise. At how she frowned, not understanding why her daughter was backing up their lie. She also eased her grip on the mattress.

"Melissa, what're you doing there?" Socorro held her hands to her mouth. "Turn around, don't look at this."

The teacher ran to Melissa and blocked her vision with a hug that buried Melissa's face in breasts that suffocated her. Melissa turned her face so she could breathe.

"What a situation you've put me in." Socorro's bust reverberated when she spoke. She was looking at Iris, her eyes narrow. "You told me they were letting him die."

"She also says she's in love." Dad sat on the bed, beside Mom. "With a thief capable of firing a gun at a mother of three, at my wife." He kissed her forehead. "To take what? A twenty-year-old truck? A jar of coins?" He paused to underline the absurdity of every alternative. "How right we were to live so far away from everything. Sometimes I think the world's full of bad people."

Hearing him say that, Melissa burst into tears. She cried because of the way Rick had smiled in the bed when he felt Elizabeth's presence. Because of the way he'd breathed in to enjoy the honey smell of hair he'd never had the chance to touch. She also cried because of how he had stopped breathing, long before the supposed attack on her parents.

"Don't worry, it's over." Socorro kissed the crown of her head. "You're not in danger anymore, the boy can't do anything to you now."

But Melissa's crying intensified. The rate of her sobs quickened until she choked. Socorro rocked her like a little girl.

"There, there. There, there," she whispered in her ear.

"I don't know what to say . . . Dad . . ." Iris was shaking her head. "Mom, I'm sorry, I didn't think . . . he seemed so nice."

"Go on, go fetch the first-aid kit."

Mom's eyes found Melissa's as she was drying her tears on Socorro's dress. Melissa noticed slight changes in the focus of her mother's pupils, the subtle work of her eyelids. Mom was still trying to decipher the reason for her daughter's actions. The twins' voices interrupted their dialogue of looks.

"Mommy?"

"Mommy?"

They both spoke in Socorro's presence. Iris stopped sniffing. Dad cleared his throat. Mom straightened her back. Everyone's eyes sought everyone else's.

"The little one," said Socorro, speaking in the singular. "Please, don't let Lily see this."

Mom leapt up and headed in the direction of the twins' room with the key in her hand. Melissa separated herself from her teacher and took the key from between her mother's fingers.

"You deal with Rick." She gestured at the body with her chin. "I'll take care of Lily."

In Mom's eyes, she made out a flicker of wonder, of pride. Melissa herself was surprised at how grown up she'd sounded.

She went into the twins' room with a finger on her lips.

"There were gunshots again," the little girls were saying.

Melissa shushed them.

"Don't worry, everything's fine," she whispered. "But you have to be quiet—Socorro's here."

They looked at one another, frowning.

"Do we have class?"

"Of course not."

"You're sure?"

"I'm sure."

"So why's the teacher here?"

Melissa took a deep breath, preparing to lie again.

"She came to take the man away. She's going to take him to the town, so he can keep on walking from there." She said the words as if her mouth didn't belong to her. "He'll be gone tomorrow."

"Yippee!" they both yelled in unison.

Seeing them celebrate Rick's absence made her sob again.

"Why're you crying?" Daisy asked.

"What's the matter?" asked Dahlia.

Four little hands dried her cheeks, tidied her tangled hair.

"Do you have tummy ache?"

She shook her head, forced a smile.

"And now, quiet as mice." She covered their mouths with her hands.

"It's just that he was really scary," Daisy whispered, warming Melissa's left hand with her breath.

"And he wanted to steal our pictures." Dahlia's tongue moistened the right one.

Melissa hugged her sisters. She kissed their little heads, imagining how many times Rick must have wished he could kiss Elizabeth's.

Rose turned off the kitchen light. There was no need to keep it on now that the pale yellow of dawn illuminated the room. She returned to the table where Iris and Socorro were. The three of them had sat there to share some tea when it was still dark. Iris was gripping her cup, blowing on the edge, her gaze lost in the valerian infusion as if the liquid was as deep as an ocean.

"Imagine how bad my husband felt." Rose sat down, retrieved her cup, and continued the conversation where she'd left off. "But I would've run him down, too, if I'd arrived home and seen him running away with a shotgun in his hand."

"*Dios mío*, how horrible." The teacher sipped on the tea, half closing her eyes. "That must have been horrible for your husband."

"We've been caring for that boy to the best of our ability, we removed our own daughter from her bedroom so we could tend to him . . . and look how it all ended."

Rose stretched her arm out on the table, showing them the cut that she'd given herself. An ocher line revealed the wound's dimensions through the bandage. Iris came out of her trance. She stroked the dressing.

"Does it hurt?" she asked. "I'm sorry, Mom . . ."

Rose took her hand. "Don't blame yourself." She stroked it with her thumb.

"How couldn't I? Of course, I must take responsibility." The fact that Iris had renewed her elaborate way of saying things was a good sign. "If I hadn't escaped in the truck, you wouldn't have left the door open, and if you hadn't left the door open—"

"I said, don't blame yourself," Rose cut in. "It was us who invited a stranger into our home."

"But it's not your fault, either," said Socorro.

"I know, I know. He certainly had us fooled. He seemed like a good kid who just wanted to talk to people. We invited him in with the best intentions." Rose clicked her tongue. "You just can't be good, Socorro, you can't be good to people."

The teacher took her hand.

"Yes, you can. Of course you can. You have to be good. Like you are, like your girls are. Please don't lose your kindness. There're bad people everywhere. Even here, in the middle of the desert, would you believe? But we can't let their evil infect us. We win by responding with more kindness."

Iris sighed. "I don't know if I'll ever be able to trust a boy again . . ."

"Iris, please." Socorro took her free hand—the three of them formed a closed circle. "Don't let this episode torment you. What happened here, with this boy, it's an exception. Don't associate the love you felt for that young man with tragedy. Love is beautiful, it's not tragic."

"In a good book it's almost always tragic."

"And do you want to experience tragic love like in your books? Or real, wonderful, uncomplicated love, like your parents?" She squeezed Rose's hand.

Iris looked deep in thought. "I think I've had enough tragic love . . ."

In Rose's eyes, the slight smile that appeared on her daughter's lips lit up the kitchen more brightly than the dawn sun.

"I'm sorry, Socorro," Iris said.

"Sorry? What for?"

"For the fright I gave you."

"Don't be silly. You were acting through love." The teacher guided Iris's hand to her heart. "Don't ever apologize for that. Not ever."

Rose nodded, applying the message to herself.

"You're very young. You still have a lot of love to give," Socorro went on.

Iris looked out at the landscape. Rose knew that her daughter was imagining the love she would find out there, far away from the house among the cacti.

"And you have a lot of boys still to meet," the teacher added.

Iris's eyes opened wide with shock. She let go of their hands to hold in the laugh that exploded in her mouth.

"Socorro!"

"Hey now," Rose intervened. "Not *too* many."

The three women laughed over their cups, like old friends who'd met up for tea. Rose's laughter set off the pain in the bruises she had from when Elmer let Rick's body fall on top of her.

"Are you OK?" asked Socorro.

"It's nothing." She massaged her neck, pressed on the painful area of her abdomen. While she moved, she took the chance to check whether the teacher had finished her tea. "One thing I do need is some rest. It's been an exhausting night. Well, four exhausting days."

Socorro got the message. "Time for me to go," she said. "But if you want me to stay, Rose, to take care of the girls while you sleep . . ."

"There's no need, really." She took a last sip of tea. "Thank you."

"Sometimes all you need to feel better is to be alone with your family, don't think I don't understand that." Socorro got up, the chair scraping the floor. "But one thing I can do for you is call the police when I get home—one less thing for you to worry about."

Rose dropped her cup.

It was left balancing on the edge of the table.

"I'm . . . I'm going to . . . send Elmer to his workmate's house now," she said. "It's closer than the gas station, than your house, so it'll be quicker." She watched the cup teetering, about to fall. "The sooner the police are called, the better for everyone."

"That would be better," said the teacher. "Best they come as soon as possible."

Rose grabbed the cup the moment its weight tipped it over the edge, avoiding disaster. She gathered up the other two and left them all in the sink.

"We'll come with you to your truck," she said, inviting Iris to get up.

Together, the three of them went out onto the porch, which smelled like hot wood. Rose saw Melissa in the distance, near her cacti. The metal of a folding ladder gleamed in the sun.

"Is she collecting flowers?" Iris asked.

"No," said Socorro. "I think she's doing something else."

Rose was annoyed by her smile, by the fact that she understood the actions of her daughter better than she did.

"Melissa!" The teacher waved an arm in the air. "Are you coming to say goodbye?"

Rose tried to copy the gesture, but the cut on her arm prevented it.

Melissa looked at them from where she stood. "Coming!"

She gathered something up in her arms before setting off toward the porch. The ladder's metallic shine was left floating behind her. Rose realized what she was carrying when she reached the porch steps. She held her cacti's clothes.

"That's great, honey." She took a step forward. "I'm so glad you're letting go of them."

But Melissa didn't stop, she walked on to Socorro.

The teacher nodded when she saw the clothes. "You've just taken an important step." She pinched her cheek. "I'm very proud of you."

"I'm going to start being glad for what I've got instead of being unhappy about what I don't have," Melissa said.

Socorro smiled as if she recognized the words.

"That's a great philosophy to live by."

"I learned it from a very wise woman."

The special bond that existed between the two of them sparked Rose's jealousy.

"I have a wonderful family, and a beautiful house in a spectacular place." Melissa said the words with the maturity she seemed to have all at once acquired. "It's all I need to be happy."

Rose blew Melissa a kiss in gratitude for her words. Her jealousy vanished. Her daughter narrowed her eyelids, questioning her with eyes that seemed to have acquired more depth. Then she hugged the teacher.

"Have a great summer." Melissa increased the pressure with a moan, expressing just how much she was going to miss her. "I'm going to say goodbye to my rocks as well."

"Say goodbye from me," Socorro requested.

"And from me," Rose added quickly.

Melissa went into the house with such firm steps that she might have been carrying one of the heaviest rocks from the landscape.

"Where have all the little girls gone, huh?" Socorro put an arm around Iris to include her in the remark. "Your house is filling up with *mujeres*. Next term I won't have anything to teach you."

With that, the teacher said her goodbyes. Her truck moved off up the track while Rose and Iris waved from the handrail.

"I left our truck at the gas station."

"Don't worry," Rose said. "Don't worry about anything."

She took her daughter by the hand, inviting her to sit on the steps. Iris rested her head on Rose's shoulder. Together they watched the cloud of dust Socorro left behind disappear among the cacti.

"Just so you know, he wasn't tied up." Rose stroked her daughter's face, using her unscathed arm. "We immobilized him to stop him from doing any more harm to himself. We were taking care of him."

"I know, Mom."

"But if you saw that he was tied up, you must've been in the room." She noticed that Iris stopped breathing. "I was right yesterday when I came down with that hair from the bedroom. The hair was yours."

Iris took a while to respond.

"Yes, Mom," she admitted with a sigh. "Please forgive me." She hugged her with an abandon that Rose hadn't seen since her daughter was a little girl. "I really thought I loved him."

Iris let it all out, sobbing in her arms. As a mother does, Rose consoled her, stroking her hair, in love with its feel, with its shine. As Edelweiss's had, Iris's hair took on various tones throughout the day, reflecting the endless array of shades with which the sun colored the desert.

Melissa perceived the smells the clothes gave off as she climbed the stairs to her room. Needles's and Pins's T-shirts smelled like dust, like sun, like cactus sap. Thorns's hadn't been exposed to the elements long enough to absorb the scents of the desert.

Upstairs, through the half-open door, she saw Dad moving inside her parents' bedroom. He was crouching, rolling up a large form in a white sheet spread out on the floor. Seeing the blood stains, Melissa looked away. When Dad noticed her presence, he straightened. He held his fingertips together at his stomach. He lowered his head, not knowing what to say, shying away from her eyes. He ended up pushing the door shut with a finger.

Melissa went into her room.

The magazines on her desk were stacked tidily, along with the other scraps of paper. There was no medicine on the bedside table, no glass with white sediment. The wastebasket was empty. The collapsed shelf was leaning against the wall. The bare mattress showed the rhomboid motifs of its stitching, its labels. Melissa sat on the edge of the bed and set the cacti's clothes aside.

She looked at her rocks, piled up in a corner.

"I promise I'll find your eyes so we can say goodbye properly," she said to Natalie and Marlon.

There was a rap on the open door.

"Can I come in?" Mom asked.

Melissa nodded. Once inside, Mom closed the door behind her and turned the key. She sat down on the mattress, next to her. For a few seconds, they looked at each other without saying anything. Then Mom took her hand. She held it against the warmth of her lap.

"You didn't see the boy attacking me in the bedroom," she whispered.

Melissa shook her head. "Rick couldn't do anything to you. I was with him earlier on, here, in my bed, when he . . ." She preferred not to say the word.

Mom's eyes glistened. "Honey, you shouldn't . . . you shouldn't have had to see anything."

"You left the door unlocked. I just wanted to switch my rock, but Rick spoke to me."

"He spoke to you?" Her mother's neck tensed.

Melissa nodded.

"And what did he say?" She barely traced the words with her lips.

Melissa's eyelids tingled. The moisture of her incipient tears stung the inside of her nose.

"I stayed while it happened, Mom."

"Why're you looking at me like that?"

"I talked to him about Edelweiss."

"Edelweiss?" She swallowed.

"Yes, Mom."

"And why would you talk to him about Edelweiss?"

"I told him that Edelweiss was holding his hand," Melissa whispered. "So that he felt a loved one was there with him when he went."

Mom's chin began to tremble. She bit her lips, fighting to contain tears that appeared in her eyes despite her efforts.

"Our Edelweiss?" She frowned, trying to feign confusion, but they both knew there was no point in continuing the charade.

"His sister, Mom. I wanted him to know that his sister was waiting for him on the other side."

Mom screwed up her face, suppressing the sobs into which she finally exploded, collapsing into Melissa's arms. She cried on her shoulder with the abandon of a little girl.

"Honey, I'm sorry . . ."

"I hate knowing the truth," Melissa whispered.

Mom waited until she had the spasms under control before sitting up. She dried her eyes with her hands. She held Melissa by the cheeks.

"Honey"—she spoke close to her face—"the only truth is this family."

"I know everything, Mom."

Her mother's eyes explored her features as if she hoped to find some explanation in them.

"How?" she finally said.

Melissa lowered her head. She looked at the floor where she'd sat cross-legged, with a lantern, in front of the folder, casting light on the truth for the first time. She remembered her conversation with Rick the morning after. In her lower eyelids, she felt the weight of the sleepless nights reading the documents. In her hands, she felt the heat of the fire with which she'd reduced the past that couldn't exist to ashes, just as Dad had done.

"My rocks told me," said Melissa. "They were here the whole time."

She gestured with her chin at the corner where they were stacked. Mom opened her mouth to say something, to respond that what she said couldn't be true, but she closed it without a word. She accepted the explanation with a nod, the way Melissa was accepting what they had done.

"I'm sorry, honey." Mom collapsed again into her arms, crying against her chest. "Please, forgive us."

As if she were the mother, Melissa stroked Mom's hair until she was calm. As she did so, she looked at the wall of drawings. The portraits of a perfect past glowed gold in the special light with which the sun illuminated them each morning.

"Come on!" the twins yelled. "It's the last day of cactus bloom! We have to hurry!"

"Bloom?" asked Mom. "Who taught you that word?"

"The teacher!"

They ran downstairs, counting out loud the number of necklaces they planned to make. Melissa heard the scene from the bathroom, brushing her teeth in front of the mirror. Mom spoke to her reflection.

"And come on, you, don't make Dad wait." She picked up some colored beads from the floor. "Aren't you supposed to love going to town?"

Melissa nodded with the toothbrush in her mouth.

"Well, you'd never know it." Mom threw the beads in the trash can next to the sink. "Come on, hurry now, Dad's finished his breakfast."

In her bedroom, Melissa pulled out the bag she always took to town from under the bed. She usually took it empty, to fill with shopping, but not this time. From the chest of drawers where she kept the tempera, she took out a sketchbook. She tore out the picture she'd drawn of Rick in the bed. From the wall of drawings, she chose another of Edelweiss. She put them in the bag with the other things. As she went down the stairs, she tightened the buckle to the last hole.

"Ready?" Dad asked when he saw her walk into the kitchen.

"Ready."

"Then let me finish getting these floriculturists dressed"—on one knee, he was putting straw hats on the twins' heads—"and then we'll get going."

"It's true, we're flowery culchists," they repeated.

They showed Melissa the empty wicker baskets that hung from their arms.

"We're going to make necklaces for everyone," said Daisy.

"We're going to make necklaces for everyone," Dahlia repeated.

Melissa showed her appreciation for their plan with a smile.

"And now some gloves, so you don't prick yourselves." Dad put such big ones on them that they fell from the girls' hands when they lowered their arms. "Rose! You finish up here, before I go crazy."

He picked up the two pairs of gloves from the floor and left them on the table, where Iris was building wobbly towers with books she was taking down from the shelves. On tiptoes, she reached with her hand to the back of the highest section. Mom came into the kitchen through the back door, bringing four tomatoes from the vegetable garden.

"It's not here." Iris clicked her tongue. "I don't understand."

"Have you looked in the living room?" asked Mom.

"I moved everything." She gestured at a pile of cushions near the door. "It's not there."

Melissa shifted her bag behind her back. "What're you looking for?"

"My book. *Pride and Prejudice*. It's as if it disappeared from the face of the earth. And I haven't even had the chance to finish it."

"A whole month and you haven't finished it?" said Melissa. "That *is* strange."

Iris's face darkened.

"I haven't been in the right frame of mind for reading . . ." She blinked the darkness away. "Seriously now, you two," she said to the twins. "My book. Did you take it out to play with in the desert and lose it? I'd rather you just told me the truth."

The little girls shook their heads.

"Well, I don't get it."

"I bet the man stole it," said Daisy.

"I bet the man stole it," Dahlia said.

A tomato fell onto the floor, spattering Melissa's ankles. Mom bent down to pick it up. She still seemed on edge whenever anyone mentioned Rick.

"Why do you say that?" asked Iris.

The twins whispered in each other's ears.

"Because he also stole a picture from us, after all," they said at the same time. "One of our nicest ones."

"He did?"

They nodded with conviction.

"He knew how much they're worth," said Daisy.

"He must've gotten rich selling it," Dahlia said.

"Are you sure it didn't fall off the wall and get stuck behind the bed?" Mom cleaned remnants of tomato from between her fingers.

"The man stole it," they said again. "He's bought a house with the money he made selling it."

"I'm sure he did." Iris ruffled their hair. "Just in case, I'm going to keep looking for my book."

"And you two." Mom pointed at Melissa and Dad. "If you don't go, you'll be late."

"When can *we* go to town?" the twins asked.

Dad pinched their noses.

"When you're big girls."

"We're already big girls."

"You stay here with me," said Mom, "so you can help me make dinner for when they get home."

"Dinner? That's boring. We want to make necklaces."

"Making a picnic's boring?"

The twins looked at each other, and the straw brims of their hats brushed together.

"Picnic!"

They jumped up and down, the baskets swinging in their arms.

"But if we're going to do that"—Mom pushed them toward the front door—"your father and your sister Melissa have to go now if they're to get back before nightfall."

The first stop they made in the town was the supermarket.

Melissa stayed with Dad while he read some of the product labels, written in Spanish. He also spoke Spanish to the man selling fruit, and to the woman who gave him two packs of one hundred corn tortillas. Following Dad's instructions, the butcher selected a large piece of meat and got ready to slice it into steaks.

"Should I go get something?" asked Melissa.

Dad handed her the list that Mom had written.

"The last three." He pointed at them on the paper. "Get the medium-sized sugar."

She took the list and disappeared down the aisles. When she knew that Dad couldn't see her, she pressed her bag against her hip.

She began to run.

She felt her shoulders burn in the sun as soon as she left the supermarket. She let a truck go by before crossing the street, coughing when she breathed in the black smoke from its exhaust pipe. She ran to the right, to the first corner, and turned.

She was sweating as she walked into the post office. She emptied her bag on the counter. The clerk asked her something, but Melissa couldn't understand what he said. Nor did she have time to waste.

"Por favor," she said. She pointed at the addresses she'd written on three parcels. *"Aquí."*

Before leaving, she dropped a handful of coins on the counter.

Back in the supermarket, she fetched the boxes of cereal, the sacks of rice, and the sugar. She returned to where Dad was with the butcher wrapping a third package.

"Honey, catch your breath," he said. "No need to rush around like that, our friend here's taking it slow."

The butcher smiled, not understanding what Dad had said.

Melissa fanned herself with her hands. She swallowed thick saliva. The bag on her hip felt light.

Mom spread the checkered picnic blanket over the ground. To keep the wind from blowing it away, she weighed down the corners with stones.

"How was town?" asked Iris.

Melissa shrugged while she deposited the picnic basket on the blanket. In the center, Iris placed the pitcher of agua de Jamaica that she'd just made in the kitchen. Green slices of lime floated on the ice, and drops of condensation pearled the glass.

"And the twins?" she asked while she laid out six glasses.

"They're coming," Mom said. "They're so excited."

Melissa looked toward the porch. At that time of the evening the front of the house took on the same purple tone as the rest of the landscape.

The cacti's elongated shadows painted dark lines on the family's home, which seemed to camouflage itself among the rocks and disappear, as if it didn't exist.

Mom took a deep breath and stretched her arms up to the sky.

"What a beautiful evening. It smells so good."

"It can't be the flowers." Iris gestured at the cacti's branches, where there was no trace of the white flowers that had decorated them for the last few weeks. "Did they pick *all* of them?"

Mom smiled.

"I don't believe you." Iris stifled a laugh.

"Come on, sit down."

Mom took their hands, inviting them to take a seat on the blanket.

"What pretty daughters I have . . ." she said to them.

Then she threw her hair back and sighed.

"Have you seen the colors of the stones?" She looked at the landscape with half-closed eyes, as if the beauty she saw around her was so intense that it blinded her.

The screen door banged against the wall as it opened—Dad had fixed it a few days after the events with Rick. Daisy and Dahlia appeared on the porch. To Melissa, they looked like two white clouds floating over the land, approaching them.

"What *are* they wearing?"

Mom's only response was to show her left hand, the fingertips covered in needle marks.

Iris knelt forward to see better. "It can't be."

"What is it?"

Mom smiled. "You can't imagine how much work it was."

The twins reached the picnic area. Melissa let out a sigh of wonder, and Iris held her hands to her mouth.

"You look . . . gorgeous."

Daisy took Dahlia's hand to swivel her around, showing their sisters the dress she wore. Flowers covered the garment's shoulder straps, the chest, the back, the skirt. Then Daisy stopped spinning and did the same with her twin, who also wore a dress of flowers, turning her while the others showered her with compliments. The little girls thanked them with a bow.

"And these are for you."

From their necks they took flower necklaces for everyone. Daisy put one on Melissa, Dahlia on Iris. Together, they gave the most luxuriant one to Mom.

"You're the best mommy in the world," they said at the same time.

"Thank you, girls." Mom smelled the flowers on the twins' shoulders.

Dahlia took off another necklace.

She left it on one side of the blanket, where Edelweiss would've sat.

Melissa saw Mom's eyes glisten.

"And Dad?" asked Iris.

"Dad has a surprise, too." Mom's eyes went even brighter. "You're going to love it."

She gestured at the porch, onto which he came out at that moment. The twins leapt with joy when they saw what he was carrying, then sat down on the blanket with the others. Iris hooked an arm through Mom's. Melissa took the other arm. The five of them settled into a semicircle while Dad caught up with them. When he arrived, he stood in front of them, without treading on the blanket.

"Wonderful, Dad," said Iris. "At last."

He cleared his throat. His temples filled with wrinkles when he smiled.

"Here goes," he said. "I hope you like it."

The first chord he played on the guitar revived in Melissa so many memories of Edelweiss that she could see her sitting with them, wearing the flower necklace that Dahlia had left in her place.

"*I want to live with you among the flowers,*" Dad sang, his fingers so accurate on the chords that nobody would have guessed he hadn't played for more than a year, "*with them and me you'll never be alone . . .*"

The twins stood up. They danced to the music that Dad played just as they danced to the record player in the living room. Melissa smiled when she saw the two whirls of white happiness spinning among the rocks, their dresses giving off the sweet smell the flowers produced at dusk in the desert. Next, she looked at Iris. She was listening to Dad sing with her lips pressed together, humming to herself while she dreamed of a new romance in which a boy showed his love for her with a bunch of flowers. Mom exchanged a look with Dad, the man who'd given her the most beautiful bunch that had ever existed, made up of five daughters with flower names. Melissa also smiled at the floating image of Edelweiss, sharing with her a secret thought about Rick and his mother. And then she closed her eyes. She smelled the flowers, the lime in the drink. Silently, she asked her family to forgive her for her secret visit to the post office. Until they found the house among the cacti, Melissa could carry on enjoying Dad's voice, the twins' laughter, Iris's soft humming. She stroked Mom's hand, feeling proud to be her daughter. Until everything changed, she wished life could be like a drawing in which her family was happy forever.

NEVADA

From the kitchen, she saw the raised lid of the mailbox on the street while she was making her son's breakfast. A bigger envelope than usual, or a parcel of some kind, had prevented the mailman from closing it. She spilled the orange juice she was pouring into a glass.

"Are you all right?" Her husband was spreading peanut butter on a slice of bread, his tie over his shoulder to keep it clean. He was very careful with his work suits.

She went outside without replying. Something in that unusual delivery unsettled her. She didn't know why she was smiling. When she took out the parcel, other letters fell onto the ground, getting wet on the newly watered lawn. She inspected it right there, standing beside the mailbox. She could find no sign of who had sent it—not even their own address was complete. She tried to tear the envelope open down the middle, but the trembling in her fingers prevented it. She yelled her husband's name. He ran out after her, the soles of his shoes thudding as he approached.

"What is it?"

"Open it, we have to open it."

"Who's it from?"

"Open it, please . . ."

Nerves gripped her stomach painfully, and her voice sounded like a wail, but her hands were gathered at her chest, as if awaiting good news. Her husband ripped open the corner of the yellow envelope. He peered inside.

"What is it?"

He let her take it out. It was a rolled-up piece of paper, in the form of a tube. With a fingernail, she unpicked the piece of tape that kept it together. An explosion of color appeared in her hands when the paper unrolled, when the sun lit the surface covered in little plastic beads. Red, yellow, green, pink, blue. They spelled out one word:

MOMMY

As she read it, she fell to her knees, gripping the mailbox post. Her husband knelt beside her, grass and wet earth sticking to his suit pants. It was he who turned the piece of paper over.

The twins made this picture, using beads to color in the letters that I drew for them. I love having them as sisters. They are fine, they like doing everything together. They even say things at the same time. They are very happy.

—Melissa.

The woman held the picture to her face as if she could see her daughters reflected in the beads with which they'd decorated the word she'd never heard them say.

"Mom?" the boy asked from the front door. "What is it?"

She looked at her son with a smile. She let her husband hold her. They both collapsed onto the grass, not caring that it was wet. They laughed in a way they hadn't laughed for six years. They kissed each other as if they thought they would never kiss each other again. The boy joined in the celebration, leaping on top of them in an imitation of his favorite football team. They were still there on the ground when the school bus arrived.

TEXAS

The mailman's knuckles repeated the sequence of knocks that informed the recipient that today's delivery didn't fit through the slot in the door. She waited a few minutes before answering. She preferred not to have to say hello to him, or to listen to his remarks on how sad it was to see the garden so dry, when before what happened it had been filled with flowers each spring. The parcel toppled inward when she opened the door. She picked it up without looking at the barren soil in front of the house, forcing herself not to remember the happy times when she had tended that garden, imagining how her daughter would chase the butterflies that fluttered among the flowers.

She returned to the living room testing the weight of the parcel, trying to guess what it contained. Deliveries without a sender or exact address tended to be from people who'd read about her in the newspapers, who'd noted down her name and the town and had felt the need to write to her. They were messages of encouragement that really did help, but they had arrived mostly in the first few years. It had been a while since anyone had sent her something.

She sat in the armchair next to the side table, where she'd left her second cup of tea of the morning. With the parcel on her knees, she took a sip—it was still hot enough that the steam moistened her eyelashes. She pinched a corner of the envelope to open it without it breaking, as her mother had taught her to do. When she lifted up the flap, she saw the top edge of a book.

She frowned as she took it out.

She rested it on her legs.

From the side table, she took some reading glasses. Her sight had waned noticeably in the past few years. She always said that her eyes had been ruined by so much crying. She put them on, and read the cover.

"Pride and Prejudice."

As she did with any book, she held the edge to her nose and breathed in the smell of the paper. Among the smells of ink and dust, she discovered another scent. A sweet note that, without her understanding why, filled her broken eyes with tears. For years, it had been something that could happen at any moment.

She opened the cover. On the first page, she found a dedication.

This book smells of your daughter. She has spent hours with it. She loves reading and can do it all day long. She especially likes romantic stories. Sometimes it is as if she is in the clouds, but she is a very smart girl. She is sixteen, she is a wonderful sister and she has been happy all this time. Very happy.

—Melissa.

The woman closed the book before the tears that fell on the paper could blot the ink. She smelled the pages with a deep sigh that filled her lungs in a way they hadn't filled in sixteen years, since she'd smelled her baby's little head the last time she held her in her arms. With her eyes closed, she breathed in the aroma imbuing its pages. When she opened them, she examined the corner of the envelope, trying to decipher, in the blurry ink of the stamp, the name of the city from which the parcel had been sent. Through the window, she saw a butterfly fluttering in the garden.

COLORADO

On the letter that reached the post office, only a name appeared, with no address other than the town and state, but everyone in that town knew the intended recipient. The mailman who took it to her mailbox was the same one who'd covered the street for twenty years, since before the disappearance. When she heard the postman arrive, she interrupted the letter she was writing and went out to receive him. She sat on the porch swing with the envelope, in the shade of the elm trees that flanked the front of the house and cloaked in the scent that the sun-warmed roses gave off. From the cushion, she plucked one of the white hairs that now populated her blonde head, much whiter than befitted her age. Her hair had also begun to fall out. Before opening the envelope, she touched the unfamiliar childlike handwriting in which her name was penned.

From inside the envelope she took out two pieces of thick paper, which she identified as belonging to a sketchbook. She narrowed her eyes when, on the first page, she discovered a portrait of herself, in pencil. Unable to imagine who could have sent it, she wondered whether it had been some friend from the past, someone secretly in love with her who years later had drawn her from memory, as he remembered her from when she was young. Then she looked at the second portrait of her son, so handsome, sleeping on an unfamiliar b

"Rick," she whispered, her hand on her chest, "I was writing to you. Where are you?"

Hearing her own voice, an impossible idea flickered in her mind. She looked at the woman in the first drawing again. Hypnotized by the face rendered in pencil, she went back in time with each blink of her eyes until she recognized in the portrait the little face of the baby she'd kissed every morning, the one in the single photograph she had of her daughter.

"Elizabeth?"

It had been a long time since she'd said the name aloud.

"Eli—"

The rest of the syllables were swallowed by her tears. All at once the whole world tasted to her of salt. She examined the two portraits, searching for a signature. She turned over the one of Rick. She turned over the one of Elizabeth. She dried her eyes to read the text written in the same handwriting that was on the envelope.

Rick found his sister. Now they are resting together in the most beautiful landscape that exists. She had a happy life in a family that loved her a lot, she was the best sister I could have had. I miss her every day and think of her whenever I hear a guitar. She had a beautiful voice and always smelled like honey. Rick told me she looked just like her mother, like you. I ᵉ you can see this in my drawing. I'm sorry for what hap- ᵗ I wish I could do something to change it. I hope we can ᵈay, I would love to tell you more things about her.

—Melissa.

ABOUT THE AUTHOR

Paul Pen is a Kindle top-three bestselling author, as well as a journalist and scriptwriter. His novel *The Light of the Fireflies* has sold more than one hundred thousand copies worldwide, and an American film adaptation is under way. Following the Spanish digital publication of *Trece historias* (*Thirteen Stories*), a powerful collection of short tales, Pen returned with another international release in 2017, *Desert Flowers*, bringing his unmistakable brand of literary suspense to readers around the globe. For more information, please visit www.paulpen.com.

ABOUT THE TRANSLATOR

Simon Bruni is a translator of fiction and nonfiction from Spanish, a language he acquired through "total immersion" living in Alicante, Valencia, and Santander. He studied Spanish and linguistics at Queen Mary University of London and literary translation at the University of Exeter.

His literary translations include novels, short stories, and video games, while his nonfiction portfolio spans fields as diverse as journalism, social geography, early modern witchcraft, food security, and military history.

He has won two third-place prizes in the John Dryden Translation Competition: in 2015 for his translation of Paul Pen's harrowing short story "The Porcelain Boy," and in 2011 for Francisco Pérez Gandul's slang-driven novel *Cell 211*. His translation of Paul Pen's novel *The Light of the Fireflies* has sold more than a hundred thousand copies worldwide.

Simon serves on the executive committee of the Society of Authors' Translators Association (TA) and is a member of the American Literary Translators Association (ALTA). For more information, please visit www.simonbruni.com.